THE RED FURY

A MEDIEVAL ROMANCE

BY KATHRYN LE VEQUE

Table of Contents

AUTHOR'S NOTE

Welcome to the very first historical romance I ever wrote – long-hand!

Those were the days before computers – at least, readily accessible home computers. I believe I started this book around 1988 or so. I have dozens of notebooks I wrote "practice run" books on, learning my craft, and this is a version of the very first historical romance I ever wrote.

I say version because this one went through a few iterations. There were at least three, and each one was a little different. This version was the last one, and the most complete (and the one that was actually really good), so it's really exciting to me to finally see these characters come to life after so many years. For so long, they were just words on a spiral notebook that I never thought would be published.

A few fun/interesting things to note about this story because it's gone through an evolution. This book was originally set in 1378 A.D., but because Andrew made an appearance in The Wolfe (simply because I wanted to use the character), I had to move the original date of his book back by over one hundred years. This book also contained the original Bose de Moray, who was the captain of the guard for the Scottish king. Well, I thought Bose was pretty darn cool, so I gave him his own novel but set it back a century, too. So, Bose had to become someone else – Ridge de Reyne, whose family had a lot of activity in Scotland on or before this time. Ridge is a grandson of Creed de Reyne (GUARDIAN OF DARKNESS) and will have his own novel next year, a story called THE BLACK STORM.

A few other things had to change – locations, some names, things like that, either because I used them in other books or given my current research, they simply didn't work. In fact, the leading lady's name was originally Jeniver – a name I liked so much that I used it in the Lords of Thunder series. So, "Jeniver" became "Josephine" (although I briefly toyed with calling her Elizabel). Why Josephine? Because I like it, and also because it belonged to a tiny old woman, who died many years ago, and she was one of the strongest women I'd ever known. But, as you can see, I cannibalized a lot of this book and used characters and names in other stories, thinking this story would never see the light of day. Boy, was I wrong!

You're also going to notice that the "Scots Speak" in this book isn't very heavy. It's very minimal because we're talking about the border areas where some regions had more of an English accent than a Scots one. Much of this book is set near Ayr, which is far south as far as Scotland goes.

But foremost, I need to thank my assistant, Kris Newberger, for her skill and patience in typing out dozens of hand-written spiral notebooks (that I'd very poorly put in order!) to make sense out of this story. The woman has the patience of Job. She went to a huge effort to put this book together, including the places where there were plot holes so I could fill them in. Without her, this book probably would have never seen publication and I am extremely grateful for her diligence. This book is really for her – she has begged me to finish it so, for her, I have done just that.

Now, this book is pretty much in its original form, although it has been heavily edited by me to bring it up to par. Still, I didn't do any massive rewrites (unless it badly needed it), because I'm a firm believer in presenting stories as they were meant to be read. This is a fast-paced story that moves very quickly, which is good – nothing to drag down the storyline. However – my writing style has changed dramatically and you will see that within these pages. This book is more along the lines of THE WOLFE and the other early novels I wrote. It's definitely a time capsule of Le Veque history.

But I will say this – this book was probably the most difficult one I've ever had to work on because of the missing gaps in the storyline. Since I wrote it long-hand on spiral notebooks, over the years, some of those notebooks have gone missing. It was a very big story that was literally a puzzle to piece together, as I mentioned, and very labor intensive. But, for Andrew and Josephine, I think it was well worth the effort. I hope you think so, too.

Get ready to fall in love with The Red Fury...

Hugs,
Kathryn

DEDICATION

I don't normally do dedications because, with the number of books I have published, I would soon run out of people to dedicate my books to. I'd be dedicating them to the homeless guy on the corner or the mail man. In any case, this book is a little different in that I must dedicate it to my assistant, Kris Newberger, who did something truly remarkable for this novel.

There have been few people in my life other than close family that I could depend on as much as Kris. She's my biggest fan, my biggest critic, and the most efficient, skilled assistant anyone could ever ask for. Without her, I probably wouldn't have published books like *The Wolfe, Rise of the Defender*, or *The Dark One: Dark Knight* because she not only typed up those manuscripts from very old hard copies, but she was the one who said they were good enough to publish.

I'm so glad I listened to her.

So, it is to Kris that I dedicate this novel, with the deepest affection and gratitude.

And I looked, and behold a pale horse: and his name that sat on him was Death, and Hell followed with him.

Revelation 6:8

PROLOGUE

"*R*UN, *ANDREW, RUN!*"

It was dark as he heard the cry. Heart pumping, his breath caught in his throat as he tried to run, but he was boxed in by tall walls with tiny windows. There were walls everywhere he looked, big gray stone blocking him as he tried to run.

There was nowhere for him to go except for a long corridor that stretched out in front of him. It seemed to be twisting and undulating. Even as he tried to run, the floor was moving as he struggled to keep his footing. He heard someone screaming to him, telling him to run faster. Over and over – *run faster, Andrew*! He was trying – God help him – he was trying, but the shifting corridor and rolling floor made it so very difficult.

Light!

He saw light at the end of the corridor and he ran for it, propelling himself out of the building that was jerking and rolling. As he landed heavily on the dirt beyond the corridor, he turned to see that that building he was in – the one with the twisting corridor – was breaking into a million pieces, shattering as he watched.

He couldn't even stop to breathe. Stones were being thrown at him as the building collapsed, giant stones hurling at his head. He no longer heard the voice telling him to run, but he didn't need to. He continued to run, as fast as he could go. He had no idea where he was going, only that he had to break free of the disaster that was trying to swallow him up.

Around him, everything was distorted by the storm raging overhead and disaster happening around him. He was so scared. God, he'd never known such fear. Something – *someone* – was trying to kill him. He knew that.

He had to run for his very life.

Sinister laughing now filled the air. He could hear it behind him, a booming sound, like thunder. In fact, it rolled like thunder. The sound undulated, almost as if it were coming from under water. Overhead, lightning crashed and that crazy laughter could be heard again. It was terrifying.

He was trying to pick up speed. As the ground lurched beneath his feet, he could see a gateway of some kind ahead. If only he could make it. But then the laughter came, louder than before, making him feel as if it were right behind him. In a panic, he turned to see if the threat was upon him and that's what he saw her…

Mother….

He came to an unsteady halt. His mother was simply standing there, smiling at him. But it wasn't a normal smile – there was fear in her eyes. He took a step in her direction, to go to her, but, suddenly, she screamed at him.

Run, Andrew, run!

The cries had been coming from her. Behind her, a dark figure rose up, as if bursting forth from the very ground. A shadow of extreme size enveloped her and she began screaming again as the shadow swallowed her up.

In the midst of that murky shadow, he caught a glimpse of black, wicked eyes.

God, he knew those eyes.

He turned on his heel and began to run again, running as fast as he possibly could while the wicked laughter rang out behind him and his mother's screams were drowned out. Grief swamped him; why didn't he try harder to get to her? He'd left her to die and by the time he reached the gate he'd been striving for, he was gasping with agony.

His mother… his sweet, gentle mother had been consumed by the monster and he couldn't save her. Just as he reached the gate, the twisting and trembling gate, the entire thing collapsed and everything went black.

… nothingness…

With a start, Andrew d'Vant suddenly sat straight up in bed, sweating profusely, feeling as if he'd just had the fright of his life. Taking a deep breath, he struggled to calm himself. He was in his familiar tent, with his familiar possessions around him, trunks of valuables, fine furnishings, coinage, and plate.

It was dark and damp this night, with the moon periodically hidden behind dark clouds that were blowing across the glittering sky. It gave the illusion of a curtain being lowered and raised as the light from behind his tent flickered and undulated.

Somewhere in the distance, thunder rolled. A storm had blown through, perhaps feeding that terrible dream. But the truth was that he'd been having that dream for as long as he could remember, ever since being chased from his home at a young age and left to fend for himself. Those days were long gone now, and he'd made a success of his life.

Even if his brother had tried to kill him.

But his mother… he'd had this dream so many times and he'd never been able to save her. Perhaps it was that sense of loss, of failure, that fed his drive and made him what he was today – a sword for hire. He was paid to fight other men's wars, proving himself the most powerful mercenary the world had ever seen. He always had to be better, stronger, and more intelligent than everyone else because, long ago, he'd been powerless to prevent the incident that had shaped his entire life.

In a sense, every sword stroke, every victory, was a victory he'd wished he'd had those years ago when he hadn't been victorious, not saving his mother. He'd failed when she'd needed him the most.

He didn't fail any longer.

Wiping his hand over his sweaty face, he happened to see a half-open missive lying on the table next to his bed. The candle was burning very low, barely illuminating the missive he'd received from yet another man who wanted him to fight his war for him. Only this missive hadn't come from a man. It had come from a woman, and she was begging for his services to save her family home.

Torridon...

That's what made this missive different from the others he'd received over the years. A woman was asking for his help, and that was unheard of. But, somehow, it meant more to him than any other missive he'd ever received. His mother had asked for help once, and he hadn't been able to help her. But this woman... he *could* help her. He had to. Because maybe in some small part, it was a victory struck for his mother from those years ago.

Aye, he knew now why he'd had that dream again. It was the fact that a woman had once again asked him for help. Even though he had offers for other jobs, huge-paying jobs, he was going to ignore them all in favor of helping this woman.

And this time, he wouldn't fail.

PART ONE:
TORRIDON

CHAPTER ONE

Torridon Castle
Five miles southeast of Ayr, Scotland
September, 1233 A.D.

"LADY JOSEPHINE! *WATCH*!"

The warning came in the nick of time. Lady Josephine de Carron brought her heavy sword up with amazing speed and grace, stopping what would have surely been a deathblow from the avenging Dalmellington soldier.

With a grunt, she dropped to the ground and rolled directly into the soldier's legs, throwing him off balance enough to topple him. Leaping to her feet, which was no easy feat considering the heavy chainmail she wore, she pounced on the man and drove her sword into the leathery skin of his neck. Withdrawing the blade with a grunt of effort, she charged towards the outer bailey, not waiting to hear the enemy soldier's last bloody gurgle of death.

Here she was, again, facing a battle.

Facing death.

God, it was a nightmare. The outer bailey of Castle Torridon was in shambles. If it was wood, it was burning. If it was stone, it was crumbling. The sounds of death and destruction assaulted her senses, and the smell of smoke and blood filled her as she searched for her second in command. Fatigue pulled at her body and mind as her eyes scanned the yard.

But it was more than exhaustion she felt; it was devastation. The battle had been long and bloody, and the anger at the Dalmellingtons for yet again another attack on her home of Torridon Castle was eating at her. They seemed determined to destroy what they could not have. The Dalmellingtons had once been allied with the House of de Carron, a long time ago. But that was so long ago, and times had changed.

Changed from the glorious alliance that had once been in place, now reduced to ashes.

It hadn't always been like this. Gazing over the destroyed bailey, Josephine retreated to those times when her home had been peaceful. It all started with Josephine's father, Hugh, when he had left his home in the north of Scotland and traveled south to Dalmellington to stay with his mother's cousins when he was very young. Several years and several colorful campaigns later, including the granting of an earldom from King Alexander, Hugh had been given a small stronghold. He had taken the stronghold, renamed it Torridon Castle from his home in the Highlands, and built it into one of the most powerful fortresses in Scotland.

With the title, Earl of Ayr, came the usual privileges, and Hugh in his prime was courted by the father of every eligible woman in Scotland. Of course, it didn't hurt that Hugh was distinguishingly handsome and had a tongue from whence flowed words of honeyed wine. Women seemed to swoon at the sight of him. Eventually, he was courted by the king himself on behalf of the king's niece, Afton. Hugh hadn't been too keen on the match until he saw the lady.

One look was all it took.

Hugh and Afton had a love match from the start and their first child came less than a year later, a son named James. Their happiness only seemed to take on an increased dimension when, the following year, Afton gave birth to a daughter, Josephine, and two years later, a daughter named Justine.

But with Justine's birth, something went terribly wrong. After the midwife delivered the lusty infant, Afton began to hemorrhage. Within minutes, she was gone, leaving Hugh with three very small children and a grief that ate at his very soul. He never recovered from his lovely Afton's death, and he never married again.

Instead, he preferred to lavish attention on his children, especially Josephine, for she was a mirror image of her mother. Whereas James was a strapping and handsome blond and Justine a dark-haired beauty, Josephine had a beauty so uncommon that it brought a sigh of joy from any man who was fortunate enough to lay eyes on her. She was perfection.

Hugh took comfort in his daughter and in his children in general. Life, for the most part, was good. When James de Carron had reached sixteen years of age, he was betrothed to young Marie Dalmellington. It was a very desirable contract, for the Dalmellingtons were very wealthy, as were the de Carrons, and it promised to strengthen an already strong family bond. Fortunately, James and Marie liked each other very much, and the contract looked as if it had created a love match.

But it was not to be. That very reason was why Josephine was standing in her bailey, looking at the destruction and agonizing over the cause behind it. Two years after James and Marie's betrothal, James de Carron drowned trying to save a young peasant from the river that flowed near Torridon Castle.

Hugh had been devastated, as had been Josephine and Justine. They felt his loss to the core of their existence, but to Hugh it was much more. He had lost his male heir and feared for the continuation of the de Carron line. His only choice, though he loathed the very thought, was to take another wife and produce another son.

Young Marie Dalmellington had taken the news of James' death with no outward emotion. After accepting the news from her Uncle Colin, who was the head of the House of Dalmellington, she quietly excused herself to her room. Once inside the chamber, she went immediately to her great cedar chest and withdrew the bejeweled dirk her grandmother had given her. Without as much as a prayer, she plunged the blade deep into her chest, and was dead before she hit the ground.

In that action, Marie cemented a permanent rift between the Dalmellingtons and the de Carrons, for Colin openly blamed the de Carrons for her death and set out to destroy his cousin.

There was blood on his mind, as bloody as the dirk in Marie Dalmellington's chest.

But he was too late. Hugh de Carron, on the road to Edinburgh to see the king and discuss the death of his heir, was attacked and murdered by common bandits. He, one of his knights, and three men-at-arms succumbed to the group of outlaws that swarmed upon them like vermin on a dog. Hugh had fought valiantly, but even his strength and experience wasn't enough against their sheer number.

In an instant, he was gone.

Now in command of Torridon, Josephine dealt with the deaths of her brother and father in her own way; silently and stoically for the benefit of her subjects. But as time passed, she realized she must take the reins of power decisively so that none would question who truly ruled Torridon. Her father had worked exceedingly hard for this magnificent fortress, and she felt his spirit filling her with courage. She'd been born with the will of ten head-strong men, and with the intelligence to accomplish most anything she set out to do, and she was determined to carry on in her father's stead. She firmly believed that he would've wanted it that way, and she swore that none other than a de Carron would rule Torridon while there was breath left in her body.

If nothing else, she was foolishly determined. But she had to start somewhere.

Summoning her courage, she'd had Sully teach her the finer arts of swordplay and fighting. At her initial request, the man had had been speechless. Sully Montgomery was her father's closest friend as well as the captain of his guard. He was also a soldier to the core; the only women he had ever seen fight were more man than most men, not refined ladies like Josephine de Carron. But when he opened his mouth to refuse, he caught a look of such resolve in her eye that he promptly shut it.

If his lady wanted to learn to fight, then so be it.

Josephine spent the next few weeks intensely training with Sully and the other knights; from sunup to sundown. Sully had never seen anyone work harder and struggle against difficult odds. When she was knocked down, she would bounce back up again. And when she was hit, she wouldn't shy away. Josephine knew she had to be strong, especially in the eyes of her father's men, because she needed their respect not just as their lady, but as a warrior.

She got it.

Sully and the other knights' opinion of Josephine de Carron doubled and they looked at her with new eyes in those weeks of training, and swore new loyalty to her. Only Hugh de Carron's offspring could fight with such raw courage and awakening tactical intelligence. It was a good thing, too, because, soon enough, the trouble started to come.

The first Dalmellington attack came five weeks after the death of Hugh de Carron. Colin Dalmellington decided that two females running Torridon made it ripe for the picking. His arrogant mind decided that Torridon Castle should rightfully be his through his dead niece and her departed betrothed, the heir to Torridon. Colin's mind became twisted with his only niece's death, and he vented his rage on Torridon. But what he didn't count on was the unity between Hugh de Carron's daughter and the knights of the castle, and the fierce determination they possessed to defend what was theirs. He withdrew the first time, but he kept coming back again and again, like an evil plague.

And they were back, again, on this day.

That was why Josephine found herself standing in her destroyed ward yet again. It seemed like these attacks never ended, as if there had always been battles between the de Carrons and the Dalmellingtons. Two years after Hugh's death, Josephine could hardly remember a time when there was peace. She was a seasoned soldier after all of these battles. As she stood in the demolished outer bailey of her home, she reflected upon those days of peace when her father was alive and the hell that had followed in the wake of his death. There was still fighting going on around her as the sun set, giving the courtyard a ghostly atmosphere as gray figures continued to grapple. Soon it would stop, the dead would be hauled away and the wounded tended, but then it would start again at some point soon.

But today, she'd lived to fight another day.

Shaking off her sense of reflection and focusing on her duty, Josephine caught sight of Etienne, the master French swordsman, over the by outer wall as he toyed with an inferior Dalmellington soldier. She headed directly towards him, calling his name. He heard her, and finished humoring the enemy by driving his sword into the man's abdomen. He then went immediately to his lady.

"My lady." His heavy French accent was edged with concern. "You are well?"

"I am," Josephine replied steadily, trying to mask her weariness. "Where is Sully?"

Etienne shook his head, only his eyes and mouth visible through his helm. "I have not seen him for some time."

Josephine glanced about the fading battle and let out an exhausted sigh. She was tired of death this day, tired of fighting yet another battle. Every time she fought, she felt as if she lost another piece of her soul.

As if another piece of herself chipped off and died.

"You will find him and send him to me," she said. "I am going to see to the wounded in the great hall."

Etienne saluted smartly as she marched off, watching her pass into the inner bailey. He knew how tired she must be. She had fought hard since early morning. Now that the Dalmellington army was either retreating or dead, she was retreating to the castle and leaving the clean-up to the knights.

Etienne strode off on his long legs in search of Sully with his mind still thinking of his pretty, forbidden mistress.

The woman with the heart of a soldier.

SULLY MONTGOMERY HAD seen his mistress head into the inner courtyard, having no idea she was looking for him. He, too, was weary from the battle, and the sight of his lady lifted his sagging spirit and boosted his sapped strength.

Tipping his helm up, he wiped the sweat and dirt from his brow, letting out a heavy sigh as he surveyed the damage to the outer walls. Anger and disgust were partners in his chest at the thought of rebuilding the wall again. With a heavy heart, he began to head towards the inner ward and the keep.

Sully had seen thirty summers and two. He was not large, but was rather average in height, but he was exceptionally muscled and was stronger than he appeared. His jaw was square and his face handsome. He also possessed ice-blue eyes that were piercing enough to send fear into any man who should have the misfortune to provoke his wrath, yet he could look at his Josephine with such tenderness that his eyes could melt the soul. His receding blond hair was cut very close to his scalp, and was as prickly as a porcupine.

Sully's respect was hard-won, but once held, he was loyal until the end. That was why Hugh had held Sully with such high esteem – Sully very nearly worshipped the ground his lord walked on. He had been guilt-ridden that he had not accompanied Hugh on his trip to Edinburgh, for Hugh had explicitly forbidden him to leave Torridon at that time. He wanted his trusted captain overseeing the castle in his absence. Hugh's trust in Sully was what had saved his life.

But there was some guilt in that. Now, he felt obligated to stay, and knew that he would always remain at Torridon, despite Hugh's death. Some of the other knights spoke passingly of leaving to seek their fortune elsewhere, but not Sully. He had been with Hugh too long, and Torridon was as much in his blood as it was in the blood of the de Carrons.

But it was more than that... he wouldn't, and couldn't, leave Josephine, not when she needed him the most. He had been unsure of his role at Torridon until Josephine made the announcement after her father's death that she was now in command of Torridon. When her father died, and in the absence of any male heir, his title and wealth passed to her.

That was mostly why Sully had to stay.

To help Josephine in this strange, new world.

Colin Dalmellington, of course, had petitioned the king to make him the rightful Earl of Ayr, but his blood relation with Hugh was distant. Alexander hadn't been apt to grant his petition and Josephine remained the Lady Josephine, Countess of Ayr. Josephine's sister became her chatelaine, a seemingly odd arrangement, but never had Torridon Castle run so smoothly. Had it not been for Colin Dalmellington laying siege to Torridon every few weeks, Torridon would truly be a paradise.

But wherever Josephine was, as far as Sully was concerned, was paradise.

He was jolted from his train of thought as he passed through the remains of the inner gate and into the inner ward. Tall, blond, Etienne was calling his name and thoughts of Josephine faded.

"What is it?" Sully called to him.

"Lady Josephine requests your presence," Etienne said as he approached. "She is in the great hall with the wounded. I am sure Dewey and Justine are with her."

Sully shook his head. "I do not like Justine around the wounded," he said warningly. "She is of virtually no help. All she does is pass from man to man with those damn cards and sheep's knuckles to tell them their fortunes. If she tells a man he will not live, then they lose all hope and die anyway, even if their wound is but a scratch."

"The men believe she possesses great power," Etienne said faintly.

Sully snorted. "What she possesses is a gift for persuasion and storytelling," he said pointedly. "She is no more a witch than I am."

Etienne shook his head with a wry smile on his face, for he knew

Sully spoke the truth. Sully caught his expression and laughed a little himself.

"I will attend her and make sure she does not steal the hope from the men," he said finally. "You will see that the clean-up proceeds quickly. All Dalmellington bodies are to be burned. Leave no trace. And get the men on the outer wall immediately. We must rebuild the breach."

"Aye." Etienne was in motion.

Sully left him, marching on to the inner baily amongst the smells of the evening fires and the stench of the decaying corpses. Glancing over in the direction of the stables, he saw two of his knights directing some men-at-arms and a few villeins in the clean-up.

"Burl! Albert!" he bellowed.

The knights were to him instantly, ready to do his bidding.

"Round up as many men as you can," Sully ordered quickly. "The main gates, I fear, are beyond repair. But see what can be done. And I want the entrance secured before the sun is gone from the sky, one way or another. Make your assessment and report back to me. I shall be in the great hall with the wounded."

Burl was the oldest knight of forty and two years. Albert was considerably younger and darkly handsome in a lanky sort of way. They saluted smartly and were off.

Sully continued on through the mud until he reached the three massive steps that led into the keep of Torridon. Inside, the long foyer was dark and cool, and more torches were being lit by the servants as he passed through. His boots clanked sharply against the stone floor as he turned to his right at the end of the foyer and entered what was the great hall of Torridon.

The two massive stone fireplaces were blazing with a warming fire, illuminating the bodies strewn about on the rushes. Sully removed his helm, placing it carefully on the ground near the door. His weary eyes searched for his mistress amongst the servants tending to the sick and the dying.

Over the by south wall, he spotted ancient, decrepit Dewey. The man was old, perhaps having seen eighty or more years. He was the size of a large child, and was balding and bent, but his knowledge of herbs, flowers, and potions were limitless. How he came to be at Torridon, Sully didn't know. Perhaps he had always been here, for he was as much a part of Torridon as the walls or the roof. Dewey's reputation was legendary throughout Scotland, and even the king had tried to lure him away. But Dewey had declined on the explanation that if he were to leave Torridon, he would surely die; for he was too old to start elsewhere.

Not far from Dewey was Josephine, kneeling beside a soldier as she gently removed his armor. Sully felt a sense of contentment sweep over him at the sight of her, and his heart lightened as he approached her. She always had that effect on him. She stood up as he approached, wiping her hands on her tunic.

"My lady," Sully greeted.

Her eyes flew up to meet his; she had not seen him coming. Her eyes locked with his, as each saw that the other had survived yet another battle. After a moment, Josephine smiled.

"Good, Sully, you are here," she said with relief in her voice. "Tell me of the situation of my fortress."

Sully followed her over to one of the giant hearths so they could take their business away from the men.

"I have Etienne on the outer wall blocking in the gaps, and Burl and Albert are on the main gates, although I cannot guarantee their repair anytime soon," he told her. "It seems that most of the damage is confined to the outer bailey this time."

She nodded, some relief in her expression. "Good," she replied. "But what will we do tonight about the open outer entrance?"

Sully didn't hesitate. "I will order the gates to the inner bailey se-cured and double the guard," he said evenly. "I will post as many men-at-arms at the entrance as we can spare, while the work proceeds through the night."

"Archers?" she inquired.

He crossed his arms. "They shall be tripled."

Satisfied, she nodded. "Very well. Then I shall leave you to your duties."

Sully could see how exhausted she was from the way she carried herself. He reached out and put a gentle hand on her arm. "You are weary, my lady," he said gently. "Why do you not retire to your chamber?"

Josephine shook her head emphatically and almost lost her balance. Her beautiful hair was secured in a knot behind her head, and tendrils came loose and tumbled free to her mid-back. Irritated, she pulled out the remaining pins that stuck in the tangle. Sully watched her; *God's Bones, how he longed to run his hands through that hair!*

"I cannot, Sully, you know that," she said insistently. "I must make sure that every man is tended for the night. Then, perhaps, I will retire while Justine and Dewey keep vigilant watch."

Justine. Sully's ears twitched at the sound of her name. Ever careful, so as not to offend his mistress, he chose his words.

"My lady," he said evenly. "I am well-aware of Justine's… uh… powers but, mayhap, she should retire when you do. The men should sleep and not be distracted by Justine's… skills."

Josephine's eyes flashed for a split second, and Sully feared he had upset her. But he soon discovered her anger was not directed at him.

"Justine's only skill is annoyance," she said. "But she is learning much from Dewey, and I wish for her to continue learning. And as for her powers… *ha!*"

Sully choked off a laugh at her last word and the expression accompanying it. Then they both glanced over at Justine, who was in the middle of the room sitting on the rushes between two wounded men. What she was telling them had their undivided attentions, as they watched her with intent awe.

"… and distilled rose potion will attract the woman you long for," Justine was saying with great exaggeration.

"Aye? Is that so?" one of the soldiers said.

"Absolutely," Justine said emphatically. "And then, root of mandrake will increase your virility once you have her. It never fails!"

Josephine shook her head at the topic of conversation. Justine, at seventeen years of age, fancied herself a physic as well as a mystic. She lacked any sort of modesty when it came to her knowledge of herbs and potions, as she was displaying with her open discussion of love potions and male virility. Her honesty and forthrightness were redeeming qualities in a girl who could quite easily be perceived as a lunatic.

But she had little tolerance for her sister. Josephine rolled her eyes in exasperation as she turned back to Sully.

"God's Bones," she muttered. "The woman has no shame. Fear not, Sully. She will retire when I do. Mayhap even *before*."

Sully bowed graciously, but a grin was playing on his lips. "As you wish."

As the weary captain of Torridon's forces walked away, Josephine gave her sister a second glance. Justine's hair was a rich brown color and her face was pleasingly oval. Her eyes were unspectacular in a shade of blue and her lips were sweetly curved. She was, at best, almost pretty. But she was skittish, selfish, and could be exceedingly odd. Yet, she made a superior chatelaine, in that she was a consummate perfectionist, and demanded the same from the servants. The servants, in turn, feared her because she was a self-proclaimed white witch. None wanted to find out on their own if she truly possessed the power.

But Josephine avoided her sister, at least at the moment. She hadn't the strength to deal with her. With a weary sigh, she made her way over to Dewey to ask him the general condition of her men. It seemed she was always asking that question, always asking after the condition of men who were tested time and time again. She'd lost so many, but she hadn't lost count. She still remembered their names and their faces. Knowing the cause of their death was something of such great waste, it made those deaths more difficult to bear.

But bear it, she did.

The long day was about to turn into a long night.

CHAPTER TWO

I T WAS WELL after midnight when Josephine retired to her room. Justine almost had to help her up the stairs, but ever-independent Josephine would not allow it. Her thirty pounds of chainmail felt like one hundred pounds as she reached her heavy oak door. She pushed it open as she bid her sister a good night.

Inside, the comfortable room was lit and warmed by a blazing fire in the hearth. Her maid, Ola, had already filled the large iron tube with steaming water, and she could smell her precious rose oil emitting from it. It filled her senses and with the implication of great relaxation and cleanliness away from the horrors of the day, she couldn't wait to get her clothes off.

Ola came in through the door, her arms laden with linens. She was surprised to see her mistress in the room.

"Oh!" the plump little maid cried. "My lady, let me help you!"

Josephine was too tired to even utter a word as Ola dropped the linens and began to strip her mistress of every scrap of clothing. The chainmail landed in the corner with a loud clank, followed by the tunic, undertunic, and breeches. Finally, Ola helped her weary mistress into the huge tub.

It was a routine they went through quite often, a bathing ritual that Josephine relished. But as she allowed the hot water and precious oils to steam away the sorrow and weariness, there was envy in the heart of the little maid. There always had been.

Ola had been with her mistress a very long time. As she oiled and scrubbed the woman, she found herself wishing for her mistress' perfect body. Josephine wasn't tall, only of average height, but she possessed a shape that would make God himself lustful. Her slim neck gave way to soft, white shoulders and well-shaped arms. Her breasts were round, full, and perfect. A taut torso blossomed into shapely hips and a deliciously rounded bottom. Oh, how Ola envied her mistress!

But it was a quiet envy, something she'd always kept to herself, as one does when one admires something unattainable. Finally, when every inch of Josephine's body was scrubbed clean, Ola gathered her things and vacated the chamber.

Oblivious to her maid's envious thoughts, Josephine lay back in the tub, her eyes closed. For the first time in over a day, she was alone, with no sounds of battle or anguish filling her ears. It was quiet and peaceful. But, God's Toes, she ached to the marrow in her bones. Even her aches had aches. But the warm water soothed her tired body and made her incredibly sleepy. So before she fell asleep, she carefully pulled herself out.

Ola had left a large piece of drying linen warming by the fire, and Josephine quickly dried off. Over on the bed lay her white lamb's wool robe, and she pulled that on. The robe was soft and sensual with the way it clung to her feminine curves as she went back over to the fire to dry her hair. Laying crosswise in a sling-back leather chair, with her neck resting on the armrest and her damp hair cascading down to the floor in front of the warm fire, Josephine meant to dry her hair that way. But she was asleep before she took two breaths, unable to hold off the exhaustion that was clutching at her.

And this was how Sully found her.

He had come up to tell her of the progress on the damaged section of wall and found her door slightly ajar. Upon entering, he could see the back of the chair and the hair spilling over one side. Rounding the chair, he was hit with the vision of the peacefully sleeping Josephine, her lips moistly parted in slumber. With stolen minutes, he watched her sleep and allowed himself the luxury of exploring his feelings for her.

He simply couldn't help it.

Sully had loved Josephine for as long as he could remember. Even if she hadn't been the earl's daughter and had simply been a peasant girl, he would have loved her. There was something about her that had always drawn him to her. But now, it was a difficult situation. He knew her feelings were not the same for him, simply because she considered him her very best friend. She'd told him so many times. It had been Sully who had always protected her, Sully who had comforted her when her favorite horse died, and Sully who lied to Hugh on Josephine's behalf when she snuck out of Torridon disguised as a boy to attend the faire in the village. He had been with her through the good and the bad, and that only made him love her more.

But there had been dark times in that one-sided love affair. Josephine had almost been betrothed two years prior to the fat, old Earl of Kilbrennan, but it was Sully who saw through the old bastard's façade and convinced Hugh that the earl would have treated Josephine less than desirably. There had always been rumors, but it was Sully who had done some digging. He had discovered that Kilbrennan had a deviant sexual streak. The earl used to like to watch his now-dead wife and daughters as they engaged in sexual acts with more than one man at a time, and sometimes with objects of the earl's choosing.

It had been a disgusting discovery and Hugh had been exceedingly grateful to Sully for that information. Josephine had never known about it, of course. But yet again, Sully had saved her from a horrible fate.

He was always there for her.

Josephine stirred in her sleep, disrupting him from his thoughts, and a portion of the robe fell away, revealing one shapely leg and a portion of the other as they hung over the side of the chair. Sully was only human. He would have liked nothing better than to run his hands up the silken limbs, but he knew he couldn't. His main duty in his life was to protect Josephine, especially from himself.

There was something in him that wanted to nurture and pamper her. Even take care of her. Like now, he knew she would sleep much better on a bed and not a chair, so with infinite tenderness, he picked her up and carried her over to her bed. Gently laying her down, he pulled the coverlet over her, and Josephine snuggled down in her sleep and sighed contentedly. Sully smiled at the sight, wishing with all of his heart that he could have crawled into the bed next to her.

But he couldn't. She was an heiress, and he was not of her station. Josephine was as she always was – unattainable.

Quitting the chamber, Sully shut the door quietly behind him, leaving his mistress her well-deserved sleep.

The next morning

JOSEPHINE SAT AT the head of the massive oval table in what used to be her father's chair. The chamber was the Knight's Haven, a long, rectangular room that was located off of the great hall where Hugh would meet with his knights. Now, it was the place where Josephine met with the very same men, men that had become *her* knights.

The room was rich with the heritage of Torridon Castle. The de Carron banner of two black serpents facing each other against a field of white hung high above the head of the table. It smelled of smoke, of rushes, and of the special aromatic wood her father had liked to burn in the hearth. Josephine always felt closest to her father here, and today that feeling was especially important. She prayed that Hugh would understand what she was about to say.

She'd come to a decision.

It wasn't an easy decision, but a necessary one. She'd been mulling it over for months. But after yesterday, she knew she had to do something. She could no longer sit back and watch the Dalmellingtons destroy her beloved home.

Dressed in a rich surcote of emerald silk over a white underdress, Josephine's beauty hid the power of her distress. The dress hung low on her shoulders, revealing their tempting lines and a hint of cleavage. A gold linked belt hung low on her hips, and her thick hair was pulled back loosely at the nape of her neck and was secured with a golden ribbon. It was a beautiful picture, deceiving to the men who were now entering the chamber.

There was something on the wind.

The knights entered the room in a group, taking their usual places about the table. Josephine sat straight in her chair, waiting until all were seated before she spoke. But first, she glanced at the faces of her most loyal knights – Sully, Burl, Albert, Henly, Simon, Rickard, and Bruce; sitting on her right. Etienne, Severn, Geoffrey, Stephen, John, Quig, and Christoph were to her left. There were fourteen of them, a rather large number, but the Earl of Ayr's estate demanded such skilled protection. Hugh had made sure his lines were well-fortified with expensive knights. It was something that he could afford. Each one of the knights looked at Josephine with unquestioning loyalty, which made what she was about to say more difficult.

But the time had come.

"My faithful friends," she began. "I realize the hour is early and you have your duties to attend to, but thank you for coming at my summons. I wanted to say that you were all magnificent yesterday in the latest Dalmellington attack, and you have my undying gratitude. But the damage we sustained yesterday was beyond anything we have seen up to this moment and the task of rebuilding is sorely stretching our resources and our subjects. I fear that it will only get worse."

Josephine paused a moment, watching their reactions. Everyone seemed to agree. Folding her hands, she collected her thoughts and continued.

"I love Torridon with all of my heart, and to see it and my loyal subjects so badly assaulted pains me deeply," she said. "Therefore, I beg you to understand what I am about to say. We cannot take any more of these barbaric attacks. We are losing men-at-arms by the tens and, very soon, we will have no one to defend our walls. And you, my brave knights, I fear I will lose one or more of you at any time. And that, I cannot bear. My reason tells me to fight until there is nothing left for Colin Dalmellington to take, but my heart says to save Torridon any way that I can. I choose to listen to my heart."

Sully stiffened in his seat. She had said nothing to him about this, but he knew she'd been agonizing over the situation for quite some time. Yesterday's battle had been particularly bad. Now, a warning bell went off in his mind.

Good Lord, he thought. *What is brewing inside that pretty little head?*

She didn't keep him waiting.

"I have decided to travel to Burnton Castle and discover what will pacify Colin Dalmellington," she said firmly. "Whatever it is, within my power, I shall give it to him."

The knights bolted to their feet, all loudly protesting her decision and declaring their intention to fight until there was no breath left in their bodies. Josephine had expected this and she stood as well, holding up her hands for silence.

"Gentle knights, please," she begged. "There is no other choice, as I can see it. But if any of you have suggestions, now is the time."

They quieted somewhat as if contemplating alternative plans, looking at each other in discussion or yelling across the table. Only Sully was silent, watching his fellow knights in their animated conversations. Still, his mind was working swiftly – he truly wasn't surprised to hear of her decision, and it wasn't as if he entirely disagreed. It was obvious that she meant to do something to spare her castle and her people, but what would be the least dangerous option for her? Would walking into the Dalmellington lair be her best choice? He didn't think so.

"Dalmellington will demand a marriage," Albert, a burly and younger knight, was almost yelling. "The bastard will marry her to some lout-headed relative!"

"No, no," said fair-haired Severn. "He'll demand all of Torridon's riches *and* her title!"

"Ye're both wrong, laddies," Quig, the ruddy Scotsman, cut in with his usually calm fashion. "He'll demand her maidenhead. He never could keep his eyes off our mistress."

Josephine's bile rose at that thought. *Oh, Sweet Jesus, would he really? Would the man be low enough to demand such a thing?* She stepped away from the table as her men argued and wandered to the wall where the swords and shields of her father hung. She was still so young, never having any true responsibility in life until Hugh died. She'd never had to make a serious decision in her life.

And that inexperience was showing.

Josephine had awakened in the dead of darkness last night, her mind churning with worry. That happened often but, this time, it had been different. She had had a dream that her father stood on the drawbridge of Torridon, looking at his devastated fortress with such sadness that Josephine sensed he believed all of Torridon's problems were her fault. She had taken his once-magnificent castle and run it right into the ground.

Naïve as she was to the ways of the world, somehow Josephine believed that reasoning with Colin Dalmellington would solve the situation. *Sweet Jesus, she had tried!* She had tried so hard to keep Torridon running as smoothly as her father had, but she had one thing to contend with that her father hadn't – Dalmellington attacks.

She wasn't even sure Hugh could have defended the castle more ably than she had.

Josephine turned from the wall and walked back to her knights. Her usually confident self was damaged, but her pride still was intact. They were still arguing over the best course of action and she found herself sincerely hoping they would come up with a better solution than she did, because she most certainly didn't want to surrender her virginity to Colin Dalmellington. The mere thought made her ill.

Returning to the table, she stood by her chair as her knights continued to debate the issue. She wasn't hearing anything that seemed like a better solution to the problem but, out of the arguing, Sully's voice could be heard.

"I may have a solution," he said.

Instantly, the other conversations ceased, all eyes turning to him. But Sully only had eyes for Josephine.

"I believe the problem lies in the fact that we have lost so many men," he said matter-of-factly. "In the beginning, when we were eight hundred men strong, we were only concerned with defending Torridon and not launching counterattacks. We assumed, wrongly, that Dalmellington would tire of his game. But he has chipped away and chipped away until we now only possess enough men to barely defend ourselves, to say nothing of a counterattack. Our villeins are fleeing and our remaining men are discouraged. What used to be one of the strongest fortresses in all of Scotland is now in shambles."

The knights were silent. Sadness was reflected in their eyes. Josephine looked as if she were about to cry. Sully continued.

"What Torridon still possesses, however, is her last coffers of wealth," he said. "Money is not lacking, so I contend that we hire a mercenary army to help us rebuild and launch an attack that will wipe out Burnton Castle and the Dalmellingtons once and for all."

Josephine's lips parted in surprise. *Of course! Hire an army! Why hadn't she thought of that before?* With growing eagerness, she took her chair and fixed her eyes on Sully.

"Do you know of one?" she asked eagerly.

"Not personally," he said. "But it is well known that The Red Fury is the fiercest mercenary in all of England and Scotland. He commands over a thousand men and there isn't an army around that can best him."

The Red Fury! Of course, Josephine had heard that name. Hardly a person in England and Scotland hadn't. The man was English, she'd heard, but he did a great deal of business in Scotland fighting wars for Scottish lairds. It was said that The Red Fury could lick any army, anywhere. Most sane men feared him.

Was it possible she could hire him to defeat Dalmellington?

"Do you think he would assist us?" Josephine asked. "For the right price, of course."

A lazy grin creased Sully's lips. "My lady," he said. "He would assist the devil himself for the right price, to be sure."

Josephine's mind was working furiously. It was an astonishingly simple solution and she was truly ashamed she'd not thought of it herself.

"How much will it cost?" she inquired, perhaps a little hesitantly. "Will it be expensive?"

Sully cocked his head, glancing at Etienne before answering. Etienne gave him a quick lift of the eyebrows.

"Perhaps ten thousand marks," he said finally. "Mayhap more."

Josephine's mouth fell open in outrage. "Ten thousand ma…" she sputtered. "God's Toes! I could buy half of Scotland for that amount of money! They shouldn't call themselves mercenaries; they should just call themselves thieves and do away with the veil of deception!"

She threw herself against the back of the chair, her expression a cross between anger and disbelief. If the mercenary would really cost ten thousand marks, then hiring him would take everything they had.

"My lady," Sully said, seeing that she was discouraged. "Ten thousand marks for a one thousand man army. That is, at the very least, worth the money. Think of the security and stability they will bring to Torridon."

"But it will take everything we have," she said passionately. "And that is not where it will end. We will have to feed and house them here with our people. My God, when I think of all of the bastards we shall have running around next summer, it makes my head spin. Oh, Sweet Jesus…!"

She put out a weary hand over her eyes in a gesture of despair. What Sully was proposing was the best possible solution and she knew it; they all knew it. Josephine had been in favor of the idea until she found it would cost her ten thousand marks. Mayhap it wasn't as good an answer as she originally thought, but she seriously wondered if it was the *only* answer. A mercenary in their midst.

There was no other choice.

Josephine sighed heavily and looked at Sully. Her lips formed a straight line in a gesture of resignation as she came to the conclusion that they'd all come to; this was the only real solution. They'd already tried to fight off the Dalmellington forces themselves and they were near collapse. What they needed was a bigger army.

A professional army.

"Very well, Sully," Josephine said finally. "If you feel this is the right thing to do, then… then I suppose we have little choice. Find The Red Fury and hire his army. Make it so."

Sully had to admit that he was relieved to hear her command. He'd had his doubts. But even Josephine could see that it was their only answer, even if it would drain their coffers. But at least they'd have their fortress saved from the Dalmellington onslaught.

And a mercenary to save them.

"Aye, my lady," he said quietly. "I will do what I can."

The decision had been made. Josephine watched her knights leave the room and wondered if she made the right decision. *Sweet Jesus, a mercenary army at Torridon!* She'd have to make sure all of the valuables were hidden away, and that none of the women were ever alone or without an escort.

And then there was her sister.

Justine would be in her glory with all of the soldiers to tell fortunes to, but not if Josephine could help it. She wondered how Justine would react to being locked up in the tower indefinitely.

She snickered bitterly at the thought.

IT WAS TOWARDS mid-afternoon on the day after the battle, and repairs were in full swing under a bright blue sky and soft winds. Seated in her solar and repairing a pair of her breeches that had been torn in a previous battle, Josephine heard a shout from the inner ward. Visitors were arriving, and she set her things aside and quickly headed out to the keep entry where several servants were congregating.

"Who is here?" she demanded.

A young maid with bad teeth and hair bound up in a kerchief snapped her head in her mistress' direction and curtsied quickly.

"Donald Muir, my lady," she said.

Josephine looked in the direction of the entry door as if to see the inner ward beyond. "Excellent," she said, pleasure in her expression. "Find Lady Justine. Inform her we have a guest. I want the great hall prepared for a grand feast this evening. Now, run!"

The servants scattered and Josephine went to stand in the entry. Outside, in the inner bailey, the entourage of young Muir was just coming to a halt. Josephine smiled at Donald, who caught sight of her immediately from atop his silver-gray destrier. The wind caught her emerald silk surcote as she descended the stone steps, causing it to billow out behind her and revealing her pretty legs from the knees down.

Young Donald was pleased at the unexpected view of her legs but said nothing. He dismounted with a smile on his face, chivalrously extending his hand. Josephine placed her hand in his, and he flipped it over and brought the tender side of her wrist to his lips. She smiled reproachfully at the devilish look on his face. He was blond, tall, very handsome, and was two years older than she.

"Master Muir," she said. "What brings you to my humble, if not slightly destroyed fortress?"

Donald removed his gauntlets and slapped the leather against an open palm. "I would say Torridon is more than just slightly destroyed," he said, passing a practiced eye over the ward. "We received word of yer attack late yesterday. Father sent me with one hundred men-at-arms to see if we could be of assistance."

She smiled gratefully. "How I wish you had come yesterday," she said softly. "But the siege ended at dusk. Your father is very kind to have sent you but, as you can see, the storm has passed. But you will stay, of course, and feast with us tonight."

"Of course," he said agreeably. "Ye do not think I really came to fight, did ye? I only came to gaze on yer beauty."

He was arrogant, and a flatterer, but a good friend and Josephine liked him a great deal. Donald extended his arm and she took it, leading her off across the compound as his followers disbanded. It was a well-known fact that the son of the neighboring lord was wildly in love with Josephine, but she considered him nothing more than a childhood friend. Pity, too, for they made a handsome couple.

Sully entered the inner bailey from the stables in time to see Josephine and Donald stroll leisurely towards the opening into the outer bailey. He could tell that Josephine was showing him the damage. She was pointing to the destruction as Donald nodded his head. An expression of impatience crossed Sully's face; as much as he liked young Muir, he felt a distinct twinge of jealousy at the sight of the two of them arm-in-arm. He knew Donald's feelings for Josephine; everyone knew. Although she showed him no interest, the lad wouldn't give up. Perhaps that's what bothered Sully the most; the fact that Donald never seemed to understand Josephine's position on the matter. He thought he still had a chance.

Foolish whelp.

Casually, Sully followed the pair just to make sure young Donald behaved himself.

EARLY IN THE evening, a sumptuous spread was served of roast venison, mutton, roasted pigeon in plum sauce, and waterfowl. Whatever problems Torridon Castle may have had, food was not one of them. With their own herds and gardens, they always had plentiful fare. Fresh loaves of bread with butter and honey crowded the tables.

The enormous great hall was warm and brightly lit. The servants moved among the boisterous diners, making sure their cups were never empty of sweet Spanish wine. A quartet of minstrels, who were actually soldiers from Torridon's ranks, played lively music from one corner of the room.

Even though the feast had already commenced, Josephine was just finishing dressing. For this evening, she had selected a gown of red silk. The gown hung dangerously low on her chest, greatly accentuating the swell of her luscious breasts. The sleeves started midway down her upper arm and extended down to her tapered wrists. A large, white collar encircled the top of the dress and the sleeves were intricately embroidered with golden thread.

The silk clung to every curve, flaring just below the hips and gracefully encircling her. Resting on her hips was a girdle of finely woven gold that came to a "V" right before her pubic mound. The dress was absolutely magnificent.

To finish the picture, Ola had pulled her great mane back, weaving it into a loose braid. Upon her head, she wore a thinly-woven net of gold. A layer of beeswax gave her lips a glossy glow. As Josephine gazed at herself in her polished bronze mirror, she didn't think she looked much like a woman who was killing men and wielding a broadsword only the day before. She looked like a true lady, a countess in fact, who ruled a prosperous earldom.

But it was all a façade; the beautiful picture masked the weariness, the hopelessness that she felt. The eyes that looked back at her couldn't conceal the sorrow. Perhaps an evening with her friend, Donald, would change that reflection. She was hoping so, ready for some pleasantness after such terrible times. Rising from the stool she'd been sitting on, she heard an audible gasp from Ola.

"Oh, my lady!" she breathed. "You look lovely!"

Josephine smiled, with a blush creeping into her cheeks. "Thank you."

As if on cue, there was a knock at the door. Ola opened it and in swept Justine. But this was no ordinary appearance by Torridon's self-proclaimed white witch. Josephine's eyes bulged at the sight of her sister, and then she looked at Ola in disbelief. Ola's face was a mirror of her mistress' distress.

Justine was dressed in a black silk dress that was so sheer, that one could see her skin right through it. And she wore nothing underneath it. Some sort of strange silver girdle encircled her hips with odd occult markings on it. Over her shoulders, she wore a long, silken black shawl. Her long brown hair was pinned up in an elaborate style. Josephine circled her sister in disbelief.

"I will *not* allow you to wear such a garment," she finally said.

Justine stiffened. "I will wear what I please, my sister, with no instructions from you."

"Then do as you please," Josephine said angrily, "but only in your own boudoir. Not in the dining hall surrounded by oversexed soldiers!"

"I am not ashamed of my body," Justine informed her with self-righteousness. "It is as pure as the heaven and the earth, and to gaze upon it will bring them good fortune. And, in fact, there is not one man down there that has not seen a woman's body."

"Oh, God's Toes," Josephine rolled her eyes in exasperation, letting a hand slap her thigh. "Ola, send Sully to me immediately."

As Ola slipped out, Justine flamed. "Sully cannot tell me what to wear, either," she declared. "Hear me, Sister. I am very powerful and you would be wise not to a-flame me."

"Spare me the empty threats, Justine," Josephine said, unimpressed. "Your mind works in such mysterious ways that I cannot believe you and I sprang from the same loins. Just once – just one blessed time – I wish you would stop this pretending to be something you are not and assume your true position as chatelaine of Torridon. How on earth do you expect to find a husband if you continue acting like a brainless nymph?"

"Who wants a husband?" Justine seemed genuinely repulsed. "I must remain pure if my powers are to remain strong."

Josephine scowled. "You will not remain a virgin if you continue to dress like that."

Justine stepped into her sister's face. "I am untouchable," she said threateningly. "No man would dare touch me and risk provoking the powers of the universe."

"Aye, Justine," Josephine said as she put up a hand as if to push away her foolish sister. "You must be sure to remind them of that as they rip off your sheath and drive their manhood deep into your womb."

Justine's blue eyes flashed furiously and she opened her mouth to retort when the door opened and Sully calmly entered the room. Josephine turned to him, her face wrought with exasperation; she didn't need to tell him anything because he'd already heard some of it. At Ola's urgent message, he had raced from the dining hall in a matter of seconds and stood outside of Josephine's door. The only reason he chose this moment to enter was because he was afraid they had reached the hair-pulling stage.

That had happened before.

"My ladies require me?" he inquired casually.

"Sully," Josephine said, pointing a finger at her sister. "See what she plans to wear at dinner. Tell her that it is most inappropriate."

Sully honestly hadn't noticed anything about Justine; his eyes were riveted to Josephine as they always were. But after her statement, he managed to tear his eyes away long enough to give Justine the once-over. The first thing he saw was the dark thatch of hair between her legs, clearly seen through the sheer fabric. After that, he tried not to look any further but morbid curiosity kept his eyes where they should not be. He could not believe that Justine would actually wear the dress in front of hundreds of drunk, leering men. He crossed his arms and lifted a fatherly eyebrow.

"You intend to wear that... *garment*?" he asked.

Justine's chin shot up defiantly. "I do."

Sully cocked a thoughtful eyebrow before turning to an irate Josephine. "A word, if you please, my lady."

Josephine cast Justine a triumphant expression as she went to the opposite end of the room with Sully. Justine, in turn, cast her sister her very best evil eye.

Sully moved close to Josephine. "Will you trust me?" he whispered.

She nodded eagerly. "Implicitly."

He looked her in the eye. "Let her wear it."

Josephine looked stunned. "*What*?"

"Let her wear it," he repeated patiently. "Let her see just how untouchable she really is. You can yell at her until your tongue falls out, but she will never relent because she believes she is right. Some people must learn lessons the hard way."

Josephine looked at him dubiously, then looked at her sister, and back to Sully again. Her jaw muscles were flexing as she thought on his words.

"Very well," she said reluctantly. "I would be in favor of that. But what if the situation gets out of hand? Will you save her?"

"Do you want me to?"

There was a twinkle of mirth in her eye. Despite her anger, she found herself fighting off a grin.

"I almost do not," she said.

The subject of the conversation began to fade in Sully's mind and all he could think of was the smell of Josephine's rose perfume and the swell of her bosom. Why on earth should he think of Justine when this glorious creature was in front of him? But Josephine turned with a wink and was gone. That ended Sully's daydreams.

Oblivious to Sully's mental worship of her, Josephine walked over to her sister and looked the woman up and down. Hands on her hips, she faced off against Justine's stubborn stance.

"Sully feels you should be allowed to wear the gown of your choosing," she said evenly. "So be it. We will attend our guests now."

Justine's chin jutted out triumphantly and she stomped from the room. Josephine looked at Sully with uncertainty in her eyes.

"I hope you are right," she said quietly. "Or I will have lost all control over her."

Sully came over to her, a reassuring smile on his face. He offered her his arm and she accepted. As they descended the stairs, he didn't say what he was thinking; he knew that Justine's shocking costume would be quickly forgotten when Josephine, in all of her glory, entered the hall. Any normal man would look at her over her foolish sister.

Sully wondered if his plan would, indeed, backfire.

JOSEPHINE COULD BARELY eat. With Donald on one side of her and Sully on the other, her trencher was filled to overflowing with food, but her appetite was gone.

Around her, the hall was alive with music and laughter. The smells of roast meat filled their air as hungry dogs wandered the room. But Josephine's eyes watched her sister's every move as she sat at the end of the table, surrounded by salivating soldiers who pretended to be interested in what she was saying. But their bloodshot eyes were fixed on her small breasts with large brown nipples that showed obviously through the fabric.

Josephine was deeply embarrassed for her sister, but Justine seemed not to notice the reason for their attention. She was going on and on about the deadly benefits of the nightshade plant.

"Justine has certainly dazzled the men with her... charms," Donald spoke in Josephine's ear.

Josephine glanced over her shoulder at him. "I pray that the floor will split wide and swallow her up."

"Is she truly yer flesh and blood?" Donald asked with mock seriousness. "Or did yer mother find her growing on a vine in the forest?"

Josephine visibly sobered. "My mother died in childbirth for that... that *woman*."

Donald wished the floor would split wide and swallow him, too. He had not meant to sound insensitive. Josephine turned away from him and focused on Sully.

"Your plan is not working," she whispered, singsong. "Not once has anyone made a move to touch her and she is enjoying the attention immensely! Now what?"

"Patience, my lady," he reassured her. "Have you ever known me to be wrong?"

Her pause made him turn to look at her. "Not very often, but it has been known to happen." His eyes twinkled at her and she pointed a finger at him in a threatening fashion. "But this better not be one of those occasions!"

Suddenly feeling ravenous, Josephine turned her attention to her trencher and began to hungrily devour a piece of stringy beef. The music grew more lively and a few couples rose to dance to the swift beat. Before Josephine could finish her food, Donald had her by the hand and led her to the floor near the hearth where the others were dancing. It was a fast-paced old folk dance and Josephine was soon breathless and laughing as Donald swung her endlessly in his arms.

Sully watched from his seat on the dais. It was so good to see her laughing again; Lord knew, there had been little enough to laugh about lately. Her laughter sounded like chimes; clear, pure, and tinkling. But his eyes darkened with the jealousy he had no right to feel.

God in heaven, what was he going to do when she married? How in the hell was he going to handle a husband touching and loving Josephine? *Get a hold of yourself, man,* he scolded himself. *Who is to say that you will not be the one holding and loving her?* He comforted himself with that thought. He always thought that if he was patient enough, his patience would come to fruition. Josephine would see who loved her the very most. Not Donald or the other fools who fawned over her, but the stoic and strong knight who had devoted his life to her.

The man who had treated Torridon as if it were his very own castle.

In fact, Sully comforted himself further when he remembered that he had news for Josephine. News that they had been waiting for had come right before the feast began and Sully intended to deliver it to Josephine personally.

Alone.

Aye, she'd know soon who loved her the very most.

As Sully pondered what the future might bring for him and his lady, Justine was dancing furiously with several men, being passed from man to man as they swung her roughly. They were laughing loudly in their revelry but, soon, hands began to touch places they shouldn't. Justine stopped laughing and tried to stop dancing, but momentum kept moving her from one man to the next. Finally, one particularly burly soldier grasped her around the body and pulled her close to his sweaty, smelly face. Justine squealed and pushed at him as he brought his stinking mouth close to hers.

"Aw, c'mon, girl! Do not be shy!" he rasped.

Josephine stopped her dancing and raced to her sister's side. She pounded the man's broad chest.

"Let her go, you swell-headed lout!" she yelled.

Sully was on the move. He vaulted over the dining table and hit the floor running. Etienne, Burl, and Christoph followed on his heels. But he wasn't fast enough to prevent Josephine from wrapping her arms around the man's neck and hanging on for dear life in her attempt to choke him.

Between Josephine's yelling, Justine's screams, and the soldier's grunting, it was hard to tell just who was assaulting whom. Donald, rushing to assist Josephine, was summarily flattened by one of the soldiers who had been dancing with Justine. His nose was gushing blood as he pushed himself up from the floor and shook off the bells ringing in his ears.

Sully bounded over the flailing Donald to wrench Justine from the man's grasp. He thrust her into Burl's waiting arms.

"Get her out of here!" he ordered.

The soldier was struggling to breathe with Josephine's arms wound tightly about his neck. She managed to remove one arm long enough to pound him solidly on the side of his mangy head, all the while hurling insults at him. Sully lunged and grabbed Josephine about the waist, tugging her hard at least twice before he managed to dislodge her.

"Josephine!" he bellowed. "Josephine, release!"

Etienne had the soldier by the hair, pulling him away as Josephine was pulled off of him. She was still angry and fighting until Sully, with one arm wrapped tightly around her small waist, clamped his other hand over her mouth. Then, with Josephine silent, he turned with a clenched jaw to his knights.

"I want the offending soldier and his cohorts sent on their way," he growled to Etienne.

"Och, my lord!" the man whined. "We were just 'aving a li'l fun! Besides, she was jus' askin' fer trouble with that invisible dress she's wearin'!"

His friends chimed in loudly, implying all sorts of unladylike things. Sully had to struggle to keep Josephine under control. She writhed, twisted, and grunted under his iron grip. But the man's argument didn't affect Sully; he continued to stare at the man with an unwavering gaze. Then, with a nod of his head to Etienne, the soldier and his four accomplices were forcibly escorted from the room. As they were exiting the door, Sully looked over at the musicians.

"Play!" he commanded.

Without so much as a pause, the music began again, as lively and melodic as before. People began to turn back to their conversations and the dancing resumed. Slowly, Sully removed his hand from Josephine's mouth.

"Are you calm?" he asked.

Her mouth was twitching. "Aye."

He still had her about the waist, pulled close against him. Just inches below his mouth was the tender nape of her neck and her creamy white shoulders. The temptation was almost overwhelming, but Sully forced himself not to think about it. Still, he didn't let her go.

"Can I trust you not to run after those men if I release you?" he asked.

Josephine pulled herself irritably from his grasp. "Of course, Sully," he snapped. Then she caught sight of Donald Muir being attended by Christoph. "Donald! What happened to him?"

Sully's eyes followed her as she ran to Donald and fussed over the man. The lad had gone down quickly in the fight, he noted with a bitter chuckle. He was a good swordsman, but not much with his bare knuckles. Josephine had fared better in the fight than young Muir had. God's Bones, she was feisty.

Sully rather liked that.

But Sully was forgotten, as was the feast, as Josephine helped Donald to his feet. She had greater concerns on her hands now than a foolish sister and a lascivious soldier. With her guest of honor injured, she felt terrible about the entire event and escorted him to a guest room to recuperate. She suspected that his nose was broken with the pain he was experiencing. Donald tried to joke about it, but she could see the blue circles forming underneath his eyes already. Deeply concerned for her friend, Josephine left the chamber to seek the old physic, Dewey.

The old man who had been at Torridon long before the House of de Carron took charge of the castle was in his room at the top of the east tower of the keep. It was a dark and eerie tower, smelling of strange odors, and most people avoided going into the tower altogether. But not Josephine; she knocked loudly on Dewey's door and entered hesitantly, peering into the room as the ancient oak door squeaked open. As children, she and James and Justine had been absolutely terrified of coming up here, and they used to threaten each other with the prospect of it often. It was a cold, dank, and weakly-lit room; even on the brightest of days.

Josephine called Dewey's name softly and slowly entered into the forbidden chamber. It was a large room littered with tables, and the tables were heaped with paraphernalia she did not recognize. Among

Dewey's many talents, he also practiced the ancient art of alchemy. She gingerly examined the contents of the nearest table, noticing the foul odor emitting from it.

Disdainfully, she backed away and called Dewey's name again just as the old man appeared out of the darkness behind her. When he put a hand on her shoulder, she jumped with fright.

"Oh!" She put her hand to her chest. "You startled me. Dewey, Master Muir has been injured and requires your attention."

"Of course, my lady," he smiled his ancient crooked grin at her. "Let me get my medicaments."

Josephine waited while he retrieved his enormous woven basket laden with potions, herbs, and mysterious salves. With a swish of his cloak, he preceded her out of the room and she followed eagerly, glad to be out of his private abode. Glancing over her shoulder as she descended the stairs, she could swear unseen eyes were watching her from the walls of the old tower. Dewey's tower had that effect on everyone. Shaking off her uneasy feeling, she continued quickly down the steps, following the tiny physic all the way to Donald's chamber.

As it turned out, the young man did, indeed, have a broken nose, according to Dewey, who tended the young man as best he could. Josephine stood by, helping the old man if he needed it, all the while feeling a building rage towards her sister. Justine and her ridiculousness had caused all of this, after all, and the more she watched Donald wince, the angrier she became.

By the time Dewey was finished with him, Josephine had worked up a righteous fury. As far as she was concerned, this would be the last time Justine behaved so poorly. This time, Donald was injured but, next time, there was no telling what the consequences would be.

Josephine made a decision that there were to be consequences, no more idiocy, even if she had to throw her sister in the vault to prove it.

This night, Justine's foolishness was at an end.

WHEN JOSEPHINE RETURNED to her chamber after helping tend Donald, Sully was waiting for her in the corridor outside of her room. But she swept past him without so much as a glance on her way to Justine's room, next to hers. Sully watched her breeze by, then followed her.

He had a feeling what was coming.

Reaching Justine's door, Josephine pounded on it loudly. Her sister screamed for her to go away, but Josephine ignored the command completely and burst into the chamber, seeking out Justine. She spied her huddled up in a ball in a chair by the fireplace. Justine's eyes were red-rimmed as she looked at her sister in surprise.

Josephine's anger was unchecked. She intended for Justine to feel the full force of her wrath. Marching up to the chair, she put her balled fists on her slim hips and glared down at her sister.

"Well?" she demanded. "Are you satisfied with the havoc you have wrought? Who needs Dalmellington when we have you around to destroy us from the inside?"

"Cease," Justine propelled herself from the chair, trying to get away from her angry sister. "I will not hear your insults. Leave me alone and attend your guests!"

"I have!" Josephine fired back. "Because of your willful stubbornness, Donald Muir is now abed with a broken nose and we are less five men-at-arms. Justine, why did you not listen to me? I was not speaking just to hear my own voice, you know. I happened to know what I was talking about."

Justine glared frightfully at her sister and, for a moment, Sully again feared that they would come to blows. But Justine, showing a ray of intelligence, turned away from her sister and stared into the fire.

"Leave me, Joey," she said dully. "I have no wish to listen to your words tonight."

"Is that all you have to say to me? That you do not wish to listen to my words?"

Justine was starting to tear up again. "What would you have me say?" she asked. "That you were correct? That I should have listened? That I am sorry for what happened to Donald? Of course I did not plan that. I am more sorry than you know."

"Are you? Enough to listen to me the next time I tell you something for your own good?"

Justine sighed heavily and looked away; there was such defeat in her features. As Josephine looked at her sister's expression, she began to calm down. She could see that Justine was repentant and she was coming to suspect that there was nothing she could say that Justine didn't already know. Perhaps, the humiliation of the evening was enough of a lesson for one night. God's Bones, she could only hope so.

Therefore, she was coming to think it was best if she simply left. As she reached for the door she paused, her gaze moving to her sister's profile.

"Justine," she said hesitantly. "I only want the best for you. I do not try to make your life miserable. You are my sister and I love you. No matter what... please always remember that."

Justine turned to her and, for a brief moment, Josephine caught a glimpse of a normal, rational woman who would someday make a fine wife. That woman was there, buried deep inside Justine's complex persona. Josephine hoped that she would come out someday, sooner rather than later.

"I love you, too," Justine whispered.

In silence, Josephine quit the chamber with Sully on her heels. He escorted her back to her chamber and poured her a cup of mulled wine, thinking that she probably needed it. Josephine accepted it absently, her mind still on her sister.

As she went to sit by the hearth, Sully poured a cup for himself, watching his mistress' face as she sat. He knew she was taxed with Justine adding to her already insurmountable burdens. It was a large load for one so young to handle, but she was strong. And she had to continue being strong until a permanent solution was found to the

Dalmellington problem. As of tonight, Sully hoped he had the answer.

This was the moment of privacy he'd been hoping for.

"My lady," he said quietly. "I sent out four messengers today; one in each direction. They are instructed to find The Red Fury and deliver the message that five thousand marks await him and his army if they will defend Torridon Castle against the Dalmellington onslaught. The Red Fury is usually encamped this time of year near Dumfries, so we may get lucky. He may get our message quickly and respond."

Josephine pondered that information for a moment. "I thought you said it would cost me ten thousand marks," she said, staring into the flames of her hearth.

Sully shrugged lightly. "I left room for negotiation."

She tore her eyes away from the fire and looked at him with wide, frightened eyes. "But what if it is not enough?" she asked. "What if he will not come?"

He puckered his lips in a silent whistle and went to stand by her chair. "Five thousand marks is still a great deal of money," he said. "It will be enough to get his attention. I believe it will be enough to garner his attention."

Josephine looked at him with uncertainty, but so wanting to believe him. Sully was always right, wasn't he?

"Oh, Sully," she looked into his ice-blue eyes as she lifted her cup to him. "May you always be right."

Sully found himself lost in her eyes, her lips, and her hair. The dress, in a sitting position, strained against her breasts. Common sense screamed at him to get the hell out of the room before he did something they would both regret. Swiftly, he turned away from her and deposited his cup on the table as he hastened for the door.

"Sully!"

Josephine called to him and he froze with his hand on the door latch. Josephine set her goblet down and rose from her chair. In the next second, she was standing next to him and he could feel the heat radiating from her body.

"Thank you," she whispered sincerely. "Thank you for taking such good care of Justine and me. I shudder to think what would have become of us had you not been here."

Suddenly, she threw her arms around him and hugged him tightly. Sully was plunged into a tumultuous abyss; he had no idea how to respond. She was warm, soft, and fragrant, and the only thing between their bare bodies was a silk dress and his linen tunic and leather doublet.

This was where he'd always wanted to be.

Still, he wrestled with keeping his arms to himself. He was afraid of what would happen if he let himself go. Yet he knew she was expecting some sort of response and his arms came up, hesitantly, and wrapped themselves around her waist. He squeezed her quickly before releasing her, moving away so that she was forced to release him, also.

God in heaven, he had to get out of there!

"Sleep well, my lady." It was the only reply he could manage.

Sully left her without another word. Outside in the corridor, he rushed to the stairs and descended them two at a time. His cheeks were hot, his heart pounding in his ears, and he just had to get the hell out of the keep.

In the great hall, the feast was still going on, as it most likely would all night. Sully could hear faint strains of the flute as he strolled out into the night on his way to the knight's quarters. He found himself wondering which one of the whores would fill his bed tonight. They were women who warmed the beds of the knights and who gave them a particular peace in a world that didn't have much. There were seven of them and Etienne had named each one after the seven deadly sins – Gluttony, Lust, Greed, Pride, Sorrow, Wrath, Vanity, and Sloth.

He was feeling particularly lustful tonight.

CHAPTER THREE

North of Dumfries, Scotland
Along the River Nith

I T WAS THE nooning hour and the camp was filled with the smell of roasting sheep. Three were splayed over the pit, with their juices dripping onto the fire and creating an almost acrid smell. The men stood around waiting hungrily for their portion, conversing heartily. But they were hearty men, used to the harsh elements, harsh women, and harsh food.

Mercenaries were not men akin to luxury.

These were men that slept on their saddles and traveled with everything they owned, for they were men without homes and, in most cases, without families. These were professional soldiers and worth every penny of their fee. Yet, with all of their rugged toughness, the one thing their leader insisted upon was decent clothing. Their breeches and tunics were of durable fabric and their vests and doublets were of excellent leather. Most of them wore thigh-high boots, for they were better protection when mounted, and their chainmail and helms were always in good condition; their commander made sure of that. He wanted them to look like an army that was worth the money spent.

It also meant they were a well-fed army, but the mutton at noon was an unusual occurrence. Usually it was stew and hard bread, but they would be breaking camp in a few hours and their commander wanted them traveling on hearty fare. Therefore, the men stood around and wiped saliva from their lips as they waited for their meat.

Andrew was not one of them. The morning after his horrific nightmare, he didn't have much of an appetite. Although he had ordered the sheep butchered, he would wait until his men were fed before eating himself. Andrew sat in a collapsible chair under a vast oak tree, leaning back against it on two legs of the chair as he sharpened the non-serrated side of his broadsword. Sunlight filtered in between the leaves and cast rays that fluctuated as the wind blew. They reflected off of his sword as he tended it under expert hands.

It was a fine day, considering the storm that had blown through the night before. It was warm and bright, and was almost too warm for the season, especially this far north. He lowered the sword; his clear brown eyes looked off towards the camp where he could see soldiers sitting in groups, eating their meal.

The camp was a large one, stretching for nearly a half-mile, housing a thousand men. But for all the men-at-arms, they traveled light and fast with six wagons, three hundred horsemen, one hundred archers, and six hundred soldiers. It was the biggest mercenary army in all of England and Scotland, and Andrew was extremely proud of what he'd built.

But it was something he'd had to do as a matter of survival.

The recurring nightmare the evening before had been the spark to this empire he'd created. As the second son of the Earl of Annan and Blackbank, Andrew had been the son who'd had to earn his own way in life for the most part. His father had been a kind man who genuinely loved his only two sons. Alphonse was the eldest by three years, and never did a more lecherous, greedy, and selfish person walk the face of the earth.

The earl knew this, but it was Alphonse's birthright as the eldest son to inherit the titles and lands when the earl passed on. This distressed him greatly, for Alphonse lacked everything Andrew possessed – fairness, sensibility, uncanny intelligence, and compassion. The earl attributed his eldest son's disposition to the fact that his mother had Plantagenet blood in her, and Alphonse was very fair, plain, and petty, just like the Plantagenets.

Andrew, however, was different. He had the d'Vant strength and common sense, the d'Vants being an ancient bloodline from the wilds of Cornwall where some of the family still lived to this day. But along with that strength and common sense came the d'Vant comely looks; in a completely masculine sense, he was the most beautiful man God had ever created. His auburn hair was cropped near his skull, although he was lazy about cutting it. Sometimes it grew long enough that with sweat and grime from his warring ways, it would stand straight on end. His face was finely featured: auburn brows arched over the most soulful of brown eyes fringed by thick lashes. His nose was straight and well-shaped, and his chiseled cheeks descended to a square jaw.

Women went absolutely mad for the likes of Andrew and he knew it. He had no shortage of bed partners, but he made sure he never had the same woman twice because that threatened emotional attachment. Women were nothing more than objects of lust or bearers of children and he had no trouble seeing them as such, for he had never met a woman he had even remotely considered forming an attachment with. His life revolved around his sword and his army.

And he meant for it to be that way.

But his path had been decided for him long ago. That's where the nightmare came in, why it was something that repeated itself again and again. The moment his father had died, brother Alphonse had taken firm control of the d'Vant properties. He'd greedily devoured the title and the lands, imprisoned his own mother, and had threatened Andrew with his very life unless he left immediately. Young Andrew, still grieving for his father, ran out with only the clothes on his back. He was afraid that his newly titled brother, the earl, would send his newly commanded soldiers to make good on the threat.

His departure was not an act of cowardice but rather it was an act of wits. Still, those nightmares were his guilt talking. He swore that, someday, he'd return and avenge his mother's imprisonment and punish Alphonse for every unkind deed and barbarous act he ever committed.

But he needed help. Andrew believed it was truly fate that brought him to a man named Trey. Trey led a small army of mercenaries that traversed the wilds of northern England and southern Scotland, preying on travelers and small villages. Trey was older, having traveled from France several years before, and Andrew believed he was the most worldly man he had ever known. He fell in to Trey's group, eventually becoming his page and learning everything he could from him. Trey took the place of his late father to young Andrew, and opened up a whole new world of education to him.

Trey le Bec saw something truly special in his young friend. Not only was Andrew a quick learner, but he handled a sword with extraordinarily raw talent; for from the size of him, someday he would make the best of soldiers. Even so, Trey sensed a great sadness in the lad, for he was silent almost to a fault, and only spoke when spoken to. Questions about his past and heritage were usually met by answers that were completely off the subject. Trey respected the lad's unwillingness to speak of his past and, in spite of everything, the two became the best of friends. He even discovered a devilish sense of humor which lurked within young Andrew.

One day, Andrew had cut undetectable slits in Trey's cup. That evening at dinner when he sipped his wine, the red liquid seeped out all over his tunic. Only he didn't realize it until everyone began laughing loudly. Enraged, he realized he had been made a fool, and he grabbed the man nearest him and put a dagger to his throat as he roared at the top of his lungs. At that point, Andrew flew up and over the table, and placed himself between the innocent man and the wild-eyed Trey. Although he did not confess in so many words, it did not take a man of great brilliance to realize Andrew had played the joke.

The boy had a tricky streak in him.

The relationship grew from there. Andrew eventually rose to become Trey's general, the best fighter anyone had ever seen, and he earned a reputation in the heat of battle for fighting so furiously it was as if he were fighting the devil for his very soul. He treated all of his enemies in the same fashion, as ruthless against a smaller man as he was against a larger one. His standard rule was to never underestimate anyone.

It was a mantra that served him well.

Still, there was a fire that fed him. Everyone who knew him could see it. It was the fire of vengeance, the hatred against his brother that was fuel in his veins. It was what made Andrew such a vicious fighter, as if every man he battled was, in fact, his hated brother. *The Red Fury*, the men called him. Even so, Trey grew to heavily depend on him because, in spite of that cancerous sense of vengeance, Andrew related to the men better than Trey did. He was a cunning negotiator and he was excellent at recruiting. He would incorporate smaller bands of mercenaries into Trey's army with his silken tongue, making the army bigger and stronger than ever before. The ranks swelled, as did the coffers, and Trey was generous with Andrew.

As a grown man and a full-fledged commander of Trey's mercenary army, Andrew wanted for absolutely nothing, but creature comforts were not his main concern. He did very nicely with just what he needed. It was a good life for all concerned, and Andrew's taste for revenge on his brother seemed to fade with time. He became more focused on his skills, his men, and his wealth.

But things soon changed.

Fifteen years after Andrew joined le Bec's army, Trey was killed in a battle and Andrew grieved for him as he had for his father. But, unlike his father, Trey had left him a legacy. The massive army now numbered close to one thousand men and they all looked to Andrew as their leader now. He stepped up into the role magnificently, yet without fanfare. But the word soon spread that Trey le Bec's army was now under the control of his general, Andrew d'Vant.

Some said he had been in control all along.

It was something that had only grown more powerful over the past few years, bringing them to this moment in time. Now, Andrew had an entire empire he was in control of, although it was a transient empire. They moved from place to place with no real home base. They were gypsies in the most basic sense of the word.

But thoughts of Trey, of transient empires, and of recurring nightmares faded from Andrew's mind as he sat under the tree, watching the men around him. He caught sight of a figure approaching him and he recognized his general, Thane Alraedson, as the man approached with his sword scabbard smacking against his thigh-boots. Thane flashed a grin at Andrew as he squatted down beside him and began picking at the grass.

"The men will be ready to move within the hour," Thane said. "Have you decided that we shall definitely accept the task at Torridon?"

Andrew looked down at him. Thane was flamboyantly handsome with his cropped, blond hair and granite jaw. He wasn't as tall as Andrew, but he was wider with muscle. He was a knight, but he had been chased from the lord he'd once served by the irate lord whose daughter Thane had deflowered. With nowhere else to go, Thane had joined up with Trey and Andrew right before Trey's death and was closer than a brother to Andrew. He could be childish, and not always very bright, but he followed orders without question and could command capably.

"I have," Andrew replied in his deep, rich voice. "Torridon is several miles north of our location and I should like to make the castle by midnight."

Thane thought that might be the answer. Moreover, it wasn't unusual for Andrew to move the army in darkness. Sometimes it was better that way; less chance of confrontation with other armies or nervous fortresses.

"Very well," he said, then threw down the blade of grass he was toying with. "Are you sure you wish to accept Torridon's offer? We have other offers that will pay us more."

"We will fight for Torridon," Andrew said decisively. "Tell me what you know of it."

Thane shrugged. He generally knew a great deal about most fortresses in the border and lowland region. "It is a mighty fortress," he said. "Big and rich, from what I have heard. That is why I find it hard to believe you would accept their contract for only five thousand marks."

This time, Andrew shrugged. "I have yet to learn the terms of the contract," he said. "I would like to know what they want us to do. We could be making this trip for nothing."

Thane cocked an eyebrow. "But you told the messenger to return and inform the master that you would come," he said. "That will lead them to believe that you have accepted their money."

"But I have not," Andrew said, as he rose on his long legs and sheathed his broadsword. "Until I take their money, there is no commitment. Besides… I hear the Dalmellingtons are fierce fighters."

Thane stood next to Andrew, bracing his fists on his slim hips. "I also hear that they were once a part of the de Carron Clan," he said. "I have lived my entire life in this area, so I know the tales that abound. Blood feuds are always the worst."

"What else have you heard?"

"That this is a battle that has been going on for the past two years," Thane said. "Quite bitter, from what I'm told. Truthfully, I'm surprised it has taken Torridon this long to seek our assistance."

"Anything else?"

Thane grinned. "Only that the most beautiful woman in all of Scotland resides at Torridon."

Andrew cocked an eyebrow in mock interest. "I wonder if she is the one who has sent the missive?" he said. "Lady Josephine? Someone told me that the earl and his son died two years ago, leaving only women. Call me foolish, but this job has my curiosity."

Thane looked at him quizzically. "Me, too," he said. "I would like to know who is in command of Torridon."

Andrew looked off towards the camp. "That," he said steadily, "is a very good question, one I am sure we will quickly find the answer to."

Thane thought so, too. But he wondered if the answer was to be a complicated one. It seemed to him that if two women were the heiresses, then it must, indeed, be complicated. Women always were.

Within the hour, the army of The Red Fury had pulled up stakes and headed north towards the mighty bastion of Torridon Castle. With the promise of compensation on the line, the men were all eager to move, and this was all about the money.

In the minds of the mercenaries, there could be nothing else.

Blood feud be damned. What the mercenaries did, they did for profit.

CHAPTER FOUR

JOSEPHINE WAS JOLTED from a sound sleep by someone pounding on her door. As Josephine rolled over and sleepily sat up, Ola rushed from her pallet in the alcove and unlatched the door. Sully burst in, dressed to the hilt in chainmail and leather, with his helm underneath one arm.

"An army approaches, my lady," he said quickly.

Instantly, Josephine was awake, her green eyes wide with fear. "At night?" she gasped. "But the Dalmellingtons have never attacked us at night. The wall and the gate are not even…!"

He cut her off. "My lady, the army is far larger than the Dalmellington force," he told her. "I believe it is The Red Fury."

"God's Toes!" Josephine exclaimed, jumping to her feet. "Why did you not say so to begin with? I will greet him in the Knight's Haven. Go, Sully, *go!*"

Sully saluted her and was gone, with Severn at his heels. Severn, quiet and thoughtful, was usually the one to shadow Sully on his rounds. When the door closed, Josephine ripped the nightshift over her head and went to the dressing table where Ola was preparing a quick toilette.

"Sweet Jesus, Ola," she exclaimed softly as her maid splashed rose water on her face, cold with the night's chill. "He actually came… and so *soon.*"

Ola nodded in silence as her mistress rattled on. It was obvious that Josephine was greatly relieved, but was very anxious about the mercenaries themselves. *What kind of man was a mercenary?* She wondered. And she was wildly curious about The Red Fury himself. She imagined him to be huge and grizzled with a halo of wild orange hair. Why else would they call him "The Red Fury"?

She was soon about to find out.

There was a sense of apprehension in the air as Josephine dressed to receive the mercenary she hoped would save her castle and her people. She was dressed in a gown of garnet-colored wool. Her long, silken hair was left loose and free, and was curled gently down her back. Taking a last passing look at herself in the mirror, Josephine headed out the door, leaving Ola standing nervously by the dressing table. The little maid worried for her mistress and the negotiations that were about to take place.

But Josephine would not be alone as she faced the fearsome mercenary. Justine stood by the top of the darkened stairwell, dressed in what looked like a black bedsheet. Her brown hair was pulled severely back, making her blue eyes look large. When she saw Josephine approach, she went to meet her.

"I have read the cards, Joey, and I do not like what I see," she said.

The greeting that had been on Josephine's lips disappeared, and she rolled her eyes at her sister, pushing past her.

"I do not have time for this, Justine," she said.

"Wait!" Justine grabbed her sister's arm. "You must listen to me. I fear that The Red Fury will destroy you. I spread seven cards in an arch, beseeching them for guidance in your present and future. The first card, Eight Swords and a Maiden, was correct in its description of your past grief. The second was Seven Swords, indicating your determination and hope for the future."

Josephine jerked her arm away from her sister. "Cease," she hissed. "I do not believe in your ridiculous cards."

Justine followed her sister down the stairs and ignored her protests.

"The third card was the Queen of Swords, telling your future of womanly sorrow, need, and separation," she said. "The fourth card…"

Josephine whirled around when she reached the bottom of the stairs, her cheeks flushed with anger. "Justine, I do not believe in your charlatan fortune-telling," she spat. "I have enough on my mind without your insane babbling."

Justine was stubborn; she pretended not to hear her. "The fourth card was the Knight of Swords, indicating courage and war and defense; possibly destruction and ruin," she said quickly as she followed her sister across the foyer. She felt a true sense of duty to tell her sister what her cards had foretold, whether or not Josephine believed in them. "The fifth card was the Three of Swords and tells me that you will have a happy relationship with someone, yet it indicates the presence of a third person, but does not necessarily threaten the happy relationship."

Josephine was truly at a loss as to how to shut her sister up at this point. "My only confusion is to why I have not cut your tongue out prior to this moment," she growled as they crossed through the great hall. "I may yet if you do not shut your yap."

Justine was not deterred. "My puzzlement, however, comes from the sixth card," she continued urgently. "It was the inverted Four of Swords, and indicates wisdom and prudence. I do not understand it."

Josephine stopped one final time and turned to her sister with controlled anger.

"And I do not understand *you*," she hissed. "I have told you to cease your insane chatter, yet you soundly ignore me. Have you gone deaf, Justine? I have no time for you. I am trying to save Torridon!"

With that, she turned away and headed for the Knight's Haven, moving as quickly as she could without running, but Justine gave chase. She wasn't about to let her sister get away.

"And I am trying to save *you*," Justine said grimly. "For the seventh card, the card of Prophecy was the King of Swords. The decisions and power over your own life do not rest in your hands, Josephine de Carron. Crosswise over it lay the Ace of Swords. That denotes extreme love or hate. It is the most powerful card."

Josephine heard every word her sister said but ignored her as she marched into the Knight's Haven. There were a few servants milling about, lighting torches and setting out bread and wine. The room was soon bathed in a yellow glow as Josephine took her seat at the head of the table, completely ignoring Justine as the woman lingered near the door before finally turning away and disappearing. A servant poured her a cup of wine and she took a healthy gulp. She was not too proud to admit she was nervous, but she'd be damned if she let on to The Red Fury. She sat back in her chair with her eyes fixed on the doorway, waiting. She fleetingly wondered why Justine had not followed her in, but was relieved she hadn't. She'd had enough of her sister for the night.

Best appear calm and in control from the very first, she told herself. *I shall inspect him when he enters and let him see that I do not fear him or his lusty reputation. Then let the negotiations begin!* She sat a little straighter, perhaps a bit more confident with herself. But in the back of her mind, she prayed that Sully would do the bulk of the speaking. Her confidence and experience did not encompass negotiating with soldiers of fortune.

It was not long before she heard voices and footsteps approaching. There were the hard, sharp clicks of war boots on the cold stone and, suddenly, the doorway was filled with her knights, dressed for battle. *Her knights.* They fanned out into the room, with their shadows dancing eerily on the walls as they took their traditional seats at the table. They acknowledged her with a grin or a nod, and she nodded coolly, her eyes not missing anything.

Soon, men she didn't recognize entered the room and were told to sit in the chairs that were placed away from the table, against the wall. They looked older and, perhaps, more rugged than her own knights. She eyed them; there was something earthy and different about them, something she couldn't put her finger on. But just the sight of them set her confidence back a notch or two.

Where in the hell was Sully?

Josephine focused on the doorway feeling great anticipation. Had she not been so caught up in the heat of the moment, waiting for Sully to appear, she would have realized that every mercenary solider in the room was eyeing her as if she were the most delectable morsel.

Yet, she saw nothing but the doorway. With each passing second, the anxiety grew, and she soon reached the point where all she wanted to do was stand up and scream away her apprehension. But she continued to sit, swathed in garnet wool in a room full of both familiar and unfamiliar knights, and waited for what was to come.

The Red Fury.

ANDREW HAD BEEN mildly surprised as Torridon Castle loomed into view.

It was an incredibly massive structure, rising several stories above the moor upon which it sat. The outer bailey wall was exceedingly tall as well. But the closer they got, they could see chunks missing from the wall and men working on the gates in the light of a thousand torches. It gave the appearance of a busy hive of activity, for as they drew closer, they could see the wall lined with archers and a line of foot soldiers around the wall's perimeter.

Yet one thing with this picture was painfully plain – Torridon was obviously low on manpower. The commotion inside both baileys was relatively low because everyone who could use a sword or shoot straight was on the perimeter.

Knowing that they would be skittish, Andrew halted his humongous army about a quarter of a mile away and rode the rest of the way with Thane, a couple of pages, six men, and another of his generals, a big German by the name of Hans d'Aurilliac. They came storming up to the broken gates with the hooves of their large destriers throwing mud and rocks as they pulled the horses to an uneven halt.

"I am Andrew d'Vant!" he called out. "We are expected!"

One of the knights at the demolished main gate looked at him with a sneer. "*Who?*"

Andrew cocked and eyebrow. "Tell your liege that The Red Fury has arrived."

The knight's eyes went wide with recognition and he yelled to one of the men, who immediately dropped what he was doing and took off at a dead run. The knight turned back to Andrew.

"My name is Simon," the knight said, far more politely. He was an older man with receding gray hair. "Follow me into the bailey."

They did. Except for a few men running here and there, it was quiet at this hour. Andrew and his men dismounted, with the two pages remaining behind to hold the horses while the rest of the men entered the inner bailey. There was a feeling of trepidation as they did so, feeling the stares of uncertainty from those around them, but they continued on. Not that they blamed those who were feeling trepidation at the sight of strangers; with the state of the castle, it was clear they'd been pounded and pounded yet again. Men under such stress had every right to be suspicious.

But the knight leading them into the inner bailey wasn't uncertain. In fact, he seemed more than eager to assist them. Once inside the inner ward, Simon was joined by eight more knights, all seasoned men in well-used armor and protection. Simon briefly introduced each of the knights, but introduced Andrew as The Red Fury and not as Andrew d'Vant. Andrew chuckled inwardly as he wondered if any of them believed that it was his birth name.

The Red Fury was a much bigger name than Andrew d'Vant, a somewhat unspectacular name.

And it was the name, The Red Fury, that made the biggest impact. Once introductions were complete, they were about to head to the enormous keep when the massive oaken doors swung open, purging two men from the innards. Both were dressed in full battle gear, with helms underneath their arms. The man slightly in front of the other was of average height; older than Andrew, with his square jaw set grimly. The second man was big and was very blond, with sharp and intelligent features. They approached with force, yet their eyes were guarded as they regarded Andrew, whose expression was one of self-assurance and slight impatience.

"I am Sir Sully Montgomery," Sully said. "You are The Red Fury, I assume?"

Andrew nodded coolly. "Andrew d'Vant," he replied. "Your message was received."

"Five thousand marks to defend Torridon until you are no longer needed," Sully said, eyeing the man. "The amount is acceptable?"

"It was enough to bring me here," he answered steadily. "But I do not discuss monetary amounts or contract terms out in the open air. We will proceed inside and accomplish the task."

There was something about the way he spoke that made Sully want to comply immediately. Andrew d'Vant had a natural command ability that caused men to do his bidding. But he caught himself and felt a wave of anger wash over him. No one gave him commands inside the walls of his own fortress!

"Of course," Sully replied, very controlled. "But first, tell me how many men have you brought with you."

He was attempting to gain the upper hand in the already rapidly escalating negotiation, with a man who had already given him a command. But if Andrew sensed the competition already, he didn't let on. His gaze lingered on Sully.

"Nine hundred and ninety-six," he replied.

Sully acknowledged the number with a nod of his head, intently studying d'Vant just as he was being studied in return. It was the expression of men who were sizing one another up, trying to determine who was the most dominant.

So this is The Red Fury? Sully thought to himself. Somehow, he pictured a huge, violent red-haired man just one notch back on the evolutionary ladder. But this man was tall, evenly groomed, and intelligent-looking. His hair was a reddish-brown, reflecting in the torch light. He was very strong and capable-looking but, in truth, Sully couldn't see why they called him "The Red Fury".

But then again, he had yet to see the man fight.

"Your fortress looks in shambles," Andrew said after a moment's silence.

"You noticed," Sully said dryly. "Considering what we have been through, it is little wonder the entire structure is not razed."

Andrew's gaze moved along the top of the inner wall, with great soot marks from flaming projectiles. "I had no idea that the Dalmellington army was so formidable," he said.

Sully shook his head, beginning to relax just a little now that the initial inspection phase was over and the conversation had begun.

"In truth, they are not," he said. "But constant barrages, week after week, for the past year have taken their toll. And we lose men, which makes holding the fortress harder and harder. Even our mistress has taken up arms to help defend it."

Andrew's eyebrows rose lazily. "Only one mistress? I thought there were two?"

"There are," Sully replied. "Lady Josephine chooses to fight, while Lady Justine hunches over a crystal ball in hopes of conjuring up dark powers to defeat the Dalmellington army."

He'd said it before he could catch himself. *Why was he telling a perfect stranger this? The Red Fury will believe both women are as crazy as birds!* But as he looked at Andrew with some chagrin, he caught a twinkle of amusement in the man's eyes.

"Has it worked yet?" he asked.

"Has what worked yet?"

"The crystal ball," Andrew said, as he shifted on his big legs. "Have the dark powers converged to beat back the Dalmellingtons?"

Did he sense... humor? Sully was surprised at one with such a fierce reputation having room for a joke. But the corner of his mouth twitched as he replied.

"I do not know," he said. "But you have come, have you not?"

Andrew grinned. He might possibly like this man, Sully. "God's Bones!" he exclaimed. "Do you mean to say the rumors are true? That I am spawned from the bowels of hell?

Sully's face lit up with a reluctant smile. "Crystal balls do not lie," he said. "Only hell's powers feed it."

"I would accept that as reasonable," Andrew conceded.

Before Sully realized what was happening, he felt himself warming to this professional soldier. Sully, who was always on his guard and was always coolly detached, rarely warmed to anyone. He would have to be aware of that in the future, for this man had a manner that could disarm Lucifer. Negotiating terms of contracts were not going to be easy for Josephine.

… *Josephine!*

God in heaven, she was probably in the Knight's Haven right now wondering where in the hell they were.

"Come," Sully motioned to them and turned to go inside. "My mistress awaits you."

With that, everyone turned for the keep and the Torridon knights preceded Sully and Andrew into the dimly lit castle. Sully and Andrew walked side-by-side as they marched into the cold foyer, a faintly dank smell assaulting their nostrils. Andrew glanced about him with some interest, noting the old but rich tapestries that lined the foyer, the furnishings that were costly and fine.

Off of the foyer was a corridor that they passed into, and at the end of the corridor was a wide, yawning cavern of a chamber. It smelled heavily of smoke and dogs. Down at the opposite end, however, he could see an arched doorway cut into the wall and a warm light emitting from it. As he and Sully walked towards it, Andrew spoke.

"Then it is true that Torridon has no master." It was not a question.

Sully shook his head. "True – no male heir," Sully concurred. "But there are two mistresses, daughters of the earl, and you are about to meet the eldest, Lady Josephine. She is the Countess of Ayr in the wake of her father's death and commands Torridon quite capably."

"She was permitted to inherit the earldom?"

"Aye. She was granted the succession."

Andrew nodded, satisfied with the answer. It was at that point that they entered through the brightly lit doorway.

The room was long and narrow, and was lined by flaming torches on either side. Andrew noted that the knights of Torridon were seated, while his men either stood or sat along the wall. He noticed Thane against the wall up by the head of the table, and was aware of a strange expression on his friend's face as he looked at the figure seated at the head of the table. Also near the head of the table, Sully indicated a chair to Andrew and, as he took it, he happened to look to the woman at the head of the table as he sat.

It was the most beautiful woman in Scotland.

JOSEPHINE SAW HIM enter the room with Sully.

It was hard to miss him, for he was tall and muscular, and his rich auburn hair caught the firelight as he walked. With his proud stance and potent presence, it could be none other than The Red Fury himself. Initially, she was surprised that he wasn't a hideous ogre. Quite the contrary, she realized, as he drew closer.

As the man took a seat, all she could do was stare, hoping her shock wasn't too obvious. And she had to concentrate to keep her mouth from gaping open. Never in this life had she seen a man as beautiful as The Red Fury. As he sat, their eyes met and, for a moment, she forgot how to breathe. She felt her cheeks grow warm as his brown eyes were riveted to her, and it took every ounce of willpower she possessed to tear her gaze away from him. She didn't want to look at him.

The man was already casting a spell on her.

"Lady Josephine de Carron, this is Andrew d'Vant," Sully said, then added, "The Red Fury."

Hesitantly, Josephine returned her gaze to him. "My lord."

Andrew nodded his greeting. "A pleasure, Lady Ayr."

Josephine was hit by the quality of his voice; the graceful, deep flow of it. She was sure that if she closed her eyes and listened to it, she could quite easily be charmed by it. But the fact that this man affected her so strongly frightened her so, immediately, her guard went up.

"Thank you for coming," she said stiffly. "How many men have you?"

"Nine hundred and ninety-six," he repeated. "They are camped over the rise. I would like permission to camp them around the perimeter of the fortress."

Josephine cocked a well-shaped eyebrow. "Not until contract terms are agreed upon," she said. "Now, the initial offer was five thousand marks to defend Torridon until such a time that we no longer require your services. The five thousand will be paid upon termination of your services, and not prior to the commencement. Also, should we decide on an offensive, the fee will cover that as well. Have you any questions so far?"

Andrew's face was impassive as he answered. "The first two items are acceptable as stated," he said. "However, should you decide to launch an offensive, the fee will immediately increase five thousand marks more. That is my fee for a successful campaign."

Josephine's mouth fell open. "*Ten* thousand m...!" she sputtered. "You are not a mercenary, you are a thief. How dare you add another five thousand marks to an already exorbitant fee? I would sooner...."

Sully cut her off. Her anger was quick to flare and they were not going to get anywhere if she continued. "Three thousand marks," Sully said evenly. "There will be an additional three thousand marks should we launch an offensive and a share of the plunder when we assume control of Burnton Castle."

Andrew's full attention was on Sully. He regarded the man a moment, obviously mulling over the offer.

"My choice of booty," he said finally.

Sully nodded slightly. "Your choice of the booty," he agreed. "But only with my consent. Do we have a contract?"

A smile flickered on Andrew's lips. "I believe so."

"Good," Sully replied, then looked to Josephine. She was sitting back in her chair, her pretty face stormy and her eyes were riveted to Andrew. She was angry at his boldness, Sully knew, and not the money.

"Is that acceptable, my lady?" he asked her permission.

"Aye," she said reluctantly, then looked at Andrew and stuck her chin out. "But, by God, Andrew d'Vant, you had better be worth every last cent."

Andrew's smile broke through, amused at the lady's irritation. "I can assure you, my lady, that I shall meet your high expectations," he said. "And there will be no need for you to ever raise a sword in defense of your castle again."

That had been an unexpected comment. Josephine's eyes narrowed at him in disbelief. "Thank you for your concern, d'Vant," she said evenly, "but I shall decide as to whether or not I shall fight in Torridon's defense."

Andrew stood up from his chair, his features awash with bemusement as he pulled tight his gauntlets. "Lady Josephine," he said. "I will be commanding a sizeable force in defense of your castle. It would make it considerably easier if I did not have to worry about you becoming one of the dead or wounded because you chose to fight against men twice your size and strength."

It was clearly an insult and every Torridon knight at the table groaned inwardly, especially Sully. But he bit his tongue; better Josephine deal with d'Vant's arrogance now and establish the boundaries. This was her fight, and her fortress, and Sully would let her do what she needed to do.

But he didn't envy d'Vant one bit.

Unfortunately, Josephine had a temper that she didn't often control, and a tongue to match. She bolted out of her chair, the skirt of her garnet-colored gown billowing as she rounded the corner of the table and came to stand in front of Andrew. He was so tall she had to tilt her head back to look up at him, nothing but rage in her expression.

"You conceited, piss-hearted lout!" she barked. "How dare you insult me?"

Andrew's eyebrows went up. "Conceited?"

Across the table, Sully's eyebrows went up. "Piss-headed?"

Josephine ignored the comments, stomping her foot angrily. "Let me tell you something, Andrew d'Vant," she seethed. "You will not order me about in my own home. I have been fighting and defending Torridon since my father died, and not once have I even received a nick. This is *my* castle and should I choose to bear arms to defend it, then it will be *my* choice and not yours. Is this in any way unclear?"

Andrew was watching her rather impassively, although he was thinking that she was quite beautiful when she was enraged. She was also quite unruly. He wasn't about to let this woman order him about, even in her own home. She wanted his help? Then she was going to have to do as he asked.

"I would have you safe in the tower in the event of another attack." It was not a request.

Without hesitation, a little balled fist came up and caught him squarely on the jaw. There was a dull popping sound when the fist made contact and Andrew's head snapped to the right. His hand came up and he began rubbing his jaw as he eyed her. Across the table, Sully was on his feet, his hand on the hilt of his sword as he prepared to defend his disorderly mistress.

But Josephine didn't care how angry Andrew was. All that mattered was that the man understand her position, on all things. She was nothing to be trifled with but, by God, he was certainly trying.

"And I would have you keep your stupid male notions to yourself," she said, jabbing a finger at him. "I can fight with the best of them, Andrew d'Vant, and I'll not have you tell me otherwise."

With that, she breezed past him and flew from the room, leaving everyone in stunned silence. No one knew quite what to say, or how to react. They could not believe that little Lady Josephine de Carron just punched The Red Fury. Sully seemed to find his legs first, and went over to Andrew. Their eyes met and he looked at the tall man questioningly. Andrew continued to rub his jaw.

"She has a good strike," he admitted. "Did you teach her that?"

"No," Sully shook his head. "She learned that on her own. Now, I believe, we need to get you and your men settled for the night. You may move your army to the perimeter now, as you have requested. Will there be anything else you require?"

Sully was desperate to change the subject away from his rowdy mistress, hoping that encounter didn't change d'Vant's mind about taking on the defense of Torridon. He hoped if he pretended that it was simply business as usual, Andrew would be more focused on the job, and the reward, rather than the little spitfire he was working for. It must have worked because d'Vant motioned to his men, still standing in the shadows, and the group began to head to the chamber door.

"Not that I can think of, but I shall let you know," he said. "And Montgomery?"

"Aye?"

"Do not think I shall forget this."

With that, he walked away, leaving Sully to wonder what, exactly, he meant. He would not forget that Josephine struck him? That a woman refused to lay down her arms now that he was here?

He wondered.

CHAPTER FIVE

S ULLY TOPPED THE stairs just as Justine came from her sister's room, quietly closing the door behind her. She looked up and saw Sully coming close, and their eyes met. Justine could see his face etched with concern and she felt a tug of jealousy.

But it was a familiar feeling, especially where her sister was concerned. That was because Justine had loved Sully since she had been very young and the years had only served to deepen and enrich it. Justine was not foolish, nor was she blind. She knew Sully had eyes only for her sister and, perhaps, that had driven Justine's attention to the magical arts – it was a way to ease her pain and occupy her mind, to forget about the man she could never have.

The man whose heart belonged to another.

"Is she asleep?" Sully asked her.

Justine nodded. "Aye, I gave her something to help her sleep," she replied softly. "What on earth made her so angry? I have never seen her so agitated."

He ignored her question. "Something to help her sleep?" he repeated suspiciously. "What did you give her?"

"Poppy," Justine told him, hurt by the tone of his question. *Didn't he trust her?* "I made a sleeping potion from one of Dewey's powerful medicine books. It promises to promote a deep and peaceful sleep. To the poppy you must add a bit of hemlock and...."

"Hemlock?" he said with shock. "But that is poison."

"Not if given in small doses. But I gave her a little more because she was so restless."

Sully shoved past her. "Mother of God," he hissed. "Are you *trying* to kill her?"

He threw open the door and rushed to the bed where Josephine lay. It was dark in the room, the fire burning low in the hearth. He looked down upon Josephine, noticing she was still in the garnet wool dress. But she was very pale and her breathing was labored. Sully dropped to his knees, grasping the woman by the shoulders.

"Josephine?" he whispered urgently. "Josephine, awaken!"

"Sully?" Justine asked fearfully, standing behind him. "What are you doing?"

He ignored her, trying to rouse Josephine. "Josephine?" he said. Then he hissed, "Joey? Wake up!"

Josephine didn't stir. Sully lifted up an eyelid and saw that her eyes were rolled up to the top of her head. His heart jumped into his throat with nothing short of panic. He turned to Justine.

"Go get Dewey," he commanded, trying hard to maintain his control.

"But…!" Justine started to protest.

"*Go!*" he roared and Justine visibly jumped. Quickly, his eyes sought out Ola, standing quietly in the doorway of the alcove where she slept. "You, Ola – go with her. *Run!*"

The women rushed out without hesitation and Sully cradled Josephine's neck on his right forearm. He was in a fear-stricken haze as he looked at the woman he loved so much. *Oh, God in heaven… hemlock! What in the hell was Justine thinking? Curse that little novice witch!* His left hand came up and grasped Josephine's limp left one. He simply sat there and held her; he didn't know what else to do.

Sully never felt so helpless. Grief and anxiety tore at his gut and he could feel sweat starting to bead on his forehead. *If she died… if she died…. what would he do?* His head began to spin with the thought, but he shook it off. He couldn't think about that; not now. He looked back down at her pale, unconscious face and felt his throat constrict.

One thing was certain… Justine would answer for it.

ANDREW WAS IN the outer bailey with Thane, beneath a blanket of stars as they walked towards the main gates, when they happened to overhear one of the Torridon knights. Lady Josephine was dying and he was frantically looking for someone named Dewey. Andrew came to a halt, looking at the knight who had been wandering the outer ward anxiously. It was John, the youngest knight of Torridon, and his youthful face was on the brink of panic. Instead of heading out of the ward as he'd planned, Andrew made his way to the young knight.

"You, there," Andrew said, catching John's attention. "What is this nonsense about Lady Josephine dying?"

John's wide blue eyes bespoke of his terror. "Her sister says she was poisoned," he gasped. "I must find Dewey!"

"Poisoned? By whom?"

The young man shook his head vigorously. "I do not know," he said. "Lady Justine is in the inner bailey with some other women. She will tell you more."

With that, he was gone. Andrew turned a perplexed face to Thane, who shrugged at his commander.

"Let us go find this Lady Justine," Andrew said. "I wonder if they think I poisoned her."

Thane shook his head as they started towards the inner bailey. "Lord knows, you had enough reason to."

Andrew grinned. "It was a love tap," he said. "Baby's breath is more forceful than her fist."

"Love *tap*?" Thane looked at him. "I saw no affection in that gesture. Mayhap you are wishing there was, eh?"

Andrew snorted. "I think we would likely kill each other with our love taps," he said. "But I must confess that she is the most beautiful woman I have ever had the fortune to look upon."

He sobered suddenly and he did not know why. Perhaps it was the thought of that feisty, beautiful woman now evidently at death's door. But Thane didn't notice Andrew's sudden change in demeanor; he was in the process of heartily agreeing with Andrew's last statement.

"She is that, my lord," he said. "I could not believe my eyes when I saw her. Who in the hell would want to poison such a creature?"

Andrew shook his head as they entered the inner bailey. For the middle of the night, there was quite a bit of traffic. Villeins and servants seemed to be scurrying about in a frenzy. The only people who were stationary were a few women standing atop the front steps leading into the darkened keep. Their faces were agitated and worried. Andrew could hear one woman crying. He assumed Justine was in the little group, and he approached purposefully.

"I am seeking Lady Justine," he said.

The women all turned to him, suspiciously. Only one spoke, eyeing him hesitantly. "I am Justine," she said. "Who are you?"

"Andrew d'Vant," he said, as he rested a massive boot on the bottom step. "My army is in camp around Torridon. Tell me – what ails your sister?"

Whispers rippled through the women. *The Red Fury*! Justine was momentarily distracted by the flutter, but she put up a hand to silence them as she took a couple of steps down to look Andrew in the eye.

"My sister spoke of you," she said. "You are the man they call The Red Fury?"

"Aye."

Justine eyed him a moment before continuing. "She was quite angry after her meeting with you."

Andrew remembered the smack on his jaw; the spot was sore. "So it seems."

Justin glanced at the women behind her, nervously, before returning her attention to Andrew. "I gave her a potion with poppy and hemlock to make her sleep after her meeting with you," she said. "It was meant to calm her nerves, but I poisoned her instead."

Andrew looked at her strangely. "Hemlock?" he echoed. "Why on earth did you give her hemlock?"

Justine clenched her jaw. She hated admitting her failures and this one could cost her dearly. "Because I... I read of a potion in one of Dewey's books and made a sleeping drink for her," she said. "I know hemlock is deadly, although the book said that mixed in tiny quantities it was very beneficial to the mind. I was trying to help her."

Andrew listened to her explanation and he believed her. She didn't seem the malicious type, at least from what he could tell. Silly, aye, but not malicious. She certainly wouldn't be confessing that she'd poisoned her sister if her intention had been malicious. However, if what she said was true, then he knew that Josephine needed help. Every moment that passed was another moment that the hemlock could be doing serious damage.

"Is your healer with her?" he asked.

Justine shook her head. "Nay," she replied. "We are searching for him. Sully is upstairs with her now."

Andrew turned to Thane. "Find Oletha," he said. "Bring her to Lady Josephine's chamber. And be quick about it."

Thane barreled off across the inner bailey as he headed for the soldiers' camp and Andrew turned back to Justine. She was looking at him with a mixture of fear and curiosity, and he found himself wanting to ease her apprehension. She looked so young and confused. He smiled a little, treating Justine to a glimpse of the big dimple in his cheek.

"All will be well," he said quietly. "I have sent for my healer. She will know what to do."

"That is kind of you."

"Will you take me to your sister?"

"I will if... if you promise not to anger her again."

Andrew fought off a grin. "I swear it."

Justine was in motion before he finished his sentence, calling for

Ola to follow. The plump little maid dashed after them, following the enormous mercenary into the keep. They entered the cool, quiet foyer and traveled up the narrow stone stairs, built into the thickness of the wall. Josephine's chamber was on the third level and Justine opened the door quietly and entered, with Andrew following closely. Ola slipped in behind them and stood silently by the open door.

Above all else, Andrew was immediately struck by the soft femininity of the room. Rushes carpeted the floor and two massive tapestries graced opposite walls. Above the huge hearth hung a flowered piece of *petit poi*, an elaborate scene with animals and a banquet of colorfully-clad women. As he approached the elaborately-carved bed, he saw that she had hung a massive bouquet of dried heather on the wall and it was gaily tied with colorful ribbon. He smiled inwardly at the significance. In Scotland, that meant good luck.

As Andrew inspected the room curiously, there were eyes on him. Sully rose stiffly from his kneeling position beside her bed, his eyes on the big mercenary. He didn't like the idea of the man in Josephine's chamber but, more than that, he noted that Justine was without the little physic that everyone was searching for. He looked pointedly at the woman.

"Where is Dewey?" he asked.

Justine could hear the stress in his voice. "The castle is in an uproar searching for him," she said. Then, she looked at Andrew. "Sir Andrew has sent for his own healer in the meantime."

Sully's gaze moved to Andrew. He didn't want anyone but Dewey touching her, especially with her life hanging in the balance. But he didn't want to offend the mercenary; at least not now. He had enough to worry about and he needed Andrew handling Torridon's defenses while he was preoccupied with Josephine. Still… he was grateful. Any healer was better than no healer. Therefore, he nodded curtly at Andrew.

"Thank you," he said quietly.

Andrew's gaze lingered on the man, noticing the nearly hostile manner in which Sully was regarding him. *Why?* He wondered. Then, he looked down at Josephine; she was as white as the sheet she laid upon. Her luscious hair was stuck to her clammy skin and, if her chest hadn't risen every so often, one would have believed her to be dead. The deep red dress in which she was clad made an even greater contrast against her white skin. He felt a strange sense of sorrow as he looked at her.

Before he could speak, however, the chamber doorway was filled with Torridon knights. Quig, Severn, and Albert were breathing heavily as they stumbled into the chamber, their focus on Sully.

"My Lord," red-haired Albert spoke, breathing as if he'd just run up several flights of steps. "We have sighted a Dalmellington scout party not far from here. There appears to be several men on horseback."

Sully's nostrils flared. "In the middle of the night?"

Albert shrugged. "It is possible they saw the approach of the mercenary army and followed," he said. "You know they are never far from us. They have spies everywhere."

That was very true, and Sully began to realize that he may have another serious problem on his hands. "Damnation," he hissed, passing Andrew as he made his way to his men. "I want twenty-five men-at-arms saddled in the outer bailey in five minutes. We've got to stop those bastards before they return to Burnton Castle with what they have seen."

The knights were gone in a flash. Sully's jaw muscles flexed as he turned to the bed where Josephine laid. *God in heaven, he couldn't leave her now.* He didn't want to chase down Dalmellington spies; he wanted to be here with Josephine. But he had little choice. He had to be present when they engaged the Dalmellington spies. His duty was to protect Torridon. Josephine would live or die whether or not he was at her side.

Much as Sully had studied Andrew when the man had first entered the chamber, now it was Andrew's turn to study Sully and his reaction to a night patrol. He saw the turmoil in the man's eyes and that was his first clue that all may not be business-related when it came to Sully

Montgomery and his lovely mistress.

"Would you prefer I go?" he asked.

Sully looked at him, sharply, as if suspicious of the question. Was it magnanimous? Or was he suggesting he could do the job better than Sully could?

"Nay," Sully said. "I will go. I know their tricks and where they hide. You would not know this."

Andrew simply nodded. "Then I shall remain here with your mistress," he said. "I will not leave her."

Sully looked at him a moment before giving a reluctant sigh. He did not have any choice; his duty called. But, God in heaven, he didn't want to leave Josephine's fate with a man he didn't even know.

"Very well," he agreed. "Stay with her. I shall return as soon as I can."

Sully blew past Justine as if she were a ghost, and her eyes turned to follow him longingly as he left the room. She knew this was all her fault, and she knew that Sully blamed her. If any chance had ever existed to win Sully's heart, she was positive that it was gone now.

She'd poisoned the woman he loved.

Justine had never felt such despair as she turned to look back at her sister. In the process, her eyes fell on Andrew. He was watching her like a hawk and, simply by his expression, she knew that he had discovered her secret. *Her love for Sully.* Justine thought she might die from embarrassment from Andrew's knowing gaze, but he turned away quickly and focused his attention on Josephine.

Justine was very relieved.

There were strange forces at work at Torridon; Andrew had quickly come to that conclusion. Just in the past few minutes, he'd witnessed Sully's longing expression for Josephine and Justine's longing expression for Sully. It all seemed rather foolish to him, but none of that mattered. As long as they paid him what they promised him, he didn't care what these people did.

He had a job to do.

Now, his focus was on Josephine. She hadn't moved a muscle since he'd entered the chamber. With Sully gone and the other two women in the room standing back in the shadows, he had his first opportunity to get a good look at the lovely Mistress of Torridon. For a few stolen moments, he looked his fill of her.

If God could have asked Andrew his idea of a perfect woman, he would have described Josephine down to her ladylike ears. Her face was absolutely perfect, and he felt an impulsive urge to run his fingers through the silken tresses and inhale their scent. His eyes drifted to the creamy white swells that disappeared beneath the tight silk bodice. Even lying on her back as she was, her breasts were pleasingly large. Beyond the narrow waist, he could tell no more, but he somehow knew the rest of her was just as perfect. He decided that should she survive this bout, he would not forgive her for hitting him. He would, however, allow her to make it up to him.

People were entering her room now, distracting him from thoughts of Josephine. He turned to see Thane entering, his sword rattling against his side. Behind him, almost hidden within the folds of a huge gray cape, was a small figure. Andrew pointed swiftly to Josephine on the bed.

"She has been poisoned," he said to the figure. "See what you can do for her."

The shape moved quickly and knelt beside the bed, with the cape billowing to form a wide circle. A fragile white hand shot out from the cape and checked the breathing, the heart, and the eyes.

"How long since the poison has been ingested?" the voice said; it was tiny and fairy-like.

Andrew looked to Justine, who stepped from the shadows, her eyes wide. "About a half of an hour," she said, concerned.

The figure pulled the hood from its head as it turned to Justine. A tiny woman with a mass of wild white hair fixed her beady eyes on Justine, and the girl felt a bolt of something shoot through her. Whether it was from the shock of seeing a dwarf or from the actual power emitting from this woman, she didn't know. But she was suddenly afraid and confused.

"What did you give her, darling?" the tiny woman asked gently.

Justine's mouth popped open in surprise. *How did she know?* Then it dawned on her. The other man, the blond giant, had been present when Justine confessed to Andrew. He must have told her. Yet, even that knowledge did not erase the eerie feeling she had, like the tiny woman could read her mind.

"Poppy in straight wine, laced with hemlock," Justine replied. "I only meant to help her sleep."

The woman did not seem the least bit upset by the knowledge. She calmly removed her gloves and cape as Justine watched with growing anxiety. *Why was she not doing something?* She wondered. Why is she being so calm? Justine glanced at Andrew anxiously, who also appeared to be calmly watching the woman as she settled herself down on the bed, all quite calmly moving about.

Justine could not believe her eyes. Where was the sense of urgency? Had they all gone mad?

"You did not give her hemlock," the woman finally announced.

Justine's eyes widened. "Of course I did!"

Andrew interrupted, his voice full of concern. "How do you know, Oletha?"

"Simple," Oletha said as she stood up from the bed and moved to pull a small stool over to the bed. "If she were given even the slightest amount of hemlock, with her size, it would have killed her within minutes. Hemlock is an extremely fast-acting toxin."

Andrew glanced at the pale woman on the bed. "Are you certain?"

Oletha nodded as she sat on the stool. "Of course," she said. Then, she looked at Justine. "Now, we must determine exactly what you did give her. Can you show me what you used?"

Justine nodded unsteadily. She was overwhelmed at this revelation. Was she really so stupid and incompetent as to not know what hemlock was when she saw it? Dewey had it in a jar, clearly labeled. When she drew it forth, she believed it to be hemlock. She'd seen it a thousand times.

But if it wasn't hemlock, what was it?

Justine turned on her heel and ran from the chamber, her head swimming. She just couldn't have been that idiotic! She was a wise sorceress. She knew about plants and herbs! Didn't she?

Well... didn't she?

Back inside the room, Oletha had her fingers on Josephine's wrist as she felt the lady's pulse. It was strong and steady. Oletha smiled as she pulled her hand away. Andrew was standing above her, hovering somewhat anxiously and the old woman looked up at him.

"Not to worry, Sir Andrew," she squeaked. "Lady Josephine is merely in a deep sleep. I suspect she will rise with the rest of us come the morning."

Andrew cocked an eyebrow. "But she will not awaken," he said. "Would poppy make her sleep so?"

Oletha nodded, lifting one of Josephine's lids to check her eyes. "Some people are very sensitive to certain herbs and potions," she said. "Perhaps lovely Lady Josephine is one of them. However, she will have a terrific headache on the morrow and will not be much company to be around, I will venture."

"But what about the sweat?" Andrew wanted to know. "She is drenched in it."

Oletha cocked an eyebrow. "You would be, too, if you were swathed in heavy silk in this warm room," she said. "Where is her maid? We will remove this clothing."

Andrew stepped back as Ola rushed forward, very nervously, and began assisting Oletha. As he watched, he began to wonder why he felt such a tremendous sense of relief at Oletha's words. Crossing his arms, he looked over at Thane, and Thane lifted his brows as if to say *"well... that is the end of it."*

And it was, if Oletha said so. Andrew, in truth, was reluctant to leave Lady Josephine because he told Sully that he would not. There was a sense of responsibility there, in keeping his word, but there was also a strange surge of elation at the thought that he didn't *have* to leave her. But why? He had no idea why he should be happy to remain.

But then, he knew – he simply did not want to leave a beautiful girl's boudoir.

He was only a man, after all.

Several minutes passed while Ola and Oletha stripped Josephine down to her thin linen shift. When they were removing the dress, Andrew cleared his throat loudly in Thane's direction, and the two of them discreetly moved to the other side of the chamber, to the door, to allow for a little privacy. As their backs were turned, Andrew leaned his head towards Thane.

"Why is a Torridon knight not up here guarding their mistress from us?" he asked. "I find that peculiar that he would not post a Torridon guard here."

Thane glanced sideways at him. "Sir Sully took nine knights with him," he said. "The other four are at the main gate. It would appear, my Lord Andrew, that they are going to trust us to honor our knightly vows."

"I never took any," Andrew stated flatly. "But they need not know that. I will honor my word just the same."

Thane eyed his master; there had been something in his expression as he looked at the lady of Torridon. Something of interest, if Thane didn't know better. But he said nothing. Instead, he turned his attention back to the lady on the bed as two women worked over her. In truth, he didn't blame Andrew in the least for showing the slightest interest towards Lady Josephine.

He just might have some interest himself.

"Sir Andrew," Oletha called out, breaking the men from their thoughts. "We need your help, milord."

Andrew moved to where the women stood and Oletha looked up at him. "Lift Lady Josephine so that we may turn back the bed, please," she instructed briskly. "It will make it much easier for us to make her comfortable."

After a moment's hesitation, Andrew reached down and gently scooped up the limp form. She was so soft and warm; hell, his saddle weighed more than she did. He found himself cradling her gently against his chest as Oletha and Ola fussed with the coverlets. He could smell Josephine's hair; it smelled like flowers. *Roses*, he thought, a fragrance of delight, like the joy of a warm spring day. And her face; it was upturned to him and her lips parted softly in sleep. Inviting, full lips. He wondered what it would be like to taste them.

The temptation was almost too much to bear. He had to put her down before he did something foolish.

"Are you finished yet?" he snapped impatiently. How many women did it take to prepare one bed, anyway? "I cannot stand here all night."

Under him, the women worked swiftly, but there was evidently a need for clean linen, so they bolted from the room and left him standing there with the temptation still in his arms. They even pulled Thane with them, and Andrew was left alone with the unconscious lady. It would have been an enticing situation had it not been such a serious one. Josephine was quite a lovely creature, though, and he found himself staring at her, if only for a moment. But that was the last peaceful moment between them as a fist he was most familiar with came flying up at him again, this time catching him in the throat.

After that, the fight was on.

JOSEPHINE HEARD A voice in her warm, dark world.

It was a man's voice; deep, rich, and melodic. She tried to shut it out and ignore it, but it seemed to reach forward and grab her, pulling her into the light. She couldn't resist the soothing tones. They caressed her sensually, gently coaxing her from the haven of sleep. Unable to fight the voice any longer, she followed it willingly.

Then, she awoke in someone's arms. Her left cheek was pressed against something very warm and firm and, upon opening her eyes, she realized it was a chest. A *man's* chest. Looking up, she saw the face of a man she didn't recognize, sending panic into her heart. But after a terror-filled second, she realized it was the mercenary leader.

Andrew d'Vant was holding her.

God's Toes! What was she doing lying cradled in his arms? The last thing Josephine remembered was drinking a cup of wine Justine gave her and laying upon her bed. Now, she found herself in Andrew d'Vant's arms. Surely, he must have abducted her from Torridon and was planning some sort of horrible fate for her. What else could it be?

Well, the bastard wasn't going to take her without a fight!

In his arms, Andrew felt Josephine twitch but he had no time or opportunity to defend himself as a balled fist came swinging up and caught him squarely on the throat. She dropped from his arms as he staggered back, coughing and sputtering, clutching his neck with one hand.

Josephine missed the bed entirely and landed on the floor, scrambling away from him as fast as she could. Then, she leapt onto her bed in a panic, her hand shooting under her pillow in search of her bejeweled dagger.

Terror was causing her breaths to come in short gasps, and her hair hung about her wildly in her struggle. She was positive that any second Andrew was going to jump on her and try to squeeze the life from her. After a hysteria-filled moment, her hand closed over the hilt of the blade, and she swiftly drew it forth.

As Andrew struggled with the blow to his throat, he saw Josephine struggle onto her bed and thrust her hand beneath the pillow, and he guessed what she was searching for. Most fine women slept armed. It was simply the way of things, and he suspected Lady Josephine was no different. Still rubbing his throat, he staggered over to the bed just as Josephine drew forth a rather large dagger with a nasty-looking blade. As she brought it up, he grabbed her right hand and flipped her easily onto her back, pinning her down with his body weight while one hand grasped both wrists and deliberately removed the dagger with his other hand.

The dagger ended up on the floor, several feet away.

"Now," Andrew said with an exhale. "Please tell me what this display was all about?"

Josephine was still very groggy. As he watched, frightened tears welled in her eyes and started to course down her temples.

"What are you doing in my room?" she demanded.

"Believe me, my lady, it was not by choice," he assured her coolly. "I was summoned here by Sir Sully. It seems your sister gave you a sleeping potion that she claimed contained hemlock and no one could rouse you."

That brought Josephine's struggles to a halt. Her eyes widened. "I do not believe you," she said flatly. "Justine would never do that. She knows the properties of hemlock."

"That may be, but it was apparently impossible to awaken you." He looked at her curiously. "What finally roused you?"

Josephine blinked, trying to process his question in her foggy mind. "I do not know," she replied. "I… I heard a voice. A man's voice. That's all I remember, then I awoke in your arms. Why were you holding me so?"

She didn't seem so apt to fight him now and Andrew released her, pushing himself off of her. Josephine watched him for a moment as he moved away from the bed before propping herself up on her elbows, still watching him intently. She assumed that if he was going to attack her, he would have done so by now. Instead, he was eyeing her with some amusement.

"I was not holding you for my pleasure," he said. "The women were preparing to change the linen on your bed, though why they picked this moment, I do not know. They asked me to lift you from the bed and that was exactly what I was doing."

"What women?"

"Your sister and my healer."

She looked around the room but there were no women to be found. In fact, somehow, his casual statement disappointed her and she had no idea why. His attitude was very detached, as if he were performing a service for any village wench. It didn't seem to matter to him that he had been intimately touching the Lady of Torridon.

Wasn't she worth holding?

She was only being foolish now. Idiotic, even. Whatever Justine gave her was clearly still affecting her thought processes. Glancing to the chair beside her bed, she spied her red silk robe and modestly snatched it up as Andrew pretended to busy himself by pulling tight the leather gloves on his big hands.

Josephine rose quickly and put the robe on, tying it lightly about her waist. When Andrew turned around at the appropriate moment, having been fully aware of what she was doing, a wave of pleasure rolled through him at the sight of her. God, the woman was all shades of lovely, even when she wasn't feeling particularly well. But he made sure she was unaware of what was going through his head; his expression was completely neutral.

"Well," he said finally. "It would seem that I am no longer needed here now that you are clearly no longer in danger. I shall bid you a good evening."

As he headed for the door, she followed him with her eyes. "You were never needed in the first place," she said coolly. "I am not paying you five thousand marks to spend time in my chamber. Where you are needed is on the walls of Torridon, protecting my castle."

He stopped and turned, looking her over with haughty amusement. God's Bones, the woman was as changeable as a chameleon. As he opened his mouth to reply, Justine rushed into the room and almost ran into him in the process. But when her gaze fell on her conscious sister, her eyes widened in surprise.

"Josephine!" she gasped. "You are awake! Praise God!"

Josephine's eyes narrowed. "What do you mean 'praise God'?" she asked. "Why is it so amazing that I am awake?"

Justine took a couple of steps towards her, wringing her hands. "Because I gave you a sleeping potion with what I thought was hemlock in it, and…"

Josephine flew at her, outraged. "Hemlock?" she gasped. "I knew you were angry with me for not listening to your cards, but to actually try and kill me?"

Justine was flabbergasted. "*Kill* you?" she repeated. "Never! I merely laced your wine with a little too much…"

Josephine cut her off. "Justine, you know nothing of the powers you so freely profess to be well-versed in," she snarled. "How dare you try to experiment on me with your feigned-witch powers? Never again feed me your boiled weeds!"

"Boiled weeds?" Justine choked, forgetting the fear she had experienced when she thought she had killed her sister. "I know the powers of herbs and potions, and they are anything but boiled weeds. You should take heed of who you are speaking to, Josephine."

"Nay, *you* should take heed!"

"You are not nearly as grand as you think you are!"

"And you are a fool!"

"And you are a reeky harlot! I really *should* have poisoned you!"

That was all it took for Josephine to fly at her sister, knocking over her tapestry loom as the two girls fell together with grunts and cries. After that, the slaps began to fly.

Andrew knew he was forgotten in that singular act. He was amazed to see the two of them writhing on the ground, apparently very intent on bruising each other. But in that realization, a smile came to his lips. It was actually quite funny. He contemplated, for a split second, as to whether or not to intervene, but he quickly decided he should. Both girls were not holding back as they punched each other with hard-clenched fists and he feared someone might truly get hurt.

Ah, what a shame, he thought as he took the steps necessary to reach the squabble. He did so enjoy watching women fight.

It was great entertainment.

"Ladies," he admonished sternly. "Cease this instant."

Josephine was on top of the pile, and he reached down effortlessly to pull her off by the collar of her robe. She struggled and twisted, still shrieking obscenities at her sister as he held her far enough away that he was able to pull Justine up by her sleeve.

But they were still yelling at each other and he found it took every ounce of his willpower to keep from laughing. Instead, he informed Justine it might be a wise choice for her to leave and was thoroughly surprised when both women turned on him like wild dogs, in essence telling him to mind his own business.

Andrew grimaced in confusion, praying that Thane and the women would return soon. He wasn't sure how he would deal with the two of them physically turning on him. The last thing he wanted to do was hurt them. But, God's Bones, he could not think with all of the screaming going on.

It was no longer the humorous situation he had been enjoying.

Swiftly, he pulled Josephine against him and clamped a gloved hand over her mouth. A half-second later, Justine was in the same vise-like grip; silent but breathing heavily through his splayed fingers. Andrew sighed heavily.

"Now," he said quietly. "That is much better. You two sound more like a couple of she-dogs fighting over a bit of meat rather than the mistresses of Torridon."

Josephine uttered a sound and put her hands up against his side, but he only gripped her tighter to silence her.

"Now," he continued, "I believe the best thing for both of you is to retire to your respective chambers and prepare to deal with this calmly come the morning. Lady Justine, if I release you, you will promise to leave this room and not fight any longer. Agreed?"

Justine rolled her eyes but she didn't try to nod or even shake her head, and Andrew was momentarily unsure as to how to proceed. She just stood there, stubbornly, and Andrew began to feel foolish. He was a man who handled a thousand men with ease, yet now he was befuddled by two small women. This was uncertain territory for him, not something he ran into every day. But he had to show that he was in command here or he was certain these women would run all over him. He knew for a fact that Lady Josephine would. But he had to be honest with himself – he was afraid that if he released one or both of them, the fight would start up again.

But he couldn't show that concern. He had to trust that the ladies would at least be sensible and was preparing to release Justine when Thane and the two women came back into the chamber.

"Thane," Andrew said with relief. "Attend me."

Thane was at his side instantly, his face a mirror of confusion. "Lady Josephine has awoken?" he asked with surprise, but it was more than that. He was looking at Andrew with Justine and Josephine clutched in each arm, his hands over their mouths. This wasn't how he had left them. "What has happened?"

Andrew gave him a lopsided smile. "Just a little sibling rivalry," he said. "Please escort Lady Justine back to her room and see that she stays there."

Andrew removed his hand from Justine's mouth and Thane took firm hold of the girl's arm as he led her from the room. Then, with the younger sister safely out, he turned to Oletha and Ola.

"Out," he said quietly.

The women fled. When the door shut softly behind them, he released Josephine.

Rubbing her face where he'd clamped a hand over her mouth, Josephine stepped away from Andrew, her expression wary. He saw her expression but it had no impact; he crossed his massive arms over his chest and set his jaw, looking disapprovingly at her. Still, Josephine was uncomfortable under his gaze. Uncomfortable... but strangely intrigued.

"You should not be in here with me, alone," she said after a moment. "Please leave."

He suddenly grinned and Josephine's heart jumped at the sight of the big smile across his face. Straight, white teeth and a large dimple in his left cheek made him unexpectedly appealing.

Handsome, even.

"I am pleased that you find compromising my reputation so humorous," she said defensively.

Andrew sobered, knowing she was serious about the two of them alone in her room with the door closed. To compromise her was not his intention, at least not at this point.

But that lovely woman had possibilities.

"Forgive me, Lady Josephine," he said apologetically. "I was not laughing at the possibility of damaging your reputation. I was laughing at your idea that I would wait until now to attempt to ravish you, considering how long I have actually been alone with you. If I was going to do it, I should have done it while you slept. To do it now would guarantee me, at the very least, a blackened eye. You are not the least bit reserved in the use of your fists."

Josephine considered his statement. Since he had arrived three hours earlier, she had hit him twice and had fought with her sister in his presence. To him, she most certainly was a bit of a ruffian and a hesitant grin crept over her lips.

"You must believe me quite the brute," she said, perhaps with a bit of embarrassment.

"Quite," he replied, rubbing his throat. "But I truly believe you defend Torridon, mayhap singlehandedly."

A chuckle escaped her. "Nay, not singlehandedly. I do have some help." She paused and looked up at him, perhaps allowing herself to openly inspect him for the first time. Perhaps, it was time. "I… I fear we got off to a bad start and I apologize for striking you – both times. When my emotions run high, which they do on occasion, I become very… demonstrative."

Andrew could see her guard go down, as if someone had lowered a curtain. The change in her manner was dramatic. Pleasant, even. Now, he thought he might be seeing the real Lady Josephine – the intelligent, caring, and sensitive side. He had already seen the no-nonsense, feisty side, and he liked this new side just as well. Well, almost.

He liked a woman with fire.

"There is no need to apologize," he said. "No harm done, although you have a powerful punch. I rather enjoyed it."

Her eyebrows flew up in surprised amusement and she snorted. He was either flirting with her or simply being humorous; she couldn't tell which. Either way, he was causing her to blush, something she was quite uncomfortable with.

But it was rather fun.

"You are a fool, Andrew d'Vant, jesting with me as such," she said. "Now, get out before I enjoy you to death!"

Andrew had to chuckle at the woman. He could see her red cheeks, appreciating that he had put that color there. He'd seen it creep in. He rather liked teasing her because she was quick to respond. He realized very quickly that he liked to get a rise out of her. But he dutifully moved for the door, intent on obeying her command. With a gloved hand on the latch, he turned one last time to the figure in red silk standing in the center of the room.

God's Bones, she was lovely.

Josephine saw his gaze as he stood by the door, a rather appraising expression on his face. There was such heat in his eyes that she could feel her limbs tingling at the mere look – it was saucy, cocky, and seething with mischief. She wanted to run, melt, or slap him all at the same time.

She'd never known anything like it.

"Now, get to bed and go to sleep," Andrew commanded with mock seriousness. "I expect a full tour of Torridon on the morrow."

Josephine lifted an eyebrow. "Then be sure to inform Sully," she said. "I would not want you wandering Torridon alone."

So she was not going to fall for his charm. That was something that amused Andrew greatly. He was used to women falling at his feet. But it was of little consequence; there would still be time for him to put her under his spell. Therefore, he cast her a rather bold wink as he exited the chamber and closed the door quietly behind him.

With Andrew gone, the chamber was abruptly still and quiet. Josephine stood a moment, looking at the closed door, lingering on the memory of that bold wink. Oh, but he was a devil and he knew it. She could see it in his face. He was a scoundrel and he didn't care. But none of that seemed to matter; somehow, she couldn't fight off a grin as she removed the red robe and crawled into bed.

The clean linen bedding that Ola and Oletha brought in lay folded carefully at the foot of the bed, but she ignored it as she snuggled down under her coverlet and closed her eyes. It couldn't have been an hour or two at most before dawn, and she was exhausted. It had been a very busy night.

Sleep claimed Josephine almost in an instant, a sleep so deep that she didn't even hear Ola come back in the room and glance timidly at her mistress before retiring herself.

Ola went to sleep wondering why Lady Josephine had a smile on her face.

CHAPTER SIX

WITHIN THREE DAYS, the wall had been repaired and the main gate reset. Andrew had put his men to helping Torridon's men in the repairs, for it was evident that there were woefully few for such a large job. Fortunately, several of Andrew's soldiers were handy craftsmen and carpenters, and the task was completed with relative speed.

The past three days had also been an adjustment period for Andrew, and he spent most of his time with Sully, Thane, and various other Torridon knights, learning all that he could about the Dalmellington army and their tactics. He ate, slept, and pissed Dalmellington. He talked to everyone he could, even the lowliest soldiers, to learn everything he needed to know. In order to fight an enemy, he had to know the enemy, so Andrew spent his days learning about the army he was being paid to destroy.

In fact, he found himself almost wishing that the Dalmellington army would come again and lay siege, for he wanted to see them in action to confirm what he had been told. But three days of peace passed, and so did a fourth, and Torridon was repaired to withstand another battle. But Andrew knew, instinctively, that the peace wouldn't hold. If everything he'd been told was true, then the Dalmellingtons would come again, soon enough.

The Dalmellington patrol Sully had ridden to intercept the night

Andrew had arrived had managed to send an advance messenger to Burnton Castle. They'd discovered that very quickly when a Dalmellington man they captured was quick to inform them. It was therefore assumed that Colin Dalmellington knew of The Red Fury's army at Torridon, which changed the dynamics of the situation considerably. What Colin would do with that knowledge remained to be seen.

So they watched and they waited, Torridon men alongside d'Vant men, and Andrew and Sully right along with them. There was a tension in the air that never seemed to go away, the apprehension of men who found themselves in a battle every time they let their guards down. Andrew understood that apprehension well. But all the time he was spending time with Sully and Etienne and the knights of Torridon, there was one person he wasn't spending time with.

That little spitfire who liked to slug him in the throat.

Josephine hadn't been around much at all, much to Andrew's disappointment. He never saw her during the day, only at night when they would feast on any number of culinary delights from Torridon's stores. She would sit on the dais, the lord's table, in the most resplendent of gowns while he sat down the table or across from her, hardly speaking with her, mostly speaking with Sully or any number of other men.

He was rather tired of speaking to other men.

Justine, in direct contrast of her sister's fine gowns, always sat on her sister's right hand and always looked as if she were wrapped in black sheets. But the two girls constantly seemed to be isolated, talking only with each other or, occasionally, to a Torridon knight. For Justine, it was probably true to character. But for Josephine, he wondered why.

The day he'd arrived, she seemed to be very much aligned with her knights, and they with her. She did not seem to be the withdrawn type. He wondered if her bout with her sister's potion was still affecting her, though it turned out to be harmless. Through Oletha, Andrew discovered that Justine had mistakenly put dill in the potion rather than hemlock, for the two flowers looked very similar, yet dill was yellowish-green instead of white. Oletha had had a good laugh at Justine's amateurish mistake, though she never let on to the young witch-hopeful.

Still, Andrew thought Josephine seemed withdrawn and tired, at least from the little he saw of her. He was disappointed, hoping to at least pick up with the flirtatious repartee they'd had the night of his arrival. But the days passed and there was no interaction, and he was coming to wonder if Josephine's health was poor in general, although she appeared robust enough. He mentioned it in passing to Oletha, but the little woman had shrugged and stated gaily that the mistress looked well enough to her.

This brought him to the subject of the mysterious Dewey. He had yet to be found, but nobody seemed particularly concerned. Sully mentioned that, sometimes, Dewey would disappear for days on a supply hunt, combing the woods and hills in an attempt to restock his vast array of herbs, flowers, and fungi.

Sully also mentioned that Dewey was quite ancient, an old man who had learned the art of healing and alchemy from his father, who had learned such things from his father. Dewey evidently had ancient books bound in human skin, and some whispered that he had a ghost in a bottle hidden somewhere in his chamber. It was enough to keep people from wandering into his rooms, in any case.

A withdrawn lady notwithstanding, Andrew thought it was all quite curious. Truly, what an interesting place Torridon Castle was turning out to be.

JOSEPHINE HAD, INDEED, been remote, she knew, but it wasn't for the reasons people thought. It had nothing to do with the arrival of the mercenary army, or even Justine's attempt to poison her. It all had to do with the fact that the day following Andrew's arrival, she had received a dispatch from King Alexander. A royal rider had come and gone, leaving a message that Sully had inquired about, once, and

Josephine had refused to elaborate on. He'd dropped the subject but, to Josephine, it wasn't a subject easily put aside. In, fact, it was quite important. The message she'd received had informed her that the king would be visiting around the third of the next month, which was a mere week away.

At first, she had been thrilled with the prospect of entertaining the king, her distant cousin through her mother's side of the family. Colin wouldn't dare attack so long as the king was at Torridon. But the euphoria soon gave way to darker emotions, for she began to suspect this would not be a social call to resolve the feud between the Dalmellingtons and the de Carrons. At her age, and unmarried, a sure way of resolving a feud was marriage. If King Alexander ordered her to marry Colin Dalmellington, which had been proposed before, she could not refuse.

Frightened, and sickened at the thought, the next few days passed in a blur for Josephine. Only she and Justine were aware of the contents of the letter, for she had not even told Sully. To be truthful, she was afraid to. With the hatred he had for the Dalmellington, she was unsure of what his reaction would be and she wanted to think through all of the possibilities before broaching the subject. It wasn't as if he could fight off the king, either.

They would both be at his mercy.

And then… there was The Red Fury.

Good Lord, the man was proving to be a tremendous distraction for her. The second day after his arrival, she had watched from on high in the west tower down to the practice field in the outer ward where Andrew d'Vant was mock sword-playing with a few Torridon knights, as well as a few of his own commanders.

What she saw utterly amazed her.

For such a large man, he moved with the speed of a hummingbird and had the skill to match God Himself. He was so quick and so strong, that most men didn't have the chance to see what had hit them before they fell to the soft earth. Josephine had always considered Sully the best knight she'd ever seen, but not any longer. She was certain The Red Fury could outfight even Sully.

Yet, as she watched, there was something more she sensed in Andrew's movements. He seemed so... angry. There was violence behind every thrust and every parry. It was as if he were truly trying to kill someone and kill them again, with every movement of the sword. In his business, he had to make every effort count, and it was obvious that he did just that.

Still... it seemed to her that it was more than a business to him. What he did, the way he moved... it was personal.

But he was enthralling to watch. She was riveted to the flash of his sword as he fought with a madness that set an uneasiness in her chest. He frightened her with his intensity. And then, it hit her – *fury*. He was fighting with fury. Now, it became clear how he received his nickname. It was clear in every move he made. It was then that Josephine began to believe that, mayhap, the man called The Red Fury was worth five thousand marks. There was something about the man that made him seem worth every pence.

And she felt interest in him that wouldn't seem to go away.

The only time Josephine was ever in the same room with him was at the evening meal in the great hall, where she had had an unobstructed view of Andrew as he sat with his men at the same table. But he seemed not to notice her. Instead, he was very engaged with the big blond general that followed him around like a dog. Or, he was engaged with Sully. Although she was not in a particularly social mood, somehow it irked her that he did not so much as acknowledged her presence at the meal.

Not that she was going to be the first one to make a move.

Therefore, the evening meal was an odd standoff, but Josephine had more important things on her mind. Now, on the fourth day of The Red Fury's arrival, she was coming to feel resignation with the king's impending arrival. Andrew d'Vant or no Andrew d'Vant, that would not change the motive behind Alexander's visit. In Josephine's mind, she was convinced it was for a marriage to bring together two houses and end their nasty feud. In this case, there were two choices – Colin could either marry her or Justine, and she knew that it had to be her.

And there was nothing she could do about it.

It would be with great reluctance that she would marry Colin if the king wished it, but she would never love him. She couldn't. She might even present him with children for the rest of his life. So what if she was miserable? She had to think of the greater good – Torridon, her sister, and her knights would be spared. But she wondered how Sully would react to taking orders from Colin Dalmellington. Most likely, he would do something foolish and get himself killed. She shuddered at that thought. She would have to talk to him and convince him, for her sake, to behave.

On this rather cool and blustery day, it was just before the nooning meal and Josephine descended into the foyer and crossed into the great hall on her way to the kitchens. The kitchens of Torridon were on the ground level of the keep, a low-ceilinged series of rooms that were always hot and smoky, at any given time of the day or night. The cook was just setting out huge platters of boiled beef. She looked up as her pretty little mistress entered, her attention on the steaming meat and huge bowls of peas and onions. Josephine caught the woman's eye as she looked up.

"You know that I love boiled beef," Josephine grinned. "Is there enough for the evening meal, too?"

The woman nodded. "This is from the meat we butchered last month, the same meat that has been in the cold vault since then," she said. "There is plenty for tonight, too."

That pleased Josephine greatly. Dora was the best cook who ever graced a kitchen and could make a spiced crab apple pie that sent Josephine into a virtual feeding frenzy. As children, she and Justine and James would practically thrash each other for the largest piece.

But now, there was no such competition and Josephine picked up a large hunk of freshly baked brown bread, dipping it into a bowl of honey before taking a healthy bite. The door to the kitchen yard was open, emitting light into the dingy kitchens and giving the smoke somewhere to evacuate, and Josephine chewed on her bread and engaged Dora in a light conversation. It wasn't often that she was able to come to the kitchens with Justine as chatelaine. But she was so preoccupied with food and conversation that she didn't see the two little villein children stealthily creep in through the open kitchen door.

The two young children stood quietly by the table near the door, the one harboring cooling meat pies that Dora had just baked. Moreover, Dora's back was turned to the door and she had no idea they were there. Children of the servants often frequented the kitchen, which was why Josephine gave no thought to the children until they snatched two of the nearest pies and dashed out the door.

Dora and Josephine quickly turned in time to see the children racing off. Dora was already howling as Josephine ran after them.

"I'll retrieve the pies, Dora!" she said as she blew by the flustered cook.

The little boys were fast. They rounded the corner and flew with unnatural speed into the inner bailey. Josephine, however, was closing the gap behind them. She rounded the corner as well, her dress flying out behind her as she pounded the dirt with her slipper-clad feet but she found herself hoping that the children would not drop the pies in their panic. Dirty meat pies would be a sad loss, especially Dora's pies. She began to run faster, hoping to catch them.

Sully, Andrew, Etienne, and Thane were entering the inner bailey just as the children ran past them, almost plowing into Etienne. He jumped awkwardly out of the way, and all four men turned curiously to watch the children run off towards the main gate. They shrugged and started to proceed again, but then Josephine ran between the four of them in a pounding flash of braided hair and purple wool. That glimpse caused more of a reaction from the knights, and they were surprised at their mistress running after two children at top speed. It was Sully who moved first.

"God's Bones," he muttered, putting his hand on his sword to hold it steady. "This will prove to be interesting."

He took off, followed by the other three in a close pack. Everyone in the outer bailey was frozen in mid-movement, watching their mistress run after two small children, and then watching two knights and two mercenaries running after her. Albert and Burl stood with their arms crossed and grins on their faces, shaking their heads at the humor of it. They had no idea what was going on, but it was great entertainment. But Christoph, John, and Severn, at their posts on the wall, gave the parade exiting the front gates uninterested looks. Whatever had happened was no concern of theirs.

The children were tireless as they tore down the road and, miraculously, the pies were still intact in their grubby little hands. A quarter of a mile down the road, however, they veered sharply to the left and headed into the woods. By now, Josephine was growing tired and was no longer amused by their little chase. She considered stopping, but rather decided it was the principle of the situation that she didn't. To let them run free would constitute a success in their thieving little minds and would encourage them to try again. Besides, she was curious now – they had turned away from the village.

Where were they going?

Josephine stumbled a little as she entered the woods, but not bad enough to trip, yet enough to slow her a little. Ahead, she could see the little boys growing smaller in the foliage. Growing increasingly irritated, she started to run again, picking up speed, determined as ever to catch the little louts. They were not going to make a fool of her!

But the undergrowth was slowing her considerably. She plummeted through a thicket and splashed across a small stream, all the while growing angrier. Those little buffoons were ruining a perfectly good dress! As she went deeper into the growth, she began to slow, realizing the kids had lost her. It was difficult for her to admit that. Coming to a panting, sweaty stop, she stomped her foot in frustration.

"Damnation!" she muttered, planting her fists on her hips.

She glanced about, looking at the trees and surroundings, but there was no sign of the children. The smell of moldy leaves was heavy in her nostrils, causing her to sneeze once or twice. With a reluctant sigh, she turned to go, but something up ahead in the trees caught her attention. There was something moving through the trees in front of her. Smiling craftily, she drew up her skirts and stepped quietly towards the movement, being very careful to make no noise.

She was going to capture those boys yet.

Josephine could see a small group of people in a clearing up ahead, sitting around a small fire. It was difficult to tell who or what they were, but her better sense told her to turn around and leave as quietly as she came. Generally, a group of people camping far deep in the woods was never a good thing. It indicated thieves, outlaws, and the like. Suddenly, her enthusiasm to catch those young thieves wasn't so strong anymore.

Cautiously, she stopped behind a large tree, peering around it and watching the people in the distance. They looked like wanderers, dirty and unkempt. Decidedly uncomfortable, Josephine decided the best course of action would be to return to the castle, quickly, and she kept her eyes on the clearing while she began to back away. But it was already too late; her path was abruptly blocked by a warm body, and as she started to scream, a dirty hand went over her mouth.

Blind panic filled Josephine as she was dragged into the clearing by her neck, kicking and fighting all the way. She still had not seen her attacker, but she could hear him mumbling something unintelligible with his stinking breath. He had her by the neck and by the hair, and she was unable to even make a fighting attempt to flee.

He had her solidly.

As they approached the group of people in the clearing, everyone seemed to panic at the sight of her at first until they realized that she was, in fact, a prisoner. They suspiciously eyed Josephine, looking at the person who held her questioningly. Josephine's heart sank as she realized these people were the scum of the earth, uneducated and without sense or morals. They taught their children to steal but the older ones did worse than that. Taking the possessions she had on her, her shoes and jewelry, would probably be the very least they would take.

She was going to have to think fast to get herself out of this one.

God, why did she run after those boys?

As Josephine looked anxiously at the people around her, the two little boys she had been chasing stepped out from behind the adults, smiling mischievously and chewing sloppily on a hunk of meat pie. She would have liked nothing better than to wring their little necks.

"Och, whatch got, Zef?" one of the men asked.

The man holding her laughed lewdly. "Mayhap, one of the wood nymphs I have heard stories told," he said. His accent was not Scot; it was very, very English. "She's pretty like one, isn't she? Smells good, too."

He took a long smell of her hair and Josephine cringed, trying to pull away as the men standing around laughed lewdly. But the man who had spoken before pointed at her.

"If she were a nymph, she'd be naked as a baby," he said. He was fat, dark, and dirty. "Mayhap she's a fae, come to grant our wishes!"

The group laughed loudly and Josephine felt sick with fear. She had been so stupid to let her determination get the better of her. She should have never followed the boys into the trees, and when she saw the dirty wanderers in the clearing, she should have run at the mere sight of them. What a foolish female she was. And now, what would her silly woman's curiosity cost her? No doubt, they would strip her of her clothing. But most likely, she would relinquish her virginity as well.

How could she have been so stupid?

A woman burst forth from the small gathering and rushed straight at Josephine. The woman was disheveled and her black hair was dirty and unkempt. Reaching out with long, filthy fingers, she yanked the pendant Josephine had been wearing right off of her neck.

"Ha!" she crowed triumphantly, holding the jewelry up for all to see. "She has already granted my wish!"

The clan roared wildly and Josephine's first urge was to grab the woman and pound her face into the ground. But, wisely, she refrained, for she knew she was heavily outnumbered. But she vowed she would get that necklace back and that little witch would pay.

They would all pay.

But that was providing she ever had the upper hand. As she stood there, fearful and angry, the fat man stepped forward and motioned to the man holding her.

"Let her go," he ordered. "I'm interested to know who she is."

The man let Josephine go but shoved her when he did. She fell forward onto her knees, almost pitching onto her face. But she caught herself and, deliberately brushing off her hands in a gesture of pure disgust, she remained on her knees. She wasn't one to cower, but she wasn't going to stand up and give them a target to strike at. With disdain, she glared up at her captors.

The fat man read her expression, but he was more interested in studying her fine curves. She was a delicious, ripe morsel, ready to be plucked. He sauntered over to her and stood directly in front of Josephine, appraising her openly. She stared back angrily, her cheeks flushing a rosy color.

"What's your name, lass?" he finally asked.

She looked at him a few long seconds before answering. It was her way of controlling the situation. She was going to make him wait.

"Josephine," she finally said.

"Josephine," he repeated slowly, rolling it on his tongue. "Josephine. What were you doin' in the woods, Josephine?"

She looked at the two little boys, grinning back at her. They all probably knew what she was doing in the woods, so she couldn't lie. She straightened her back and looked back up.

"I was running after two little thieves," she said.

A small chuckle bounced about the group; somebody tousled one boy's hair. The fat man smiled.

"They were simply hungry," he said. "They stole to feed us all. Is that still thievin'?"

"It is," she shot back. "They did not have to steal. I would have given them the pies and more had they only asked."

The man's smile was fading. "You are too kind, my lady," he said, but his tone was menacing. "You are a saint. Tell me, are all castle servants as gracious as you?"

"Castle servant?" she said in outrage. "I am the Mistress of Torridon, not a castle servant."

The man's eyebrows shot up in surprise. "Mistress of Torridon?" he repeated with mock courtesy. "Oh, I beg your forgiveness, my lady."

She knew immediately telling him had been a grave mistake. She cursed herself for her annoying habit of speaking before thinking. Damnation, she hadn't done a single thing right since she left the kitchen in pursuit of those two guttersnipes. She prayed that the knights that saw her leave had enough sense to come looking for her before too much time had passed, because it did not appear that she was doing too well on her own.

She needed help.

As Josephine knelt on the grass and struggled not to tremble, the fat man was staring at her. He had no doubt she was telling the truth, for she was as fine and pretty as any queen. But she was the Mistress of Torridon, which meant her husband was probably very aware his wife was gone and, perhaps, was hotly searching the area now. If she was located with a group of outlaws, it could go very bad for the outlaws.

Daume was a gypsy and a thief, but he was not stupid. He knew if her husband found her here with them, he would most likely kill them all. They could flee, but they'd either have to take her with them or kill her so she couldn't tell her husband.

He had to make a choice.

"Bind her hands," he said finally.

Josephine looked at him in shock. He had been almost pleasant talking to her, but now he ordering her restrained. In truth, she had almost been expecting it, but was hoping he wouldn't. The disgusting man that had captured her in the woods gleefully grabbed her arms and bound her wrists tightly in front of her, touching her cheek with a dirty finger before rising.

"Gag her until we decide what is to be done," Daume instructed.

A grimy rag was shoved in her mouth and tied snugly. Josephine was absolutely terrified at this point; she truly had no idea what was going to happen next. Would she even make it out of this alive? She found herself worrying about Justine. What would happen to her without Josephine's guidance? And Sully... what would he do without her? Certainly, he could run Torridon quite adequately, but she wondered if he would even miss her.

Then... there was Andrew.

God, why was she even thinking about the man? She had known him exactly four days and wasn't sure if she even liked him. He was conceited, arrogant, pompous... but he had let it slip that he could be caring and sensitive as well. And watching him train with the men had excited her more than she would care to admit.

As much as she told herself that her interest in Andrew was purely for the fact that he was a new and interesting face at Torridon, she found herself sorry she might not ever get to know him better. The Red Fury seemed to be the antithesis of his formidable reputation, but she wanted to find that out for herself. He intrigued her, as much as she hated to admit it. Anyone who took two punches from her without hitting back couldn't be all that ferocious.

A big, grubby male grabbed her by the upper arm and roughly pulled her to her feet, jolting her from her train of thought. He pulled her over to the other side of the campfire and cruelly pushed her down. With a grunt, Josephine landed heavily on her left side, but slowly pushed herself up as he walked away. All the while, her eyes were shooting daggers at the people who were now very much her enemy. Her thoughts began to turn to escape. She would have to be very aware of any opportunity. Perhaps, she would even have to form a plan.

She wasn't going to go down without a fight.

As Josephine struggled to come up with a plausible escape plan, there was some commotion in the trees to the west. The gypsies jumped to their feet and began running about in a panic. Josephine was sitting on her knees, straining her neck to see what was transpiring. She was not frightened, only tremendously relieved that the attention was diverting away from her. Maybe this was the opportunity she had been looking for.

Maybe it was time for her to run.

She was looking for an escape route when she saw two men emerging from the woods. She saw them and heard them, but it wasn't until they actually approached the camp that she realized the two men were none other than Andrew and Thane. Neither one seemed to notice her, so intent on the conversation they were having with Daume.

There were greetings being tossed about and Andrew seemed quite amiable. Josephine watched with increasing confusion as Andrew and Thane proceeded to sit heavily on a log directly across from her, graciously accepting the cups and the platters of fatty meat offered to them. Still, they didn't look at her.

They ignored her completely.

It was fortunate that Josephine was gagged because she would have given both men a piece of her mind. She could not believe her eyes. There was The Red Fury and his general, as large as life, consorting with the enemy.

At first, she wondered if this wasn't some sickening trick and that, perhaps, Andrew and his mercenaries were in cahoots with these criminals. They were chatting animatedly with her captors, as if they had everything in common, even laughing at the buffoon's crude jokes.

Was it possible that this had been their plan all along, to get her out of Torridon?

But, no. That kind of collusion didn't make sense on too many levels. Josephine may have been frightened, but she wasn't irrational. Whatever was happening now was improvised, but she couldn't understand why Andrew wasn't trying to save her.

Shock gave way to full-blown anger. How dare Andrew ignore her in her time of need? He hadn't so much as cast her an uninterested glance and the anger in her belly began to burn. If she was fortunate enough to make it out of this, Andrew wasn't going to get a single mark out of her. Not one bloody pence. He'd be lucky if she didn't throttle him with her bare hands.

Anger was a miraculous motivator. Josephine shot to her feet, unable to speak, but unintelligible sounds emitted from her throat as she told Andrew d'Vant exactly what she thought of him. Andrew and the others looked at her in surprise, startled by her sudden movement, but Josephine didn't care. She was so angry at Andrew that the gypsies were all but forgotten in her rage. God's Toes, she was going to thrash him even if it cost her greatly. He wasn't going to get away from this.

But Andrew seemed to have something else in mind and Josephine was about to find out what, exactly, that was. Perhaps, he wasn't ignoring her so much, after all, when he pointed to her and asked about her. Somehow, the subject of a price came up and the next thing she realized, someone was yanking her to her feet.

Josephine quickly discovered that she had underestimated Andrew.

CHAPTER SEVEN

T HE KNIGHTS IN their mail and heavy swords had fallen far behind their nimble young mistress as she ran after the two children with the stolen meat pies.

Despite the knights' individual strength, which was considerable, the weight of the metal and leather dragged them down. By the time Josephine and the two children disappeared into the woods, the knights were quite far behind them.

She'd simply been faster.

But once the knights entered the woods, Josephine's trail was not difficult to follow. That was fortunate for them, for it was even slower going as they moved their bulk amongst the trees with the swords banging and branches slapping at them.

They followed the trail that led them through hedges, undergrowth, and across a small stream. Only Andrew seemed to be gaining any headway through the thicket, staying a few steps ahead of Sully, Etienne, and the floundering Thane. Men in armor were not designed for swift movement or traveling through undergrowth.

It was Andrew who saw Josephine first as she stood behind the tree, watching people in what seemed to be a small clearing. He was immediately uncomfortable with the situation; he didn't like the idea of people hiding deep in the woods, as it could only mean one thing – outlaws, transients, or worse. And he thought that Josephine should know better, too – why wasn't she turning and heading right back where she came from? Whatever those children stole certainly wasn't worth what these gypsies would do to her if they discovered her.

He had to get her out of there.

Andrew was crouched low in the brush when Sully reached him. He, too, squatted down, creating a low profile as his gaze fixed on his mistress in the distance. He, too, could see the people in the clearing and felt a tremendous need to get to Josephine before the gypsies did. His urge bordered on panic.

"What in the hell is she doing?" he hissed.

Andrew shook his head, his eyes scanning their surroundings. "I do not know," he whispered. "But we must get her out of there."

Sully took a couple of small steps in Josephine's direction, hoping to come up behind her and steal her away. But she seemed to be mesmerized by the activity in the grassy clearing and she was too far away for the men to risk calling out to her. Therefore, Sully crept stealthily through the floor of the forest, inwardly raging at his mistress for her foolish actions. He would like nothing better than to take her over his knee and bruise her sweet little bottom.

But he had to get to her first.

Unfortunately, he wasn't fast enough. Andrew was the first one to catch motion out of the corner of his eye and he turned to see a big, bear-like man heading towards Josephine, well ahead of Sully. He was coming straight for her from inside the ring of trees, while Sully was several yards back in the undergrowth. There would be no possibility of Sully reaching Josephine first. God help her, she was about to be captured.

And there was nothing they could do about it.

As Andrew watched the kidnapping unfold from a distance, Sully had sense enough to duck low behind a tree trunk as he saw the man close in on Josephine. He wasn't nearly close enough to rush him and they couldn't risk alerting the others. Therefore, he had to stay where he was, but his heart was in his throat when he saw the man grab her by the neck and clamp a hair hand over her mouth. She squealed only once initially, then was silent as the man yanked her savagely into the clearing.

In a half-second, Sully was back to the others.

"Etienne!" he ordered. "Back to Torridon. Get help!"

Etienne fled. Andrew watched the big, blond man rush off but, much like Sully, his attention was on the gypsies, who now had Josephine in their midst. It appeared that they were simply talking to her at this point, which was good. Things seemed to be calm for the moment. But Andrew was so tense with apprehension at that point that had the gypsies tried to harm Josephine, he would have rushed the camp against his better judgement.

As ridiculous as those thoughts were, he knew he couldn't fight that instinct. He had to save that silly woman who liked nothing better than to throw a punch at him. Now, his mind was working furiously on a plan to remove her with little or no bloodshed. After a moment, he turned to Thane.

"Do you have any money on you?" he asked quickly. "Any valuables?"

Thane looked surprised. "Of course," he insisted. "I always carry my money with me. You do not think that I would leave it in camp with our people, do you?"

Andrew gave him a lopsided grin. "Good lad," he said. "Now, remove your mail and your helm."

Thane looked curiously at him. "What?"

Andrew ripped off his helm and then pulled off his heavy hauberk. "Do it quickly," he urged. "Hurry!"

Without another question, Thane did as he was told. Sully watched in growing alarm as Andrew finally pulled off the chainmail coat and cast it aside.

"What are you going to do?" he asked.

Andrew rose to his knees, trying to smooth out the heavy linen tunic against his broad chest. It was dirty and damp with sweat.

"I am going to rescue your troublesome mistress," he said.

"Then I am coming," Sully said as he began to remove his armor as well.

"Nay," Andrew said firmly. "You must remain should our attempt fail. We cannot risk all of us falling captive."

"But Etienne has gone for help," Sully said. "He will return with a force."

"And he will need someone here to direct the forces," Andrew responded firmly, looking Sully in the eye. "They are *your* men. They will need to be directed by you. Thane and I will enter the camp under the guise as renegade soldiers. With Thane's money, I will attempt to buy Lady Josephine."

Sully couldn't believe what he was hearing, any of it. He just looked at Andrew in astonishment.

"Are you serious?" he said. "You are mad!"

Andrew flashed a grin. "I am that," he said. "I am mad for risking life and limb for a woman who has struck me twice, with virtually no provocation. There has to be an easier way to earn eight thousand marks."

"Five thousand," Sully reminded him.

"It will be eight thousand when I get through with this."

With that, he headed off, pulling Thane along with him. Sully watched the two men traipse off towards the camp indirectly, wondering if any of this was going work. He knew their plan was only half-formed, but he also knew it was imperative that they free Josephine before something occurred that would make them regret not attempting a rescue plan sooner. Perhaps it was only logical that Andrew and Thane attempt to infiltrate the gypsies. They were mercenaries, after all, and were accustomed to dealing with that element.

Sully was a proud man and did not like to admit he lacked knowledge in any area, but he wasn't a fool. He knew when to swallow his pride. Yet, it disturbed him that virtual strangers were rescuing his mistress, the woman he was so wildly protective over, but he felt it was the wisest path to follow.

As Andrew and Thane entered the clearing where Josephine was being held, Sully crept forward and crouched behind some growth, his eyes glued to the clearing. He couldn't hear what was being said, but he could certainly read the body language. Hand on the hilt of his sword, he sincerely hoped that Andrew could buy Josephine's freedom because if something dire happened before Etienne and the rest of the troops arrived, then it would be Sully's one-man army rushing out to save them all. He hoped it wouldn't come to that.

God help them all.

CHAPTER EIGHT

A GYPSY HAD grabbed a hold of Josephine, holding her tightly as he dragged her in Andrew's direction. The subject of a price came up again, clearly meant for her. Andrew's eyes were locked on her as if he had never seen her before but, in truth, it was an expression that Josephine would always remember.

There was great interest there… and great confidence.

But Josephine was quivering with fright, with anger, and was still trying to understand why Andrew wasn't helping her. But when she got past that expression on his face, she realized that he wasn't dressed in his usual style. He was without any protection at all, not even his broadsword. Instead, he was clad in heavy leather breeches and big boots. His linen tunic was open down his broad chest, revealing his tanned, slightly hairy skin beneath. She'd only ever seen him in mail, so to see him so casually dressed was something of a surprise. And, if she admitted it, pleasurable.

The man's male beauty was unsurpassed.

Yet, her opinion of his comeliness didn't stop her anger. There was still great confusion and angst. When the gypsy man brought her to a halt, Andrew came towards her as if to inspect her as a prize, stopping inches from her as his eyes raking over her curvaceous form. When his gaze came to rest upon hers again, Josephine thought she might start shouting obscenities at him again, but nothing seemed to come forth.

Something in that intense gaze was mesmerizing.

But in his eyes, she saw something else, something that brought her anger to cool. Somehow, she saw protection, loyalty, and gentleness in the clear brown depths. Whatever she had initially thought about his presence here, she knew she was wrong. Down to her heart she knew it. He was here, and he was here to help… but how?

What was he planning?

There was more confusion in her heart now. How had he known she was even in trouble? She'd run off so quickly that no one knew where she'd gone, but Andrew evidently did. Perhaps he'd even followed her. Her eyes must have relayed her confusion, for she saw his face soften slightly. His eyes began to glimmer, with a message only for her if she dared look hard enough to read it…

Do not fear, my lady.

Andrew did, indeed, see Josephine's expression. It was hard not to see it on her innocent face. He knew how frightened she was and he felt mounting rage at the gypsies for bringing the fear upon her. He tried very hard to convey comfort to her and he began to see that she understood him. That was good. But the anger he felt at the situation was something he wrestled with, and he suppressed the feeling, for it could very well jeopardize what he was trying to accomplish.

He was, in fact, playing a role and he had to be convincing. He was a buyer and she was his prospective possession. He put a hand up, grasping Josephine's chin between his thumb and forefinger. He turned her face from side-to-side, inspecting her.

"She is exquisite," he said finally. "Where did you find her?"

Daume came to him. "Eli found her in the woods," he said. "She claims to be the mistress of the nearby fortress."

"Indeed?" Andrew's eyebrows rose. "Take the gag from her mouth."

Daume nodded to the man holding Josephine, who complied. The gag fell away and Josephine licked her lips, again looking to Andrew. He smiled seductively at her.

"What's your name, lass?" he asked.

As she looked at him doubtfully, he prayed to God that she would be smart enough to play the game. There was something in his expression beseeching her to understand what he was trying to do. Not really knowing the woman, he wasn't sure if she'd be sharp enough to understand.

Fortunately for them both, she was.

"Josephine de Carron," she said. "I am Lady Ayr."

"How old are you?" he asked.

"I have seen nineteen summers."

He cocked his head at her. "I like them younger."

Josephine's eyes blazed. Before she could stop herself, she retorted. "That is probably because an older woman is smart enough to know about the likes of you!"

The group of gypsies gasped, Daume coughed, and Thane and Andrew laughed out loud.

"She has spirit!" Andrew announced, then turned to Daume. "I must have her. How much will you take?"

Daume looked surprised, but quickly his mind began to churn. "To be truthful," he said to Andrew, "I was plannin' to keep her myself. She is just my taste."

Andrew put his hand on Daume's shoulder. "Come, come my friend," he said. "You have many women in your camp. My brother and I are alone with no companionship. Surely we can agree on a price."

Daume was reluctant to part with his trophy but Andrew pressed the point. He began to point at Josephine, scrutinizing her. "She is not so grand a prize after all," he said. "Look at her; she is small and pale and is bad-natured. Do you really want her with your people, causing problems? You know that she will only be trouble to you. I will pay you to take her off your hands."

Daume was fairly limited in his intelligence. He couldn't see beyond the moment and, at the moment, money for this captured woman was very appealing. With a long glance at Josephine as if to confirm what Andrew had said, he looked at the muscular, auburn-haired man.

"Two hundred marks," he said finally.

Andrew didn't miss a beat as he motioned to Thane. Outwardly, he appeared highly confidant, but inwardly he was praying that Thane had enough money with him. He then caught the expression on Thane's face as the man approached; he didn't have enough. So Andrew turned his head to Josephine.

She was looking at him openly, her big eyes wide with apprehension. What was he going to do next? She didn't have to wait long for an answer because in four long strides he was directly in front of her. Any closer and he would be standing in her shoes. Her head was tilted far back as she looked up into his eyes with uncertainty and, perhaps, with a little fear. She had no idea as to what he was going to do, or how he was going to rescue her from the clutches of these outlaws. But looking into his eyes, she knew instinctively to trust him. Unspoken words passed between them and her heart calmed.

In truth, she had little choice.

Andrew's entire body was trembling as he stood ever so close to her. He'd felt the same way when he'd held her while she'd been ill and the attraction he'd felt to her had nearly overwhelmed him. God's Bones, she was so beautiful. Thank God, Daume was more interested in money than in her. Now, he regretted what he was about to do.

But it was necessary.

Josephine's hands were still bound so she offered no resistance as Andrew's hand entwined in her hair and yanked her head back savagely. She yelped in pain and surprise, but was cut off as his mouth clamped over hers. But before his lips touched her, she heard him utter two words.

"Forgive me."

Andrew's lips were hard and insisting, bruising her soft lips. Josephine tried to pull away, but his hand in her hair made that impossible. The kiss became stronger and deeper, his tongue prying her lips open and licking the soft, pink insides of her mouth. Had she not been so frightened, she might have enjoyed it, for it wasn't in any way repulsive.

But his grip on her head scared her, and her mind began to race. He'd begged for her forgiveness, but for what? What he was doing or what he was about to do? In a surge of panic, she bit down with her sharp teeth on his lower lip.

Andrew didn't utter a sound, but he pulled back with a start. His eyes were wide with surprise as he tasted his own blood. His gaze lingered on her a moment, as if to ask her why she bit him, but he already knew why. He took a step back and, with his eyes still lingering on her, he spoke.

"She is not worth two hundred marks," he stated.

Turning abruptly, he marched over to Thane and jerked his head sideways in a silent command to follow him. With Josephine and Daume looking on, surprised with the swift motion, Thane fell in behind his commander and began to follow him away from the fire. Daume began to sputter and looked back to his group for support, thinking he'd just lost a good deal of money, when Josephine took a couple of steps forward and began to follow Andrew as he walked away.

She was sorry! She had been frightened and reacted the only way she could think of. *Oh, Andrew, please do not leave me... please!*

"Andrew!" she cried.

Andrew froze and Thane almost plowed into the back of him. Both men turned around slowly, with Andrew slower than Thane. The expression on his face was unreadable, but Thane looked like a child who just got caught stealing sweetcakes. Guilt was written all over him.

But Daume wasn't looking at the men; he was looking at Josephine. He didn't look suspicious, only terribly confused. He scowled at her.

"Andrew? Who is Andrew?" he demanded.

Josephine was on the verge of tears of frustration and of fear. She had destroyed Andrew's rescue plan with one word; God help her, she knew that. Whatever came now, she deserved. She wouldn't blame him if he simply walked away. She looked at Daume, her mouth working.

"He... I mean he..." she stuttered. "He looks like someone I knew once. I do not know why I said that. I am mistaken."

Daume looked at her, dubious, and for a split second, Andrew thought Daume might just be dense enough to accept her lame explanation. Still, he knew he had to do something before it all tumbled down on them, so he decided to take action. He stormed over to Josephine, bent down in front of her, and tossed her up over one broad shoulder like a sack of grain.

"She comes with me," he said angrily. "No wench is going to bite me and get away with it. And I'll only pay one hundred marks for her. She's not worth anything more."

Daume found his wits and his mouth. "Two hundred marks!" he roared. "No less!"

Andrew could sense a fight coming. He looked at Thane and knew the man was ready; he could see it in Thane's body language. The two men were quite a bit larger than the gypsies, but the man-to-man comparison was at least seven to one. If Sully came on cue, then the ratio would be cut in half. But his primary concern was getting Josephine to safety before any blows were dealt. He motioned to Thane, who was at his side quickly. With a bit more care, he handed Josephine to his second.

"To the woods," he growled.

Thane understood. Andrew meant get her the hell out of here before she got caught in the middle of a fight. As Thane moved quickly away from the growing hostility, Andrew squared off with the short, fat gypsy. He smiled threateningly.

"The whore goes with me either way," he said in a tone that made the hair on Daume's neck stand on end. "One hundred marks or nothing. The choice is yours."

Daume's face flushed. "How dare you steal from me?" he sputtered. "I graciously open my camp to you, give you food and drink, and you have the gall to steal from me! I ought to cut your heart out!"

Andrew's smile faded and he glared at the man. It didn't take long before some fool made the first move, so Andrew flew into action. He caught the man square in the face with a backhanded fist, sending him sprawling. After that, the whole camp was moving in on Andrew.

Just inside the edge of the trees, Thane deposited Josephine with Sully, who quickly cut off her leather bindings. Thane barely had time to look back over the clearing just to see Andrew throw the first blow.

"Damnation!"

Thane took off at a dead run, heading back into the clearing to help Andrew. Sully forgot about Josephine for the moment, looking to see where Thane was heading in such a hurry.

"God Bones…" he muttered.

Now, Sully went barreling after Thane, rushing out to help Andrew fight off men who were clearly trying to kill him. Still in the thicket, Josephine pulled way the leather bindings and rubbed her wrists as she stood up, watching Andrew, Thane, and Sully in a vicious fight with several gypsies and feeling a good deal of concern for their safety. They'd come to save her, but at what cost? Three of them against the entire camp? They risked themselves to rescue her. She couldn't let one or more of them come to harm.

She had to help them.

Josephine knew how to fight. She wasn't a weak female, by any means. Quickly, she looked around for a weapon and her gaze came to rest on a small log on the floor of the forest, right at her feet. It had broken branches at the top of it, like spikes, and she picked it up without hesitation. Wielding it with two hands, she charged back into the clearing. She was going to kill those slimy sons-of-whores for laying a hand on her and then she was going to find that little bitch and retrieve her mother's necklace.

There was vengeance in her heart this day.

As Josephine entered the clearing with the wood held high, she never gave a second thought to her own well-being. All she could think of was Andrew, Sully, and Thane, and the fight they were facing because of her.

Quickly, she engaged one man and one woman, people who charged at her. But she faked them both out, turning one way but swinging another, just as Sully had taught her. She brought the log down on the man's skull, quickly disabling him, while she used the same motion to slam the woman in the face. As the woman ran off screaming, Josephine began swinging her club in a frenzy.

It was a nasty fight from the beginning, unfortunate because neither Andrew nor Sully realized Josephine had entered the fray. In fact, Andrew had his own problems at the moment; a screeching woman hung on his neck as he traded blows with a big, hairy man. The man, due to Andrew's human cargo, was able to land a good blow to Andrew's ribs, but as he closed in for a more devastating blow, Andrew turned around and thrust the woman on him as he pried her arms from his neck.

Kicking and yelling, the two went down in a pile and Andrew moved on. He was turning to see what had become of Sully and Thane when a man jumped out at him, but Andrew threw a punch that sent the man to the ground. As he pushed his way through the writhing crowd, he was growing amused. The gypsies, for some reason, were fighting each other more than they were fighting the enemy. Apparently, the excitement of a fight was all they needed.

It was bedlam.

But his humor vanished when he caught sight of a purple dress. Josephine was swinging her log at men's heads, pounding those who came too close to her, and Andrew felt a surge of panic at the sight. God's Bones, she was in the middle of this fray! But even as he began pushing people out of the way on his quest to get to her, he came to realize that this was no ordinary woman in a fight. He knew she'd wielded a sword for Torridon but that didn't have an impact on him until this moment.

She was fearless in her fight. He could see that in an instant. Her bravery was beyond compare. What was it he'd told her? That she no longer had to protect her fortress? He could see now that it had been a mistake for him to say that. Cleary, she was at home in a fight.

His respect, and his attraction, grew.

Oblivious to the fact that Andrew had her in his sights, Josephine was beating the brains out of a man until someone grabbed her club. Furious, and frightened, she looked up to see that Andrew had a hold of it. He was fixed on her, but before he could say a word, two men rushing at him from the crowd.

Josephine saw them coming.

"Andrew!" she cried. "Behind you!"

Instinctively, Andrew's fists balled up and he swung to his right, catching one man in the stomach as the other man managed to hook an arm around Andrew's neck and pull him to the ground. While the first man lay gasping in the dirt, Andrew wrestled with the other man, trying to dislodge him.

The gypsy was furiously throwing his fists about and Andrew was doing no more than fending him off, trying not to get hit in the face. Weary of grappling with the man, Andrew brought up a knee and caught the man in the crotch. With a scream, the man rolled off.

Staggering to his feet, Andrew went to Josephine, who still stood grasping the log with white knuckles. He grabbed her firmly by the upper arms.

"What are you doing here?" he demanded. "You were to stay out of sight!"

"I came to help!" she said breathlessly. "You three were grossly outnumbered!"

Andrew caught movement in the forest and looked up. A look of satisfaction crossed his face.

"Not anymore," he said flatly. "Help has arrived."

Josephine turned around, seeing her men spilling out through the trees towards them. She let out a sigh of relief and turned back to Andrew, but several feet to her right, she could see Sully pounding the hell out of the burly gypsy. The man had sense enough to roll away from Sully's merciless fists but when he came around again, he was grasping a wicked-looking dagger.

"Nay!" she breathed, and broke away from Andrew. "Sully, *watch out!*"

Andrew reached out to grab her, but she was fast on her feet and halfway to Sully by the time Andrew started after her. But she was too late; Sully took the dagger in his upper arm and Josephine screamed, dropping the log and rushing for him as he stumbled backwards.

Andrew intercepted the gypsy before he could move on Sully again. His rock-like fist caught the gypsy in the jaw and the man's head snapped sideways, but he didn't go down. Andrew's other fist pummeled him again and the man's head jerked in the opposite direction, with blood and spit flying everywhere. Still, he did not go down, but he was weaving dangerously. With the final blow, Andrew brought up a huge booted leg and kicked the man right in his soft belly.

He went down like a stone.

Andrew ripped the dagger from the man's hand and tossed it away, far away, before turning to Josephine and Sully. Sully was on his feet, watching the approach of the Torridon army as Josephine wrapped his bleeding arm with a strip of purple wool from her surcote.

"It is not too deep," she announced to Andrew. "A few stitches and he shall be as good as new."

Andrew nodded, watching her grimace as she tore the wool and tied it tightly. She seemed greatly concerned for Sully, which spurred Andrew oddly. She was showing concern for another man and, somehow, he didn't like that. Not even though it was Sully. Not a man prone to jealousy, he refused to admit that he might actually be feeling some. Impossible! He'd never felt jealousy with regard to a woman in his life and he wasn't about to start now.

Still... it would be nice for her to show him the same concern, too.

Pulling himself away from Josephine and Sully, Andrew's attention turned to the fight at hand. The Torridon forces had infiltrated the group, quickly quelling whatever resistance there was. Two Torridon knights – Etienne and Burl – were on horseback, with their massive war horses snorting and dancing, knocking about men and snapping with their big teeth. Etienne reined his steed to a halt and dismounted.

"You are injured," he said to Sully. "How badly?"

Sully shook his head. "It is a scratch," he assured him. "But I want these people rounded up and sent on their way. They are not to spend another moment on Torridon lands."

"Wait!" Josephine cried, putting a hand on Etienne's arm to stop him from following through. "When I was brought to the group, one of the gypsy women took a pendant from around my neck. It belonged to my mother and I want it back."

The knights all began looking around. "Which woman?" Andrew asked.

Josephine craned her neck, searching the crowd. "I do not see her," she said, her voice laced with disappointment. "Etienne, collect all of the women into a group. I must find this woman *and* my pendant."

Etienne saluted smartly, bellowing orders as he walked away. Josephine brushed a stray lock of hair from her face, her features etched with concern as she watched her men carry out her orders. They were not gentle with the gypsy women by any means; any attempt to resist was met by a sharp slap or a pull of the hair. But that wasn't Josephine's concern – she wanted her necklace back and she had yet to see the woman who took it.

Finally, Josephine saw Albert dragging the scraggly young woman from back beyond the wagons. She fought the tall, gangly knight like a wildcat until the usually gentle man grabbed her hair and pulled her the rest of the way to where the women were now corralled. As they came nearer, recognition dawned.

"That is the one!" Josephine cried out. "The woman with Albert!"

She dashed towards Albert, and Andrew and Sully followed close behind. Fearlessly, Josephine went up to the rebellious young woman.

"Where is the necklace you stole from me?" she demanded.

The woman gave her a defiant smile, evidently not caring or too stupid to realize that Josephine commanded the army around her.

"I lost it," she said lazily.

Josephine stepped closer to the woman. "Listen well, you cocky little wench," she hissed. "I intend to find that necklace, so do yourself a favor and tell me where it is. Do you see these men around you? They are at my command. I can have them punish you a thousand ways, so much so that you will wish you were dead. Now, *where* is my necklace?"

The woman looked to the stone-like faces of the men that surrounded her. She did not doubt Josephine's words for a moment, but she was proud and was not going to let Josephine belittle her in front of her own people. More important than anything, she was not going to lose their respect.

"I do not remember where I put it," she shrugged, still blatantly defiant.

Josephine flamed. She took a step towards the woman and raised her hands in a most threatening fashion, but Andrew stopped her.

"Wait," he said. "If you will allow me to reason with her, my lady."

Josephine, clenching and unclenching her fists, turned her back to the woman. She was so angry that she was genuinely afraid of what she might do. Andrew went to the gypsy girl.

"Rise," he told her.

The wench glanced over to the other women smugly, as she drew herself up. Her eyes twinkled seductively at Andrew, knowing she had more of a chance conning him than she did Josephine. She would pull out all of her tricks for this big man.

Josephine forced herself to turn and watch what Andrew was doing, but she didn't like what she saw. The woman stretched and posed like a cat in heat, and she found herself angrier, but on a different level. She was appalled to discover that she didn't like this woman's attention on Andrew in the least and she didn't like it at all that he seemed to be eating it up. He wasn't even trying to retrieve her pendant. Instead, he was trading flirtatious looks with the whore.

"Do you know where I can find Lady Josephine's pendant?" he asked politely.

She stuck out her small chest and batted her lashes at him. "Now, I might," she said. "If you were to ask me properly, I might."

He reached up a hand towards her and Josephine was about to burst with anger and outrage. Her breathing became fast and hard, and Sully put a hand on her forearm to quiet her. He wanted to see what Andrew was going to do. But what happened wasn't what he or Josephine expected.

Andrew smiled at the gypsy woman, who was nearly salivating as she waited for his touch. Then, quick as a flash, Andrew grabbed the front of the woman's blouse. With a loud, ripping noise, she was laid open to the waist and her tunic was in tatters. Her tiny breasts were exposed to the world and she yelled in surprise, trying to cover herself up, as women around her loudly voiced their protest. But the Torridon soldiers were even louder – voicing their approval.

Whistles and cheers filled the air as Josephine watched the woman's humiliation, stunned by what Andrew had done. Next to her, Sully couldn't keep the smile off of his face. He was coming to like The Red Fury, just a little. The man had ballocks, that was for certain.

Andrew heard all of the revelry, but his eyes were fixed on the woman in front of him. And he was no longer smiling. As she yelped and tried to cover herself up, Andrew pulled at the bodice, pulling it off of one side of her body as she struggled. He spun her around as if looking for something.

"It does not seem to be there," he said. "I wonder where else it could be?"

The men screamed with laughter. In spite of herself, Josephine felt like giggling as well. The woman was utterly humiliated. Had Josephine not been so angry, she might have felt a twinge of pity. But she silently applauded Andrew for his application of persuasion without the use of physical force. That haughty, nasty woman was bound to give in faster this way.

"Has your memory returned?" Andrew was asking politely. "Or shall I help it along?"

The woman's eyes were black with fury. With a toss of her black hair, she sneered at Andrew.

"Bastard!" she spat. "How dare you…"

She never finished her sentence, for Andrew reached out and grasped a corner of her dirty skirt and yanked so hard, she was tripped by the force of it. She was screaming, the men were laughing, and Josephine watched in amused shock as Andrew reached down for the bottom of her shift. Although she was kicking him with all of her might, he barely felt it.

"Very well!" the woman screamed. "Very well, very well! Stop and I shall give it to you!"

Instantly, Andrew stopped pawing at her, crossing his arms expectantly. Huffing and puffing with humiliation, the gypsy woman rose as carefully as she could without exposing anything. She looked at Andrew, verging on tears. Then she covered her breasts with one arm and thrust her hand into a hidden pocket in her underskirts. With her grubby fingers, she drew forth the dazzling pendant.

Josephine charged forward and snatched the necklace before Andrew had a chance to accept it. Then it was Josephine who smiled smugly at the gypsy woman. She was twitching and her mouth was working as she formed her final reply. Her hand itched to slap the little witch, but she didn't. She had her necklace and that was all that mattered in the end.

"Thank you," she said through clenched teeth. Then she spun around, walked away, and spoke to no one in particular. "I want them off my land and out of my sight."

Andrew smiled sweetly at the shaking, filthy woman before turning to follow Josephine. He had expected her to flatten the woman, but he admired her for showing restraint. Given her passionate nature and her fondness of punching, he was proud of her for showing some hard-fought self-control. As he stood there and watched her walk away, Sully interrupted his observations.

"Take Lady Josephine back to Torridon, if you would," he said. "I shall make sure the woods are cleared."

"As you wish," Andrew said. "I'll need a horse."

Sully waved a hand at Etienne, whistling loudly between his teeth. "Your destrier!"

Etienne motioned to the soldier holding his steed, and the man immediately brought the muscular animal to Andrew. Without even using the stirrups, Andrew swung himself onto the horse and, using his massive thighs to guide the animal, he moved it in Josephine's direction.

But Josephine wasn't paying any attention. She'd had enough excitement for one day and her emotions had the better of her. Moreover, she was trying to put her necklace back on, but it was broken. She felt a great deal of sadness at that. She was distracted from the broken chain by a big horse next to her and she looked up to see Andrew riding Etienne's blond beast. She held up the necklace.

"It is broken," she said glumly.

He held out his hand. "May I?"

She gave it to him and he examined it carefully. She stared at his actions, alternately watching his face and watching his hands as they moved nimbly over the beads.

"See here," he held up the broken ends of the necklace. "The silver latch only needs to be repaired. I can do it when we get back to Torridon."

Her face brightened. "You can?"

"Indeed."

She smiled gratefully. "You are a man of many talents, then," she said. "Not only do you fight battles, but you repair jewelry as well."

He grinned. "It is nothing, really," he said. "It just needs to be bent back into place. It is simple."

Josephine watched his face, the strong lines of it, and she began to feel the pangs of attraction again. Something about the man had attracted her from the beginning, whether or not she realized it, and it was something that was only growing stronger with time.

Thank you," she said after a moment. "That would mean a great deal to me."

Andrew carefully put the necklace in the money pouch on his belt. When he looked at her again, he couldn't help but notice she was still looking at him with that same soft expression. *Gratitude*, he thought. *Or... something more...*

Perhaps that was only wishful thinking.

"It would be my pleasure," he said after a moment. "Now, Lady Josephine, may I escort you safely back to Torridon?"

Josephine returned his smile; she couldn't help it. She placed her hand in his extended one and he lifted her effortlessly onto the saddle in front of him. When she was settled, he squeezed the horse lightly and it walked forth into the forest, heading back to the main road. As the animal picked its way among the bushes and roots, Josephine was very conscious of Andrew's own warm body next to her.

It was making her heart race simply to experience it.

The forest around her was alive with sunlight flickering and birds singing, and she smiled as a pair of butterflies flitted past her. But among it all, she found herself enjoying Andrew's presence. It was comforting, warm, and settling. She felt safe, as she'd never felt in her life. Her eyes wandered up to the trees as the horse carried them into the shadows, and the situation they left behind them seemed like a wild, impossible nightmare.

Andrew had been magnificent from the start. From the moment he appeared and had charmed his way into the camp, he had been in complete control, only Josephine had been too blind to see it. She had been too wrapped up in her own outrage to even realize that he had come to help her. That had taken some time, but she was still sorry she'd doubted him. Like a white knight, he'd ridden to her rescue.

How he even found her didn't matter. The only thing that mattered was that she had trusted him completely. And she had; well, after a few minutes, anyway, once she figured out that he'd come to help her. Then, her own foolishness nearly destroyed his attempt, but he'd salvaged it beautifully. And the fight; it had been like watching him at practice as he'd neatly dispatched the men thrown at him. To watch him made her chest feel strangely tight, her heart beating in her ears. It had been pure excitement to watch him, despite her concerns and the danger involved.

Josephine would admit, only to herself, that she was glad The Red Fury had come to Torridon. He was proving to be a welcome diversion for her during a period that seemed to hold little more than anxiety and grief.

As Josephine was lost to her thoughts, Andrew had some thoughts of his own with her sweet body pressed up against him. He, too, was secretly glad he had come to Torridon. Much to his surprise, he had never felt more at peace than he did now, riding through the peaceful trees with a gentle breeze lifting tendrils of Josephine's hair until they tickled his cheek. Feeling her against him was the most natural thing in the world. He had never in his life experienced such things, not with any woman he'd ever known. Somehow, Josephine was different. He found himself looking forward to the coming months and wondered what they would bring.

He wondered how long he could stretch out his contract at Torridon.

"How did you find me?" Josephine's question distracted him from his thoughts.

He had to focus on what she was asking, so carried away with daydreams he was. "We followed you as you chased after the two children," he said. "Why were you chasing them, anyway?"

She felt foolish explaining what had started the ruckus. "They had stolen two pies from the kitchen," she said. "I did not want them to get away with it, so I ran after them. I would have caught them, too, had I not been hindered by this heavy surcote."

He smiled, looking off into the forest. "All of that was over two pies?" he asked. "I thought they had stolen the family jewels, at least. Or, mayhap coin. Or, Christ, the gold plate straight from the great hall, or even...."

"I get the point," she said, cutting him off with a grin and turning in the saddle to look at him. He was dangerously close, closer than was advisable. Her initial intent had been to throw him a threatening look, but the expression faded at the sight of his beautiful face and she found she had to turn away quickly lest he see the blush in her cheeks.

But, in retrospect, the taking of two pies by two hungry children did seem like a foolish reason for endangering her life and the lives of those sworn to protect her. She began to feel a little sheepish and decided to change the subject.

"Where were you born, Andrew?" she asked.

Andrew hadn't missed the flush of her cheeks when she'd turned away. He thought he might have had a bit of a flush in his, as well, mostly because the last time she'd been that close to him, he kissed her with a hunger he'd never before experienced. He'd like to try it again sometime, hoping she wouldn't bite him again if he did.

Somehow, he suspected she wouldn't.

"England," he said after a moment.

"Where in England?"

"Near Haldane," he said distantly.

She should have picked up on his reluctant tone, but she didn't. To her, it was a pleasant conversation. To Andrew, it was dredging up things he worked hard to forget.

"Haldane is almost in Scotland," she said. "You look decidedly more Scot, with your red hair. You do not speak like a Scots."

"Nor do you."

Josephine shrugged. "My mother thought we should not speak so," she said. "She had an English lady-in-waiting who taught my brother and sister and me how to speak the way of the English. And what of you? Why do you not speak like a Scots?"

"Because I fostered in England."

"But you seem to be based in Scotland," she said. "Do you have kin in Scotland?"

His soft brown eyes darkened. "My mother was Scots, but she spent most of her time in England," he said. "My father was English. That is how they met."

"Oh?" Josephine's eyebrows lifted in interest. "Where was your mother from?"

"Dumfries."

"But she lives in England now?" Josephine asked, oblivious to the dark memories she was awakening in him. "What says she to your mercenary way of life?"

He didn't want to talk about things that upset him, and he most certainly didn't want to talk about his mother. Her chatter was growing annoying now. "I have not seen my mother in several years," he said, his tone bordering on sharp. "I believe she is dead and we will not speak on her."

Josephine was a little shocked at his tone and shut her mouth immediately. Realizing he'd sounded harsh, Andrew was sorry he had snapped at her. He'd not meant to, but where his mother was concerned, he was emotionally unsteady. The last time he'd seen his mother, she was being dragged to her chambers by his brother's men and there wasn't a damned thing Andrew could do to help her. Nay, he didn't want to talk about the gentle Elaine.

The woman he'd failed those years ago.

The destrier came out of the woods and stomped up onto the dirt road, heading towards Torridon, which loomed in the distance. For a ride that had been so pleasant a short time ago, Josephine could not wait for it to end. She had no idea why Andrew was angry with her and, in truth, he had hurt her feelings with his sharp tone. But why did she care if he was angry? Whatever she'd said to anger him, she didn't care any longer. She wanted to get back to Torridon, off of the horse, and away from the moody Andrew d'Vant.

So much for the warm attraction she felt for him. It had been a fleeting thing.

They rode to the castle in silence and entered the outer bailey. People were milling about, hurrying to their destinations, and a flock of loose chickens squawked in panic as the horse walked through them.

Somewhere overhead, she heard a knight bellowing orders up on the wall.

A sense of relief and familiarity flooded into her as they crossed into the inner bailey. She was glad to be home. But her anger and confusion had not abated and, immediately upon crossing the threshold into the inner bailey, Josephine pulled herself from Andrew's grip and slid to the ground. Without so much as a word, she marched off across the mud and straight into the keep.

Andrew watched her ramrod-straight back as she mounted the stairs and disappeared into the bowels of the castle. He knew he had hurt her feelings, but he could not apologize without including an explanation and he wasn't ready to do that yet. His past, his secrets… they were for him and him alone. They weren't for him to share with someone he'd only known a few days.

Even if he *was* wildly attracted to her.

As Andrew turned the destrier towards the stables, a smile played on his lips. All was not lost; he would see Josephine at the evening meal and, mayhap, he could make amends without apologizing for his shortness with her. Women had always told him that he possessed uncanny charm. If that were truly so, then it would come in handy tonight, as the thought of Josephine angry with him strangely disturbed him. He didn't want her to be angry with him.

Tonight, he would do what he could to change that.

CHAPTER NINE

OME THE EVENING, everyone in the castle and most everyone in the village knew of Lady Josephine's afternoon adventure. But, at what usually happens with a tale, it transformed as it passed from person to person, and soon villagers were chatting excitably about the rape of Lady Josephine and how the mercenary lord, The Red Fury, had charged in to save her by chopping off the heads of fifty gypsies single-handedly. By nightfall, it was a truly unbelievable tale.

As the sun dipped behind the gentle western hills, and the sky be came rich hues of purple and pink, torches were lit about the castle and the village to the south. The villagers still talked of the ordeal and of the larger than life Andrew d'Vant while their suppers inside their warm huts went cold.

Inside the castle, now locked up against the night, everyone was converging in the great hall where tantalizing smells of venison and pork beckoned them. The hall was alive with torches and musicians, with people taking their seats as servants rushed forward to assist them. Several knights already sat at the head table but did not eat, as they were correctly waiting for their mistresses. They spoke quietly between themselves as to the events of the day, clarifying what had actually transpired and speculating as to the very reasons in the first place. The fact that it had ended well made the situation seem almost comical in retrospect.

But there were a few who weren't laughing, Donald Muir being one of them. He sat with the knights, his eyes blackened and his swollen nose bandaged. He listened with awe and regret that he had not been able to assist Josephine in her hour of need. That was what his father had sent him for, after all. But he had spent last night and all day sleeping off the poppy Josephine had given him. He'd missed all of the excitement and felt rather worthless for it.

As Donald wallowed in guilt, Josephine was up in her bower as she prepared for the evening meal. She sat at her dressing table clad in a magnificent pink silk. It turned the tint in her cheeks and lips to an almost identical color. Her hair was pulled back and was secured in a bun at the nape of her neck, covered by a glittering silver net that started at the crown of her head and swept down the back like a glistening waterfall. A few tendrils of hair caressed her chin and neck.

It was a beautiful image, in truth, but Josephine's expression was anything but pleasant. She stared at herself in the mirror, reluctant for what she must say this night.

She was back to where she was before the escapade of the stolen pies. She was back to delivering the news of the king's visit to Sully and the rest of the inhabitants of Torridon, and she was back to feeling nervous and uncertain about it. In desperation, she had sent Ola for Sully – she had decided it was best that she inform him first, before the rest. She would need his wisdom and guidance, hoping he could give that to her and not rage out of control.

Josephine's stomach churned as she looked at her reflection. How could the king ask her to marry Colin? Especially when he knew the long, bloody history and the deep-seated hatred the families harbored against each other? He was as much as condemning her to death. Of course, she didn't know if that was what the man was going to ask of her, but to travel all the way from Edinburgh simply to visit her... something was in the wind. The king was coming with a purpose.

It was her wild imagination that told her what the purpose was.

A knock at the door roused her from her thoughts and Josephine rose from her dressing table. Taking a deep breath for courage, she bade the caller to enter and Sully opened the door, closing it softly behind him. When his gaze fell upon her, he smiled warmly.

"Three days of events seem to not have an adverse effect on you," he observed. "How are you feeling?"

Josephine shrugged. "I am weary," she said. "But I did not send for you to speak on my health. I have something I wish to discuss with you."

He saw the expression on her face and felt a twinge of apprehension. "Of course, my lady," he said. "I am at your disposal."

Now, the time was upon her. Nervously, Josephine looked away, as if trying to find the correct words.

"I received a dispatch from King Alexander three days ago," she said finally. "He is coming to visit next week."

Sully's eyes widened. "The king? At Torridon?"

"Aye."

Sully was at a loss. "Why was I not notified of this before now?"

Josephine turned to him. "Because I told the gatehouse guards not to tell you," she said. "A missive from the king is worrisome enough without you breathing down my neck to know the contents."

He looked at her, perhaps a bit cut down by her words. "I did not realize that I breathed down your neck."

She relented a bit. "I did not mean that," she said. "I simply meant that I wanted to read the missive and digest it before speaking to you about it."

"And have you?"

She nodded, looking the slightest bit sickened. "It simply says he is coming to discuss important matters, but I believe I know what they are," she said. "You know that Colin Dalmellington has been pestering the king to name him as rightful heir to Torridon and I believe he intends to inform me of his decision. Personally."

Sully looked at her suspiciously. "*What* decision?"

Josephine looked long and hard at him before answering. "Sully, you are sworn to obey me, are you not?" she asked firmly. "You will do whatever I ask of you?"

He didn't hesitate. "To the death, my lady."

"Then if I comply with the king's wishes, you will do as you are told?"

He read defeat in her eyes and felt his heart sink. "I will always do as you wish."

She lowered her eyes, feeling so very disgusted at what she was about to say. "I believe our king will wish for me to marry Colin and turn Torridon over to him as my dowry," she said, her voice hollow. "That is not what the king's missive said, but something inside of me tells me that is his purpose."

Sully could feel the blood drain from his face as realization dawned. Marrying Colin Dalmellington had never entered his mind, probably because the very thought of Josephine marrying anyone crazed him. But marriage to evil Colin? He thought, mayhap, that the king would simply demand she turn over Torridon and end the bloodshed once and for all… but marriage to an enemy?

Sully's mind reeled at the mere thought. He had to turn away from her. No wonder she had made him swear his loyalty first; she knew exactly what his initial reaction would be. But he couldn't help himself. God help him, all he could feel was blind rage.

"I shall kill him," he finally growled. "Before I witness any such union, I shall kill him."

Josephine wasn't sure if she meant the king, or Colin, or both. She knew he would react in this fashion and she had dreaded it. But because she was prepared for his outrage, she was able to deal with it and not buckle under.

"Nay, Sully," she said calmly. "You will be of no use to me dead, which is exactly what you will become should you defy King Alexander's wishes. I need you alive."

His jaw flexed as he looked away from her. Josephine knew the dilemma and she knew his pride. She also knew his undying loyalty to

Hugh, and allowing Josephine to marry Colin Dalmellington would be failing his master. Her heart ached more for his internal conflict than it did for her own future.

Josephine went up behind him quietly, putting her arms around him and laying her cheek on his warm back. It was a gesture of friendship, of family, and of sadness. But to Sully, it was far more than that; it was a touch that took his breath away, that doused the anger in his heart. It was a touch he would have given the rest of his life for had it been a touch of affection or even love. He closed his eyes tightly, feeling her touch down to his very bones.

"Please, Sully," Josephine begged softly. "You and Justine are all that I have left. I lost my father and my brother. I do not want to lose you, too."

He shook his head. "You will never lose me, my lady," he said huskily. "This, I promise."

"Then you will swear no violence towards the king or his directive."

Sully hesitated. "No violence, I swear."

Josephine wasn't sure she believed him, but she didn't press him. "Whatever the king asks of me, we will obey peacefully. Agreed?"

"As you wish."

Josephine released him and he turned to look her. She was so lovely in the flickering light. A tug-of-war ensued in his mind, a fight between rage and softness. Rage at the king and his horrid agenda, and softness towards Josephine. She was in no position to defy the king and they both knew it. He wished he could think of a way to help her out of it.

Sully had been a soldier since his youth. The ways of court and diplomacy did not come easily to him. Military tactics and planning were as natural as breathing, and he was always correct in his judgment. Therefore, it was very difficult for him to stand helplessly by while his mistress was at the mercy of the king, and there was nothing he could do to protect her. But that didn't mean he wasn't fully prepared to risk his life for her.

Without a word, he knelt down before her and took her right hand into his. His pale blue eyes were intense as he gazed up at her.

"You are my commander, Lady Josephine de Carron," he said hoarsely. "I have been and always shall be yours. Whatever you ask of me, I shall do without question. But if that should include serving under Colin Dalmellington, know that I will do it under great personal protest. But I will never, ever leave you."

Josephine could hear that angst in his tone. She could see it in his eyes, and she hurt for him. "It pains me to ask you to serve Dalmellington when you have as much hatred for them as I do," she said. "Believe me, I derive no pleasure from the thought of sharing Colin's bed."

Sully's jaw ticked at the mere thought. God, he was sickened by it. But looking up into her pale face, it occurred to him how selfish he was acting. Josephine would be the one at the center of the storm. He was only a bystander, yet he was acting like he was to be directly affected.

"Hopefully, it may not come to that," he said softly. "Mayhap, God will grant us a miracle."

Her smile faded. "Mayhap," she said wistfully.

But she wasn't counting on it.

THE MOOD OF the Knight's Haven was, to say the least, somber.

The knights of Torridon, plus Josephine, Andrew, Thane, and Donald had taken the evening meal in the great hall and, upon the conclusion of it, Josephine proceeded to inform the knights of the king's visit and her suspicions as to the reason. Once she was finished, the room was deathly still with shock and disbelief. Josephine had never felt more like crying in her life. For Torridon to come to this end was sorrowful.

Such a terrible, somber end.

But her men would not surrender so easily. Soon, the table was abuzz with ideas and solutions. More than relinquishing Torridon, the thought of their pretty mistress in Colin Dalmellington's clutches horrified them. The more the after-dinner wine flowed, the more animated and full of ideas they became.

"My friends!" Severn rose and gestured wildly. "Have we forgotten we have The Red Fury at our disposal? Should we defy the king, not even the royal armies could defeat us!"

"Do not be ridiculous, Severn," old Burl said sharply. "We have over one thousand men and the king commands all of Scotland. The combined forces would sweep over us like a plague of locust and scatter our bones to the wind."

The room roared with arguments and counterproposals, with each man talking all at once. The noise level was deafening and Josephine was overwhelmed and confused by it all. Even though the situation directly involved her, no one seemed to be talking to her. They were screaming and yelling at each other. Even Donald was involved, with his swollen face, arguing for reason as the knights lobbied for action.

Feeling left out and confused, she stood up from her seat. No one noticed as she walked the length of the table, behind the chairs of gesturing men, and exited the room. No one, that is, except Andrew.

He had been sitting passively in his chair since the riot started, initially caught off guard by Lady Josephine's announcement, but he wasn't completely surprised. Torridon was valuable, as was a maiden heiress, so he was inclined to agree with Josephine's assumption. Still, his mind began to work on a solution. A new twist thrown into an already volatile situation. If he didn't help her figure a way out of this, then he wouldn't get his money.

And he might not ever see her again.

Therefore, when she left the room, he followed. And as he followed her, he realized it wasn't just the money that disturbed him, but the thought of Josephine with a man he had heard only terrible things about. He remembered how he felt when he had seen her at the mercy of the gypsies; it was an overwhelming feeling of protection. But was it money-inspired? He would have liked to believe it was, but he knew better.

The problem, as he saw it, was that he liked Lady Josephine. He liked her beauty and her spirit. He liked that she wasn't afraid of him, much less anything else. She was an extraordinary woman who seemed to have been dealt the short end of the stick over the past few years. But she was strong of character and intelligence, even if she was a little naïve. She was different than every woman he had ever met. She wasn't throwing herself at him in a constant barrage of flirtation.

In short, she was a challenge.

He followed Josephine into a portion of the castle's rambling keep that he had never been to. He looked about him as he traversed the corridor, noting the level of dirt and black mold. It seemed to be a very seldom used wing and, in a keep this size, that probably wasn't an unusual thing.

Up ahead, he could see Josephine entering the very last room at the end of the hall. She didn't bother to close the door and he came up in silence, standing in the doorway. The room was immaculate, tidy, and clean, and it had a large alcove in one corner and a beautiful Persian rug under the great mahogany bed. It was a delicate and completely feminine room, and he felt completely out of place in his heavy leathers and sword, as if his mere presence might somehow damage the fragile aura.

Josephine still hadn't noticed him. She sat in front of a huge dressing table, staring at herself in the polished bronze mirror. Slowly, Andrew entered the room and came up behind her, looking at her through her reflection. Josephine didn't start when she saw him. She simply looked at him, her face devoid of any emotion, but the gloom in the air was palpable.

"My mother's name was Lady Afton de Carron," she said quietly. "Her father and King Alexander shared the same grandfather. The king arranged the marriage between my mother and father. My father said that he was not too keen on the idea at first. But after he saw my mother, it was love at first sight."

Andrew's voice was gentle and deep. "This was your mother's

room?"

"Yes," she responded. "She died in childbirth with Justine. I was so young when she died and I do not remember her, but I feel her presence very strongly in this room. I talk to her often here about things at Torridon and I know she hears me." She looked at herself a little more closely in the mirror. "My father used to tell me that I look just like her."

"Then she was extremely beautiful," Andrew said.

Josephine lifted her eyes slowly to him, trying to read his expression. It took her a moment to realize he was referring to her. When their eyes met, she felt a spark run through her veins. Of what, she wasn't sure, but it frightened her and thrilled her at the same time. The attraction she was feeling for Andrew was turning into something else, something she had no idea how to deal with or control. She wasn't sure she *wanted* to control it. But, clearly, it was all very one-sided. Surely a man like Andrew d'Vant had no need for a naïve heiress and a broken-down fortress.

Distressed, she stood up and began to wring her hands.

"I am failing them – do not you see that?" she said. "My parents loved each other. They built Torridon into what you see and raised their children in the hopes that my brother would carry on the family line and maintain the integrity of the castle. But the castle has fallen to me and I've done nothing but run Torridon into the ground. Now I must pay the ultimate price by marrying my enemy to save my home. I am glad my parents are dead and cannot see my failure."

Andrew cocked an eyebrow. "Hold," he instructed sternly. "You, Lady Josephine, are the bearer of nothing more than bad circumstances. Had you not been as strong and determined as you are, Torridon would have fallen long ago. You are to be commended for holding a fortress of this size against a formidable enemy, and I am proud to have been commissioned to serve you."

"There will be *no* battle," she said bitterly. "At least no battle that you will be able to assist in. The battle now will be decided in King

Alexander's court, but the war will continue in Colin Dalmellington's bedroom. God's Bones, I would sooner wed the devil himself."

With that, she wandered over to the massive bed and sat heavily. Slowly, Andrew went over and sat down beside her. He truly felt her despair, but he knew that her self-confessed failure was not her fault. From what he'd seen, she was anything but a failure. He just wished that she would realize it as well.

But he was coming to see a problem. He'd only been at Torridon for a couple of days but, in that short time, he was feeling a pull to this place and its lovely mistress. He'd already come up with a plan as a result of the speech she'd given to her men, but it was a plan borne of haste and desperation. He wasn't even sure if he wanted to suggest it because it would mean great sacrifices for both him and Josephine. All the while, as he was thinking of his plan, he kept questioning himself as to why he should even involve himself in any of this.

It wasn't his castle!

Andrew knew he should remain a bystander. The first rule in Scotland was not to involve oneself in clan wars, and that was exactly what this was. He would be smart to simply forfeit the contract and leave. There was no shortage of work for his army, so why was he staying?

God help him, he knew why.

Josephine.

As he sat there and deliberated over his involvement in all of this, and the plan he was afraid to mention, Josephine abruptly stood up from the bed and faced him.

"I apologize for bringing you and your army here," she said. "It would seem that it was a waste of time on your part and a waste of money on mine. I will pay you your five thousand marks and you are free to leave. With the king coming… I fear there is no reason for you to be here."

Andrew eyed her, hearing the surrender already in her tone. He didn't like to see such a fiery woman admit defeat.

"Lady Josephine," he rose slowly on his big legs, with his eyes fixed on hers. "I believe I have an idea that may be a solution to all of this. Would you permit me to suggest it?"

She looked at him a little curiously. "By all means."

He paused a moment, hardly believing he was about to propose his idea. But he'd come this far.

"The king cannot betroth one who is already married," he finally said.

The simple solution hit Josephine like a ton of rocks and her eyes widened until they nearly popped from her skull. She took a few steps in Andrew's direction, not realizing she was moving, for her mind was reeling with realization of his suggestion.

"Of course!" she gasped. "Andrew, you are brilliant! If I marry someone else, the king cannot betroth me to Colin!"

"Indeed, he cannot."

She was beside herself with glee. "But who can I marry in the next two days?"

Andrew hesitated a split second before opening his mouth again, but he couldn't get the words out fast enough before she was moving away from him, thinking aloud in her zeal.

"It will have to be someone close by, someone of rank or a noble birth," she said. She spun around to Andrew with a sudden look of horror. "But what of Justine? Even if I am married, King Alexander can still betroth Justine to Colin; therefore, she must be wed, too. Andrew, I must find *two* husbands!"

He shook his head. "Nay, my lady," he said. "There is no need to search, for what you seek is within these walls of Torridon."

She stopped her pacing and her brows knitted together curiously. "Who?"

His gaze upon her was intense. Slowly, like a predator stalking its prey, he went to her. For a moment, he simply stood there, gazing down at her, hardly believing what he was about to say but, in the same breath, nothing had ever seemed so right. Josephine de Carron was the only woman who had ever caught his attention in such a way that he could hardly go a minute without thinking about her. She had may fine qualities, as he had seen, and she was exquisitely beautiful. Perhaps they were shallow reasons but, to him, they were reasons enough. He couldn't stand the thought of her married to another.

With great deliberation, he took a knee before her.

"My father was the Earl of Annan and Blackbank, a title inherited by my older brother," he said. "When I said I born north of Haldane, I neglected to tell you that my family's earldom is from Gretna Green to the east all the way to Dumfries. The heir apparent to the earldom is Viscount Brydekirk, a title which I technically hold unless my brother has a son I am unaware of. We are descended from the ancient kings of Cornwall on my father's side and Kenneth MacAlpin on my mother's. I have wealth to match your own, and an army of men to protect your holding. I will offer myself to you in a marriage of convenience, if you will accept me."

Josephine was stunned. She hadn't seen his offer coming and the more she thought on it, the more astonished she became. The Red Fury was offering for her hand to spare her the king's betrothal to Colin?

She could hardly believe it.

"What… but what of Justine?" It was all she could think of to ask.

In truth, Andrew had been holding his breath, waiting for her reply. At least she hadn't refused him outright. Much to his surprise, she actually seemed to be considering it.

"Justine can marry Sully," he said. "Surely he must come from a good family, and it is not so important that the second daughter marry well. I suspect that he is already as good as a member of the family and marriage will make him permanently so."

Josephine was beginning to see his plan clearly. It was simple and seemingly foolproof. But as her astonishment began to fade, several questions began to form.

"How will I explain to the king that I married secretly and quickly?" she asked. "And Justine, too? He will become suspicious."

Andrew shook his head. "We will explain to the king that it was necessary to marry quickly, for you are with child," he said. "As for Justine, she and Sully were betrothed by your father before he died because they were deeply in love. It was kept secret because your father wished to marry you off first."

He seemed to have all of the answers. Josephine put her folded hands to her lips, pondering his plan and all of the angles of it that she could see. It *could* work. Better still, she liked Andrew. She was deeply attracted to him. Even a marriage of convenience to a man she found attractive would be better than spending the rest of her life in a hate-filled marriage with an enemy. Furthermore, Torridon would be safe because no man in his right mind, not even Colin Dalmellington, would attack property belonging to The Red Fury.

God, could this *truly* work?

But there was Justine; the woman would have to get used to the idea of marrying Sully. And Sully! Poor Sully would have to get used to the idea of being saddled with Justine the rest of his life. She felt a genuine twinge of pity for him, her very best friend, but it couldn't be helped. He would make a fine husband for Justine. Perhaps Justine would even grow up with his guidance.

Josephine's thoughts turned back to Andrew. He was still kneeling chivalrously before her, his eyes searching her face. It seemed to her that he was looking for her answer in all of this. She gave him a weak smile.

"It would seem, Andrew, that a wife could come along with the five thousand marks," she said quietly. "But why would you do this on my behalf? We hardly know one another. There is nothing at stake between us."

Andrew had to admit, he was relieved. He'd never asked for a woman's hand before and was hoping his first attempt wouldn't end in failure. Thankful that Josephine saw his reasoning, he stood up, a twinkle in his eye as he looked at her.

"Nay," he said. "There is nothing at stake between us. But as I see it, you are in need of a husband to save your castle, and I believe it would be a mutually beneficial arrangement. Besides, I am sure that taking a wife would please my mother, wherever she may be."

"But I thought you believed your mother to be dead?"

As soon as Josephine said those words, she was sorry. Andrew's smile disappeared and he stiffened. His first impulse was to throw a curt answer back at her, but he forced himself to calm and realized that she had not asked out of malice. Moreover, he was the one who had brought the woman up. If he was to marry this woman, it would only be fair that she know something of his past.

With that in mind, he forced himself to calm. He didn't like to speak of his past; it was a forbidden subject to those who knew him. Therefore, to speak on it was both awkward and painful.

"'Tis true, I do believe that," he said quietly. "I… I suppose it is only fair that you know something of my past, of where I come from. But I warn you, it is not an easy tale."

That was a clue to Josephine as to why he'd become brusque with her earlier in the day when the subject of his mother came up. Patiently, she nodded.

"I hold no judgement," she said. "If you wish to tell me, I shall listen."

With a sigh, Andrew sat down on the bed again, next to her. He was silent a moment as he gathered his thoughts. "When my father died, my brother Alphonse inherited everything," he said. "Alphonse is a dim-witted, greedy bastard, and he ordered my death before my father was even cold in his grave. In fear of my life, I fled my home and joined up with a band of mercenaries. I was just a lad at the time, not yet a man. Even so, I was forced to grow up quickly. A mercenary named Trey took me under his wing and I learned well. I learned well enough that I now have the largest and most powerful mercenary army in all of England and Scotland. But I always swore that I would return someday to my brother's home of Haldane Castle, seat of the Earl of Annan and Blackbank; someday when I could stand and meet my brother face-to-face, and call him to answer for all of his misdeeds."

It was quite a story and Josephine was naturally heartbroken for him. She could hear the distress in his voice. He was letting her to see a glimpse of the man beyond The Red Fury persona, to the beating heart of the man beneath, and that touched her.

"I am so sorry to hear that," she said sincerely. "But what of your mother? Did he force her to flee, too?"

He shook his head. "The same day he ordered my banishment, he locked my mother away when she tried to protect me," he said. "That was almost nineteen years ago. I suspect she is no longer alive, so any mention of her for me is… painful."

Josephine felt sorry for the man. Instinctively, she put her soft hand on his well-muscled shoulder, trying to give him some comfort. Although the touch was as light as a child's, Andrew felt it as though it were reaching through to his soul. He looked up at her, with his defenses down and all of the self-assuredness gone from his eyes. To Josephine, he looked as vulnerable as a child.

"Why haven't you gone after her?" she pressed gently. "With all of your money and manpower, surely you have enough strength to go after her and find out if she is still alive?"

He lowered his gaze and shook his head. "My brother commands an earldom and all who reside within it," he said. "That's thousands of men, Josephine. I am not nearly powerful enough. Not yet."

"But you are The Red Fury," she said, as she gripped his shoulder. "You are the most feared man in Scotland and England; you have said so yourself. Surely your brother will concede rather than fight you? One mercenary is worth ten regular men."

He smiled at her encouragement. He was deeply touched by it, too. But she was too close, too young, and too naïve. His rough, callused hand reached up and gently touched her cheek. It was baby-soft and as rosy as a petal. The issue at hand suddenly faded as he found himself consumed by the warmth radiating from her.

The effect on Josephine was equally as jolting. His gentle touch sent shivers bolting through her body and she found herself pleased at the prospect of getting to know him better, and of marrying him. If the man could make her feel like this at a mere touch, she was willing to spend a lifetime seeking his magic touch.

Magic, indeed.

"I am sorry about your mother, Andrew," she said softly, dropping her hand from his shoulder. "And I appreciate both your candor and your generous offer. Are you sure this is what you wish to do?"

"I have no reservation."

"Then I accept your offer. I will marry you."

And with that, he was a man betrothed. There was some excitement in that thought, the thrill of an unexpected future with a woman he was very much attracted to.

"We shall wed as soon as you are ready, mayhap sooner rather than later if the king's visit is imminent," he said, realizing he sounded rather happy about the whole thing. "And, might I suggest we make it a double ceremony?"

Josephine nodded. "Absolutely," she agreed rising to her feet. "Now, I must inform Justine and Sully. And I fear I must prepare myself for a good argument from them both."

Andrew grinned, rising from the bed beside her, towering over her. When they stood next to one another, she came to his chest. "Allow me to accompany you to deliver the bad news, my lady," he said, as he offered her his arm. "They might be less apt to argue with my menacing presence."

Josephine returned his smile. "You are quite menacing, aren't you?" she said as she accepted his arm. "But, nay. The news must come from me. And, please... now that we are betrothed, you will call me Josephine."

Andrew felt as if he'd been waiting for that invitation since the day he'd met her. "It would be my pleasure," he said genuinely. "You will address me as Andrew. Call me what you wish; I will answer."

It was a sweetly giddy moment and Josephine found herself fighting off a grin. She'd never been giddy in her life, but Andrew certainly made her feel silly and foolish enough.

She liked it.

They walked out into the corridor, heading for the great hall in warm silence, traversing halls with wide, arched ceilings, halls that generations had tread before them. There were grooves in the stone floors from the traffic. Josephine's thoughts were still quite giddy and she found herself watching her feet as they moved, feeling his big arm warm and firm in her palm.

"What's your full Christian name, Andrew?" she asked, purely to make conversation.

"Andrew Albert Deinwald d'Vant," he said. "And yours?"

"Josephine Alys de Carron," she said. Then, she grinned. "When I was very small, however, I did not want to be called by my name. I insisted that everyone call me Joey. I suppose I wanted to be a boy at that time in my life. Even until his death, my father would call me Joey. Justine calls me that, too, on occasion, when she is not annoyed with me."

"Joey," Andrew repeated, a glimmer of a smile on his lips. "I like that."

She chuckled and looked away. "It is a boy's name."

He was grinning at her even though she couldn't see him. "Not in this case," he said, "for you are most definitely not a boy. It is rather sweet. May I call you Joey, then?"

She shrugged, both embarrassed and flattered. "Call me what you wish; I will answer."

He heard his own words repeated back to him, something that made him grin all the more.

"Joey it is," he murmured.

CHAPTER TEN

S ULLY AND JUSTINE were corralled in Josephine's sitting room; each
one having no idea why they had been summoned.

Ola had been the summoner and she didn't give either one of them
a clue. Therefore, they sat in awkward silence, eyeing each other on
occasion but not really speaking, until Josephine entered the room with
Andrew in tow.

Although Sully was glad to see Josephine, he found himself wondering why Andrew was with her. He had just spent the past hour in the
Knight's Haven butting heads with other knights regarding Josephine's
situation, and he was in no mood to deal with his jealousy of Andrew.

As always, he banked it well, but it was becoming increasingly difficult, especially with Andrew now in the mix of things. Although he
appreciated the lengths Andrew went to in order to save Josephine
from the gypsies, he was coming to wonder if the man wasn't looking at
Josephine as more than simply a job. Even now, as he watched
Andrew's expression, there was something in it that suggested his
attention towards Josephine was more than common politeness.

And then, there was Josephine herself – as she took a seat next to
her sister, Sully read her like a book. She seemed calmer, much more
herself, and he wondered why. Did Andrew have something to do with
it? Confused and suspicious, he waited for what was to come.

Josephine, for her part, felt for all the world like a bowl of jelly. She was oblivious to Sully's suspicions, far more concerned with her own feelings at the moment. She'd been quite calm until she saw Sully and Justine, looking at her expectantly. Now, her insides quaked and her palms were moist. She knew that Sully and Justine were going to be angry about this; she knew it intuitively but there was nothing that could be done about it. Clearing her throat quietly, she embarked on news of the king's visit and her suspicions, for her sister's benefit. Sully already knew but, by his expression, it wasn't any easier to hear the second time around.

Justine was quite naturally outraged, loudly voicing her opposition to her sister's interpretation of the king's visit. She swore vehemently that she would call forth the powers of darkness to curse the king. But as she raged, Sully sat in silence, eyeing Andrew intermittently.

There was something not quite right in all of this. He suspected there was a reason behind The Red Fury's presence, but he couldn't quite put his finger on it. He partially shut out the conversation between Josephine and Justine, and began mentally searching for various reasons as to why Andrew d'Vant was trailing Josephine like a shadow. He needn't have strained so hard for, in little time, the answer fell in his lap as Josephine cut to the heart of the matter.

She stood abruptly, cutting off her sister's argument with a sharp wave of her hand. When Sully finally looked at her, he realized he'd never seen her look so determined.

"Because the king is giving me no choice in this matter, it seems that I must make drastic decisions to save Torridon, and all of us, from Colin Dalmellington," she said in a tone that left no doubt as to who was in charge. "Justine, I know you are angry, but shouting curses at the king is not helping the situation, so kindly shut your mouth. Since I am convinced that the king's visit will result in a betrothal to our greatest enemy, it is apparent that the only way to avoid a marriage is to already be married. I have, therefore, decided to marry immediately."

"What?" Sully asked, shocked. Now, she had his full attention. "*Marry*? Marry whom?"

Josephine could see the astonishment in his eyes, both the fear and the hope of it. Her manner softened somewhat. "I just do not see that there is any other option," she said. "Justine will marry immediately, too. We must both be married so King Alexander cannot contract either of us to Dalmellington."

Justine flew at her. "Married?" she screamed. "I will not marry, not by the king's command or by yours!"

Josephine, surprisingly, didn't explode. She looked at her sister with as much patience as she could muster. "I do not like this any more than you do," she said evenly. "But I truly believe I have come to the only possible solution.'"

"It is *not* solution," Justine argued. "It is a sentence for a doomed existence!"

Josephine's anger was mounting. "What would you have me do, Justine?" she hissed. "Marry Colin? Condemn you and all of Torridon to living under his sadistic rule? Please tell me if you have any other ideas, for now is the time!"

Justine's jaw flexed while she thought on those words. It was as if only she and her sister existed; Sully and Andrew faded far into the shadows. This was between the two sisters. Justine didn't like the fact that Josephine was choosing the path of her life and she couldn't honestly see that her sister was only trying to protect her. Justine only knew what she wanted from life, and marriage wasn't a part of it.

"And just *who* are we to marry?" she finally sneered.

"You will marry Sully," Josephine said quietly. "And I shall marry Andrew."

Justine looked at her sister as if she had not heard correctly. Her eyes bulged and her mouth popped open, but strangely, she didn't argue. Then, with painful confusion, she looked at Sully.

He still sat by the window, his blue eyes riveted to Josephine. He didn't move or speak, but his eyes screamed with disbelief. He honestly could not believe what had just come forth from Josephine's lips, and the air in the room seemed to stand still while Justine and Sully digested the news.

Finally, he rose to his feet. His motion was slow, which was unlike Sully at all.

"How did you decide on this... match, my lady?" he asked hoarsely.

Josephine needed him to understand. "Andrew's father was the Earl of Annan and Blackbank, and he would be more of a suitable match for me," she said. "You are born of a good family, Sully, and you are a very suitable match for Justine. In fact, you are almost like family as it is, so the marriage would be a mere formality."

Sully's gaze lingered on her a moment longer before glancing at Andrew. "And he has agreed to it?"

"It was his idea."

Sully wasn't surprised by that; he really wasn't. All of his suspicions about Andrew's behavior towards Josephine came to a head; *the man has wanted her all along. With her, comes Torridon.* Did he even realize that the woman was more valuable than the fortress? Perhaps; perhaps not. Either way, Sully would now have a mercenary for a liege.

But it was better than the alternative.

With a sigh of resignation, he turned away. Josephine went to him, praying the man wasn't deciding on just how much he hated her at the moment.

"Please tell me your feelings, Sully," she said softly. "I must know."

He shrugged, unable to look at her. "It would seem that you have already made your decision."

"I have," she said. "But I truly feel there is no other alternative if we are to keep Colin Dalmellington out of Torridon. What would you rather do, Sully – serve him? Or marry my sister to keep him away?"

Sully didn't know which he would rather do. Both seemed like hellish futures to him. He looked to Andrew, standing silently by the chamber door, and he felt a stab of both jealousy and anger.

As much as Sully's mind raced to discover an evil streak to Andrew d'Vant, his good sense could not believe that there was anything nefarious to Andrew's suggestion of marriage. It was, in fact, a very logical solution. And although Sully didn't know Andrew well, he simply didn't seem like a man with an ulterior motive. His reputation, even as a mercenary, was an honorable one. But the price to keep Colin Dalmellington away for good was that not only would Josephine marry Andrew, but Sully would marry Justine. Never in his wildest night-mares did Sully ever imagine himself being married to the crazy younger sister he seriously disliked.

But Josephine wished it.

His beautiful, sweet mistress, the woman he deeply loved, wanted him to marry her sister. God, he knew his hopes to marry Josephine had been foolish. He knew he wasn't of her station, so there was no possibility for a match. It hurt his heart to realize that, once and for all. If there was a silver lining in all of this, a marriage to Justin would forever tie him to Josephine, even if he wasn't married to her. He would become part of the de Carron Clan, and Hugh's son.

It wasn't how he'd always hoped it would be, but it was something he would have to be satisfied with. Taking a deep breath, he turned to look at Justine.

The woman was dressed all in black, looking as strange as she usu-ally did. He'd known her most of his life and although she was an odd one, she did have redeeming qualities. And she was young enough so that a husband could mold her.

At least, he hoped so.

"If Lady Justine will have me," he said softly, "then I would be hon-ored."

Josephine smiled with great relief and turned to her sister. "Jus-tine?" she said encouragingly.

Justine's mind was reeling. While Sully was watching a dream die, she was watching one realized; her most far-fetched dream was to come true. *If she would have him?* Sully was the only man in the world Justine would consider having, as much as she vehemently denied any and all marital aspirations. But he would never, ever know. To let her guard down and admit she had feelings would be admitting weakness, and she had none. At least, that's what she wanted everyone to think. She was proud and perfect. Taking on a rather arrogant stance, she looked at Sully.

"Since it is so important to Josephine," she said stiffly, "I will marry you."

"You are, indeed, wise, Lady Justine," Andrew said as he finally stepped forward. "Sir Sully will be a fine husband."

Sully chuckled ironically and turned away. Josephine watched him a moment, hoping the man didn't hate her overly, before turning to her sister.

"I expect the king within the next day or two," she said. "He is very close. Therefore, our marriages must take place right away. I will make the arrangements for the ceremony to take place at noon in the great hall. Sully?"

He swung around to face her at the sound of her voice. He'd spent his entire life jumping when she called to him, and would continue to do so.

"My lady?"

"Send someone to fetch the priest in Ayr," she ordered. "Father Delmo at St. John's. He will do."

"Aye, my lady."

"And, Sully?"

"My lady?"

"After you marry my sister, you may call me Josephine or Joey, as you used to when I was younger," she said with a twinkle in her eye. "I realize that when James and Father died, your address became formal with me, as was proper, but soon you will be my brother. There is no place for titles."

Sully couldn't help the grin. "Aye, my lady."

So far, Andrew had remained mostly silent throughout the entire exchange. But now that the situation was starting to ease, at least as far as the decisions that had been made, Andrew suspected the two sisters had much to discuss and he would give them their privacy.

"I will accompany Sully and assist him in his duties," he said. "Good eve to you, Lady Justine. Good eve, Joey. See you on the morrow."

Justine looked at her sister curiously as Andrew followed Sully from the room. She waited until both men had left before speaking.

"Joey?" she whispered. "You told him Father's nickname for you?"

Josephine tore her eyes away from the closed door and looked a little guiltily at her sister. "It came up in conversation," she said. "I told him he may call me by the name if he wishes."

Justine eyed her sister for a moment longer before going in search of a chair. She sat heavily, much calmer and quieter than she had been earlier. Josephine sat in a chair opposite her sister, also lost in her thoughts. So very much had happened this day that she was still trying to absorb it all.

"I cannot believe that tomorrow at this time I will be Sully's wife," Justine finally said.

"Nor can I believe that tomorrow at this time I will be married to The Red Fury," Josephine said. "It does not seem possible."

Justine looked at her sister. "My poor darling," she said as compassionately as she could muster. "Married to a man you hardly know, and a mercenary at that."

Josephine fought off a smile as she turned away. "He is not all bad," she said, remembering the tale he told her earlier and even the heated kiss they'd shared in the midst of the gypsy's camp. "He can be rather… pleasant."

Justine simply cocked an eyebrow in disagreement. "Although I haven't noticed personally, the women around here swear he's somewhat of a god," she said. "It seems he has taken a couple of our servants to his bed. When I think of…"

Josephine cut her off, her eyes wide with shock. "What do you mean by that? He has been bedding our servants?"

"The man is a pig, Josephine," Justine insisted. "Surely you have realized that."

Josephine flamed. "How dare you speak of him like that!" she said.

"He is nothing of the sort. But then again, you were always a terrible judge of character. Listen to me, Justine – I suggest you reform your opinion of Andrew d'Vant, or at least keep your stupid opinions to yourself. He is to be your brother-in-law, whether or not you like it."

Justine cocked her head, her eyes narrowing at her sister as if something had just occurred to her. "I understand now," she said. "You like this… this man, don't you? You are pleased at this marital agreement!"

"Still your tongue, woman!" Josephine waved her hand irritably. "I do not even know the man. And as for the marital arrangement, I would rather marry a stranger than Colin Dalmellington."

Justine simply eyed her sister, disbelieving everything she was telling her. With a shrug, she finally turned away, but not before the damage was done.

Josephine was angry – angry at her sister's wild claims and angry at Andrew's hot blood. Why on earth should his liaisons bother her? She didn't know. She felt a distinct sense of betrayal and he wasn't even her husband yet.

Hurt, even.

"And what about you, Justine?" she countered, wanting off the subject of Andrew and the rumors of his bed partners. "You seemed not to protest too much when I told you of your future marriage. Is it possible that you might like Sully even though you have sworn off marriage?"

Justine felt the barb right in her heart. "I'm only marrying Sully for the good of Torridon," she insisted. "I have no emotions towards him one way or the other."

"Ha!" Josephine scoffed as she turned away from her sister. "He is a kind and gentle man and far better than you deserve. Hear me, Sister. Treat him well or feel my wrath. Do you understand?"

"Now who has feelings for Sully?" Justine taunted.

Josephine shot her sister a look of pure disdain. She had no time or patience to argue with Justine. She was more concerned with seeking out Andrew and discovering the truth about his indiscretions. If they were to marry, then that would have to stop immediately. She couldn't have him married to the Lady of Torridon and bedding his wife's servants.

"Sully is my captain and my friend," Josephine said as she headed for the door. Once she reached it, she turned to her sister. "And I wish to God that our mother had made me her last child!"

Dramatically yanking open the door, she fled from the chamber.

Justine stared at the empty doorway for a few seconds, feeling the force of her sister's words. But she was also feeling the force of the entire conversation, wondering why her cards never said anything about the king's visit or the dual marriages. Surely her cards should have said something about these drastic events in their lives.

Pushing way her feelings of regret for her words tonight, and the hurt her sister's own words had inflicted on her, she headed for her room.

She would see what her cards had to say.

CHAPTER ELEVEN

L ATER THAT NIGHT, Andrew sat inside his tent on the perimeter of Torridon, sipping a great goblet of red wine.

His thoughts were on his actions of the day, of the decisions made, and on Josephine's effect on him. He had finally reached the point where he could admit to himself that he wanted her. Her beauty and the body that undoubtedly accompanied it roused him more than any woman ever had.

He propped his long legs on a stool and took another drink. He and Thane had a long talk after he had informed his second-in-command of the impending marital plans. At first, Thane had been shocked and had made several points as to why marrying the heiress of Torridon might not be such a good idea. But the reasons were fairly weak and, eventually, he had laughed slyly and congratulated Andrew of his cunning in his betrothal to the Mistress of Torridon, and all of her wealth.

But after that, the conversation turned uncomfortable for Andrew. Thane said several things that greatly disturbed him. He spoke of bleeding Torridon, of acquiring the dowry and using it to increase the size and strength of the army. *No wife was going to tie The Red Fury down!*

Indeed, Andrew was planning to continue his lifestyle. When he was sure Josephine and Torridon were safe from any more Dalmellington attacks, he would leave and continue with his army and his vocation. Josephine, of course, would remain at Torridon, and he would visit when time permitted. It would be a good arrangement, for neither of them had any interest in a marital relationship.

… did they?

But foremost was the question of why; *why did he do it? Why did he offer to marry Josephine de Carron to save her from marriage to her enemy?* Andrew had to laugh at himself because he really didn't know why. He was very attracted to her, more than he had been to any other woman. And, of course, the fact that she was very wealthy didn't hurt. But that wasn't his chief motivation. Then, there was Torridon, one of the largest fortresses in Scotland. But strangely, that wasn't a factor either.

So… what was the chief reason behind his offer? Andrew had re-membered his initial reaction when he saw Josephine in the grips of the gypsy man. *Joey.* He had felt such a sense of protectiveness towards her that it had threatened to destroy his cover. He wanted to rush forward and strangle the bastard with his bare hands for even touching her.

Andrew had been surprised at himself for so strong an emotion. The only person in his life who had ever managed to provoke feelings of such power had been his mother. Andrew came to the conclusion that, for the reason of his own sanity, he had to offer to marry Josephine rather than see Dalmellington abuse her. He knew that if she did marry her enemy, he could not sleep at night wondering at her fate.

He couldn't let Josephine suffer.

Therefore, it was a most noble sacrifice coming from a man who never thought of himself as being very noble. Perhaps by preventing Josephine's imprisonment, he was somehow compensating for being unable to control his mother's.

Odd that he would look at it that way.

Lost in thought, he was gradually aware of a commotion outside his tent and his hand went to the hilt of his sword. Straining his ears, he could hear snippets of a soldier's voice and then an angry female voice.

He thought he recognized the female voice.

Andrew's feet came off the stool and he rose on his powerful legs, but his sharp ears were still focused. God's Bones, it *was* Josephine. What in the hell was she doing in a mercenary camp? With a frown, he took a step towards the door just in time to see Josephine propel herself in through the tent flap.

Her cheeks were flushed and her nostrils flared with exertion. She was still dressed in the same dress she had been wearing for the evening meal, rather thin of fabric, and with the evening's chill, her erect nipples showed obviously through the material.

Surprised to see her, Andrew nonetheless looked at her with a mixture of curiosity and desire. His hand came away from his sword.

"To what do I owe the pleasure of this visit, my lady?" he asked pleasantly.

Josephine didn't mince words. She'd had time to work up a righteous anger between the keep and Andrew's encampment.

"I have been told that you have sought… comfort with my servants," she said.

He looked amused. "And if I have?"

Her jaw fell open in shock. "Then you do not deny any of the rumors?"

He shrugged and laid his sword on the table. "I do not confirm them, either."

"Do not play me with riddles, Andrew d'Vant," she told him angrily. "Tell me if the rumors are true."

He crossed his arms as he faced her. "Why is it so important that I admit that I slept with a maid?"

"Ah!" she crowed. "So you admit it? Allow me to inform you that I will *not* permit you to bed any more of Torridon's female servants."

"Why?" he asked, not at all concerned with her outrage. In fact, he found it rather amusing. "Would you prefer I bed the mistress?"

She scowled. "You'll not lay a hand on me," she seethed. "I'd just as soon bed a stable hand; it would bring me as much pleasure."

He cocked an eyebrow at her. "We are to be married tomorrow," he said. "Do you think you can keep your husband from your bed?"

She stood her ground, pointing a finger at him. "And may I remind you that this is a marriage only of convenience?" she said. "I intend to remain…"

He cut her off. "Remain what? A virgin?" His face and voice took on a hardness. "Josephine, we are to be married. Whether or not I deflower you is not the issue. Do you think that anyone decent would marry a divorced woman, providing the church and I grant you a divorce? Is that what you think?"

She was stunned into silence by his words. She hadn't thought of it that way. Aye, she was attracted to him, terribly so, but she realized that she didn't want to marry a man who would look at the union as a business arrangement. That's never what she wanted. God, she didn't know what she wanted now. All she knew was that she didn't want a man who would bed the servants as well as her. It was wrong; shockingly wrong.

She wanted a man who would remain true to her.

Tears sprang to her eyes and she turned from him while her mind mulled over his words. Then, wiping the tears before they rolled down her cheeks, she turned back around.

"Then there will be no wedding," she said hoarsely. "I will hold off the king and his men until I discover his true intentions. Andrew, you will choose two hundred of your best men and prepare them to ride at dawn. We will meet King Alexander on the road and, there, I shall discuss his intentions. While we are out, Sully will position the rest of the men in defensive positions in anticipation of our return and a massive attack by the king's forces. I will die and see Torridon in ruins before I marry you or Colin Dalmellington."

He fought off a smile. He knew she was angry, but he also knew she wasn't serious. Torridon meant too much to her. Still, there was something at the bottom of her fit that rather touched him. Was it possible she was jealous he'd bedded the help? Was it possible she wanted him all to herself, as a wife would?

He rather hoped that was the case.

"As you wish. I'll get my money either way." He reclaimed his wine goblet in a thoughtful move. "I wonder if Dalmellington can use my services after Torridon has been purged of the de Carron Clan."

That was enough for Josephine. She flew at him in a rage, with her little fists. But Andrew caught her by the arms before she could do any damage, pinning them behind her and pulling against his warm, hard body. Josephine twisted and squirmed. But she eventually realized her resistance was futile.

He had her exactly where he wanted her.

"Let me go," she growled.

"Nay."

Furious, she looked up, realizing that he was bent over her and his face was an inch from her own, his breath warm on her forehead. But his expression was not one of rage; there was something warm and seductive in his face. In spite of her fury, Josephine found herself relaxing against him because he felt so good. There was something about being held close to the man that made her heart leap wildly, the joy and comfort of a man of extraordinary strength.

She liked it.

"Now, Joey, my sweetling," Andrew purred. "Listen to me and listen well. There will be a wedding because I want you, and you want Torridon. Tomorrow, you will become my wife and by tomorrow night I will take you bodily. We will truly become man and wife. And if the king and Dalmellington still want Torridon, they will have to go through me to get it."

His words made her heart race faster and she was spellbound by his eyes. She tried to respond but found she couldn't. There was nothing she could say by way of argument or anything else. What he said was exactly what she wanted… wasn't it?

As she watched, his face loomed closer and, suddenly, his lips were covering hers, softly and gently as if he had all the time in the world. His stubble tickled her skin as his lips did marvelous things to her mouth. *Warm... soft... delicious....* his tongue opened her lips to lick the pink insides of her mouth and run itself along her straight, white teeth.

It was more than she could take. Josephine collapsed against him completely, totally oblivious to anything else but the delight of his kiss. He was holding her close, possessing her for the first time, truly making his mark on her. She could've cried with the sweetness of it.

In his ardor, Andrew released her arms and Josephine immediately wound them around his neck, with their kisses growing in fervor. Andrew wrapped his thickly-muscled arms around her body and lifted her, carrying her swiftly to the furs that constituted his bed, and laid her gently down.

God's Bones, he couldn't seem to get enough of her.

Josephine was so caught up in the heat of the moment, she barely realized he had laid her down. His hands roamed her body freely, rubbing her hard nipples through the fabric. His mouth left hers, blazing a trail down her neck and gently brushing the tops of her full breasts. The sensations were so utterly incredible that Josephine had not the mind to stop him if she wanted to.

She should... but she couldn't.

But abruptly, he stopped. Lifting his head, Andrew looked deep into her eyes with a passion-strained expression. Josephine gazed back at him with her mind at a standstill. But she did wonder, fleetingly, why he had stopped and why he was looking at her. She was greedy in that she wanted more; more kisses, more of him. She didn't want him to stop. Finally, Andrew's mouth moved as if he were going to speak but, instead, he simply went back to kissing her. Josephine responded eagerly.

"My lord!" someone yelled from outside the tent. "Lord Andrew!"

Andrew was on his feet and raced to the tent flap before Josephine even had time to open her eyes. But as she scrambled up and tried to look as regal as possible, the tent flap opened and in swept Thane.

Thane opened his mouth to speak, but caught sight of Josephine and hesitated a split second. Andrew saw his surprised look and sighed impatiently.

"Well, well? What is it?" he demanded.

Thane tore his eyes away from Josephine and focused on his lord. "Riders," he said quickly. "About three miles out."

"How many?" Andrew asked.

"About twenty," Thane replied. "Wearing uniforms and flying green and yellow colors."

Andrew looked at Josephine for her opinion. She stepped forward towards the men, her eyes wide.

"Those are Kennedy colors," she said. "Are they bearing weapons?"

Thane shook his head. "Nay," he said. "It looks like an escort of some kind."

She and Andrew passed perplexed glances.

"This time of night?" he asked her. "Who would be riding at this hour?"

She shook her head, perhaps a bit apprehensive. "It must be extremely urgent for Methuselah Kennedy to be exposing himself in the dead of night."

Andrew didn't waste any time. He turned to Thane. "Send a party out to meet them," he instructed swiftly. "Bring them directly into the inner bailey, and say nothing of the events of today. Understood?"

"Aye, my lord," Thane said, and was gone.

Andrew turned to Josephine. "Any idea as to why they should come?"

She shook her head, increasingly concerned. "I would not know," she said. "But I am certain we will find out soon enough."

It was a true statement. But Andrew realized he was nearly as apprehensive as Josephine was. Whatever it was, he was certain it could not be good.

But there was no time to waste. With guests on the approach, Andrew went to the corner of his tent where his mail and protection hung on a frame and donned his mail coat. He also had pieces of plate protection and Josephine watched as he deftly donned the protection and secured his sword. Picking up the big leather gauntlets he always wore, he pulled them on.

As Josephine watched it all curiously, it occurred to her that this was the true professional soldier that he was. Big, fearsome, and deadly. It sent a shiver of fear up her spine, for he was truly formidable. She had seen him many times before in his armor and gauntlets, and she didn't know why this particular time was so different. It was as if she just realized she was gazing at the legend of The Red Fury.

There was a prideful feeling about it, too. It was this legend, this man, who was to be her husband. Such warm, giddy feelings filled her chest. Pulling herself from her daydreams, she gathered her skirts and moved to the tent entry.

"I will ride out with them," she said. "I must have my horse brought around."

He turned to her with lightning speed, a command to remain at Torridon on his lips. But he knew she wouldn't tolerate that well, so he paused before replying carefully. "I am sure that will not be necessary," he said. "You have enough men to do that for you. Surely you would rather remain here, where it is warm and safe."

Josephine shook her head. "As the heiress of Torridon, it is good manners to greet other clans personally," she informed him patiently. "No need to fear; the Kennedy are allies. You may join me in greeting them if you wish."

He regarded her steadily, not at all pleased with her decision, but understanding her reason. But in the back of his mind, a voice was screaming a warning to him... riders on a dark night... in armor... bearing colors... it just didn't make sense.

It was a custom that the chief of a clan greet allies personally; everyone knew that. With all of the trouble Torridon had been experiencing, the word "ambush" flashed in Andrew's mind. If a man could control Josephine, then he could control Torridon. But Andrew knew no amount of pleading would change her mind. He had no choice.

"Very well," he said begrudgingly. "I will ride with you."

"Bring thirty or so men with you. Will you leave Thane here to assist Sully?"

"I will."

He didn't seem happy about any of this, but Josephine didn't care. She turned for the tent flap and as she pushed it back, she stopped and turned around to look at him one more time. He wasn't looking at her as he adjusted the tunic over his mail. Josephine admired how the light from the brazier made his hair dance with color. God, he was a glorious man.

"Andrew?" she said softly.

He stopped and looked up at her. "Aye?"

"I will ask you only this once and I would appreciate an honest answer," she said. "Did you bed my servants?"

He straightened, gazing into her angelic face. It suddenly dawned on him that she was jealous, and she didn't even know it. There was insecurity there, something that made her seem vulnerable and womanly. It was good to see, and his heart softened.

"Nay," he said softly. "I have not even had the time. But if I had the time, I think I might've spent it with you."

She smiled modestly and lowered her gaze, pushing through the tent flap.

He looked down at the empty doorway for a few moments before a smile appeared on his lips.

It had been the right answer. And it had been the truth.

PART TWO:

NEMO ME IMPUNE LACESSIT

CHAPTER TWELVE

S ULLY BALKED AT the idea of Josephine riding out in the dead of night to meet incoming riders. No amount of pleading seemed to deter her as she pulled on her heavy leather boots over her woolen hose and heavy black woolen tunic with the de Carron insignia sewn onto it. He might as well have been speaking in tongues for all of the response he got out of her, for she acted as if she didn't hear him. He followed her across the room and finally fell silent as she pulled her hair to the nape of her neck and secured it into a tight bun.

With Sully pacing nervously beside her, Josephine took her helm from its stand and plopped it on her head. Her helm was different from the knights. It was a basic style, cutting down over the ears and running higher along the base of the skull to allow for her hair. Chainmail hung from the ears and around the neck and extended to her shoulders. There was a hook in front where she could secure the mail to completely protect her neck, but she rarely did. Extending from the top of the domed helm was a four-inch spike, designed to ram victims if all else failed.

Josephine rushed from her chamber, securing her sword and dirk as she went, and tied on her heavy black woolen cloak. Sully followed, hoping against all hope that she would change her mind. But given the fact that she wouldn't even look at him, he didn't think that was much of a possibility now.

"Fortify the wall after I leave," she instructed Sully as they exited the keep and headed into the bailey. "Andrew is riding with me, so you will command his men until we return."

"What of his second, Thane?" Sully asked. "What is his role?"

"He is at your disposal," she said. "I'm taking Etienne, Albert, Burl, Severn, Henly, and John with me, plus forty men-at-arms. Andrew is bringing thirty of his men since he has more to spare. It will be a big escort party, Sully. You have nothing to fear."

Sully doubted that seriously. A soldier brought up her beloved war horse and Josephine's attention turned to the beast. She paused a moment, stroking the hugely-muscled neck and tickling the silky nose. Calibas snorted in recognition of her scent and voice, shaking his gigantic head that was at least as long as Josephine's entire torso.

With a slap to his chest, she pulled herself nimbly onto the broad back. The darkness of the night dimmed the silver coat of the horse, but it could not blot out the glorious color entirely. He wasn't white, nor was he gray, but the luxurious silver that came in between. His thick mane had streaks of black in it, as did the tail.

Calibas was twelve years old, and had been Hugh's horse for all but two of those years. Josephine had taken the horse after her father died, working with the animal that everyone considered meaner than Satan himself. After much hard work and coaxing, the horse finally seemed to take to her, much to the surprise of the other knights. Being an excellent horsewoman, Josephine controlled the huge beast with soft-spoken commands and leg pressure, as well as any man twice her size. In battle, the two fought as one.

Josephine gathered Calibas' reins and, immediately, the horse began a nervous dance, excited to be on the move. Keeping a tight rein, she looked about her for Andrew and his men, but had yet to see them.

"Where is Andrew?" she asked to no one in particular.

"Outside the gates, my lady," one of the soldiers told her. "He awaits you."

It was the answer she'd been looking for. "I shall return shortly," she called to Sully from atop the prancing beast. "Bolt the gates when I leave!"

Sully nodded as she and over forty men pounded across the inner bailey and headed for the gatehouse. He frowned to himself as she disappeared from view, deeply unhappy that she was possibly putting herself in danger.

But arguing with her would do no good. It never had. In a huff, he turned around to go about his duty but almost plowed into Justine instead. She stood behind him in her nightshift. It was a thin woolen gown. Her straight brown hair hung loose to her waist. Her blue eyes looked curiously at Sully.

"I heard the commotion," she said. "Where is my sister going?"

"Incoming riders," he said in a hard voice. "She is riding to meet them."

Justine's eyebrows drew together. "Who is it?"

Sully shrugged. "They are flying green and yellow," he said. "Most likely the Kennedys."

"Oh." She looked beyond him, out to the outer bailey. "And she is going alone?"

Sully pursed his lips irritably. "She is not," he said. "D'Vant is going with her."

Justine simply stood there and nodded her head, still looking towards the outer bailey, but that's not where Sully was looking at all.

He noticed that Justine was starting to shiver and her hard nipples were rising through the fabric. The slight breeze caught the gown, gently caressing it against her body and lifting tendrils of her hair. He'd never really looked at her like that before – like a man looks at a woman – but given their intertwined destinies, he supposed he had a right to look at her like that now. As a woman.

As a wife.

And he had to admit that her hard nipples were rather tantalizing. But before he burst forth with a demand that she retreat back into the castle, he found himself evaluating the rest of her. With her hair loose, and her cheeks slightly colored from the chill, she was rather pretty. Quite pretty, actually. At closer scrutiny, he noted that her eyes were a darker shade of blue; like a warm summer sky. In this light, she looked a bit like her sister. Nearly every bit as lovely.

But the fact remained that she needed to go inside before any of these soldiers also enjoyed the fact that her nipples were poking through her shift. He cleared his throat.

"Inside, my lady," he ordered quietly. "It is too cold out here for you."

But Justine put up her hand. "Wait," she said, some concern in her tone. "Shouldn't my sister be…"

Sully cut her off by grasping her by the shoulders and spinning her in the direction of the door. "Do not argue, Lady Justine." He gave her a shove, perhaps a little harder than he should have.

But Justine wouldn't be pushed around. "I am not arguing," she said. "I am simply concerned for Josephine. Stop pushing!"

He put a hand to the small of her back firmly. "One more word, my lady, and you go over my shoulder."

She jumped away from him and stomped her foot. "Stop shoving me, Sully," she said angrily. "You are an ill-mannered clod and if you ever lay a hand on me again, I'll…"

She didn't quite finish her threat and he crossed his big arms expectantly "You'll *what*?"

Justine scowled at him, forgetting her concern for her sister and focusing on Sully's taunting face. A handsome taunting face. Truth be told, she couldn't think of a threat serious enough. Her scowl turned into a smug expression.

"I'll turn my sister loose on you and then you'll be sorry!" she finished.

Sully feigned fear. "Say it is not so!"

Justine didn't appreciate his humor. It was then he realized she had been serious. Uttering a small cry, she flew at him in a white blur. He dodged her easily, squatting down in the process so that she fell conveniently across his left shoulder like a sack of flour with the force of her momentum.

With his bundle screeching in outrage, Sully carried her into the keep and up to her chamber, waiting until she was in the room before depositing her onto her bed. But Justine wasn't finished with him; she glared at him furiously, pushing her hair out of her eyes.

"Get out before I take a sword to you," she growled.

Instead of arguing, he bowed gallantly and turned for the door. He liked her much better when she wasn't pretending to be a witch. She had spirit like her sister and she wasn't willing to surrender easily. Perhaps this marriage wouldn't be so much hell after all. It might actually be rather fun. With his thoughts lingering on the coming marriage, he turned for the chamber door but paused before leaving.

"May I ask a question, my lady?" he requested.

She looked at him, her angry expression having turned into a pout. "What is it?"

Sully tried not to grin at her expression. "What are you planning to wear for our wedding tomorrow?"

The question took Justine by surprise and the petulant expression faded. "I… I do not know," she said. "I haven't given it much thought."

It was a lie. Ever since she'd agreed to the marriage, her wedding gown was all she had thought about. She didn't know why she lied; maybe it was because she didn't want Sully to think she was looking forward to the union. But when he simply nodded and opened the door, preparing to leave, she stopped him.

"What would you have me wear?" she asked, somewhat eagerly.

Sully looked at her a long moment, then Justine swore she caught a glimpse of color in his cheeks.

"Don't brides usually wear pink as a symbol of purity?" he asked.

"Yes," Justine said hesitantly. "But I do not own anything pink. Will blue do?

"Blue?" he repeated thoughtfully.

She nodded as she took a step towards him. "It is the most delicate shade of light blue," she said. "Of course, if you hate blue, I can always wear black."

"Nay!" Sully put up his hand as if to stave off the mere thought. When he saw her rather startled expression, he forced a smile. "Blue would be most acceptable, Justine. I am sure you will look beautiful in it."

I am sure you will look beautiful. Justine's heart began to race. Was it possible he actually thought she might be beautiful? Her Sully, the man she had dreamed of for so long?

"Then I shall wear it if it pleases you," she said, fighting off a rather giddy smile.

Sully simply nodded, smiling in return before quitting the chamber. If he hadn't known better, he might have thought Justine was just the least bit pleased by all of this.

ANDREW WAS WAITING outside the gates for Josephine's arrival, clad in his gray and black leather and sitting astride his magnificent red destrier. The horse snorted and foamed as the party approached, but he controlled it as if he were holding nothing more than a goat on a leash. It was a true testament to Andrew's skill and strength, the manner in which he controlled a nearly uncontrollable animal.

Josephine approached quickly, her big silver horse tossing its tail about, a flash of light in the darkness. Her men had torches, as did his men, giving the entire party a rather eerie appearance. To the incoming riders, it would be intimidating, indeed.

"We ride!" Josephine cried over the noise of the riding party.

Andrew and Thane flanked her as they rode off into the night. The countryside around them was deathly still with the half-moon in the glittering sky above. This part of the country had softly rolling hills interspersed with heavenly valleys that were covered with wild heather and hemlock in a dazzling display. It was also a part of Scotland heavily controlled by rival clans including the Stewart, Kennedy, and Douglas clans.

Given that de Carron wasn't from one of the dominant clans, it made them, and the entire Ayr earldom, rather an island unto itself. But Hugh had known the value of the clans and he'd made sure to have good relationships with them, even the Dalmellington until the deaths of James and Marie. Still, the de Carron Clan was considered by most of their neighbors to be friendly and generous.

Josephine wanted to keep it that way.

The riding party was silent as they traversed the hard-packed, uneven road. Although Josephine's mind was focused on the possible confrontation ahead, she found her attention drifting to Andrew beside her. She didn't dare look at him.

Josephine knew this road like the back of her hand, as did Calibas. She did little else but sit astride him as he cantered along, charging off into the night. Her mind wandered a bit, going back to the events of the day, and she saw Andrew again when he strode into the gypsy camp. He was so tall, so beautifully muscular, that it had been all she could see. He consumed her entire attention. Andrew, of course, had been his usual disarming self, but somehow through all of the charm, no one doubted his threat.

It had been enough to save her from the gypsies, at any rate.

Josephine's stomach tightened to think of the first kiss they had shared. And the second. But she could not comprehend or even know what lay in store for her on her wedding night. She wondered what it would be like, progressing beyond that kiss and giving herself over to the man she had married. Still, it seemed like a wild, impossible dream.

One that would soon be a reality.

"Riders!" came a cry.

Josephine was jolted from her train of thought. In the faded moonlight, she could, indeed, see a riding party heading towards them, about a quarter-mile down the road. They were just coming through a bank of black trees and they were, indeed, flying banners, but she could not make them out.

"Halt!" she called.

The party pulled to a stop, with the horses snorting and dancing. Josephine was focused on the mystery riders.

"Andrew," she said. "Hold here. I shall ride alone to meet them."

Andrew gave her a long look before replying. "As you wish," he said, unhappy. "But humor an old soldier. Should hostilities seem imminent, give a signal by latching the protective neck guard of your helm. We shall come."

"You can see me that far ahead?"

"Take a torch and I can."

Josephine's jaw muscles flexed, but she agreed. Digging her spurs into Calibas, she galloped down a slight hill and onto the level road, racing towards the incoming riders. As she drew closer, she could see the banners rippling.

Blast! She still couldn't make out the insignia. But it didn't take long before the riding party halted at the sight of her and sent forth a rider to meet her.

The rider carried the standard and as he came upon her, she could see it was the king's banner. Her heart sank. Josephine reined Calibas to a stop, waiting for the rider to reach her. When he did, it was a young knight, not unhandsome, but very determined looking.

"Let us pass in the name of the king," he demanded. "We ride to Torridon."

She remained cool. "I am Lady Josephine de Carron, heiress to the Ayr earldom," she said evenly. "You are approaching my home. Who are you?"

Even in the dim moonlight, she could see the young man's face wash with an incredulous look. He stared at her a moment as if he could hardly believe what he was seeing. After a few awkward seconds, he nodded his head sharply.

"Nicholas de Londres, nephew to King Alexander," he said proudly. "'Tis an honor, Lady Josephine."

Shock filled Josephine at the announcement, but she covered well. "The king has arrived?"

"Aye, my lady."

"You are early. We were not expecting the king until the day after tomorrow."

Josephine thought he smiled, but it was hard to see in the dark. "We made excellent time," he said. "The king was anxious to reach yer fortress."

"How far behind you is the king?"

Nicholas looked over his shoulder. "About a half-hour at a hard gallop."

That was much closer than she had imagined and her shock was starting to turn to panic. *Not much time to prepare,* Josephine thought with disgust. *Damn!* But she couldn't convey what she was feeling, not in the least. If she did, it might make the messenger suspicious and that suspicion would get back to the king.

She had to make the man feel welcome.

"Will some of your men accompany me back to Torridon and help us prepare for the monarch's arrival?" she asked. "We should like to show the king all due respect."

Nicholas nodded. "It would be my pleasure, Lady Ayr," he said. "Let me collect some men and we shall join ye shortly."

He spurred his horse back to his party. Josephine did the same.

Thundering back to her waiting men, Josephine was confronted with Andrew's curious face.

"Well?" he demanded. "Who is it?"

Josephine exhaled sharply as she slapped her helm against her thigh. "It is the advance party for the king," she said. "The king himself is less than an hour's ride away."

Word rippled through the men. They had not known the king was coming, as it was something Josephine had only shared with those closest to her. She could hear the ripples of surprise but she couldn't tear her eyes from Andrew's. Silent words passed between them.

The king is here!

Andrew was feeling the same shock that she was. All of their plans; everything, would never be. The king was less than an hour from Torridon and there was hardly time to accomplish what needed to be done.

Andrew could see the fear and defeat in her eyes before she tore her gaze away. Quietly, he reined his great animal next to hers. But she wouldn't look at him; she kept her eyes averted.

"I must stay and escort the party back to Torridon," she said when she realized he was next to her. "You take half of the men and return now. Tell Justine the king approaches and to prepare."

His jaw muscles flexed as he watched her lowered head. He knew what her concerns were now that the king was nearly at her door. Truth be told, he had the same concerns as well. He couldn't stand seeing the defeat in her eyes.

"How long will it take the priest to arrive at Torridon?" he asked quietly.

"Not soon enough."

"How *long*?"

She looked up at him, hearing determination in his tone. She could see that he didn't have the same resigned attitude that she did.

"Mayhap an hour," she said.

Andrew's mind was working quickly, desperate to salvage the situation. An hour away? Much could happen in an hour.

"Justine and Sully can still be married," he said. "We can do it right under the king's nose. He will never know how swiftly we moved heaven and earth to accomplish it."

Josephine couldn't help but feel some hope. He was taking charge and she needed that at the moment. "That would create one less worry. With Justine married, I would only have to worry about myself." Suddenly, her face lit up. "And I could give Justine Torridon as a dowry. It is within my rights as mistress!"

Andrew could see that the spark of hope was back in her eyes. It fed his own sense of determination, that the king's visit should not be the end of their plans.

"Thane!" Andrew barked, turning to his second as the man rode up. "Take a few men with you and ride for Torridon. Inform Lady Justine the king approaches and tell her to prepare for her wedding within the hour. Inform Sir Sully as well."

As Thane nodded sharply and went about his task, Andrew turned to one of the Torridon knights that had ridden with the group. Andrew was a man who never forgot a face, or a name, even of someone he'd only met once, so he addressed the knight by his name.

"Albert," he said evenly. "Ride to St. John's Church in Ayr and find the priest. Bring him to Torridon before the end of the hour and you shall receive one hundred marks."

Young Albert's eyes bulged and he looked to his mistress as if in disbelief of the offer. But Josephine merely nodded and the young knight dug his heels into his horse, shooting back down the road the way they had come. There was no mistaking the knight's sense of urgency.

Now that things were in motion, Andrew turned back to Josephine. She was looking at him with hope again and it fortified his heart. He'd spent his entire life making decisions on his own, decisions that affected only him. But now, he was making a decision that would affect her as well.

She trusted him.

"Josephine," he said quietly. "Do you still wish to marry me?"

The hope in her eyes flickered, then dimmed. "It is too late for us," she said softly. "There is no time."

"You have not answered my question," he said. "Do you still wish to marry me?"

A feeling of sadness washed over Josephine. Of course, she still wanted to marry him. She had become accustomed to the thought of becoming The Red Fury's wife. Perhaps she had even been excited about it, anticipating a future she never thought to have.

Even now, he was still offering to marry her. The king was upon them and, still, he was willing. She thought that, perhaps, he was simply taking pity on her and offering her an easy solution to a complex problem. He was being chivalrous. But the situation was far more complex than they both realized.

He had offered her an easy out – now, she would offer him one.

"Nay, Andrew," she replied quietly. "I no longer wish to marry you. Your offer was most kind, but it is no longer necessary. Please return to Torridon, and I will pay you your money this night. You are free to leave whenever you wish."

Pulling back sharply on the reins, she turned Calibas around and headed back towards the group of men, now gathered behind them, waiting for the king's advance party to arrive. Andrew watched her go, but he wasn't going to let her get away so easily. Spurring his horse after her, he managed to catch Calibas and roughly grind the horse to a halt.

"Give me those!" Josephine jerked the reins from his grasp. "Why did you do that?"

Andrew pulled his horse close until he was right next to her; the horses were bumping into each other.

"You did not allow me to finish our conversation," he said quietly. "You do not wish to marry me? Then that is your misfortune. You agreed to it. I will tell you this, now. I told you once that I wanted you. Now I will tell you again. My body cries for you, Josephine de Carron. My heart lightens at the mention of your name. Say that you will marry me, and I will fight God Himself for that right. Now, do you still wish to marry me?"

Josephine was stunned. She searched his face for any hint of doubt, but was met only by rigid determination. God's Bones, was he serious? Was it really true? His words lifted her spirit more than she ever imagined words could. Was it possible that the man was as attracted to her as she was to him? His words would seem to prove that theory.

"You may only have to fight the king," she said after a moment. "As I do not believe God would quibble with you when He, too, believes I should be married."

The corner of his mouth twitched. "Then perhaps, it is by divine intervention that I am here."

Josephine continued to stare at him in the darkness, feeling her heart race until it was nearly close to bursting. As it stood, she would rather marry him than any other man on earth. They seemed to be two pieces of a puzzle that fit perfectly with one another to form a thing of beauty – he gave her strength and wisdom, and she brought out feelings in him he never knew were possible. Each, individually, were formidable, but together they were invincible.

The Red Fury had found his mate.

"I would marry you, then," she whispered finally.

He reached down and removed a heavy leather glove from her hand. Raising the soft white fingers to his lips, he warmly kissed them, lingering for a moment while his eyes locked with hers in the moonlight. After what seemed like an eternity, he released her hand.

"A wise decision, Joey," he said, watching her grin. "Have faith that all will be as it should. We shall be married and the king will simply have to accept it. Do you believe me?"

"I do."

"Then return to Torridon and ensure that your sister marries Sully as soon as the priest arrives," he said. "As your betrothed, I shall escort the king to Torridon. It would be my privilege."

Josephine smiled at the man, a smile brighter than the sun. "As you say," she said. "I shall prepare Torridon for the king, personally."

He flashed a grin at her. "Obedience becomes you."

"Do not get used to it."

She heard him laughing even as she turned her horse around and raced back to the group of men, some of which headed back with her to Torridon.

But she, too, couldn't wipe the smile from her face.

There was much to smile over.

CHAPTER THIRTEEN

EXACTLY FORTY MINUTES after discovering the king's visit was imminent, Justine stood in her room before her full-length mirror in a gown of pale blue silk. She stood silent and immobile as Josephine and two maids fussed over her, flittering around like frightened chickens.

Josephine was not even out of her leather and mail as she strung a belt of gold around her sister's hips, with the center of each square implanted with a large sapphire, ruby, or emerald. Justine's brown hair was brushed until it gleamed, then a gold diadem inlaid with small sapphires were rested gently on her head.

Josephine stood back a moment, inspecting her handiwork. Justine looked beautiful. She turned one of the maids.

"Go down and see if the priest has arrived," she said quickly, and the girl bolted for the door. "And make sure Sir Sully is in the hall!"

When the girl was gone, Josephine turned to her sister and tried to smile reassuringly.

"Now," she said quietly. "Before you enter into this marriage, there is something I must tell you. I want you and Sully to be happy. I know you love him and, someday, I am sure that he will come to love you."

Justine's eyes threatened to pop from their sockets. "Wherever did you get such a… a ridiculous idea that I love Sully?"

Josephine smiled knowingly. "You forget who you speak with, my dear little sister," she said. "I know how you feel about him. I have for some time. Why do you think I suggested you marry him? In the years to come, he will be much happier with someone who loves him, who worships him. It would be better for you both."

Justine opened her mouth to protest yet again, but she thought better of it when she saw the look on her sister's face. There was no use in denying it. And she thought she'd been so cool in her admiration for the man. She was coming to feel like a fool.

"Have I been that obvious?" she said, embarrassed.

Josephine chuckled softly. "Not at all," she said. "I began to realize your feelings for him when you took on a glassy stare every time he came near you. You pretended that you did not care, but your expression said otherwise. I do not blame you, you know. Sully is a fine example of a man."

But he is only in love with you, Justine wanted to say. But she didn't. For once, she kept her mouth shut because there was no point in starting an argument about it. Perhaps, Josephine already knew how Sully felt about her; perhaps not. In any case, Justine saw no reason to point it out.

"He does not wish to marry me," she said after a moment.

Josephine took her sister's arm, giving her a squeeze. "I think, at this point, no one wants to marry anyone," she said. "This plan has come about so quickly that no one has had time to become accustomed to it. But do not fret; give it time. I am sure Sully will come to appreciate you."

Justine wasn't so sure. She'd been worrying about that very thing but, now, it was too late to give her concerns any validation. She had to marry the man regardless.

"Mayhap," she said quietly.

Josephine could see her sister's apprehension. She understood her fears, for she was facing some of those fears herself. But she put forth a brave face.

"Do not be afraid," she said. "I will stand with you."

Justine shook her head. "I am not afraid," she said. "But you were correct when you said this was all happening very quickly. I can hardly believe it."

Josephine smiled. "It will be wonderful for you. I am certain of it."

Justine wasn't so certain; she simply shrugged. "I suppose we shall find out."

"Aye, we shall," Josephine said, giving her sister's arm another squeeze. "Come along, Justine Afton Louisa de Carron, and let us attend your wedding."

Justine didn't resist as her sister pulled her towards the door of the chamber. Josephine turned to the maid still in the room, who was starting to clean up the mess they'd left in their wake.

"Cassia," Josephine said. "Please escort my sister to the great hall. I must quickly change clothes and will join you as soon as I can."

The woman dropped what was in her hands and preceded Justine and Josephine through the chamber door. The sisters started to part as they reached the top of the stairs, but Justine came to a halt.

"What of Andrew, Josephine?" she asked. "Will you still marry him, too?"

Josephine paused at her door. "Aye," she said. "I do not know when, but I will."

Justine shook her head in disbelief; disbelief at the whole situation. Her sister's defiance of the king, her own marriage to Sully, and she had great fear and uncertainty where the future was concerned.

"Do you... *like* him?" Justine asked with genuine concern.

"I do."

"Do you... *could* you... love him someday?"

Josephine looked at her sister as she thought on that question. *Love?* It had crossed her mind, but she had always dismissed love as a silly child's fantasy. The very fact that her parents had been madly in love was a fluke. And then her mother died, and her father had never been the same. Having never experienced love for herself, Josephine drew forth from the only experience she had ever known, and deduced love was a very self-destructive emotion.

Love?

She wasn't sure she wanted to risk it.

"Nay," she whispered finally. "I admire him and respect him, and I am sure he will make a fine husband, but I will never love him."

With that, she went into her chambers and closed the door softly. That act left Justine standing there at the top of the stairs, thinking that her sister was in for a sad life if she couldn't bring herself to feel more than admiration for her husband because Justine knew for a fact that she would always love hers.

In a sense, that gave her more hope and joy than her sister would ever know.

As Justine and the little maid headed down to the great hall, Josephine went about removing the leather and mail she wore. She also forced herself to put aside her sister's question. *Could you love him?* There was too much to do and she didn't want to be distracted by the seed that was now planted in her brain. Ola emerged from her alcove as Josephine went to her wardrobe and began roughly pulling through the garments on pegs.

"I need to wash, quickly," she said to Ola, who went scurrying. "And put plenty of rose oil in the water!"

Within minutes, she was stripped to the skin and Ola was quickly washing her with cold water and rose oil. After a hasty drying, Josephine slipped into the most lavish dress she had, a rich purple silk with a plunging neckline and a full skirt. Gold and silver thread decorated the long sleeves and hem, and there were semi-precious stones sewn into the neck.

It was a lovely, striking dress that required no adornment. Quickly, Ola brushed her mistress' hair furiously and braided it because that was all that time would allow. With a pinch to her cheeks for some color, Josephine fled the chamber.

She took the stairs quickly and walked forward into the great hall, pulling her sleeves straight as she walked and straightening her skirts.

She felt as if she were only half-put together, but it would have to do. Head down, she was fussing with a portion of the bodice that didn't seem to want to smooth out. Entering the hall, she lifted her head into a room that was full of light.

It was nearly midnight but the hall was ablaze with dozens of torches. Fresh rushes on the floor scented the room; it smelled like a forest. The knights that had remained behind when she rode out earlier that evening stood on either side of the room in their best armor. As she walked further into the room, she saw that they had even combed their hair. Donald was there, too, with his dark-rimmed eyes and swollen nose. She forced a smile at him as she entered the room but she made no attempt to speak with him, not yet. She had business with the soon-to-be married couple.

Justine and Sully stood at the end of the hall in front of the roaring hearth. Justine actually appeared properly demure while Sully simply looked pale. He looked as if, given a chance, he might actually bolt, and she stifled the urge grin at the man.

"Hasn't the priest from St. John's arrived yet?" she asked as she approached them.

"Nay, my lady," Sully said softly. "Not yet."

He sounded so very serious. Josephine did a double-take on him. He, too, was dressed in his best armor, his squire having polished it until it was mirror-perfect. His face and hair had been washed. He looked like a little boy whose mother had forced him to take a bath in honor of grandmother's visit. Clean and shiny, he looked very handsome and, at this point, she couldn't help but smile at the man.

"Do not look so frightened," she said. "You are marrying my sister, not the devil in disguise."

He forced a smile. "I am not frightened of her," he insisted. "But I think the thought of marriage frightens all men. It reminds them of the responsibilities of this world."

Josephine understood. Reaching out, she took Sully by the hand then turned to her sister, extending a hand to the woman as well.

Justine joined their group, taking her sister's hand and holding it tightly. Josephine beamed at her.

"There is something I must tell you both," she said. "I wanted to tell you together."

Justine looked at her curiously. "What is it?"

Josephine took a deep breath. "As you know, plans have changed quickly because of the king's imminent approach," she said. "That is why you two are marrying so quickly, so that Justine will be safe. But even so, that leaves the problem of me, still unmarried and still quite eligible to any of the king's whims. Therefore, I have come up with a way to make my situation far less attractive to Alexander. Torridon, above all, must be safe."

Now it was Sully's turn to look at her curiously. "What did you have in mind?"

Josephine turned to him, looking into the face of the man she knew so well. In truth, she was quite at peace for what she was about to say. "As the heiress of Torridon, the fortress is mine to do with as I please," she said. "Therefore, I am giving it to my sister as a wedding gift. The fortress shall be yours and out of Colin Dalmellington's reach forever."

Justine gasped in surprise as Sully's eyes widened. Of all the things Josephine could speak of, that had certainly not been in his thoughts.

"*What?*" he breathed. "What are you saying?"

Josephine patted his arm. "*Think*, Sully," she said. "The king wants me because of Torridon. It belongs to me but I shall give it to you. It will be my sister's dowry, which is completely acceptable. Mayhap, now the king will reconsider his plans for me since I will no longer be a valuable commodity."

Sully still gaped at her in disbelief. Justine looked at him, equally startled, before returning her focus to her sister.

"You never said a word about this," she said, shocked and pained. "You've never said this was your plan all along!"

Josephine shook her head. "It wasn't," she said. "But when the king came so suddenly tonight, and I knew that a marriage between you and

Sully would be faster, it occurred to me that if I gave you Torridon as a dowry, then that would make me far less attractive to whatever the king wishes to do with me. That way, my fortress is safe. It is in good hands."

Justine looked at her for a moment longer as her words sank in. Then, it began to occur to her just how grand and important her sister's gift was. A smile flickered on her lips, one of joy and elation, as she looked to Sully.

"Are you not happy?" she asked him. "It is a great gift that she is giving us."

Sully couldn't even answer the question. Justine only saw the surface, the gift of a great fortress. She did not see the sacrifice her sister was making. Justine saw through the eyes of a naïve child; she thought Sully *wanted* Torridon. But he didn't.

It was Josephine's.

God, he didn't want it at all.

"Your sister is most generous," he said hoarsely. "I… I do not know what to say."

"Say you will accept it," Josephine said quietly. "*Please.*"

Looking at Josephine, Sully could see the pain in her eyes. What could he say now that she hadn't already thought of or imagined? She knew what she was giving up – her legacy. But she was doing it to keep it from someone who wanted it very badly, someone who could upend her life all in one stroke. She had to make sure it was safe and this was the only thing she could think to do.

Sully didn't take her decision lightly. He knew how difficult it must have been for her but, in truth, he saw her reason. Reaching out, he took her hand and pressed it to his lips, all the while focused on her eyes. She was watching him with fear, hope, and sadness.

"I shall take the best care of your castle while it is entrusted to me," he said softly. "This, I swear."

Josephine smiled weakly. It was such a sad moment for her but such a necessary one. Sully continued to hold her hand, looking deeply into her sweet face. The pain and anguish of what certainly was the most jolting decision of her young life tore at him like a great claw, threatening to gut him. His insides felt as if they were being twisted and wrenched from him.

But whatever Josephine must have been feeling was surely worse, even though she tried to appear brave. "My steward will draw up the contract," she said. "He will be finished by the time the ceremony is complete, if that damned priest ever gets here."

Her sharp words were indicative of the fact that she was not as calm as she appeared. God knew, she had every right to be upset. Sully simply nodded as he released her hand.

After that, the conversation between the three of them fell somewhat silent. The knights in the room were beginning to stir, looking at each other in question. They had all been summoned here so hurriedly that they scarce had time to catch their breaths and now they found themselves waiting.

The torches above their heads on the walls flickered brightly, illuminating the enormous room adequately, but phantom shadows still danced near the ceiling. Ghosts, perhaps of what had been and now what would be. They were here to witness the change. But the fresh smell of the rushes was comforting, somehow soothing frayed nerves.

Josephine moved away from the hearth, leaving Sully and Justine alone, and conversed quickly with servants as they dashed to and fro, not only preparing for a wedding but for the king's visit as well. She was trying to keep the burden off of her sister, who had enough to worry over with an unexpected wedding imminent. A feast being set in the great hall at this ungodly hour, for the king's arrival, would serve as Justine and Sully's wedding feast as well.

When the servants had gone about their duties and Josephine was finally alone, Donald made his way over to her. He'd stayed to the shadows mostly, watching the happenings but not really clear on what, exactly, was going on. All he knew was that Josephine had been very busy with the arrival of the mercenaries and now the impending arrival of the king. It was all quite confusing to him but he hadn't pressed

Josephine for an explanation, thinking that she would tell him when she had the time.

Now was that time.

"What is happening?" he hissed as he came to stand next to her. "What on earth is going on around here?"

Josephine turned to him, wincing when she saw how badly his face was bruising. "Poor Donald," she said. "Your father is going to think we've beaten you."

Donald had to admit that he looked poorly. But he waved off her sympathy. "Why are we here, Joey?" he asked quietly. "After what ye told us earlier today, about the king's visit, it looks to me as if there is some manner of action being carried out. What is it?"

Josephine sighed faintly, knowing she couldn't keep the truth from him. He would see what was going on soon enough when the priest arrived.

"I am saving Torridon," she said simply. "Sully and Justine are about to be married, if the priest ever arrives. For Justine's dowry, I am giving her Torridon."

Donald's bruised eyes widened. "*Giving* her Torridon?"

Josephine nodded quickly. "Please understand," she begged softly, putting her hand on his arm. "I have little choice. You know what I suspect by the king's visit; you know I believe he wants to betroth me to Colin Dalmellington, meaning that Colin will ultimately be in control of my fortress. And you know I cannot allow that to happen."

Donald's expression went from one of shock to one of apprehension. "But… to give it to Justine…"

"Sully will command it," she assured him. "Justine is simply the means to an end. If she has it, it cannot go to Colin. Do you understand this?"

Slowly, Donald nodded, but it was clear he was uncertain about the entire situation. "Aye," he said. "I suppose it makes sense, but what about ye? Even if yer sister is married and the fortress is hers, ye're still very valuable. The king can still marry ye away."

Josephine knew that and she nodded, with resignation. "I know," she said. "But if I do not come with a fortress, then mayhap he will think twice before doing such a thing. It is my hope that he simply goes away and leaves me alone. Besides… I will not be unwed for long."

Donald looked at her suspiciously. "What do ye mean?"

Josephine wasn't sure how happy Donald would be to hear that she would wed Andrew, the mercenary leader. She knew that Donald had always been rather fond of her. Perhaps he'd even hoped for marriage one day. She was about to quash that hope.

"Andrew d'Vant has proposed marriage and I have agreed," she said. "We will be wed as soon as possible."

She could see the shock, even disappointment, in Donald's eyes. He blinked at her as if unsure how to react. "I see," he said after a moment. "When did this come about?"

"Today."

He grunted and looked away. "If I'd known ye were looking for a husband, I could have offered," he said, sounding hurt. "But ye've never given any indication that ye were even interested in such a thing. Why did ye not come to me?"

Josephine put a hand on his arm. "Because it was not my idea," she said. "In discussing my suspicions with Andrew about the king's visit, he was the one who suggested marriage. I am sorry, Donald, I truly am. It just happened to be him."

Donald shrugged. It didn't make it any easier for him to stomach, but he understood somewhat. The more he thought about it, however, the more depressed he became.

He and Josephine continued to stand in silence as time dragged on. Josephine was sure that hours were passing when it was really only minutes. Unable to stand it any longer, she was ready to perform the ceremony herself when Albert suddenly entered the hall, half-dragging and half-escorting a haggard-looking priest.

Josephine rushed forward. "Father, thank you so much for coming," she said with great relief. "You have a ceremony to perform."

The priest adjusted his cowl and straightened his wrinkled woolen robe. "So I understand," he said irritably. "I must say that I am outraged, my lady, at being dragged here at this time of night. It is completely improper treatment for a man of God."

Josephine nodded patiently while the priest vented his rage. "Of course, you are right," she said. "Will fifty marks be enough?"

He didn't miss a beat, swiftly turning into an eager man. "Where is the happy couple?"

Josephine fought off a smile at his swift change in attitude. She took his arm.

"This way, please."

Sully and Justine looked to be frozen as they were introduced to the priest, who wanted to seem to chat, but Josephine hurried him along.

"Father, our time is limited," she said. "May we proceed?"

The priest nodded. If he thought a rushed wedding was odd, he didn't say anything. Fifty marks assured his cooperation. "Let us not waste time," he said as he waved his arms and motioned for everyone to take their place. "My lord... my lady... you will face me."

Justine and Sully did, and he began to intone the wedding mass. Josephine stood directly behind Justine, a few feet away. As the priest began reading from his weather-worn Bible, she began to wish her father and James had lived to see this. And, of course, her mother. She and Justine were the only de Carrons left, and perhaps witnessing the most important event in Justine's life.

As she watched the priest speak, she was suddenly very sorry that she forced the whole thing on her sister and on Sully. In the chain of hierarchy, they really had no choice and they knew it. Josephine got what she wanted, and what she wanted was to save Torridon and her family in the process. She hoped they truly understood that, deep down.

Now, there was no turning back, come what may.

After the liturgy, the priest pronounced them man and wife by tying a piece of ribbon, provided by Ola, around their wrists. Sully's gaze seemed to be riveted to Justine, who looked back at him apprehensively. Josephine watched the two of them as well, holding her breath for the moment Sully would kiss her sister. For a few painful seconds, he just seemed to stare at her. Then, he reached out and grasped her shoulders and deposited a quick kiss on her forehead.

With that, they were married.

Josephine was the first to move forward and congratulate the couple. She felt as if she were moving in a dream, hardly believing her sister and Sully were actually married.

"Sully, retire to your chambers and consummate the union," she whispered to the man. "Make haste!"

Sully looked blankly at her for a moment before agreeing, putting his arm around his new wife's waist and pulling her with him. Josephine walked with them as far as the staircase. There was a great sense of urgency now to complete the circle so that the union could never be disputed. Justine would be safe and Torridon would be safe.

That was all that mattered.

The king was in for quite a surprise when he arrived.

CHAPTER FOURTEEN

KING ALEXANDER OF Scotland arrived with little fanfare, surprising for a monarch who had been on the throne for many years. His arrival had been understated for the most part, and he arrived with a small contingent of courtiers and warriors, escorted into Torridon by a man who had identified himself as Andrew d'Vant. When that name meant nothing to the king, Andrew stated the nickname he was known by – The Red Fury – and suddenly, the king was quite interested in him.

He knew that name.

As she stood on the steps of Torridon dressed in her fine gown, Josephine fervently hoped that Justine was being cooperative in relinquishing her virginity to her new husband. There was no room for botched plans this night, as everything had to work on schedule or all would be lost. She could only pray the king didn't realize that everything that had taken place, so quickly, was in an effort to thwart his plans.

As the king and his entourage entered the inner bailey of Torridon, Andrew rode majestically next to the king and Josephine found she couldn't take her eyes from him. He looked more magnificent than she had remembered, and her stomach fluttered in excitement at the mere sight. Odd how a man she'd fought with on the day of their introduction had now become much more to her, very swiftly. One would have thought it was a foolish happening had it not felt so right.

And it did feel right.

Beneath the black night and dozens of torches, the inner bailey was jammed with the king's guard, wagons, and more. Josephine was a little curious as to how she was going to house all of the people in the king's entourage, because Justine usually handled that. But Justine was understandably occupied, so the duty fell to her. She watched as the king dismounted his horse a bit wearily; a tall man, with a crowning glory of wavy red hair, his face was thin but not unattractive. He had a bit of an overbite. But he bore absolutely no resemblance to the distant cousin he was visiting.

As the king approached the keep, he looked about with interest, pointing to the walls, the keep itself, and muttering to the men surrounding him. As he came to the steps leading to the keep, Josephine was waiting. She curtsied deeply.

"My lord," she said politely. "Welcome to Torridon."

The king looked somewhat amused, handing his fine gauntlets to a nearby attendant. "And which de Carron are you?"

His speech was rather continental, not Scottish as one would expect. Having been educated in England in his youth, he didn't have the heavy burr. Josephine answered his question.

"I am Josephine, my lord."

That changed Alexander's entire demeanor. "Josephine," he repeated, devouring her with his eyes. "The heiress. You do my grandfather, and your great-grandfather, a great tribute. It has been a long time since I saw you last and I am pleased."

As Josephine nodded demurely, Alexander took his eyes from her long enough to look Torridon over, making note of the obvious repairs that were going on. He was used to staying in grander castles, but he knew why Torridon looked as it did. In fact, that was the reason for his visit.

"Lady Josephine," he said finally. "You will escort me inside this monstrous fortress."

"Of course, my lord," she said, turning to go back up the steps.

As Josephine led the way, Andrew watched the king and his men as they followed her delicious backside into the depths of the castle. He had to admit that he was feeling more than just a twinge of jealousy at the way the king gazed at Josephine. The attention was more than just "family". And the king did it knowing full well Andrew was betrothed to Josephine.

Andrew had introduced himself as such when he'd ridden out to meet the king, so there was no mistake. Andrew wanted to ensure that the king knew right away what Andrew's role was in all of this. Obviously, the king either didn't care or he had a false sense of security in the way he was looking at Josephine. Perhaps, he thought he was immune to the wrath of The Red Fury, but he wasn't. And he was going to feel it if he didn't keep his attentions in check. Andrew wasn't particularly reverent of Scottish kings, being English by birth.

Thane interrupted his unhappy thoughts. "My lord," he said, catching his attention. "The men are bedded. I have ordered the escort party to also bed for the night, and I shall be joining them. Will you be coming?"

Andrew's eyes were still on the entourage entering the door. "Nay," he said slowly. "I shall be joining my betrothed and her king in the dining hall."

Thane looked at the expression on Andrew's face as the man scrutinized the king. He'd known Andrew for several years and had never seen him appear so... suspicious. Or was it jealousy? He thought it was somewhat disturbing. Remarkable, but disturbing.

"You do not trust him?" he finally asked. "The king, I mean."

Andrew gave him a look that needed no explanation. That was exactly what he was feeling. Soon enough, he headed into the castle, following the king and his men.

Thane watched Andrew go, shaking his head as he turned for the gatehouse. *Poor lout,* he thought. *He has no idea he's already gone in love with her.* But that meant that there could very well be trouble.

Men in love were volatile creatures, indeed.

HALFWAY THROUGH THE meal, Justine and Sully appeared.

Seated across the table from the king, so he could get a good look at her, Josephine was the first one to see the couple enter the hall. Josephine leapt to her feet, uttering an apology. She left the table to go to her sister, who she assumed must be traumatized by having been bedded by a man for the first time. She was fully expecting hysterics. But Justine smiled prettily at Josephine, who looked at her with open astonishment. She had never seen Justine look prettier or... *happier*. She definitely looked happier. But Justine's smile was a ruse; as she reached her sister, she threw herself forward into Josephine's arms and began to weep.

Josephine clutched her sister, looking at Sully accusingly. "What have you done to her?" she demanded.

Sully looked at her, rather drolly. "Nothing except what a husband usually does to his wife."

Josephine eyed him dubiously as she continued to hold her sister. Then, she looked back to Justine. "Darling, the king is here," she said gently. "You must greet him."

"It hurt," Justine whispered into her sister's shoulder.

Josephine's eyes flew to Sully. "You *hurt* her?"

Sully looked surprised and outraged at the same time. "It was not intentional, I swear it."

Justine sobbed again. "He... he would not stop when I asked him to."

That clinched it for Josephine. She flew into a rage, running at Sully and pounding him with her small fists. She shrieked and cursed like a soldier while he mostly tried to defend himself, wondering why in the hell she was so angry at him when she was the one who had asked him to marry her sister. Didn't she know what men did to a wife on the night of their wedding?

Andrew caught sight of the altercation and could not believe what he was seeing. Unfortunately, King Alexander saw it, too, and in a half-second both men were heading in their direction.

The king wasn't a fancy, pampered lily-soft nobleman. In fact, Alexander was a scrapper. If there was a battle, he was in it, and if there was a fight, he was fighting. He was by no means a passive observer. He had spent all of his forty years fighting rebellious barons who had no respect for his throne or policies. It was a never-ending battle, and he worked hard to keep the houses, like de Carron, under his rule.

The men nearest the door were laughing as Josephine assaulted Sully. But the laughter ceased abruptly as Andrew and the king arrived. Andrew went for Josephine, but the king shoved him out of the way purposefully, pulling the little hellcat from the soldier.

"What goes on here?" the king demanded.

Only then did Josephine realize that her little tantrum had been observed. She also realized that it was the king with his arm around her, not Andrew. Chagrinned, she looked at Andrew, then at Sully, before replying. She even laughed a little, trying to make light of the situation.

"Nothing concerning, my lord," she said. "Simply... a game, and nothing more. May I present to you my brother-in-law, Sir Sully Montgomery, and his wife, my sister, Justine."

The king's muscular arms were still wrapped around Josephine's waist. It was clear that he had no intention of releasing her any time soon. He coolly observed Justine as the woman curtsied before turning his attention back to the heavenly-smelling creature in his grasp.

"Very well," he said, reluctantly letting her go. "Nothing more than a family squabble, I am sure. Now, ladies, if you will excuse me, it has been a long day. I would retire now, but we will have business to conduct on the morrow."

Josephine nodded. "Aye, my lord," she said. "I will have the servants show you and your men where to sleep."

Servants with torches to light the darkened stairs of the keep were brought forth as the king and his entourage swept from the dining hall. Josephine and Justine watched, then looked at each other and the men somewhat nervously. *We will have business to conduct on the morrow.* But there was no hint of what that business would be, and that had Josephine – and everyone else – apprehensive. But there was nothing they could do now but retire themselves. The morning would come soon enough.

Josephine turned to Sully.

"Forgive me," she said sheepishly. "I am sorry I became angry with you. It has been a rather overwhelming day."

Sully's lips twitched with a smile. "There is nothing to forgive, Josephine," he said. "I have had a rather overwhelming day myself."

She smiled as he used her name without the usual formality. "Indeed," she said as her smile faded. "I can only hope tomorrow is not worse."

Sully could only agree with her. Things were moving quickly at Torridon and they were all struggling to keep up with it all. As he turned for Justine, to escort his new wife back to their chamber, Josephine turned to Andrew.

"We have not had any time to speak away from the king since you arrived," she said quietly. "Did he speak to you on his business here? Did he give any indication?"

Andrew shook his head; he could see how worried she was. "None," he said. "He didn't seem too concerned when I told him that I was your betrothed. Mayhap his business will have nothing to do with attempting to arrange a marriage between you and Dalmellington."

Josephine pondered that. "Mayhap," she said. "I suppose we shall soon find out."

Andrew's gaze moved over her. She seemed so very weary. He didn't blame her in the least. They were all weary. He was simply glad that the king and his men had left Josephine alone for the most part. And now that they were finally alone, his focus was on Josephine completely. His protective instincts were running strong.

"I believe the best thing for you would be sleep," he said firmly. "I will escort you, if you will permit me."

Josephine simply nodded and, with a grateful smile, they made their way up to Josephine's room. Up the darkened stairwell and onto the nearly-black landing, they had moved in comfortable silence. There was a level of comfort between them that had not been there before. When they reached her chamber, Andrew opened the door to admit her but stopped short of entering himself. Josephine stopped and turned to him when she realized he didn't follow.

Andrew was leaning against the doorjamb with his massive arms folded across his chest. He was looking at her, but his gentle expression seemed to be hiding something. There seemed to be something lurking behind those brown eyes.

"What is it?" she asked curiously.

His eyebrows twitched in puzzlement. "I do not know what you mean."

She looked at him for a moment before her eyes narrowed, suspiciously. "You do not like our king."

He shrugged indifferently. "I do not know your king."

She didn't believe him for a moment. "I saw the way you looked at him," she said. "You obviously do not like him, but I do not know why. Please enlighten me."

She was perceptive. But how could Andrew tell her that he believed the king had something else on his mind other than betrothing her to Dalmellington? It was true that the king hadn't given him any indication what his business was, but Andrew had caught bits of conversation between the king and his men. Nothing he heard had anything to do with Colin Dalmellington.

He sensed there was something else afoot.

Josephine had been right to believe the king had been here on business that would drastically change her life, but Andrew saw it as something else. He saw a man used to getting what he wanted in life, and he suspected that he was entertaining the thought of wanting

Josephine for something other than a marriage.

There was something odd about this entire situation that made him think so.

But Josephine snapped him from his train of thought. "Did you hear me?"

Evidently, he hadn't. "Hear what?"

She sighed, lifting her eyebrows at him. "I said that Alexander is 'our' king," she said flatly. "You are in Scotland."

"You forget I am English, Joey," he said softly. "My loyalty is with myself and, if pressed, with the English crown."

She turned serious at his comment. "But Scotland is my home," she said. "Torridon is my home. Are you planning to take me out of Scotland after we're married?"

He would just as soon cut out his own heart than take her from her beloved Torridon. Even having only known her a few days, he had seen what lengths she was willing to go to in order to protect her home. Yet, oddly enough, his heart ached to know she would not accompany him on his travels, for he had no intention of laying roots. He had no intention of staying in one place with her.

… did he?

"Nay," he said after a moment. "I will not take you from Torridon."

He was right; she was very perceptive, as if she could read his mind. "But," she said as she cocked her head thoughtfully, "you will not stay here with me. I can see it in your eyes. After we are married, you are planning to leave me alone, unprotected, while you go traipsing off across the countryside."

Now he entered the room. "I would hardly consider you unprotected," he said. "Besides, no man would dare threaten the wife of The Red Fury, including and especially Colin Dalmellington."

So it was true; he didn't intend to remain with her after they were married. There was a part of her hoping he would deny what she was sensing. She was hurt that he did not intend to stay with her, but wasn't stupid enough to believe marriage would change him. He was The Red

Fury, and he wasn't meant to be caged, not even by marriage.

But perhaps she didn't wish to be caged by marriage, either, to a man who had no intention of making a life with her.

"Mayhap I no longer wish to become the wife of The Red Fury," she said, turning away. "Mayhap I shall marry someone who I know will stay with me – someone like Donald Muir."

Andrew knew she was bluffing, but the marriage feasibility of Donald Muir could be considered very real. Donald was a little older than Josephine, was very wealthy, and his family held the same standing. It was such a real threat that he didn't want to hear it, even in jest. In four strides he was upon her, grabbing her roughly by the upper arms.

"He is not man enough for you," he growled. "You are a passionate, physical woman, and I suspect that tradition will continue in the bedroom. You'd have the little man Donald in his grave before the month is out."

He embarrassed her with that assessment; and she gasped and pulled away from him.

"What a terrible thing to say!" she scowled.

He stood his ground. "Does the truth upset you?"

Her scowl grew. "Do not speak of me as if I were a common whore."

He backed off graciously. "I apologize," he said. "I did not mean to infer that you were. I simply meant that you are a strong and passionate woman. Men like Donald Muir do not deserve a woman like you."

"But men like you do?"

"Without question."

She fell silent after that, making it clear that she wasn't certain whether she would forgive him or not. Andrew knew the conversation had ended and he went to the door, bidding her a good night before closing the door behind him.

She didn't answer him.

But that didn't discourage him from what he saw as his right and his duty. Taking off his sword, he sat down on the floor with his back against her door. He rested his head back, drawing up a knee and propping an arm on it.

He exhaled, trying to get comfortable for the night. There was nothing in the world that could drag him away from her door tonight, and he planned to repeat the routine like a faithful watchdog until the king left.

He had no doubt that he and the king would meet on her threshold before that time.

Andrew's eyes were closed, but he did not sleep. He heard a door close softly down the corridor and footsteps as they approached him. The footsteps slowed until they were a few feet from him, seeming to stop.

Faster than a blink of an eye, Andrew brought his sword up and pointed the long, serrated blade steadily at whoever was standing there. Somewhere in the process, he had opened his eyes.

Sully stood looking down at him.

"Do what you must," he told Andrew. "It could be no worse than what I have already been through this day."

Andrew smiled and laid the sword down. "I thought you were the king," he said. "Sit down, man."

Sully obliged, sinking wearily to the floor a few feet from Andrew. He sat for a few moments, staring out into space, while Andrew looked at him curiously.

"I never did ask why Josephine was so hell-bent on beating you tonight," he said finally.

Sully sighed. "Because Justine said I hurt her."

"Other than the obvious, did you?" Andrew asked.

"Of course not," Sully replied. "Mayhap I did get a little rough with her when she would not cooperate, but it was nothing more than tying her hands to the bed."

Andrew put his head down and his shoulders jerked with laughter. Sully looked at him, fighting off the giggles.

"What was I supposed to do?" he demanded. "She kept hitting me;

therefore I tied her to the bed. Besides, she was making consummating the marriage most difficult. She gave me little choice."

Andrew tried to control his laughter, but the mental picture was hysterical. If Sully were truly upset, he would not have laughed at all but, truly, Sully seemed to be making light of the situation as well.

"Yet, I am to assume that you won this tremendous battle and that the marriage was duly consummated?" Andrew asked.

"Aye," Sully nodded. "In the end, I carried out Lady Josephine's wishes."

Both men sobered, knowing how much the de Carron women were sacrificing to preserve Torridon. Somehow, both Andrew and Sully had been sucked into the vortex, with Sully having no choice, and Andrew *by* choice. That made a strange yet strong camaraderie between them, something that was becoming increasingly apparent.

"Are you still going to marry Lady Josephine?" Sully finally asked.

Andrew nodded slowly. "Aye," he said. "Come what may, she will be my wife."

Sully looked at him. "You love her."

It was not a question. But Andrew appeared amused. "Love?" he repeated, then looked thoughtful. "Lady Josephine de Carron is as exquisite a woman as has ever existed. She's beautiful and is remarkably intelligent for a woman, and she possesses an indomitable spirit. She intrigues me."

Sully felt a little irritated at the superficial observation of Josephine. "She is a very deep woman," he said. "She has great sensitivity and a tremendous sense of duty. I have known her since she was twelve years old, and believe me when I tell you she possesses more than simple physical beauty."

Andrew knew that, but to admit to it would be to show that he had a weakness – and that weakness was Josephine de Carron. But, somehow, in admitting it to Sully, he knew it would go no further.

"My life has been spent with a single goal, Sully," he said quietly. "That goal has been to avenge my mother and kill my brother. But with

Josephine, I find her a tremendous distraction and she brings out a side of me that wants to laugh and to love. It's a side that frightens me and excites me at the same time. Have you ever had a woman affect you as such?"

Sully knew the man was confiding in him on the deepest level. It was an awkward conversation, considering Andrew was speaking of the woman he loved, but it was also strangely empowering in the sense that Josephine deserved a man who greatly admired her, if not loved her outright. It was much easier for Sully to deal with a man soon to be Josephine's husband who actually had some feeling for her. But in that empowerment was some bitterness as well.

He wished he were the one to marry Josephine and he suspected that he always would.

"Aye," Sully said after a moment. "I have."

Oblivious to Sully's inner turmoil, Andrew found great interest in that answer. "And were you not weakened by those feelings?"

"Nay," Sully smiled faintly. "On the contrary, they inspired me. Give in to your feelings, Andrew, and you will understand. Do not be afraid of something that can give you the greatest strength of all."

Andrew stared off into the darkened corridor, digesting that statement. It seemed so alien to him. "I do not know what I am feeling," he said after a moment. "All I know is that I feel blind rage whenever I see the king for what he has brought on her and I cannot stand the thought of her in someone else's arms. I should have never come here, yet I am glad I did."

It was quite an admission coming from the legendary mercenary. Sully wasn't quite sure what to say, so it seemed best to say nothing.

For quite some time, Andrew and Sully sat in the darkened corridor, each man to his own thoughts. So much had happened to them, and between them, actions and events that had brought them together when they could have very well made enemies out of them.

That, in and of itself, was something to ponder.

With the exception of a distant voice now and again, the fortress was as quiet as a tomb. It was nearing dawn but Andrew remained wide awake with Sully beside him, keeping silent company as their respective women slept behind closed doors. But suddenly, from somewhere in the direction of the king's chamber on the floor above, came the sound of approaching footsteps. Down the stairs and drawing closer, heading directly for them.

Andrew knew the sounds of heavy war boots when he heard them. *A soldier is coming.* He shifted casually on the floor, then rose slowly. Sully followed suit.

"We have company," Sully said quietly.

"I know," Andrew murmured. "Are you armed?"

"Always," Sully replied coolly.

"Excellent, my friend," Andrew said, facing the approaching party expectantly. "Then this shall be quick and painless."

Three of the king's guards, armed and in full mail armor, approached. The flickering torches in the corridor cast dancing phantoms along the walls as they moved and the bootfalls were hard and sharp, and soon the facial features became evident.

"Who goes?" the first soldier demanded harshly.

Andrew didn't hesitate. "I am Andrew d'Vant, betrothed of Lady Josephine de Carron, and commander of the mercenary army beyond the walls of Torridon," he replied with authority. "And my companion is Sir Sully Montgomery, Master of Torridon and wife to Lady Justine."

The soldiers looked at each other. Then, the first shoulder shrugged.

"The king wishes to see Lady Josephine in his chamber," he said. "*Now.*"

Andrew had known all along that this demand would be forthcoming and now it was here. He stood his ground.

"For what purpose?" he asked.

The soldier wasn't to be dissuaded. "That is between the king and Lady Josephine."

"And me," Andrew said. "She is my betrothed."

"Then you will do well to ask the king," the soldier said. "Now, out of my way."

As the soldier took a step towards Josephine's door, he suddenly found that Andrew's sword blocked the way. He hadn't even seen it coming, but simply heard the singing sound of metal and then a thumping sound that the point made as it embedded itself in the stone wall. Andrew was attached to the hilt of the sword, his expression anything but tolerant.

"Now that I have your attention," he said in a low voice, "go back and inform King Alexander that Lady Josephine has retired for the night. She will be honored to see him on the morrow. But not tonight."

The older soldier wasn't the least bit intimidated, at least not outwardly. "Move that sword, man," he growled.

Andrew shook his head. "I will not."

The air fairly crackled with tension. For quite some time, no one dared move. They simply stared at one another, silent threats filling the air, yet no one was moving to carry out those threats. Andrew would not be the first man to act violently, but he'd be damned if he was going to let these men into Josephine's bedchamber.

But the soldiers were acting under direct orders from the king, and if they had to fight The Red Fury and the Master of Torridon to carry out those orders, then so be it. The soldier stepped back and drew forth his sword.

"You'll eat those words, The Red Fury or no," he promised.

Sully didn't remember who cast the first blow, but it was only a matter of seconds before the sounds of metal on metal filled the corridor. Sully had his hands full with one soldier. He had only a small knife and was concentrating on not being impaled by the other's sword. Andrew, on the other hand, was fending off two of the king's best.

The king's soldiers weren't like the normal soldiers, men poorly trained and even more poorly armed. These soldiers had dedicated their lives to the king and were at the height of their profession. Andrew, of course, was a professional soldier and was paid to win, but the two imperial soldiers were giving him a good fight.

The two soldiers had managed to back him into a wall, but Andrew didn't appear in distress. With a huge right arching sweep, he caught both of their swords at once and knocked them off balance. In the split second that it took for them to recover, he drove his sword deep into the side of the man nearest him.

Sully saw the soldier fall and did a flying somersault across the floor, coming up with the dying man's sword in his right hand. Now the odds were even in the fight.

Clang... clang... clang... clang! The battle grew in intensity and neither Sully nor Andrew were straining in the least, but the king's soldiers were fighting furiously. It was simply a matter of letting them wear down before turning on them, a classic battle tactic. And when the soldiers seemed to be tiring, Andrew seemed to come alive.

Andrew was a large man with a great deal of strength. He began to attack his opponent with vigor, with his sword contacting the other man's weapon so forcefully that sparks flew into the darkness. His uppercuts were double-handed, and his thrusts were well-controlled. The soldier was merely defending himself at this point as Andrew worked him down the hall.

The fighting was furious now. Andrew began grunting as he made contact. The soldier was breathing heavily, and was trying not to stumble as he backed up. Sully had to concentrate on his own match and not get caught up in watching Andrew's, for it was an awesome spectacle to witness. Sully had never seen anyone fight with such unleashed fury. He wondered how the soldier had lasted this long.

He was so caught up in Andrew's performance that when his opponent made a stupid mistake, Sully almost missed taking advantage of it. But as quick as a bolt of lightning, Sully upper-sliced right into the man's midsection, breaching the mail and plowing into the man's innards. In a second, he was on the floor dying.

Andrew, by this time, had his enemy on the ground against the wall; the soldier's sword wasn't even up anymore. Andrew hesitated a split second before killing the man; he didn't like cold-blooded killing, but he knew if the man was set free, he'd race back to the king and Andrew would be on the run, which would mean having to leave Josephine. He wasn't about to do that. Therefore, he shoved the man's head back and drove his sword right through the soldier's throat. Sully was standing by him, watching the soldier twitch in the last throes of death.

As quickly as it began, the fight was over. But Sully and Andrew knew that it wasn't really over. A battle like that made a good deal of noise and they were both fairly certain that most of the keep had been alerted to it. That made the situation rather tricky.

"We must get them out of the castle," Sully said quietly. "We cannot leave them here."

Andrew nodded. "I'll take two," he said. "Lead the way, my lord."

Sully grinned at the use of his now proper title. "Out behind the stables," he said. "But should you leave Josephine unprotected like this?"

Andrew heaved a soldier across his shoulder. "I believe it is safe for now," he said. "The king will not send out more soldiers, at least for the time being. He's probably assuming his men had to fight de Carron guards and I would wager to say he'll not send anyone to check on the situation for a time. I will be back by then."

It made sense. Sully assumed the burden of the soldier he killed. "I was hoping the king would have left Josephine alone," he said. "I am disappointed that I was wrong. These men we fought – they were simply following orders."

Andrew was somewhat solemn. "I did not want to kill them, but if I had not…"

Sully cut him off. "You would be dead now," he finished, then looked at him. "Andrew, you need not explain your actions to me. I know you are a man of character and you have yet to give me a reason to question you."

Andrew nodded quickly, grateful for Sully's words. He seldom cared what anyone thought of him, but he was coming to respect Sully. He didn't want the man to think ill of him. Gathering the bodies, they began to descend the stairs with their burdens.

"Why do I have the strange notion that I will not sleep for the duration of the royal visit?" Andrew muttered as he grunted under the weight.

Sully grinned. "Oddly enough, I have that same feeling."

The king's men were buried in the soft dirt behind the stables that night, covered up in the dark of night, never to be spoken of again.

CHAPTER FIFTEEN

JOSEPHINE SLEPT LATE the next morning, waking a little before midday. It was unusual for her to sleep past sunrise, but she was desperately tired and needed the rest.

Ola had the tub filled with steaming rose-scented water. The little servant moving about the chamber had finally awoken her. Josephine laid on her side, watching her maid as she brought linens and soap, and laid out a rich, deep-blue surcote with white panels in the skirt.

The little maid seemed to be in more of a hurry than usual, running back and forth like a scampering mouse. When she finally ceased, she faced her mistress expectantly.

"My lady, the king demands an audience as soon as you are ready," she said hurriedly. "Will you not rise now?"

Josephine sat straight up. "Why did you not awaken me sooner?" she demanded, throwing off the bed covers and yanking her night tunic over her head. "How long ago did he ask for me?"

"Not long, my lady. But Sir Andrew told me to let you sleep."

Josephine's agitated movements slowed and she peered at the woman. "He did?"

"Aye, my lady."

Josephine wasn't sure what to say to that; had he assumed too much? Or was he just being kind? But she couldn't think too much about it because the king was waiting to conduct his business with her.

She was eager to discover, finally, why the man had really come to Torridon. She had to hurry.

The bath was brief but invigorating. Ola scrubbed quickly and dried her so roughly that Josephine was certain the woman had removed skin. But there was a sense of urgency in the air and the little maid could feel it. Very shortly, Josephine was clad in the blue gown with soft slippers on her feet, and her hair was pulled to the nape of her neck and gathered in a gold net as fine as a spider web. Her neck glittered with a gold and sapphire necklace her father had given her.

When she felt presentable enough to face her king, Josephine exited the room swiftly and headed for the great hall. It was nearly noon, and she assumed everyone would be gathered there.

As she rushed, her stomach was twisting with anxiety. Before the day was through, she would know her fate and the thought of that knowledge scared her. It was the not knowing that was the worst. Once she reached the outskirts of the great hall, she took a deep breath for courage and said a quick prayer. God help her with what was about to happen. Truth be told, she was a little terrified.

The hall was crowded with people eating a meal of bread, cheese, and cold meats at midday. Donald Muir sat with the king on the dais, deep in conversation, and Josephine was almost surprised to see him. She had nearly forgotten he was still at Torridon, keeping to his room as he was because of his swollen face. Nicholas de Londres, the king's nephew, sat on the other side of his uncle, and his eyes immediately riveted to Josephine as she entered the hall.

She had not seen him at the feast last night, for he had been in charge of overseeing the king's caravan, but now that she could see him better in the light, she noted he was a very handsome young man. He was Donald's age, perhaps having seen a little more than twenty summers, with a beautiful head of red-gold hair. He had big, blue eyes, slightly droopy, but very comely. He smiled as she approached and it was a handsome smile.

But conspicuously absent were Justine, Sully, and Andrew. Josephine was hoping to find them in the great hall and was rather disappointed to realize they were not present. She couldn't go look for them because she had already been sighted by Nicholas, so it would not do for her to suddenly turn around and run off. Nay, she would have to face the king now. She'd come this far.

Reaching the head table, she bowed deeply to the king. He immediately pulled away from Donald and cast appreciative eyes on the vision in front of him.

"Ah, Lady Josephine," he said. "It is, indeed, a pleasure to see you again. Will you join me for the meal?"

She smiled. "Your majesty is very kind. Thank you."

The king shoved his nephew down a seat to make room for Josephine. She accepted the chair graciously, informing a nearby steward to bring in the meal and to send for Sully and Andrew. As the man scurried off to do her bidding, she looked around the table.

Nicholas was smiling pleasantly at her and she smiled in return. All the while, however, she was keeping an eye out for Sully and Andrew. She spied Burl and Severn several feet away and she motioned to them when they looked at her. They came quickly, saluting smartly to her and the king.

She leaned close to Burl, whispering, "Where are Sir Andrew and Sir Sully?"

"At the knight's training field, my lady," he told her.

She tried not to eye the king but she cast her eyes in his direction, hoping Burl would catch on. "Find them," she said. "Tell them I want them here, now."

Her knights obeyed instantly. Feeling somewhat comforted now, she sat against the back of her chair as a servant brought her watered wine. As she took a sip, she could feel the king's eyes on her. Bracing herself, she forced a smile and turned to him.

"You said we had business to discuss, my lord," she said politely. "Shall we discuss it now?"

Alexander had been staring at her rather heavily, the slope of her torso and the shape of her face. When she posed the question, he had to pull himself away from thoughts and feelings that were, perhaps, more lustful than they should have been.

"Aye," he said. "But after we eat. Right now, I can smell the lamb and am famished."

So much for revealing the mysterious subject. Josephine wasn't even hungry as the meal was served. Lamb, pigeon in plumb sauce, peas and onions, and pies with fruit were brought out to please the royal appetite. In truth, the smells overwhelmed Josephine and she found that she could eat something as everyone began eating with gusto. As she picked at her food, eating little bites, the conversation around the table grew loud and sometimes gregarious.

The king seemed determined to engage her and Donald in conversation, speaking on various barons, his favorite wine from France, and anything else that appeared to pop into his mind. Nicholas joined in the conversation as well, telling stories about the summer he'd spent in France with a widowed old aunt who had a mustache and liked to gamble.

That brought laughter from both Josephine and Donald, and the conversation lightened. Alexander possessed a decent sense of humor, but even if he hadn't, they would've laughed anyway. He also competed with his nephew for attention. If Nicholas told a story, Alexander had to tell a better one.

Also throughout the course of the meal, Josephine discovered that Nicholas was somewhat of a poet and spoke fondly of his love for it. But Alexander couldn't compete with him on that level. Although he was extremely fond of the lad, it was clear that he had no tolerance for the poetry and reading the boy had put so much energy into. Apparently, he believed his nephew's time would be better spent in the warring pursuit.

Once the king was finished scolding his nephew for his scholarly pursuits, he turned his attention to Donald, who was quite advanced in his warfare training. As Donald and the king discussed tactics,

Josephine looked over at Nicholas as he picked at his turnips. He looked like his feelings were hurt by the king's criticism and she felt a twinge of pity for him.

"I'd like to hear your poetry sometime," she said quietly.

He looked up at her in mild surprise. "Would ye?" he said. "I... I would be honored, my lady."

She smiled. "What do you like to write about?"

He looked a little embarrassed. "I write about many things," he said. "Things that inspire me or touch me in some way. It could be a lake, or a bird, or a meadow, or a beautiful lady."

His voice trailed off and his embarrassment seemed to grow. Josephine fought off a smile at the young man who was evidently a dreamer. "You will have to read your prose to me before you leave," she said. "I would enjoy it very much."

Her kind words soothed his embarrassment. "I would truly be honored. Thank ye."

Andrew and Sully picked that moment to enter the room. Josephine looked to Andrew and, immediately, their eyes locked. He came directly to her. Taking her hand over the table, he kissed it gently and her heart leapt wildly from his touch.

"My lady," Andrew greeted her fondly, then he glanced down at Nicholas sitting beside her. He growled. "Move, boy."

Nicholas looked completely surprised, but jumped up and moved to the next chair. He was not about to argue with The Red Fury, especially in territorial matters of a woman. Josephine, however, was mortified. She put out a hand.

"Wait," she said, looking to Sir Nicholas. "Return to your seat."

Nicholas was too fearful to obey her. "I am happy to give my seat over to Sir Andrew," he said. "Truly, it is my pleasure."

He grabbed his wine and took a healthy drink, looking away and pretending to be interested in other parts of the hall. But Josephine knew it was because he was frightened of Andrew and she turned her scowling face to the mercenary.

"You had no cause to address him in that manner," she said quietly. "You will apologize to Nicholas.'"

Andrew looked as if he were actually mulling over her demand, but the truth was that he was rather offended. Still, he would not show it, not in front of the king. To show a rift would be inviting a wedge, and he wouldn't do that. They had to present a united front, in all cases.

Therefore, he did what most normal males would have done when faced with an angry lady – he swallowed his rather large pride and bowed politely to Nicholas.

"Forgive my rotten nature, Sir Nicholas," he said. There was no mistaking the sarcasm. "I hope I have not damaged you for life."

Nicholas wasn't sure what to say in the least. All he could do was shake his head. "Not at all, my lord."

Andrew smiled thinly at him, returning his attention to Josephine. "Satisfied?"

Josephine fought the urge to smile at him because she knew he wasn't sorry in the least. He was only doing it to appease her, which was as good a reason as any. "Completely," she said. "Nicholas, would you allow Andrew to have your seat?"

Nicholas was flabbergasted at the whole situation, but managed to nod. Andrew sat in Nicholas' vacated chair and immediately demanded wine and meat. Servants tripped over each other in their haste to do his bidding. When he finally had a cup of wine in hand, he turned and smiled at his betrothed.

"You are looking well this day," he said pleasantly. "Did you sleep well?"

She turned to Andrew, her eyes roving over his handsome features. She realized that she was very glad to see him, as if his presence meant instant comfort, instant safety.

"I did," she said. "Did you?"

Andrew didn't know if she was aware he'd spent the night at her door, so he simply nodded. "As well as can be expected."

His food was placed before him, cleaving any further conversation for the moment. As he was delving into his food, Sully approached with a goblet in hand and squatted between Andrew and Josephine's chairs.

"Where is my sister?" Josephine asked him. "Did she not come to the hall to eat?"

Sully took a drink. "She is in her chamber," he said quietly. "She said she wanted to be alone, so I left her there."

Josephine's eyebrows drew together. "Why?"

He shook his head. "I do not know."

"Has she at least been pleasant since… yesterday?"

He took another drink of his wine. "It is difficult to tell."

"What do you mean?"

"She will not speak to me."

Josephine sighed deeply. "I am sorry, Sully," she said. "I am sorry she is being so difficult."

He shrugged. "She is Justine and that is her nature."

Josephine didn't say anything. She suddenly felt very bad for having done this to the man. Forcing him to marry her sister and forcing him to endure whatever Justine dished out. And he had done it just for her.

Damn Justine!

"Excuse me," she rose abruptly.

Andrew bolted out of his chair and Sully stood quickly. The king, on her right, turned to watch her as she asked his permission to leave. He nodded briefly, and she swept from the hall.

The three men watched her, with Sully and Andrew knowing exactly where she was going and wondering if they should follow.

JOSEPHINE WAS MORE than angry.

In her opinion, her sister was not only acting in a childish, selfish manner by not coming down from her chamber, but she was also risking provoking the wrath of the king by not showing her face and assuming her role as Mistress of Torridon.

Standing outside of Justine's door, she didn't even bother knocking. She stormed into the room, heading directly for the bed as she prepared to throw her sister bodily from it. The bed was mussed, but no Justine. Slightly puzzled, Josephine looked about the room but her sister was nowhere to be found. Not even her maid was present.

Josephine was befuddled as she left her sister's room; she had even looked under the bed. As she headed for the stairs, preparing to scour the entire keep for her errant sister, she noticed the door to her own chambers slightly ajar. Curious, she poked her head inside.

Justine was sitting at her dressing table, examining the contents of Josephine's jewelry box. As Josephine entered her room, she saw that Justine was dressed in her silk dress that was the color of a ripe apricot, with the square-necked bodice was embroidered with tiny seed pearls. The full skirt was also embroidered with the seed pearls in the pattern of flowers and bees.

It was one of Josephine's favorite surcotes and her initial reaction was one of outrage for having her privacy invaded. But the more she looked at her sister sitting quietly, the more she began to see the whole picture. For the first time in her life, Justine wanted to be pretty. That had never happened before. Perhaps, one night in Sully's arms was all that she needed to spur a side of her that had been kept buried; the side of a woman who wanted to feel beautiful and please a man. For certain, Justine had always ignored that side of her in favor of her black garments and witch's brews.

But now… something had changed.

Ola and Darcy, Justine's maid, were fussing over Justine as she sat before the dressing table. They were brushing her hair, arguing on the best way to dress it now that she was a married woman. But the moment Josephine stepped further into the room, they looked at her with big eyes, as if fearful for the anger to come. Josephine strongly protected her privacy against her sister.

But Josephine didn't look at the maids. She was looking at her sister.

"Leave us," she ordered, and the maids scampered out.

Justine looked at her sister guiltily, bracing for a fight. "I… I am sorry that I did not ask you," she said. "No one seemed to know where you had gone and I did not want to go downstairs dressed like… that is to say, everything I have is dark, and I wanted to… I mean, I have seen you wear this dress before and it is so pretty, so I thought…"

Josephine cut her off. "That dress never looked so good on me," she said. "I believe it was made with you in mind."

Justine looked at her in surprise. "You are not angry?"

Josephine shook her head. "Why should I be?" she asked. Then she looked down at her jewels. "Here – try the pearl collar. It goes with the gown."

She pulled forth a three-strand pearl and diamond choker and put it on her sister's neck. It was perfect. Justine looked at herself in the mirror, seeing a well-groomed, fashionably-dressed woman for the first time. Josephine brushed her sister's hair back from her face and braided it, twisting the braid elaborately at the back of her head. Then, she selected a dozen pearl pins and placed them strategically in the coiffure. Finally, she stood back to view her work.

Justine looked at her timidly, but Josephine could only smile. She looked absolutely lovely, and nothing like the strange pseudo-witch she had been masquerading as. It was as if a light had been lit and now burned brightly in the eyes of Justine, Lady Montgomery.

It was an astonishing transformation.

"Come," Josephine said softly. "The king awaits."

Justine looked down at herself. "And… and I look presentable?"

"More than presentable, darling. You are beautiful."

Justine blushed furiously as Josephine took her by the hand and led her from the chamber.

"Where are Sully and Andrew?" Justine asked as they descended the stairs.

"I left them in the dining hall," Josephine replied. "Andrew was being abhorrently rude to Nicholas de Londres, the king's nephew.

Have you met him?"

"Nay," Justine said. "Why was Andrew being rude to him?"

Josephine snorted. "Who can say?" she said. "Nicholas and I were having a pleasant conversation when Andrew demanded Nicholas remove himself from the chair so that he could sit next to me. He was quite overbearing."

Justine glanced at her sister, seeing the outrage, but perhaps also seeing an expression that suggested she might have been flattered by it. "Where you are concerned, Andrew has every right to be," Justine said, but she was unusually soft-spoken. "You are his betrothed and I believe he loves you."

Josephine looked at her sister with a great deal of shock. "Andrew loves Andrew," she said matter-of-factly. "There is little room for anything else."

Justine took on the stubborn look that Josephine knew so well. "You are so wrong," she said. "Last night, he stood guard at your door because he was afraid the king would attempt to seduce you."

Josephine shook her head, unwilling to give any credence to her sister's wild idea. "He simply wanted to keep me pure so that he could claim my virginity," she insisted. "Besides, our king is a married man."

Justine pulled her sister to a halt. They were in the foyer of Torri-don's keep and there were servants lurking about, so Justine kept her voice low.

"Josephine," she said seriously, "the king sent three soldiers to re-trieve you last night. Andrew killed two of them, and Sully killed the other."

Josephine was stunned. "What?"

"It is true."

Josephine was beside herself with shock. "How do you know this?"

Justine's expression was full of concern. "I heard the noise and peeked from my door," she said. "I saw it all. It was a terrible, brutal fight and when they were finished, they carried the bodies away. I heard Sully say something about not wanting the king to discover what they'd done."

Josephine was truly stunned. She'd never had a man kill for her honor before. "God's Bones," she finally hissed, thinking of the far-reaching implications of Sully and Andrew killing the king's men. "He is absolutely right; the king must never know this. He could punish Andrew and Sully, and we would never see them again."

Justine, surprisingly, understood that. She wasn't a fool. "I know," she said quietly. "But I wanted you to know what Andrew did for you last night. That is why I believe he feels more for you than you realize."

Josephine looked at her sister, seeing some logic to what she was saying. Was it really possible that she was right? Did Andrew, indeed, feel something for her, or was he simply protecting what belonged to him? It was difficult to know. But one thing was for certain – there were three dead men to prove that whatever Andrew was feeling must have been serious.

"I suppose it is possible," she said. "But we have known each other so short a time."

Justine simply shrugged. "I am not sure one needs years and years to know if feelings are valid and true," she said. "Sometimes, all it takes is a glance. Or so I've heard."

Josephine was at a loss for the whole conversation; she was feeling bewildered and uneasy. "Mayhap."

Justine could see her sister's expression was one of confusion. She took the woman by the hand and began to lead her towards the door.

"Come now," she said. "The king awaits, does he not?"

Josephine suddenly remembered that the king needed to speak with her, as he had requested. Her thoughts switched from Andrew's behavior to the king's agenda, and a sinking feeling in the pit of her stomach made her swallow hard. She mentally prepared herself for what was sure to come as she and her sister entered the torch-filled hall.

She would find out soon enough.

THE KING HAD retired to the privacy of the Knight's Haven, waiting for Josephine to return. She was informed of this by the king's steward when she re-entered the dining hall, but she had to speak to Andrew first. Her eyes scanned the hall quickly, searching for his auburn head.

She found him on the dais with Sully and Thane, engaged in conversation. But the words fell from their lips as Josephine and Justine approached, with each man affixed to his respective lady as Thane wisely excused himself. Andrew smiled warmly at Josephine, pulling his eyes away long enough to glance at Justine.

"Lady Montgomery," he greeted. "Marriage seems to agree with you."

Everyone in the room noticed the metamorphosis of Justine, and none more so than Sully. This was not the same woman he merely tolerated just two short days ago. She was transforming into a lovely woman and Sully took it as a sign that she very much wanted to please him. He reached out and took his wife's hand.

"Join me," he asked softly.

Justine actually seemed to blush at his attention, as much as she pretended otherwise. She took the seat beside him.

Andrew came from behind the table and stood in front of Josephine, gazing at her with appreciation. She put a hand on his arm.

"May I speak with you?" she asked.

He nodded and offered her his arm. "Of course."

Josephine took him to the small room that the servants used. It was quiet and private there, with the dark and sooty hearth smelling heavily of smoke. Once inside, she released his arm but did not stray far.

"Justine informed me of last night's events," she said quietly. "She told me you killed three of the king's guards when they came for me."

Andrew wasn't really surprised she'd heard what had happened. He paused for a moment before nodding in agreement.

"I would not let them have you," he said simply.

She put a hand on his arm. "But what if the king discovers what you have done?" she argued softly. "You have put yourself in danger."

He shrugged. "No more than usual."

He was making light of a situation she considered serious and she was afraid for him. Josephine's face took on a pained look and she gently squeezed his arm.

"I could have handled the king myself," she said. "It was not necessary for you to jeopardize yourself so. But please know that I am grateful for your efforts."

He unfolded his strong arms and tilted her chin up so that their eyes met, soft brown melding with her green. There was a significant amount of tangible emotion that poured between them, growing stronger by the moment.

"You are my betrothed," he said quietly. "What I do for you is not a service, but what any man would do for his lady. None but me shall ever touch you, and woe to any man who would try. Even the king."

Josephine was oddly fulfilled by his words. And his touch was warm; she could grow to crave it. Justine's words came back to her in that instant; *I believe he loves you*. Looking into Andrew's eyes, she could almost believe that. There was something there, something meant only for her, and her heart soared because of it.

She was feeling the very same way.

Was it possible to know feelings after having only known someone a few days at most? Perhaps there was no timeline for feelings, as Justine had wisely suggested. Perhaps, they were present in a day as much as they were present in ten days or in ten years. Who could know the unpredictable nature of emotions? Josephine didn't pretend to. All she knew was that she felt them, too.

And she was worried for what he'd done, but there was no time to dwell on it. She knew the king was waiting for her.

"For all that you have done for me and for my sister, I am touched and grateful," she finally said. "But I do wish you would be careful. I do not wish for you to be punished because of me."

He flashed her a grin. "No one would dare punish me, my lady. You worry overly."

Josephine couldn't help but grin at his devil-may-care attitude. "Mayhap," she said. "But mayhap not. In any case, the king is expecting me. I must go to him."

So far, Andrew had managed to keep the entire conversation rather light in spite of the serious nature of it. But at the mention of the king, his face darkened. He knew that she must attend him, alone, and he wasn't happy with that thought.

"Then I shall escort you and wait outside the door," he said firmly.

Josephine didn't argue with him. Truth be told, she would feel better if she knew he as nearby. The moment that she had dreaded was finally at hand and she took his arm as they headed towards the Knight's Haven. Andrew noticed her tense shoulders and taut brow as they walked.

"You are troubled," he said as they passed down the hall. "There is nothing to fear; I am here."

She didn't answer for a moment. "There is a great deal to fear," she said. "I *am* frightened."

"You?" he said, teasing her gently. "I do not believe it. You are afraid of nothing."

She sniffled and came to a halt. There was a tear on her cheek and she tried to brush it away before he saw, but he caught it. He felt his heartstrings pull as she let go of his arm and leaned against the cold, stone wall.

"I am afraid of being forced to marry a man who hates me," she said, her voice tight. "I have saved everyone but myself, and now I am sorry. I do not want to marry Colin Dalmellington."

Reaching out, Andrew gathered her hands and held them to his chest, standing very close to her.

"Josephine, look at me," he ordered, and her eyes reluctantly lifted to meet his. Her sadness was almost more than he could bear. "Do you trust me?"

She nodded, with a sniffle. "Aye."

He smiled faintly. "Then trust me when I tell you that you shall not marry Colin, or anyone else but me," he said in a tone that left no room for doubt. "Whatever the king might say to you in there shall have no bearing on our future. You shall become my wife and bear my sons, and we shall have a long and happy life together. Do you believe that?"

He sounded so very sure. "But I cannot disobey the king's directive," she said. "To go against a royal order would mean terrible things for us all."

Andrew cocked an eyebrow. "You made a promise to me before the king ever became involved," he said. "No directive he can give you will supersede the one you have with me. I *will* marry you."

She was caught up in his words, so strong and so confident. "You are used to having your way, in all things."

"I am."

"But… I do not understand why you are so determined to marry a woman you have only just met."

"I told you why. I have explained this to you."

He had but, somehow, it didn't seem enough of an explanation. Josephine sensed something more behind his determination, something stronger than he was willing to admit. Before she could think about what she was saying, she spoke.

"Justine thinks it is because you are in love with me."

Andrew was caught completely off guard by that statement. He stared at her, his eyes caressing her sweet face as those words rolled around in his mind. His first reaction was to scoff; *love?* Who had ever said anything about love? He had loved his mother and father, and what had that brought him? Only pain and grief. But as much as he found himself denying it, he knew it was true. The little witch was right.

God's Bones, he was in love with her!

Andrew dropped her hands and looked at her with a furrowed brow. Josephine stared back at him, seeing his nearly enraged expression, and she was very sorry she had even mentioned it. She should not have. But she couldn't take those words back, not now.

It became apparent very quickly that she had made a terrible mistake. Embarrassed, Josephine turned away from him and prepared to continue down the hall. She hadn't taken two steps before Andrew managed to grab her arm and stop her forward movement. When she turned to look at him, her expression full of shame, he opened his mouth as if to say something but couldn't seem to speak.

Still, his expression said more than words could. The outrage turned into puzzlement, and puzzlement to understanding. His features softened and he pulled her close, and closer still. His gaze was intense, his arms holding her fast, and he could feel her relax against him. Her warmth against his warmth, her body molding to his. Andrew had never experienced a more comforting or emotionally satisfying embrace in his life and he knew that he wanted to spend the rest of his life with this same feeling. He wanted to capture it, to savor it, and to spend his life loving Josephine.

Without a word, Andrew's lips slanted over hers softly, yet with increasing passion. Josephine gave in to his kiss immediately, swept away with the sheer tenderness behind the action, and even as his tongue licked at her pink mouth, she could think of nothing but the sheer pleasure of it. Emotions stirred so deep within her that her limbs ached with her need for him.

Indeed, she needed him.

He needed her.

Feeling her respond to him undid Andrew. It released a passion in him stronger than he ever thought possible. He pulled his lips from hers, kissing her cheeks, her eyes, and her neck. His strong hands roamed her body, exploring her with every touch, every caress. There was so much in his heart, so much that had built up in a very short amount of time that he hardly knew where to start.

"I think that I have always loved you," he whispered between fevered kisses. "I cannot remember when I have not. I have been a fool to deny it."

Joy soared in Josephine's heart. She threw her arms around his neck and, for the first time in her life, felt as if she could depend on someone other than herself. She was no longer afraid to show her feelings because she knew, with Andrew, they were safe. *She* was safe.

It was the most wonderful feeling she had ever known.

"Promise me," she whispered into his ear. "Promise that you will never leave me and that you will always love me."

He heard her wistful tone and pulled back, his hands cupping her face. "I vow on my father's grave that I will love no other but you, for now and for always," he said hoarsely. "But we must be realistic. There will be times when I will have to leave you, but I shall always return to you. Not even death can keep me from returning to you, Joey. I swear it."

Josephine believed him, implicitly. Moving forward, she kissed him sweetly and put a finger to his lips as she drew back. "Then what the king says matters naught," she said. "For I know where my true destiny lies. It lies with you."

He kissed her finger, caught up in a maelstrom of emotion that was overwhelming him. "As mine lies with you," he murmured. "Let me hear it from your lips, Joey. Tell me you love me."

She didn't hesitate. "I love you."

"Love is what life is made of."

She smiled faintly. "Truly... it is."

He kissed her fingers again and they resumed their walk down the torch-lit hall. For now, what lay at the other end of it didn't matter any longer.

CHAPTER SIXTEEN

HAD KING ALEXANDER not found Josephine de Carron so utterly lovely, he might have been truly annoyed at her tardiness. Instead, he poured her a cup of wine himself and indicated for her sit next to him at the massive table where the de Carron knights would meet.

Josephine accepted his invitation graciously, already on her guard and so very grateful that her beloved awaited just beyond the door. Although her heart was still fluttering with delight from her conversation with Andrew, she made a sincere effort to focus on the king. After all, he wanted to speak with her about something evidently serious.

She needed her focus.

"Now, Lady Josephine," the king said as he sat back comfortably in her father's chair, the chair that Josephine usually sat in. "The time has come to reveal the purpose of my visit. I know that you are unmarried, and I had not heard of your sister's marriage until my arrival. The latter revelation has disturbed my plans somewhat, but not entirely."

Josephine was somewhat disgusted to realize that, indeed, she had been right when she'd guessed the purpose of the king's visit. *Marriage!* But she sat silently, with no indication of what was going on in her mind.

Failing to draw a reaction from her, Alexander sat forward and put a clamping hand on her arm.

"I see now that you are a most valuable asset," he said. "I cannot believe that rumors of your beauty had not reached me. The men around here must be blind."

Josephine sat stone-faced through his monologue, watching him closely. Had he uttered the same words this morning, she would have hung on every word, but not now. Now she knew what her future held and whatever happened, she had the love of The Red Fury. He would be her only husband.

Although the king had been told of the betrothal, it was clear he intended to ignore it. He continued. "You see, my lady, I have been having a great deal of trouble with some of my Highland barons," he said. "They insist upon running their own clans and the surrounding country as if it were their own private country. They have no respect for their king and they fight my armies with a vengeance. It makes ruling Scotland rather difficult."

Josephine knew all of this this. King Alexander had been an ineffective ruler because the petty barons refused to acknowledge the rule of his family. But it had been the same for King Alexander's father. Neither one of them had been successful. Both had had a hard time gaining support, but being related to the man, she had to support him completely whether or not she wanted to.

"I am trying to seek support through other means," Alexander was saying. "Since I cannot depend on my own countrymen, I am going outside the realm. Which is where you enter my plans."

Josephine was still sitting ramrod straight in the chair, but her expression was no longer one of casual interest. She was looking at the king with open apprehension. He had said nothing of Dalmellington, or of Torridon, or of Burnton Castle. He was talking about an alliance outside the country and an ominous feeling filled her mind.

"Outside of Scotland?" she repeated. "I do not understand."

The king smiled benevolently at her. "My lady, you have been pledged to an English earl who has sworn his allegiance to me," he said. "He brings with him a three thousand man army. You will be a vital link between the throne of Scotland and the throne of England. Are you not pleased?"

So now, it came. This was the reason for the king's midnight visit to Torridon. Josephine could only stare at him in shock; not only because he had pledged her to an English earl, but because Colin Dalmellington had no part in the purpose of the king's visit.

"But… my lord, what of the Dalmellingtons?" she stammered. "I believed that you came to solve the feudal war between us."

"Silly lass," he chided. "Your feud is of no concern to me. It will eventually burn itself out. What concerns me is the state of my court, and your marriage to the earl will help me greatly."

Josephine was reeling. He didn't care for her or for Torridon, only his own bloody throne. Everything she had done, everything she had forced on the others had been based on a wrong assumption. But how could she have been so wrong? Now, because she jumped to a false conclusion, her sister was married to Sully. He was Master of Torridon, and she was betrothed to the mercenary, The Red Fury.

The king was waiting for her gratitude but she was struggling with her composure.

"My lord," she said as steadily as she could. "You are most generous. However, I am betrothed to Andrew d'Vant. We plan to wed soon."

That statement brought about the king's displeasure. "So I have been told," he said. "Did your father do this?"

"Nay," she said. "I did. He is a suitable match, and as Mistress of Torridon, it was my right to agree to such a proposal."

The king was impatient. "I realize that," he said. "But as Mistress of Torridon, an earl is a much better match than a mercenary leader."

Josephine was struggling against a righteous panic. She found it was difficult for her not to jump up and scream at him. "But I am no longer the Mistress of Torridon or Lady Ayr, my lord," Josephine countered. "I gave it all over to my sister as a dowry when she married. She and her husband now rule the fortress. The papers were drawn up by my steward and signed by the priest. It is done."

The king took another glance at Josephine, seeing her through different eyes. She was not an empty-headed wench, to be sure. She had a head on her shoulders. But he was angered by her seeming defiance of his wishes. Women and intelligence were an annoying combination. He was through humoring her.

"Your betrothal is dissolved," he said flatly. "You will leave with me the day after tomorrow, and I personally shall deliver you to the Earl of Annan and Blackbank, to whom you shall be wed."

Josephine knew that name; God help her, she'd heard it before. From Andrew. She had to grip the arms of her chair to keep from falling out of it. The king had not only destroyed her betrothal, but he had pledged her to Andrew's mortal enemy, his brother, Alphonse. Dear God, was this even possible? She wanted to shriek and curse and faint, all at the same time. But the only sound that escaped her lips was a strangled gasp.

"The... the Earl of Annan and Blackbank?" she repeated, just to make sure she heard correctly.

Alexander nodded. "A very powerful border laird," he said. "His father was English and his mother Scots. He has been a great supporter of mine and you will be a suitable reward."

Josephine was having trouble breathing. There had been no mistake. Of all the lords in England and Scotland, Alexander had to pick that one. *He has been a great supporter.* Josephine had never even heard of the man until Andrew came along and the story she'd heard from him was enough to terrify the hell out of her.

She wanted no part of it.

"What... what is his name?" she asked hesitantly.

"I told you," the king said with exasperation. "The Earl of Annan and Blackbank. The family name is d'Vant. In fact, is that not the same name as The Red Fury? Andrew d'Vant?"

Josephine knew she was pale. "Aye."

"Are they related?"

"They are brothers."

The king was surprised by the coincidence. "Is that so? I was not aware of this," he said. "Alphonse d'Vant has been allied with me for a few years but he never mentioned his brother, not ever."

Josephine swallowed, hard. "That is because they do not speak, my lord."

The king gave a chuckle. "Then this is an awkward situation, taking the betrothed of one brother and giving her to the other."

"Please, my lord, if I can only…" she began.

The king cut her off, rather rudely. "There will be no discussion, Lady Josephine," he said. "This is my wish and the subject is closed. Even if you do not marry one brother, you can marry the other. Now, will you join me for a ride?"

Riding with the man was the very last thing she wanted to do. It was a struggle not to tell him that.

"Nay," she said, deliberately leaving out any form of formal address. "I… I must begin preparations if I am to leave in two days."

He nodded. "Of course," he said graciously. "Then you are dismissed."

Josephine rose swiftly, rushing from the chamber on quaking legs. Spilling out into the hall, she failed to notice Andrew leaning against the wall until she was almost upon him. His smile faded when he saw the expression on her face.

"What did he say?" he demanded.

Her hands flew to her mouth and her eyes filled with tears. Then she rushed to him and threw her arms around his neck and wept pitifully. Andrew's mind exploded with the possibilities facing them. But instead of pressing her, he swept her into his arms and carried her out of the hall.

Through the bailey they went, ignoring the looks of the men they happened to pass. Into the keep they went and up the dark, stone stairs to the upper floors. Josephine's chamber was on the third level and Andrew kicked the door open, sweeping inside where he sent Ola away.

As the maid scattered, he sat Josephine gently down on a chair near the hearth and poured her a cup of wine. He forced her to take a couple of sips to calm her crying.

"Now," he said gently. "Tell me."

"Oh, Andrew," she gasped, teary-eyed and sobbing. "I-It is so horrible that I cannot fully comprehend it. He had no intention of betrothing Justine or me to Colin. He only cares about his damnable throne and who he can persuade to support it. He doesn't give a damn about me, or Justine, or Torridon, and the fact that the House of de Carron has always supported the throne."

Andrew listened patiently, but so far nothing he heard was earth-shattering. But he was not prepared for what came next.

"He dissolved our betrothal," she said, her voice squeaking. "He dissolved it because he has promised me to an English earl to form an alliance. The Earl of Annan and Blackbank, Alphonse d'Vant."

Andrew thought he had not heard correctly. He looked at her as if she were speaking in tongues. But as the information settled, assaulting his mind like an evil curse, he slowly stood up. All he could do was stare at her and try not to explode.

The Earl of Annan and Blackbank.

It wasn't possible!

"Are you certain of this?" he asked, his voice sounding oddly breathless.

She nodded. "Aye."

"When?"

"The king says that he will take me with him when he leaves in two days," she said. She was feeling desperation as well as fear. "I could not believe it myself when I heard it. Did you know that your brother was a great supporter of the king?"

In truth, Andrew had. He'd kept track of his brother all of these years, as it was always wise to know one's enemy. He'd never lost that sense of tracking his brother like a hound. Faintly, he nodded.

"I'd heard," he muttered. "I'd heard he was willing to support the king who granted him the most favor. Now, I am to understand you are part of that favor?"

Josephine simply nodded, her eyes still filled with tears. The news was so very devastating for them both. She watched him, waiting for something to happen but, so far, he'd not said anything. He simply looked shocked.

But the truth was that Andrew was more than shocked; every murderous, evil thought he had ever had now took the form of King Alexander. The man was a vile excuse for a man and did not deserve to live. Marry his sweet Josephine to his barbaric brother? Even thinking such a thought was beyond reason.

Lost to his thoughts, Andrew stepped back, stumbling on the corner of a table as he turned around. He seemed to be heading for the door. Josephine rose as well, following him. She feared what he might do once he left her chamber, and she knew she must keep him caged until his temper calmed.

Her suspicion had been correct. He was, indeed, heading for the door. He went for the door but she ran in front of him, throwing herself in front of the panel as he grappled with the latch.

"Where are you going?" she pleaded.

His face was frightening. "Get out of my way."

"Nay!" she cried. "Andrew, *think*! You'll only hasten your own death if you confront the king and then you shall be of no help to me!"

"Remove yourself, Josephine," he growled.

She threw her arms around his neck, holding on to him like a great anchor. "Please, *nay!*" she begged, then turned her head towards the cracked door. She knew that Ola was out there, somewhere. The little maid was never far from her mistress. "Ola! Find Sully and Thane! I need them! *Run!*"

Josephine knew the woman was off and running. Now, she prayed her maid found the men in time. Andrew was far too large for her to hold off for long.

But she held on to him for dear life and he stood still for the moment with his hand on the latch. Fortunately, she was greatly diminishing his resolve with her sweet body pressed next to his because he knew her words held truth. With him dead, she would be at the mercy of the king and his brother. But in his heart of hearts, he knew that he could not allow this to take place.

He intended to make the king pay.

"Please, Andrew," she was whispering in his ear. "We have just only found each other. I cannot bear the thought of losing you, not now."

His resolve took another hit. She was begging him and he simply couldn't resist her. With a heavy sigh, a big arm came up to hold her to him, and he turned his face to her hair, smelling the faint scent of rose.

"You will not lose me," he said. "But I am The Red Fury and I will fight for what is mine. Have no fear, love; 'tis not I who shall lose this fight."

She pulled back from him, looking him in the face. "If you kill the king, you'll bring the wrath of the entire kingdom upon Torridon," she said. "We shall *all* lose in that case."

He met her eyes, digesting her words. It seemed as if an eternity passed while they stared at each other. The longer he looked at her, the more his anger cooled. She seemed to have that effect on him.

"Then I shall speak with him," he said.

She shook her head. "Nay," she said. "It would do no good. You know that. It would only anger him."

Perhaps that was true, but he couldn't stand by and do nothing. Quickly, he pulled her arms away from his neck, breaking her grip.

"I will have to take that chance," he said. "And you must let me. This cannot go unanswered, Josephine."

"Nay!" she cried, terrified. "Please, Andrew, *nay!*"

Andrew heard her but he simply couldn't comply. As he threw open the door, Sully and Thane were there, and they pushed roughly into the room. Andrew fell back as Josephine wisely jumped out of the way. Andrew didn't fight back, but merely tensed up as the two men guided him well away from the door. Josephine ran over to lock it.

"Now," Sully demanded quietly, "what goes on here?"

Josephine looked like a scared rabbit, harried and somewhat disheveled. She came away from the door, moving to Andrew as he stood back by the hearth. She put a hand on his arm as if she were afraid to let go of him.

"It is all my fault, Sully," she said, the tears threatening to return. "I must beg your forgiveness and pray that it is in your heart to forgive me."

He looked puzzled. "What are you talking about?"

"I was wrong," she said miserably. "The king never planned to marry Justine or me to Colin. I forced you to marry my sister in a fit of panic to save our miserable lives. I was foolish, Sully. Please forgive me for ruining your life."

Sully wasn't angry. He had suspected all along that it was not the king's intention to marry one of the de Carrons to their mortal enemy, but Josephine had seemed convinced of it.

"There is nothing to forgive, Joey." He smiled gently at her. "I am not sorry that I married your sister. And I know you were doing what you believed to be right."

Josephine thought he was only being gallant, compounding her misery. She closed her eyes and tears fell like raindrops. Sully felt a good deal of pity for her but he was distracted. He knew without a doubt that was not the reason Andrew had been stampeding through the doorway when he'd arrived. He finally looked to Andrew.

"Where were you going?" he asked. "Why was Josephine begging you not to go?"

Andrew looked up at him with such hatred that Sully felt a chill go down his spine. But he didn't respond; it seemed as if he was having difficulty voicing the issue. Beside him, Josephine spoke.

"I shall tell you why," she said. "Because the king has dissolved our betrothal and has pledged me to an English earl, one who is in support of the Scottish king. It is the Earl of Annan and Blackbank."

Sully didn't react at first, but Thane went mad. He cursed, yelled, and threatened until Andrew ordered him to sit and be still. He slowly complied, red-faced and pounding his fists. Once Thane was controlled, Andrew let out a heavy sigh and ran his fingers through his hair, heading to Josephine's window for a breath of air.

Sully had heard Andrew's story and knew exactly who the earl was. Clearly, it was a terrible situation for all involved and his heart ached for Josephine, being in the middle of it all. But given the circumstances, cooler heads must prevail.

"Gentlemen," Sully said quietly. "It would seem that we have a bit of a problem."

Andrew chuckled bitterly as he stared out across the countryside. He was calmer now, but not much. He couldn't remember ever having been so distressed, and his best friend, Thane, along with him. His *two* best friends, in fact. He considered Sully a friend as well. Somehow, with that company, the problem didn't seem so large. Taking a deep breath, he turned to them.

"I think the best thing that we can do is go about our business and try to think of a way to salvage the situation," he said sensibly. "But if we fail, if we can think of no way out of this, then I shall take Josephine and flee the country."

Josephine looked at him in surprise. "Flee?" she repeated. "You... you would leave everything behind?"

Andrew looked at her. "My army, aye," he said. "But it will go on. Thane will make sure of that. The most important thing is to remove you to safety where we can be married so the king can never come between us."

Josephine understood. In truth, she felt as if a great weight had been lifted. And she was deeply, deeply touched. Andrew was willing to sacrifice everything he had worked for in his life to save her. She was only beginning to realize the depths and dimensions that their love would develop.

But the men weren't so convinced. "Where will you go?" Sully asked. "Where can you go where Alexander will not send men after you?"

Before Andrew could answer, Thane found his tongue. "Now, see here," he said grimly. "You mean to say that you would give up everything you have achieved? Your reputation, the respect of your men, and the money?"

Andrew looked at Josephine. Somehow, when he looked at her, all of those things Thane listed seemed so very unimportant by comparison. "Look at her, Thane," he said. "Put yourself in my place and ask your questions again. I can no longer deny my love for this woman and I shall do all within my power to keep us together."

Thane looked at Josephine for a few moments before turning away, slowly shaking his head.

"You disagree, my friend?" Andrew asked him.

"Nay," Thane said reluctantly. "I agree with you completely, but it still troubles me. All of your plans, Andrew, what of them?"

"Nothing has changed," Andrew said evenly. "I shall still kill my brother."

"What if you were to kill him now?"

It was Sully who had spoken; an unmistakable question. Andrew turned to him.

"What do you mean?" he asked.

Sully came to him, clearly thinking through his answer "Could you make it to Haldane, kill your brother, and assume his earldom within the week?" he asked. "If you can do it, then as the rightful Earl of Annan and Blackbank, King Alexander will have to honor his pledge and Josephine will be yours."

Andrew's expression went from curiosity to surprise and back again. "What you ask," he finally said, "would be difficult at best. But not unworthy of trying."

It seemed like a possibility in a situation that seemed wholly impossible. Josephine felt some hope with it. "I can keep the king here for that long," Josephine spoke up. "I can tell him that there is to be a celebration at the end of the week in his honor, and that all of our allies will be in attendance. The man is so concerned with baron support that surely he will stay."

Andrew looked at her. "Do you truly think you can?"

Josephine nodded. "It is certainly worth a try."

They were all silent for a while, each to their own thoughts. So much had happened and so much had yet to happen. It all seemed rather daunting but one could not be fearful when a life was at stake. There was much to do now and very little time.

Finally, Andrew moved away from the window, kissing Josephine gently on the temple before quitting the chamber in silence. He was far calmer than he had been only minutes earlier so she did not stop him. Sully followed shortly, with Thane the last one to leave the chamber, but Josephine called out to him.

"Wait," she said, and he stopped.

"My lady?" he asked respectfully.

Josephine looked as if she were searching for the correct words. "Have you ever met Andrew's brother?" she finally asked.

"Aye, my lady," he replied quietly. "I saw him once, in a tavern in Haldane."

"What is he like?" she pressed. "I mean, what kind of a person is he?"

Thane looked at her warily. "Has Andrew told you anything of him?"

She nodded. "He has, but his opinion is so clouded with hate that it is difficult to picture the earl with anything less than horns and a tail," she said. "That is why I want to know what you know of him."

Thane's face hardened. "I know he is a hideous beast of a man," he said. "Alphonse is at least a half-head taller than Andrew, and outweighs him by a good fifty pounds. He is absolutely massive. And he has straight black hair that he pulls back into a greasy tail, and his eyes are as black as coal. It is said that he likes to watch small children wrestle with hungry dogs, and then he eats the winner."

Her mouth popped open in horror. "He *eats* children?"

Thane shook his head. "No," he said. "The dogs. But he is evil and vile, and is the embodiment of the devil. He'd have to be to imprison his own mother. That's why Andrew wants him dead."

Josephine was appalled by the picture Thane was painting. "How in heaven could Andrew have sprung from the same loins that gave birth to a beast?" she wondered. "Is he a great warrior? Can Andrew best him in a fight?"

Thane seemed to falter slightly. "I have heard that Alphonse is a tremendous fighter," he said. "That is why his army is so great; men are afraid to fight against him, so they fight with him. But Andrew is a master swordsman; I have never seen better. I believe he can beat anyone."

Josephine didn't find comfort in those words. They just didn't sound reassuring to her. Thane saw her face and, knowing her fears, he hastened to comfort her.

"Have no fear, my lady," he said gently. "They call Andrew The Red Fury for good reason. He could fight the devil himself and win."

Josephine looked at him, appreciating his attempt at reassuring her. She forced a smile.

"Then I shall believe you," she said. "Thank you for telling me the truth."

"It is my pleasure, my lady," he said.

Turning on his heel, he was gone. Josephine stood there a moment, her mind a jumble of emotions and thoughts. *Why was love always so difficult?* she thought bitterly. But with the bitterness was a feeling of such utter elation that she was giddy from it. One minute she wanted to laugh and dance, and the next minute she wanted to collapse in despair.

As she turned for her hearth and sat slowly in her chair, she allowed herself a moment to wallow in her feelings. Oddly, she felt very alone. She had Andrew, Sully, Justine, and a host of knights at her disposal but, still, she felt alone. She was the crux of the issue, a problem with no easy answer. She found herself wishing her father was still alive for she very much needed his counsel.

If the time since his death had taught her one thing, it was that she knew absolutely nothing.

God help her.

CHAPTER SEVENTEEN

T HANE FOUND ANDREW in the stables.

Torridon had two big banks of stalls lined up against the wall in the outer bailey, walls that had seen some damage in the most recent battle with the Dalmellington forces. The big war horses were crowding up most of the stalls, individually, because they had to be separated. Put too closely together and they would fight. Thane found Andrew in one of the stable banks, right at the mouth of it with his fat, bad-tempered destrier.

"I thought I would find you here," Thane said. "What would you have of me, my lord?"

Andrew was bent over the right front leg, running his hands along the fetlock. "What do you mean?"

"I mean to ask when you are leaving to ride to kill your brother and what you would have me do in your absence. What would you have me tell the king?"

Andrew let go of the leg and stood up, pretending to busy himself with inspecting the horse when what he was really doing was mulling over the exact plans that Thane was asking about.

"Keep your voice down," he muttered. "There are king's men all over this place. I do not wish they should hear you."

Thane understood. "Then you are riding to Haldane?"

Andrew nodded, glancing at Thane as he moved around the horse.

"As fast as I possibly can," he said. "But this horse is not known for his speed. In battle, he is immovable, but when I need speed, this is not the beast."

"We have others you can ride."

Andrew nodded. "And I shall," he said. "We have several horses corralled outside in the camp. I am thinking of riding that leggy black stallion we received in payment for the job in Bonchester Bridge. Do you remember?"

Thane nodded. "A fine animal," he said. "Very fast. But is he dependable?"

Andrew shrugged. "We shall find out," he said. Then, he stopped fussing with his horse and looked at Thane. "I intend to depart before dawn. I intend to cover at least thirty miles every day, which means I shall make it to Haldane in a little more than two days. Give me a day to kill my brother and then I shall return. Josephine, and the king, must remain at Torridon for at least that long. Joey says she can keep the man here, but I have my doubts. The man is wily. She may need your help."

Thane nodded. "I shall do what I can," he said. "But… Andrew?"

"Aye?"

"What if you do not return? What then?"

Andrew didn't want to think of that. He was The Red Fury, was he not? He was as invincible as his reputation, but he knew, deep in his heart, that barging into Haldane and killing his brother would not be a simple thing. He was well aware of the risks and even though he didn't want to admit it, or talk about it, he knew it was necessary. With a heavy sigh, he leaned against the horse.

"If I do not return in seven days, assume I will never return at all," he said quietly. "Move the army out and take them to Castle Questing. My cousin, Roan, serves William de Wolfe at Castle Questing. You remember Roan, do you not? Questing would be the best place for Josephine. The king would not dare tangle with de Wolfe or de Longley, or any of those allies. Take the army there and turn Josephine over to

Roan. For mercy's sake, Thane, do not leave her here. I am depending on you."

Thane nodded sharply. "I will defend her with my life," he said. "But even if I do give her over to Roan, de Wolfe will want to know the value of the lady. If the king and your brother come for her…"

Andrew was so very disappointed by the mere thought. William de Wolfe was a man of great power, and they were loyal friends, but Andrew understood if William didn't want to risk his family against the King of Scotland. In truth, only a fool would.

"If de Wolfe will not protect and defend her, then put d'Aurilliac in charge of the army and take Josephine to Cornwall," he said. "I have another cousin, Dennis d'Vant, who lives there. He is the commander of St. Austell Castle. Tell Dennis that Josephine is my wife and that my brother wants her. Dennis knows Alphonse; he will not let him have her, not under any circumstances."

Thane knew Roan d'Vant, but he had only heard of Andrew's cousin, Dennis. He'd never met the man. "Your father and Dennis' father were cousins, were they not?"

Andrew nodded. "Dennis' father, my father, and Roan's father all shared the same grandsire," he said. "Dennis is a good man. If I do not return… you will tell Dennis that I died protecting Josephine from my brother. He will keep her safe."

Thane nodded, but it seemed to him as if he was doing an awful lot of swearing to risk his life for a woman Andrew had only known a few days. Still, he knew what the woman meant to Andrew. As Thane had known all along, men in love were fickle and foolish creatures.

But Andrew was his liege and he loved the man like a brother. There was no sacrifice too great that he would not make to preserve Andrew or Andrew's legacy.

He only hoped it wouldn't come to that.

IT WAS LATE afternoon and Josephine and Justine were in the kitchen, overseeing preparations for the evening meal.

As the men worried over how to counteract the king's directive, Josephine found solace in a normal routine, and part of that was the coming meal. The cook was in the process of making cakes in the shape of the de Carron serpent and was entertaining herself by yelling at the kitchen servants. The hot, steamy kitchens were full of targets for her to aim for.

"Now, where is my butter?" the cook asked, fuming. "How can I make the rest of my cakes without my butter?"

Justine was tasting the tangy plum sauce for the cakes and didn't hear the woman, but Josephine did.

"I shall go to the buttery," she said.

The cook appeared appalled. "With all of these lazy young things slithering around my kitchen?" she sneered. "Nay, my lady, let me send one of them. Ye there, lad! Aye, *ye*! Get up!"

Josephine was already at the door. "Never mind," she said as the small boy struggled to his feet. "I shall return shortly."

As the cook harassed the boy for not being fast enough, Justine's attention was on her sister. Josephine had told her of the king's directive and they'd both had a good cry over it. In truth, Justine was still close to tears. But she knew that by keeping busy, it helped Josephine forget the troubles of the day. Therefore, she picked up her spoon and resumed stirring the plum sauce as the cook shifted from berating the boy to screaming at a hapless young girl.

Outside of the rather loud and hot kitchen, Josephine trudged through the dirt as she headed for the buttery. Given that it was nearing sunset, the soldiers were changing shifts on the walls and the kitchen servants were rushing about madly to prepare for the coming feast. She passed by the postern gate that led from the yard out through the ten-foot thick walls and into the fields beyond. The heavily-fortified gate was open as men brought in supplies from the fields, and she slowed her pace, glancing to the green landscape beyond.

Such beauty out there and such peace. When she'd been a child, she'd run freely beyond the walls of Torridon, but those days were long gone. There was sadness with that thought, but there was also the desire to relive those carefree days. After a moment's indecision, for she knew she was expected back, she veered from the buttery path and passed through the tunnel to gaze at the freedom beyond. She was aching for just a few brief moments to remind her that all was not troubled in the world.

There was a gentle breeze coming off the rolling hills, blowing at her netted hair until she pulled off the net and shook her head, letting her hair tumble free. The wind tugged at the skirt of her cote, outlining her shapely legs as she took the first bold steps away from Torridon.

As soon as she passed through the gate, something caught her eye. She looked in the distance and saw a redheaded figure sitting under a tree, and a tall blond man sword-playing around him. She realized it was Nicholas de Londres and Donald Muir enjoying what was left of the day. Quickly, she headed in their direction.

The men saw her approach. Nicholas had a quill, ink, and a leather-bound book in his lap, but he rose from his seated position and Donald quieted his swordplay. She smiled at them, slapping her net against her leg as she walked.

"And what might you fine men be doing outside of the safety of the fortress?" she asked.

Nicholas grinned. "It was such a fine day that I had to come up here, away from the noise and smell of the castle," he said in his sweet tenor voice.

"And I followed!" Donald said wittily, bringing his sword up. "The man needed an escort. Look at him; he's as gentle as a lamb."

Nicholas smiled in embarrassment. "Would ye sit, my lady?" he asked.

Josephine folded her legs under her and the blue silk gown bellowed elegantly as she sat on the grass. Nicholas sat next to her and Donald resumed his practicing.

"Donald," she said, as she squinted up at him. "Your stance is too closed!"

Donald scowled at her, but took her advice. Chuckling at his pride, Josephine turned to Nicholas. He was watching Donald but his gaze seemed to be distant.

"You look pensive," she observed. "What are you thinking about?"

Nicholas looked at her, smiling with some embarrassment to realize he'd been observed. "I am simply examining my surroundings, my lady," he said. "It is quite lovely here."

"My name is Josephine," she informed him. "Please call me by my name. And I agree; it is quite lovely this time of year."

Nicholas looked out over Torridon, watching the activity, but his mind was lingering on Josephine. This was the first time he'd seen her since his uncle informed her of his plans for her, and he didn't want to look at her too closely lest she see the pity in his eyes. He knew about her betrothal to the earl because his uncle, the king, had gleefully told him of it the night before. He'd known much longer than she had but he'd kept it to himself.

Having grown up at court, Nicholas we well aware of the political players and he knew Alphonse d'Vant. He was a beast of a man, cruel and barbaric, and to think of sweet Josephine married to the man gave Nicholas a sour stomach. But his uncle wanted to keep Alphonse and his three thousand man army happy, so the Ayr heiress had been a spectacular match.

At least, it was in Alexander's opinion. Nicholas hadn't cared much about it until he actually met Josephine and, now, he felt a great deal of pity for her. He knew his uncle to be a selfish, petty man, but now the man was adding cruelty to the list of his attributes. As he sat there and worried over Josephine's future, he heard her soft voice.

"Recite a piece of your poetry," she asked.

Nicholas looked at her, surprised and somewhat embarrassed, as Donald snickered loudly.

"Is that what ye were doing?" he asked. "Writing poems?"

Nicholas nodded hesitantly as Josephine scowled. "Shut your mouth, Donald," she said, then smiled at Nicholas. "Please? I should like to hear how talented you are."

Nicholas nodded, quite chagrinned, and looked thoughtful as he peered down at his leather-bound book and tried to select a piece. His poetry was very private to him, so close to his heart. His uncle was so critical of his passion that he was tremendously reluctant to unveil it to anyone, but Josephine seemed very sincere in her interest. He took a deep breath.

"I know not where my destiny lies;

Beyond the blue horizon, or beyond my door; I know not.

Yet I know whatever may come, it is within my own power

To face the throes of the future

With the graceful dignity of the willow;

To bend, yet not break;

To sway, yet not fall.

My body may wither

My eyes may blind,

And my voice may silence;

But my soul will reach beyond the mortal boundaries of this world

To touch the hand of God.

I know where my destiny lies, it lies within me."

Donald had stopped swinging his sword and was listening. Josephine looked at Nicholas, astonished at the beauty of his words. But somehow, she knew he had selected the piece of prose for her benefit, and she saw the message within it. *My destiny lies within me.* It was so very true, something Andrew had been telling her as well.

She smiled gratefully at Nicholas.

"That was lovely, Nicholas," she said. "You have a great talent."

This time, Nicholas didn't blush. He thanked her graciously. But

Donald apparently didn't like being left out; he sat down heavily on the hem of Josephine's gown and kicked out his long legs.

"Touching," he said. "Are all of yer poems as lighthearted and gay?"

Josephine shot him a withering look, but Nicholas seemed amused. "Not at all," he replied. "Some are rather gloomy."

Donald laid back on the grass and folded his arms beneath his head. "I like ye, de Londres," he announced. "Ye're not stuffy or insane like the rest of yer family. Ye have sense."

Nicholas chuckled. Donald was correct in his observation of his family. He looked back to his book to see if there might be any other passages she might like as Josephine used a long stalk of grass to tease Donald. He slapped at it like an annoying gnat and she giggled. Then she beat him on his swollen face with it, laughing. It was good to see her laugh.

"What is yer pleasure, Josephine?" Nicholas asked her. "What do ye like to do, other than annoy Donald?"

She shrugged as Donald ripped the grass out of her hand and tossed it away. "I have had little time to enjoy anything since my father was murdered," she said. "But I used to like to paint and draw."

Donald looked up at her. "I remember a skinny, serious young girl who loved to paint scenery," he said. "And as I recall, ye were very good."

She lifted her shoulders modestly. "Mayhap once, I was," she said. "But that was before I assumed the responsibilities of Torridon. I have not painted since that time."

"I would like to see yer paintings," Nicholas said. "Do ye still have them?"

Josephine nodded. "Justine moved them all into the North Tower, into one of the rooms," she said. "Every so often, she'll go visit them, but I never do. They remind me too much of my carefree childhood. Somehow it hurts to remember."

"Because ye can never return," Donald said softly, as if he, too, had experienced the same.

Nicholas watched her as she resumed poking Donald. "Nonetheless," he said. "Someday I should like to see yer work."

She thought a moment. "Then I shall show it to you before you leave."

"Show me now. What else do ye have to do?"

He had a good point. Even though Josephine was supposed to be delivering butter to the cook, she assumed the cook had already sent someone else for it when she realized her mistress was not returning. Besides, she was enjoying the company of Nicholas and Donald.

"As I said, I have not visited them in a long time," she said. "But if you wish to see them..."

"I do," Nicholas said resolutely.

Since Nicholas had revealed some of his poetry, Josephine knew it was only right that she reveal her works of art to him. She was a little apprehensive to view them, but with Donald and Nicholas as company, it wasn't as if she would be viewing her paintings alone, free to relive the carefree days that she missed so much. She would have some support in her two friends. With a nod, she clambered to her feet.

A breeze was picking up from the west as the three of them returned to Torridon just as the kitchen servants were bolting the postern gate, finished with their duties for the night. But they let her in and the three of them headed across the yard and in through the kitchen entry where the cook was still harassing the servants around her.

The bedlam had only grown worse. Children were crying and the cook was raging. Justine had vanished and the cook didn't even notice when Josephine and Donald and Nicholas passed through. She should have noticed when Donald stole a serpent-shaped oat cake, but she didn't notice that, either. Donald broke it in half and gave the other half to Nicholas as they scooted out of the kitchen before they were caught.

Josephine shook her head reproachfully at men acting like naughty boys as they wolfed down the cake. They passed through the smoky hall and into the foyer but, instead of taking the stone steps to the living levels in the west wing, she took them over to a smaller stone staircase on the east side of the foyer, a spiral staircase that led them up into a single-level series of chambers that smelled very old and damp.

This was the east wing, one used only by the servants and for storage. Josephine sneezed as they ventured further into the chambers.

"I have not been up here in years," she said, sneezing again. "I am not sure where Justine put my paintings, but she said she put them up here somewhere."

The chambers were all adjoining on this level, linked together, filled with servant's beds, trunks, and other things, old and uncared for and stashed away. Passing through a pair of chambers, they came to a corner room and, suddenly, a gala of color and images confronted them.

There were many colorful pictures lined up against the floor, painted on vellum that had been stretched onto wooden frames. They were mostly of landscapes or flowers, and red roses and fields of white heather danced from the frame. Nicholas took a knee besides a group of paintings depicting water lilies, among other things. Carefully, he picked up a picture to look at it.

"These are exquisite, Josephine," he said with some awe in his voice. "Such beautiful colors. Wherever did ye learn to paint like this?"

Josephine looked at her collected works; so many hours, so many years had gone into the paintings. In truth, it wasn't as hard to look at them as she thought it might have been. In fact, it made her long to return to the hobby she loved so well. Carefully, she sat down next to Nicholas as he inspected her paintings.

"My nurse was English," she said. "The same woman who taught me to speak as the English do. She also taught me how to paint."

Nicholas was studying a particular painting that had a red flower amidst a surreal background. "Ye have a genuine talent," he said. "It is a tragedy that ye do not continue with yer painting."

Josephine looked at the artwork in Nicholas' hand. "It was just something to become proficient at, and I did," she said. "I never saw it as my life's work. But... but I do admit that I miss it. Now that I see my paintings, I long for the feel of a brush in my hand again. There is something satisfying in creating an image from my mind's eye."

Nicholas set the painting down, carefully, and went to look at another. It was a tree against a stormy sky. "I understand," he said. "That is how I feel about my poetry. It is as if my soul is speaking. But it is something I do not tell many people of."

Josephine glanced at him, seeing some distress on his features. "Your uncle clearly disapproves," she said. "He seemed very harsh with you about it on the night you arrived. Do you recall? We were speaking on it and he told you that you should be warring instead."

Nicholas nodded. "I recall," he said. "He has never been supportive of that or anything else I do. Ye see, I am the son of his bastard brother. My grandfather, William the Lion, had several bastards, but this bastard was a favorite. His name was William de Londres. My father sent me to court at a young age, hoping to work my way into the king's favor, and it has worked for the most part. My uncle has been kind to me. But he also believes I should be a great warrior and poetry has no place in that world. Writing poetry is, mayhap, the only thing I have ever done to disappoint him."

Josephine could see how sensitive the man was; Nicholas had a gentle soul, something even Donald had commented on. Josephine well understood what it was like to be misplaced, to be uncomfortable with the tasks expected.

"Your uncle wishes for you to fight and you do not want to," she said. "With me... my brother died, and then my father, and there was no one else to take up command of Torridon but me."

Nicholas looked at her, seeing a beautiful woman in a very bad situation. "Josephine," he said, his voice low. "The man ye have been betrothed to... the Earl of Annan and Blackbank... I have met him before. He vies for my uncle's favor even though he is an English lord. I know there is nothing ye can do about the betrothal, but I must say that I fear for ye. The earl is... he is not a good man."

Josephine already knew that but she hadn't met anyone else other than Andrew and Thane who knew of the earl. She glanced at Donald, who was watching her by this time, his bruised face full of concern. Although Josephine new Donald would never tell her secrets, she didn't know Nicholas well enough to know if he wouldn't go running back to tell his uncle were she to confess to him that she had no intention of marrying the earl. After a moment, she dropped her gaze.

"You are correct," she said. "There is nothing I can do about it. Much like you, I must do as I am told."

She said it because she wanted to throw him off the track if he thought she was going to rebel. Perhaps with time, she would come to know him better, and trust him, but until that time, he had to think that she was a good little soldier. Where the king was concerned, she could be nothing less.

But Nicholas' worry was clear on his features. "It is true," he said. "I… I have not known ye very long, but I feel as if I have made a friend in ye. I do not have many friends, Josephine, and I would be deeply upset if anything happened to ye. I know ye must marry the earl, but if there was a way not to…"

He trailed off and Josephine looked up at him, curiously. "What do you mean?"

Nicholas didn't want to outright tell her to run. But he couldn't stand the thought of her at the mercy of such a beast. "What I mean to say is…"

Donald cut him off. "What he means to say is that ye should run," he said. "He is right, Joey. Run with me; I will take ye away from here and the king will never know what happened to ye. Nicholas will not tell him; will ye, de Londres?"

Nicholas shook his head firmly. "Of course not," he said. "I would take ye away if I could. Ye should run; run as far away as ye can."

Josephine looked between the pair. "And what would happen to those I left behind?" she asked. "What of my sister and Sully? What of them?"

Donald was feeling rather passionate about the subject. "They would not be responsible for it," he said. "Sully is the earl now. Ye gave over yer entire inheritance to him and to yer sister. He has the de Carron wealth now and the king needs that for his support against the barons who are rebelling against him. He would not punish Sully when he needs the man and his army."

Josephine snorted, an ironic gesture. "What army?" she asked. "We barely have anyone left."

"What about The Red Fury?" Nicholas asked. "Ye're betrothed to the man; everyone knows that. Why can he not take ye away?"

He is going to! Josephine thought, but she kept it to herself. She simply couldn't jeopardize herself or Andrew in such a fashion.

"I am not certain what Andrew intends to do," she lied. "He told me he would think of something, but I do not know what he has decided upon. Please... mention none of this to the king. For now, his focus is not on Andrew and I wish it to remain that way."

Nicholas nodded solemnly, as did Donald. Neither one of them liked the future they saw ahead for Josephine, a truly kind and accomplished woman. Nicholas, in particular, thought it was sickening.

"If he needs assistance," he ventured. "If The Red Fury needs help to take ye from here, please tell me. I should like to help if I could."

Josephine could sense that he was sincere. Impulsively, she put a hand on his arm. "I could not jeopardize you so, Nicholas," she said. "Although you are most kind to offer, you must not involve yourself. It would only lead to your doom."

Nicholas smiled sadly but he understood. He appreciated that she was trying to protect him, but he truly felt as if he wanted to help her.

"At least I would be doing something well and good," he said. "My life is fairly useless as it is. I am subject to my uncle's whims, his travels, his moods. I have nothing important that I accomplish. I would like to do something good for someone."

Josephine believed him. She squeezed his arm one last time before letting go. "And I appreciate your offer, truly," she said. She thought it best to change the subject considering there wasn't much more to say on the existing one. "The evening meal will be served soon. I must go and dress, but I will meet you both in the hall. Nicholas, I would expect you to recite your poetry for me whilst I eat. Will you do that?"

Nicholas grinned. "As long as my uncle does not hear me. He says it ruins his appetite."

Josephine smiled because he was, but she thought that was a rather cruel statement about his uncle. Nicholas then stood up quickly and between him and Donald, they pulled Josephine to her feet. They proceeded to follow her out of the labyrinth of rooms and back to the small, darkened stairwell that led back to the foyer of the keep. Once there, they headed out of the building while Josephine headed to the western wing and to her chamber.

But the truth was that she had no plans to attend the meal that evening.

In fact, she planned to lock herself in her chamber and only open the door to her sister or Andrew. She didn't want to be around the king in any fashion or discuss the terrible plans he had for her. He was expecting gratitude; she would only give him displeasure. It was better that she not put herself in that situation. Gathering her skirts and taking the first step, she heard someone call her name and turned to see Andrew entering the keep. She came to a halt.

"Greetings, my lord," she said softly, affectionately. Considering the serious nature of the last conversation they had, she was hoping for a better mood between them now. "I was going up to my chamber in an attempt to avoid joining the king for the evening meal."

Andrew smiled as he reached out and took her hand, bringing it to his lips for a gentle kiss. "Wise, my lady," he said. "May I join you?"

"I was hoping you would."

He made a sweeping gesture up the stairs, inviting her to continue onward, as he followed. He held her hand as they mounted the steps, her soft fingers in his rough ones.

"I have not seen you all afternoon," Josephine said as they reached the top. "What have you been doing?"

"Visiting my horses," he said casually.

They reached her chamber door and Josephine opened it. "I see," she said, stepping into the chamber where Ola was over by the hearth, stoking the flames for the evening. "I have been with Donald and Nicholas, the king's nephew. He's a very nice young man, if you've not formally met him yet. But I do feel sorry for him."

Andrew wasn't so sure he liked her keeping company with two young bachelors. "Why is that?" he asked, a hint of disapproval in his voice.

But Josephine didn't catch the tone. She went about lighting a bank of tapers for more light in the room.

"Because he writes beautiful poetry, yet the king disapproves," she said. "He read me one of his poems. It was lovely."

Now, Andrew was increasingly certain he didn't want her keeping company with a young man who read her poetry. "You will stay away from him," he said frankly. "No man will speak sweet words to you other than me, so I will not hear of you and Nicholas de Londres being companionable."

Josephine looked at him in surprise, unhappy with his directive until she realized he'd said it because he was jealous. She could just tell by the look on his face, and she fought off a grin.

"I am not interested in him, Andrew," she assured him. "You need not worry."

He frowned as he found a half-filled pitcher of watered wine near the window and poured himself a cup. He simply made a face, emitting a rude noise from his lips.

"If I hear you have been listening to more poetry, I will have words with young Nicholas and he will not like what I have to say," he said. "Spare him my wrath. Stay away from him."

Josephine was starting to giggle. "You are jealous."

Andrew scowled. "Nonsense. I simply protect what is mine."

"If that is not jealousy, what is?"

He was grossly unhappy with the fact that she was correct in her observations and he was too stubborn to admit it. "Quiet your lips, woman," he said. "Come over here and sit down. Let us speak on something more pleasant than Nicholas de Londres."

Trying desperately to stop chuckling at him, Josephine sent Ola for food before complying with his command. But she didn't move very quickly, letting him know what she thought of his attempts to order her about.

"You should understand one thing, Andrew," she said frankly. "At Torridon, I am the one who gives the orders. There is no one who gives *me* orders."

He cocked an eyebrow at her. "That is about to change," he said. "The mere fact that we are betrothed means that I am in command. You shall do what I say."

She pursed her lips at him, irritated. "Or *what?*"

"Would you really care to find out?"

Josephine couldn't tell if he was bluffing or not. She was certain he wouldn't truly harm her, but a spanking might be in order. To be safe, she stayed out of arm's length. "I have commanded an army quite ably for the past two years," she said. "Do not think that you can sweep in and start ordering me about. We will be equal partners in our marriage and we will discuss all situations first. There will be no ordering about, from either of us."

He looked at her as if she'd gone daft. "A partnership?" he said. "Where do you get these odd ideas? There is no partnership in a marriage. The man gives the orders and the woman complies."

Josephine grew serious. "Then you do not respect my mind or my thoughts?"

Andrew had been teasing her for the most part – he did mean what he said but he didn't want it to sound cruel or demanding about it, so he was trying to jest his way through the subject to see how she'd respond. Clearly, she didn't think any of it was funny. But she had to understand that he wasn't going to go through the rest of his life clearing every order with her.

"Of course I respect your mind and your thoughts," he said. "You are very intelligent as far as women go. I have never seen brighter. But to deny my wishes and my commands shows a complete lack of respect to me. Did you not think of that?"

She sobered dramatically. "I would never show you disrespect."

"By arguing with my orders, you are showing everyone that you do not respect me," he said. "If my men see that my wife will not respect my wishes, it will give them second thoughts about obeying me as well. It could throw my entire command into question."

Josephine hadn't thought of it that way. "I would only let your men see my great respect and admiration for you, Andrew."

"Then that means obeying me, at all times, without question."

Josephine wasn't so sure she liked any of that, but she saw his point. "Well," she said reluctantly. "When we are in private, may I at least question you?"

He nodded, feeling some relief that he was gaining headway with her. "Of course you may," he said. "And there may be times when I seek your counsel. But I must know I have your obedience, love. That is very important, in all things."

She nodded, but it was with reservation. "You shall have it."

Andrew smiled at her, reaching out to pull her near the fire. When he sat down in a big oak chair, he drew her onto his lap, feeling the warmth of her soft body against him. It was incredibly arousing, and his thoughts shifted from her obeying his orders to the situation at hand. Things were coming that she had to be aware of.

"Now," he said, trying to ignore the heat blooming in his loins. "There are things we must speak of. The situation is going to change quite rapidly around here very soon."

Josephine wrapped her arms around his shoulders, her fingers tickling the back of his neck. She sensed his change in mood.

"When are you leaving to confront your brother?" she asked.

He shook his head. "Not merely confront, love," he said. "*Kill.* I am going to kill my brother."

"When?"

"Tomorrow," he said softly, reaching up to push a stray piece of hair out of her eyes. "I shall leave before dawn and it will take me a little more than two days to reach Haldane Castle. I will tell you what I have told Thane. If I have not returned in seven days, assume I am not coming at all. Thane has instructions to take you to my cousin, Roan, at Castle Questing, home of William de Wolfe. Roan serves de Wolfe and he will protect you, but much depends on de Wolfe. If the man does not want you there because of the trouble you will undoubtedly bring with you, then Thane has orders to take you south to Cornwall and give you over to another cousin of mine, Dennis. Dennis commands a very big castle and he will ensure you are protected. He will not fear the King of Scotland or my foolish brother."

Listening to Andrew speak of contingency plans made Josephine realize just what an undesirable commodity she would become should Andrew perish in his quest to save her from his brother.

"I do not want to put so many people in danger," she said quietly. "I could just as easily flee to France and lose myself there. Andrew, truly, I do not wish to put your entire family at risk from the wrath of the king."

Andrew looked at her, seeing that she was earnest about it. She was so terribly brave, this woman, something he admired so much. But there was such a large part of him that didn't want her to be brave. She shouldn't have to be brave. He should simply be able to protect her, always, so that she never had to worry about it.

But the truth was that there was a very real chance that he might not return for her. The thought of Josephine running from the king and from his brother for the rest of her life made him feel sick inside. God, he didn't want her to have to worry about it. He just wanted to marry her and get on with their lives.

"What the king is doing is wrong, Joey," he said. "Even if I did not love you, I would still figure out a way to help you. The king betrothed you to my brother, with the full knowledge that you and I were betrothed, so he is the one in the wrong. We are fighting for what is right and true and good. You must believe that. And when you are fighting for what is right, risk is not a consideration."

He made it sound so very noble. Josephine put a soft hand against his cheek, watching him kiss her palm.

"Had you not come to Torridon, I would still have been pledged to your brother with no one to warn me what a horrible man he is," she said. "Your arrival was divine intervention, I think. God knew what was about to happen. He knew I would need you."

He smiled faintly. "And if the king did not arrive but I had still come, would you still think it divine intervention?"

She grinned. "There would have been no need for Sully to marry my sister, nor me to marry you," she said. "I suppose we would still be trading insults and arguing about who would lead Torridon's defenses."

He shook his head firmly. "We would not have been arguing," he said. "I would have had command and control, in all things."

Her eyebrows lifted. "Is that so?"

"It is."

Now, she scowled. "You are an arrogant man, Andrew d'Vant. You assume too much."

He eyed her. "Not nearly as much as you do."

Josephine couldn't tell if he was serious or not, but the glimmer in his eyes caught her attention and she realized that he was toying with her. With a frustrated sigh, she turned to climb off his lap but he grabbed her, pulling her close against his chest. Before Josephine could utter a word of protect, his lips slanted over hers, hungrily.

Andrew intended to shut her up, and he did. Josephine was caught off guard by the kiss but, very quickly, she responded. Her arms went back around his neck and she held tight as the man kissed her furiously, with passion and hunger that made Josephine's heart race. When he began to caress her through her clothing, first her back and then her arms, she was hoping he might do something more, although she wasn't exactly sure what more. He seemed to be rather tame about his kisses, especially when she'd heard the maids talk about how aggressive the soldiers could be. They touched women's breasts and even put their mouths on them. She wondered if Andrew was going to be as bold as all that.

She soon found out.

As Andrew suckled her lips, his hands moved for her breasts. He was rather subtle about it at first, coming up from her torso, pretending to be stroking her ribs when his hands brushed up over her breasts. Josephine trembled but she didn't stop him, so he became bolder and put a big hand over her right breast, squeezing gently. She rather liked the feel of it; he could tell when she arched her back, pressing her breast into his hand. When he began to play with a nipple through the fabric, the woman reacted like a wanton and groaned. Her breathing began to come in pants.

Andrew took that as an invitation to disrobe her. She wasn't stopping him and he didn't want to be stopped. He'd bedded many women, too many to count, and they were all simply a means to an end – the end being his pleasure. He couldn't even recall one woman that had been remotely special to him because he simply didn't have that mindset. He'd never been looking for anyone special.

But now, he had a special woman in his arms and she consumed him like nothing else. The stays on her surcote were ties, and he managed to untie most of them, yanking the cote right over her head. The shift came next, very swiftly. Josephine gasped as he bared her naked skin to the warm, dark chamber.

Quickly, she was up in his arms, and he swept her over to the bed, laying her gently upon the mattress. Josephine was a little startled by it all, perhaps even apprehensive, but not enough to tell him to stop. She didn't *want* him to stop. In fact, when he suddenly turned and headed for the door, she was very disappointed. She thought he was going to leave. But she saw him throw the bolt on the door, ensuring their privacy, and her excitement knew no bounds. She knew that her maidenhead, the thing most of value to a woman, was about to be given over to the man she loved.

The man she would marry.

As Andrew made his way back over to her, pieces of his clothing were coming off – his tunic, under tunic, boots, and finally his breeches. He'd nearly tripped trying to pull his boots off, flinging them aside as they hit the wall of the chamber. Next, Josephine realized, he was throwing himself on the bed and pulling the coverlet over them both.

Josephine wrapped her arms around him as he fell atop her, his mouth hungrily finding hers. His hands, big and warm, were all over her flesh, touching her, caressing her, as he wedged his large body in between her legs.

She was simply moving on instinct, obeying the man's silent commands as he settled himself atop her. His mouth left hers and moved down her jaw to her neck, nibbling on her shoulders, his hand fondling her warm breast.

"I love you, Joey," he murmured, his mouth against her flesh. "Until the end of time, I will love you and only you. You belong to me."

Josephine gasped as he suckled a nipple. "I belong to you," she whispered. "All of me, forever."

Andrew's hand moved to her pelvis, touching her where only Josephine had ever touched herself. She was uncertain with it at first but, quickly, she grew to like it. He was so very gentle with her, acquainting her with his touch. Everything he was doing to her was marvelous and delicious, like nothing she could have imagined. Gone were the thoughts of gossiping maids and clumsy soldiers; what Andrew was doing was soft and beautiful. When he finally lifted himself up and she could feel his erection pushing at her threshold, she didn't even flinch. She welcomed it. She wanted it.

She wanted *him*.

Coiling his buttocks, Andrew thrust into Josephine's quivering body, listening to her gasp as he breached her maidenhead. But he didn't give her time to dwell on the shock or the pain of it before he was thrusting into her deeply, with full and measured strokes. He wanted her to know the pleasure, not the pain. Never in his life had he known such satisfaction. This was more than a primal mating act; this was his demonstration of his feelings for Josephine, of the love and admiration and respect he had for a woman who had very quickly consumed his being. It was more than taking what was his.

It was a melding of souls.

Beneath him, Josephine gasped with each thrust, but it was a pleasurable gasp now. He could tell by the way she was writhing beneath him. She was even starting to respond to him, to move her hips against his, and it was all Andrew could to do keep from releasing himself inside her. He wanted the experience to last, something for him to remember during the time of separation that was soon to come, but the way she was moving underneath him was bringing him to a climax whether or not he wanted it to.

Knowing his release was imminent, he put his hand down where their bodies were joined, expertly manipulating her. Very quickly, Josephine experienced her first release and Andrew joined her, filling her with his seed and, for the first time in his life, thinking on the strong sons she would bear him. Magnificent sons. Lads with his strength and her sensibilities. Surely no greater sons in all the land.

Bodies cooled and breathing slowed as he lay on top of her, he felt her heartbeat against his chest. He gathered her up so tightly in his arms that he was certain he was crushing her, but she didn't complain. She held on to him tightly as well, her face pressed against his shoulder. He could feel her hot breath against his skin, eventually slowing and becoming more even.

Andrew didn't even want to speak; he didn't want any words to spoil the beauty of the moment that needed no words. He just lay there and held Josephine, feeling her steady breathing against him. When he finally thought he should say something, at least ask her if she enjoyed it, the woman in his arms suddenly let out an old-man snore. Deep and loud, she was passed out cold in his arms.

Andrew had never tried so hard to keep his laughter quiet in all his life.

CHAPTER EIGHTEEN

T HE BIRDS WERE loud this morning.

At least, that was Josephine's first thought as she gradually emerged from sleep, hearing the birds outside her window, smelling the smoke in the chamber as the fire burned low. Those two events always told her it was dawn, even before she opened her eyes. Birds and the smell of smoke. Yawning, she opened her eyes.

The room was dark for the most part, with hints of sunrise coming in through her oilcloth-covered windows. It turned the room shades of gray. She lay there a moment, listening to the sounds around her and feeling more contented than she had ever felt in her life. Thoughts of Andrew immediately popped into her head and she turned her head to see if he was still in bed beside her. She knew he had been in bed with her most of the night because she'd awoken, twice, to find his arms wrapped around her and the man's soft snoring in her ear.

But he wasn't in bed with her as dawn broke, which was probably wise. It wouldn't be proper and surely he wished to preserve her dignity, even if they were betrothed. But they certainly weren't married yet and servants tended to talk, even servants that had served the family for a very long time. Ola wouldn't talk but when she went to the kitchen to bring food for two, people would wonder why.

Therefore, Josephine wasn't particularly disappointed to realize he'd left. It made her want to rise quickly, dress, and go find him.

Tossing back the covers, she called for her little maid.

Ola quickly emerged from the alcove she slept in. Josephine wondered if the woman had seen her mistress with a man in her bed. She knew that Andrew had bolted the door the night before, but he'd had to open it to leave. Perhaps that's when Ola had slipped in, but Josephine didn't ask. She and Ola had been together a long time and she wasn't quite sure how to bring it up. Did she ask the woman if she saw Andrew in her bed? Or should she simply let Ola mention it? It made for some awkward moments as Josephine got out of bed, naked, and quickly hunted down her robe.

But if Ola had seen Andrew in her mistress' bed, she didn't give any indication. She went immediately to stoke the fire and put on water to warm for her mistress' toilette. Meanwhile, Josephine went to the massive wardrobe that contained her clothing and started to sift through the surcotes hanging on pegs, looking for something pleasing to wear.

Today was a special day.

It was the first day that she truly felt like a woman, loved and possessed by a man in the most intimate way possible. When she smelled her hands, she could still smell him on her flesh and it made her heart flutter. It was a pity to wash off that smell. She could have inhaled it all day.

She located a cote of brown wool, light of weight, with a fashionable shift that went underneath it. It was very pretty with a braided belt that went with it. But she couldn't dress until Ola brought her the warmed rose water, so she walked over to the window, pulling back the oiled cloth to see daybreak over the vibrant green countryside. A new day was upon them. At least, that was what she expected to see.

But that's not what caught her eye.

An army was out there in the distance. She could see them, lined up in the distant fields like a rows of ants. Tiny, dark specs. Panic filled her. She wondered if anyone else saw the army because, down below, her men didn't seem to be manning their posts and there weren't any archers on the walls. Josephine thought that perhaps they didn't have the view she had, since her chamber was higher than the walls. It was, therefore, her duty to tell them.

"Damnation!" she spat.

Thoughts of dressing in the lovely brown cote were pushed aside as she ran for the attire she usually wore to battle. Leather breeches went on, as did a heavily-padded tunic that hung to her knees. There didn't seem to be time to dress in her full protection, as she usually did, but her mail coat was on a frame by the wardrobe and between her and Ola, they managed to get it on fairly quickly. Her heavy boots went on her feet and as Ola was fastening the ties on the boots, Josephine pulled a black and white de Carron tunic over her head, the same black and white tunic that all of her men wore.

The smell of battle was in the air.

Collecting her sword, she was heading out of the door with Ola following, trying to braid her mistress' hair and tie it off with a leather strip so it wouldn't be in her way. But Josephine had no time for hair dressing; she had to get down to her men, who clearly didn't see they were about to be set upon.

Taking the steps to the foyer far too quickly, she nearly tripped as she hit the bottom of the stairs. There was so much fear in her heart that it was difficult to breathe. Bursting through the entry door and out into the inner ward, the first person she saw was Etienne. She called to the man.

"Etienne!" she shouted. "There is an army on the horizon! Prepare the men!"

Etienne came to a sudden halt when he heard her, turning to her just as she ran upon him. "We know there is an army, my lady," he said calmly. "The sentries spied it before dawn."

Josephine was puzzled by his response. "You *know*?" she said. "We must shore up the gates! The men must be positioned on the walls and…"

Etienne cut her off, but not unkindly. He had a rather unhappy look to his eye. "The king has instructed that we not prepare our defenses, my lady," he said. "He is at the gatehouse with Sir Sully. They are currently in discussion about the situation."

When Josephine realized the king had ordered Torridon to stand down, her eyes widened. "Is he mad?" she hissed. "It is the Dalmellington army. They will slaughter us if they make it into the castle!"

Etienne sighed heavily. "I know, my lady," he said, lowering his voice. "Sully has sent me to secure the keep and the inner bailey, and that is what I intend to do. If the king wishes to leave the outer bailey exposed, then that is his pleasure. But we will protect the keep at all costs."

Josephine was pleased to hear that Sully had ordered caution in spite of the king's directive, but she was still furious. Furious *and* frightened. The king had no idea what the Dalmellingtons could do and she intended to tell him that.

"The king is at the gatehouse, you say?" she asked.

Etienne nodded. "Aye, my lady."

"Is Andrew with them?"

"Aye, my lady. They are all there."

"Then that is where I am going also," she said, pushing past the French knight. "The king is going to hear of his foolishness from my own lips."

Josephine didn't see Etienne's grin as she rushed from the inner bailey and into the partially repaired outer bailey beyond. She rushed to find Andrew and Sully, her heart pounding in her chest. Surely the king could not be serious? Not defend Torridon in the wake of a Dalmellington approach? King or no, she would fight Dalmellington with her last breath, as she knew Sully and Andrew would, as well.

She found the men standing in a group immediately outside of the gatehouse. They were all there; Andrew, Thane, Sully, Donald and Nicholas, and finally the king were surrounded by several of the king's men and several Torridon soldiers. They were all huddled together in conference.

Josephine almost felt as if she were intruding, but she squared her shoulders and charged forward, deciding to pretend as if she had never had the conversation with Etienne.

"What goes on?" she demanded sharply. "Why have you not set up defenses?"

All eyes were on her, the littlest soldier. Andrew and Sully looked angry and distressed, and she could see simply by their expressions that Etienne's words were true. The king, eyeing her, stepped forward.

"Why are you dressed like that?" he demanded.

Her chin shot up proudly. "As the eldest child of Hugh de Carron, I command the defenses of Torridon."

The king chewed his lip thoughtfully. "I seem to remember hearing rumors to that effect," he said. "But I did not believe them because they were so utterly ridiculous. Yet, I see they must be true."

His cruelty cut at her, but she didn't flinch. "My men are loyal to the core, my lord," she said evenly. "They follow me without question."

"As you follow me," the king said flatly. "And I order you to retire to the fortress where you belong. Let soldiers with ballocks decide a course of action."

He could not have done more damage if he had struck her. Josephine's first reaction was to verbally destroy him, but she bit her tongue. He was her king but she was beginning to hate him more by the minute. She felt humiliated and hurt, and it took all the willpower she could muster to turn and walk away.

What she didn't see was Sully putting a restraining arm on Andrew as the king made his crude remark. And she didn't see his eyes follow her as she walked away. Andrew's heart ached for the abuse her pride had taken, but she was handling it much better than he was.

Andrew then focused his attention back on the idiot Scot king. The man was a fool and he despised the foolish monarch. But Andrew was in his country and the man was the ruler, so he was bound to obey him.

Oblivious to the hatred he was creating in the men around him, the king turned to Sully. "Send out a greeting party to escort Colin

Dalmellington to Torridon," he said. "It would be a show of good faith, Montgomery. You will do this."

Sully's jaw fell open. "A greeting party?" he stammered. "But, sire, that man out there is our enemy! Surely you cannot…"

The king shut him up with a scalding look. "Surely you can obey a simple order from your king," he shot back. "Now, select some men and go. Fly my colors so he will know who solicits him."

Sully hesitated a split second before placing Thane in charge of a "greeting party". It was better to send the mercenaries than any of Torridon's men.

The hate ran too deep and the "greeting party" might turn into a "murder party".

JOSEPHINE DIDN'T GO back to the keep as she was told. She was up on the battlements of the outer wall, watching as the small group of soldiers charged off towards the oncoming army. She guessed it to be a scout party of some sort, most likely with a message from the king.

The man's words had hurt her, but she shook them off. She couldn't linger on a fool's words, but she also made sure to stay out of his sight. As the entire castle watched the men ride off towards the incoming army, Josephine saw Sully turn to Andrew and say something to him. Andrew leaned in slightly, listening, then turned swiftly and lost himself in his men. Sully looked up and saw Josephine on the wall. She saw him smile, perhaps pleased that she hadn't gone into the keep, after all. The woman wasn't about to let the king order her down in her own castle.

Sully motioned to her and she knew the signal well: mobilize. She turned and charged down the catwalk, yelling orders to the archers and the men-at-arms stationed along the wall. Her damaged pride was recuperating swiftly now that she was commanding once again. She needed to feel useful in her own fortress.

Far below her, she could see the mercenary army moving into ranks. The huge main gates were being shut, with the new timber creaking and popping as it moved into place. She could smell the tension in the air as the men found their places as they began to wait expectantly. She stood with them, watching the distance.

It was difficult to see what was transpiring nearly a quarter-mile away as the sun rose. She could see that the oncoming army had halted temporarily, and she could see the Torridon party speaking with the Dalmellington party. Time stood still as everyone waited with bated breath. Secretly, she found herself wishing that Colin would spit on the king's flag and charge forward. She was exceptionally confident with Andrew's army forming a tangible barrier between Dalmellington's army and Torridon.

But another part of her, the female emotional part, hoped that the army would turn and leave. She didn't want to risk further damaging Torridon and she suddenly hated the idea of Andrew on the front lines. She knew all too well she was paying him for such a service, but she was now reluctant to have him in harm's way.

Crazy woman, she scolded herself. He's survived this long doing far worse than she could ever imagine. Fighting Colin would probably be nothing short of practice to him.

But then, she saw movement on the horizon. The party that had ridden out to the Dalmellington army had now returned with several Dalmellington soldiers. As they drew closer, she could see helmless Colin Dalmellington, with his brownish hair askew. He bounced atop his black destrier as the group galloped across the moor towards the rise of Torridon.

Hatred flooded her at the sight of his ugly, bearded face. She was so angry that her hands began to shake, so she left her place on the wall. The man was coming to Torridon's gates? Over her dead body. Rushing down the ladders, she raced across the outer bailey and screamed at the guards to unbolt the gates. She was in a rage, the likes of which the men-at-arms had never seen before, and they knew why.

The Dalmellington was on their doorstep and the king refused to take it seriously.

Josephine slipped out as the gate cracked open, just in time to see the riding party reach the road and canter the remaining way. The king, Sully, and Andrew stood in an expectant group as the riders approached, having no idea a storm by the name of Josephine was blowing in behind them.

There was about to be a terrible tempest.

No one saw anything until it was too late. Suddenly, Josephine was in the middle of the road, standing between the king and the riders, and blocking their way.

"Come no further, Dalmellington bastard!" she bellowed, "or this dirt will run red with the blood from your punctured heart!"

The horses stopped, dancing and snorting. Colin rode next to Thane and peered down his nose at Josephine, his hatred of her just as evident as hers was of him. His plain features twisted into a scowl.

"I intend to go no farther, little man," he snarled. "Torridon stench is not something I wish to have on me, lest my men mistake me for you and kill me before I have a chance to bathe. I am only here by request of the king."

"Then hear him and get off of my land," she growled, fingering her sword.

Colin dismounted. Andrew had been as tight as a string throughout the venom-laced exchange but, now, he was ready to spring if the man so much as made a move towards Josephine. This time, Sully made no move to restrain him and, in fact, looked more tense than Andrew did.

Josephine stood stock still as Colin came to within a few feet of her, her eyes spitting hatred at him. Colin removed a gauntlet to scratch his head, taking a moment to look her over.

"I had heard rumor that you were a great beauty," he said, calmer now. "Your face is pretty enough, but you look like a man dressed in mail. No way to attract a husband, Josephine."

She sneered at him. "Do give me advice, Colin," she said. "This coming from a forty-year-old man who has yet to be married. I would imagine it is hard to attract decent women when your balls outweigh your brain."

"What do you know of balls?" he threw back at her. "Unless you have been doing more than just fighting with the men, Josephine. Shame, shame."

His men roared with laughter while Torridon's men seemed to get redder in the face with each passing second. Andrew was actually sweating, he was so angry. But it was Sully who decided that Colin was not free to insult his sister-in-law thusly. He opened his mouth to retort, but Josephine beat him to it.

"I hear the same is true of you as well, Colin," she said coolly.

Huge grins spread across the faces of Andrew and Sully, and it was now their turn to laugh. Colin, however, flared. His mouth worked as his eyes widened in outrage.

"You little bitch!" he hissed.

As Josephine smiled triumphantly, King Alexander stepped forward, with his hands raised.

"This is what I like to see," he said. "Good-natured camaraderie. Colin, you did not really come here to fight Josephine again, did you?"

Colin bowed deeply. "'Tis a great honor to see you, my lord," he said, then eyed Josephine. "And as you well know, Torridon should rightfully be under Dalmellington control. As Hugh de Carron's cousin, I..."

The king cut him off, with flaring nostrils. Apparently, he wasn't fond of Colin, either. "I am a closer relative than you are, Colin," he said. "If Torridon is to be under anyone's control, it should be mine. When you came to Edinburgh to petition me for control of Torridon, I thought I told you then that Torridon rightfully belonged to Josephine de Carron. I told you to leave her alone."

Colin's face was stony. "And I believe, my lord, that I pointed out that Torridon required a male to hold down such a massive structure and to control the villeins.

The king's eyes narrowed. "So you took it upon yourself to prove your point," he said icily. "And disprove mine?"

"Not at all, my lord," Colin said vehemently. "It is simply that…"

"Shut your mouth, Colin," the king said, cutting him off. "I have had enough of your lies. Now, be clear on my order – leave Torridon and the House of de Carron alone. This is not your castle. Leave it alone or face my wrath. Do you understand?"

Colin stared blankly at him for a moment. It was clear that he didn't like to be given such an order and his cheeks reddened in embarrassment, in anger. "Of course, my lord," he said after a moment. "As you wish."

Josephine watched him and knew instinctively that he was lying. Once the king was gone, he would be back to his old tricks. But she couldn't miss out on the opportunity to jab at him.

"Colin, if you are simply concerned because Torridon lacks a male, then take heart," she said. "I am no longer Mistress of Torridon. Sully Montgomery has married my sister and I gave them the castle as a wedding gift."

"Montgomery?" Colin said, outraged, as he looked at Sully. "That sow's belly? He is incapable of commanding a fortress such as this."

Sully smiled at him, but it was a warning gesture. "Better a sow's belly than its arse," he said. "And I am glad to hear that you will no longer be wreaking havoc on my fortress, Colin. Mayhap, we shall even be allies again, someday."

Colin was being goaded far beyond his reason. "I destroyed all clan ties long ago."

"That is your misfortune," Sully replied. "But the House of de Carron is strong without you. You would do well to keep your distance."

Colin's eyes narrowed. "You forget I was once a part of this house," he said. "The de Carrons were the most powerful members and look at you now – hiring a mercenary army to keep my soldiers at bay. And as for the rest of those houses who are part of the clan, I consider them weak children. They run from their own shadow."

"I am sure that my father will be pleased to know yer opinion," Donald Muir spoke from behind Sully and Andrew He'd been standing back in the shadows, watching the happenings so he could report back to his father. "As I am sure the Kennedy, Dunbar, and Fergusson will be equally as glad."

The king looked at Colin. "You provoke a mighty wrath by insulting those clans," he said. "The Kennedy alone number in the thousands."

"Then why have they not assisted the mighty de Carrons?" Colin demanded mockingly.

"Because I have not asked," Josephine said frankly. "And because they did not consider you an enemy, rather preferring to remain neutral."

"But that will change," Donald informed him. "They will not be amused with yer words because I will surely tell them."

Colin glared at everyone menacingly. He had expected Josephine to beg him for a truce but, instead, he was insulted and threatened. And the king, that horse's arse, was not supporting him in the least. After all, Colin had sworn loyalty to the throne – should he not expect the same?

As he looked at the gloating Torridon knights and the king's smirking face, Colin Dalmellington soared over the edge into complete madness. He decided then that he no longer supported the king, and that he no longer wanted Torridon for himself. He wanted it, and the de Carrons, obliterated.

Without another word, he mounted his black destrier and savagely yanked the horse's reins. The king, noting the disrespect, stepped forward.

"You have not been dismissed," he pointed out.

Colin looked down at the man he once served. "I did not ask to be," he said, then looked over at Josephine. "Lady Josephine, I shall now destroy your castle and take you as my whore. Prepare yourself for your destiny."

Andrew's tall, muscular form separated itself from the group. He looked at Colin with an expression akin to pity.

"Then you prepare to meet yours," he said in a voice that made Josephine's hair stand on end.

"Who in the hell are you?" Colin snapped.

"My name is Andrew d'Vant," he said. "But I am sure that it will mean nothing to you. Mayhap The Red Fury will."

Colin's surprise registered instantly on his face. "The Red Fury?" he repeated. "So it *is* you. My spies had told me that you had arrived, but I did not believe them."

Andrew's jaw muscles were flexing as he fought for self-control. "Then that is your misfortune," he said. "It will be a pleasure killing you, Dalmellington. No one speaks to Lady Josephine in the manner you have used."

Colin wasn't too bright; he didn't know when to stop. "Fierce loyalty from the hired dog," he quipped. "Mayhap Lady Josephine is paying you with something other than money?"

Josephine expected Andrew to explode. Instead, he dropped his head and laughed softly. "I will kill you for nothing, Dalmellington."

Colin brutally reined his horse and galloped furiously in the opposite direction. The king watched him go indifferently.

"Idiot," he remarked.

As the king and his men contemplated the warlord that was Colin Dalmellington, Andrew spun around, looking to Sully.

"And so it comes," he said quietly. Then, he turned to look at his men, back behind him and Sully and the king. "Thane! Divide the force and put half into the outer bailey. Put your archers with Torridon archers and line the entire perimeter of the wall."

Thane was in motion, as was Sully. They knew what needed to be done and there was little time to accomplish it. Only Josephine remained stationary as she watched Andrew. He went to her.

"I want you to go inside," he requested gently.

"Nay," she said. "I am not questioning your command, my lord, but I have fought in every Dalmellington battle since my father died. It is my right and I will not stop now."

She wasn't being belligerent, merely honest. He respected that. Furthermore, he knew that arguing with her would not solve anything. She was determined.

"Very well," he said with great reluctance. "But you stay with either Sully or me. Understood?"

Josephine nodded, pleased he hadn't fought her on it. With a wink, Andrew took her hand and led her back into the fortress, never imagining that he'd be fighting a battle side by side with the woman he loved.

It was a strange situation, indeed.

CHAPTER NINETEEN

ALEXANDER WAS NOT going to stay at a fortress under siege.

He entered the castle bellowing orders faster than his stewards could move. All of the wagons would have to be left behind for now. He and his entourage would have to travel quickly and on horseback, and leave within the next few minutes if they were to make it out in time.

But there was one particular man in his entourage that he wanted a moment of privacy with. His bodyguard, Ridge de Reyne, was at his side. A mountain of a man with black hair and dark eyes, Ridge was the king's shadow. He was seen but rarely heard, a defender of the most elite class.

Ridge de Reyne was a man to be feared.

He was also English, gifted to Alexander by none other than the king of England, Henry, as part of a peace overture between the two countries. Alexander had been suspicious of Ridge at first, but the man had proven himself time and time again. He could not do without him.

"Lady Josephine will depart with us," the king informed Ridge. "Find her and bring her."

Ridge looked doubtful. "She is with the soldiers in the outer bailey, my lord, and is most likely attached to d'Vant."

The king stopped abruptly. "I do not care if they are joined at the hip," he said through his teeth. "Get her any way you can. Knock her unconscious if you must. She leaves with us and we leave *now*."

Ridge had little choice, but he seriously wondered how he was going to get hold of the woman. He'd been watching her since his arrival and he knew that d'Vant was quite protective of her, as was Sully Montgomery. That never mattered until now. Now, Ridge found himself having to concoct a plan to abduct a woman who was never alone. That wasn't part of his usual duties as defender of the king but, evidently, he'd just been given the task.

With nothing more to say, he saluted the king and jogged off, his mail and sword jingling gaily as he moved. He had a woman to capture and very little time to do it in, and hopefully without bloodshed. *His* bloodshed.

Ridge was a man who followed orders no matter what they were. It was what he'd always done and how he'd become such a valued possession of a king. He was a man who never questioned an order but, in this instance, he was having to take action on something that was out of his scope of work. At least, that was the way he looked at it.

The king's bodyguard was about to become the king's kidnapper.

INSIDE THE KEEP, Justine saw the king with his stewards and noticed his haste. A passing servant told her that a Dalmellington onslaught was imminent and then the king's haste seemed to make some sense. Even as the king was preparing and the rest of Torridon was preparing, Justine had some preparations of her own to make.

She had been through battles numerous times, but now it was different. Her husband, the man she had loved since she could remember, was facing a powerful foe to defend their castle.

Their castle.

Justine had always feared for his safety and for Josephine's, but had pretended indifference. It was Justine's way of self-preservation; if she didn't admit to anything, then it almost didn't exist. If she didn't admit to fear or concern, then there wasn't anything to worry about. But now, she wanted to go outside and find Sully and wish him luck. Yet… she knew he was too busy to bother with her.

Justine remembered the night before, how Sully had gently initiated their lovemaking and how she had given in to the man as if she'd been doing it her entire life. No resistance, no protests – she'd simply let him have his way with her, a testament to her feelings for the man. He was very quickly becoming everything to her and she didn't want to lose him in some foolish battle.

Now that she had him, she didn't want to lose him.

But she had a job to do and she was determined to do it. In fact, at the onset of a siege, everyone in the keep had tasks, even the maids. Ola and Darcy, Justine's maid, brought Justine's medicines and herbs into the hall and began to heat water in the hearth so they could boil linen bandages. Justine began busying herself over the hearth with her potions when a small child swathed in cloaks entered the great hall. Justine hardly took notice until the figure threw back its hood and revealed the wild red hair.

Andrew's healer, Oletha, had arrived.

"I thought you might need help, eventually," she said to Justine in her sweet, high-pitched voice. "I offer my services."

Justine faced the woman. She had a great deal of respect for her since the night she had diagnosed Josephine's condition – not hemlock, but dill – and she was grateful for the old woman's offer.

"I graciously accept," she said. "In fact, I should most likely be assisting you."

Oletha wasn't at all sure how Justine would react to her. The last time she saw the girl, Justine was calling her an incompetent. She half-expected Justine to throw her out. Instead, Justine seemed very receptive and Oletha was a little stunned at the hospitality. This was not the same girl she had met a mere few days ago, arrogant and stubborn. She knew about the girl's marriage, but she had never seen it change a woman as such. A man, aye; but a woman? Nay. Sully Montgomery must be a great sorcerer, indeed; more than he knew.

As Oletha rolled up her sleeves and went to work preparing for the onslaught of wounded, it was clear that the smell of battle was in the air and everyone was inhaling their fill. The windows were shuttered and the bolt on the entry door was thrown. The great hall was a hive of activity, with the servants casting fresh rushes with the old to cushion the rest of the wounded that would soon litter the floor. It was a grim task; the calm before the storm, and Justine hated it. She always hated it, but she accepted it with stoic resolve because she had to.

Tying her hair back in a kerchief and pulling on an apron, she busied herself at the hearth with a kettle of healing herbs.

The death watch was beginning.

OUTSIDE, A HUGE storm bank was rolling in from the west. In the midst of battle preparations, Josephine glanced up to see the boiling clouds approaching and knew it was going to be a fierce storm, in more ways than one.

Sully was on the wall with the archers, keeping a sharp eye on the horizon where Colin was assembling his troops in formation. Colin was a student of Roman warfare and his soldiers were well-trained. Sully leaned against the cold stone, tilting his helm back and wiping his brow. He had the strangest feeling that this battle would decide the course of the de Carron – Dalmellington future.

Now that he was the official Master of Torridon, protection of the fortress took on a new, deeper meaning. This was where he would raise his own sons and, God willing, he would return it to Josephine someday. He never did intend to keep it. But Torridon was his home and it would always be a part of him.

The rain started. Far below Sully, Josephine stood with Severn and Henly as Andrew began giving orders. She was watching Andrew closely, impressed with what she saw. The man did this for a living and she could see that he knew much more of warfare than she ever could.

It wasn't simply his knowledge, but his manner with his men. A siege was imminent, but Andrew was calm and steady. He called each man by his first name. He used suggestions instead of criticisms, and a small joke instead of an unkind word. He was more a friend to them than a leader, but there was no doubt of his control.

Sully handled Torridon's soldiers just as well, and they would easily die for him. But he lacked the depth of compassion that Andrew exuded. Compassion that turned deadly on an enemy and from which there was no escape.

But the man was certainly something to watch.

The outer bailey was quickly turning into a mud pool as the rain began to pound. Helmless, Andrew's hair was turning into a dark, wavy mass as he turned from the men and caught sight of Josephine. He smiled at her and her heart leapt in her chest. But just as quickly, he was gone and she found herself moving with her knights to the wall.

Positions were about to be filled with an attack to fend off, but she had no way of knowing if it would be the last time she saw Andrew on the grounds of Torridon, now… and possibly forever.

There was no way she could have known that, at the moment, she was being hunted.

The hunter with the dark eyes had been tracking her for the last several minutes. When the woman would turn in his direction, Ridge would manage to hide himself, only to emerge when Lady Josephine was properly distracted. He lost himself in the hordes of soldiers in the outer bailey, but his gaze remained locked on to the lady.

He kept his eye on the target.

Damn the king! Ridge had known all along that d'Vant would never let the king take her away after the betrothal announcement and it occurred to him that Alexander had been planning some sort of abduction all along. The king knew he couldn't fight off The Red Fury and he didn't bring nearly enough men to fight off the mercenary army.

Therefore, Ridge was left with the dirty work.

While his sovereign and entourage had already left the castle through the gatehouse that was just being shored up, he remained behind carrying out orders that would surely provoke a mighty wrath were he discovered. Ridge was good with a sword; one of the best in Scotland, but he sorely doubted he could outfight The Red Fury.

Fortunately, Andrew was too busy with battle preparations to be able to stick close to his lady. She, on the other hand, was surrounded by several Torridon knights, and Ridge had no intention of taking them all on. Therefore, he waited, angling himself over towards the east wall where the huge ladders led to the platforms that lined the top of the fortress. He knew that eventually she would mount of those ladders and, mayhap, if he was quick enough, he could grab her. There were enough supplies, weapons, and other clutter to hide behind, so he crouched down in the sludge.

He didn't have long to wait. Lady Josephine and a young, blond knight were headed his way, talking between themselves. They were in the shadow of the wall, concealed from the walk above and from most of the bailey view, and Ridge knew his time was coming. He wasn't sure he'd ever get another chance to be this close to the woman and he knew he had to take the opportunity. As the lady and the knight drew closer, he reached into his vest and drew forth a dagger with a six-inch blade.

His eyes glittered with anticipation as Lady Josephine came to within arm's length of him. As she put her hand on the wood of a nearby ladder, Ridge's gauntleted hand shot out and yanked her behind the bushels. Severn, momentarily stunned at what he just witnessed, drew forth his sword and followed her.

The first thing Severn saw in the dimness was Josephine on the ground in front of him. The next thing he realized, a dagger was thrust into his rib cage and he suddenly felt very weak. He wanted desperately to help Josephine as she struggled to her feet. He saw a very big man wearing the king's colors move towards her, but he couldn't seem to speak. His breath caught in his throat and he saw the knight knock Josephine savagely on the side of her head, knocking her back down again.

The last recollection of Severn's life was a burly king's man gathering the limp form of his lady and carrying her off into the storm.

PART THREE:
EDINBURGH

CHAPTER TWENTY

J OSEPHINE'S HEAD WAS throbbing. She was coming out of the darkness, being jostled about in an ungodly manner, and she struggled to open her eyes.

When the world came in to view, she saw that she was cradled in someone's arms; a man's arms. She was instantly confused. *Where was she? What had happened?* She twisted about and strong arms gripped her tightly.

"So, you are awake, my lady?" a deep voice asked, not unkind. "How do you feel?"

She couldn't see the face of the man that held her, but she could see she rode atop a great roan destrier. The horse had a bristly mane, scratching her arm.

"Who are you?" she demanded weakly.

"Ridge de Reyne, my lady," he said pleasantly. "I am the king's bodyguard."

She was more confused than ever at that revelation. Fear and anger ran neck and neck in her foggy mind.

"I do not know you," she said. "What goes on?"

"I am taking you to the king, so that he may formally deliver you to your future husband," Ridge replied.

Josephine stiffened. "He will *not* be my future husband."

Ridge didn't reply immediately. "That, dear lady, is for the king to decide."

Josephine tried to sit up but Ridge held her fast. "Release me," she hissed, slapping at his hands. "Where is everyone? Where are we?"

"On the road to Edinburgh, my lady," he said, unmoved by her struggles.

Josephine's eyes widened. "Edinburgh?" she repeated in shock. "How... what... what have you done? I am not going to Edinburgh!"

Ridge had a good grip on her. "My lady, I would suggest you stop fighting," he said. "I have my orders and I will fulfill them."

I have my orders.

His jaw was set, firm, and Josephine was genuinely shocked. She was also torn between her aching head and wanting to escape. But she was, frankly, terrified. She hadn't formally met Ridge de Reyne at Torridon but she'd seen him with the king, one of the many men the king surrounded himself with, but Ridge was different. He was a very big man who moved with the grace of a cat. She hadn't known his name, but she recognized his face.

Hard-set and cruel.

As she lay there, trying to clear her spinning head, it suddenly occurred to her that there was a great battle in progress at her fortress. With the terrible pain and confusion in her head, it had nearly slipped her mind. But she was no longer torn by her confusion. She was spurred into action with the desire to return to her castle, and she twisted forcefully in Ridge's grasp. Now, the fighting began in earnest and she pounded her fists against him and kicked with all of her might until she fell from his horse.

In fact, she'd fought like a wildcat, so violently that Ridge lost his grip, and his balance, and toppled off the other side, trying unsuccessfully to grab hold of the saddle. Josephine rolled to her knees, ripping off her outer tunic and mail coat as fast as she possibly could while Ridge tried to right himself on the other side of the horse. She was soon racing back down the road, a road she knew she didn't recognize, but she knew that they had come from this direction.

She hoped it would take her home.

Josephine was being irrational and she knew it, but she had to get back to Torridon. She had no idea how long she'd been unconscious and, for all she knew Torridon was in flames and its occupants dead. But she only knew that she had to go back as her lungs began to ache and her head swam. But she didn't stop. Ferociously, she ran full-force along the rocky road.

But she wasn't fast enough. Ridge hit Josephine from behind like a runaway beer wagon and she fell heavily on the gravel with him on top of her, scratching her chin and hands as the two of them rolled down a slight incline. Before she could recover well enough to attempt to escape again, he was on top of her and pinning her hands down with his own as his heavy body lay atop hers.

Ridge's helm was gone and his black hair was wet and spiky. His square-jawed, handsome face was inches from her own, and his dark eyes looked at her with irritation.

"You knew that you would never make it," he said.

She looked at him defiantly, fighting him every inch of the way. "I have to return, de Reyne," she said through clenched teeth. "My castle is under siege. Let me go!"

Somewhere under the hard exterior, she thought she caught a glimpse of compassion. But it was gone in a flash. "I cannot," he said.

It was a simple answer, but it was also a final one. The words had impact on her. Josephine stopped struggling and suddenly, she burst into tears. "Please!" she begged. "I must return. I must save my fortress. Let me return now and I shall gladly go with you when the fighting is through."

Ridge watched the lovely features crumple and felt a stab of pity for the little soldier. He knew exactly how she felt and, under different circumstances, might have told her his story. But right now, he had a job to do.

"I doubt that d'Vant would let you return with me," Ridge countered. "It is very likely he would kill me the moment I pass through the fortress gates."

"He would not if I asked him not to." The tears were still flowing, but the sobbing had subsided. "I give you my word."

Ridge seriously considered her request. He had no doubt that d'Vant would move heaven and earth for this lady. He had seen the looks between them and he could only imagine the power of their love. In his thirty-plus years on this earth, he had never had the privilege of experiencing that emotion for himself and envied them their happiness.

But he was sworn to obey the king, even though there was a lot to be said for the pleas of a beautiful woman. Still... he couldn't weaken, no matter how distasteful the task.

"Forgive me, my lady," he said softly. "But I cannot."

He rose to his feet and pulled her with him, firmly gripping her wrists. Josephine knew by the look on his face that nothing she could say would persuade him.

"Can you not understand that I need to return?" she pleaded quietly. "My soldiers, my sister... they need me."

Ridge glanced up at the storm cloud filled sky. "My lady, it has been nearly five hours since we left Torridon," he said. "Whatever was going to happen has happened, and your presence will not change that. I understand your desire to return, but I must obey the king. I must deliver you to him."

Josephine was about to try the soft approach when the trees behind him spilled forth three men. All three of them were armed with crude swords. They were dressed in rags. Ridge heard the sounds a split second before he saw the look on her face. Drawing his sword and turning around in one fluid motion, he raised his blade just in time to prevent getting his head being chopped off.

Josephine instinctively fell in behind him, clutching his waist as he backed away from the thieves. She had no sword and wasn't much for hand-to-hand combat with anyone other than her sister. Ridge was doing well, considering he was fending off three men, but she wanted to help.

"De Reyne!" she said urgently. "Do you carry another sword on your destrier?"

"In the pack," he grunted, fending off another blow. "But I forbid you to…"

She was gone, racing off towards the distant horse. He managed to turn and see her, cursing at her flagrant disregard for their situation. He grunted loudly as two swords came down heavily on his blade, the tip of which caught his cheek.

The third man, the smallest one, ran off after Josephine. She had a good lead on him and made it to the snorting horse, patting down the pack rapidly in her search for the sword. It was there, on the top, and she drew it forth quickly.

The man was nearly at her, and she swung the heavy sword boldly in two successive upper cuts, effectively catching the thief off guard.

Josephine always made a point of looking into the face of any man she fought. It was a bad habit, for the soldier ceased to become the faceless enemy at that point and became a person. As she swung viciously at her opponent, she managed to look at his face between thrusts and saw that he was little more than a boy.

The brief stab of uncertainty she felt was replaced by self-preservation when the boy thrust recklessly at her and narrowly missed cutting her throat. In a flash, she spun in a circle and crouched low, coming in under his sword range. Before the boy could take another breath, she drew the sharp edge of the blade across his belly and effectively disemboweled him on the spot.

For a brief moment, she felt a surge of sorrow as she stared down at the dead young man. She knew if she hadn't killed him first, then she would most likely have been killed. Shaking it off, she turned her full attention to Ridge.

One bandit lay crumpled on the ground several feet from where Ridge and the final bandit fought. Despite the enemy's rotund build, he was good with a sword and matched Ridge blow-for-blow. She could see the sparks flying from their engaging weapons as she approached.

Josephine had always appreciated a good sword fight. When done correctly, it was like a well-choreographed dance, and was just as entertaining. Ridge was quite good, in fact. He wasn't launching a strong offensive. Instead, he was waiting until the bandit exhausted himself before making the kill. Josephine just stood by, heavy sword in hand, and waited.

But the would-be robber did something unexpected. He charged forward and their swords locked, but then he threw his substantial body weight forward and knocked Ridge to the ground.

Grunting and sweating, Ridge brought his sword up to block the next blow in the nick of time. The man wasn't stronger than Ridge but, with the added body weight, the swords were drifting closer to Ridge's neck.

Josephine simply wanted to end the struggle. She knew Ridge would eventually come away the victor, but she was tired and her head was aching. Almost as an afterthought, she dropped the sword and drew forth the bejeweled dirk at her waist with the serrated blade.

Marching upon the two struggling men, she lifted the dagger high and plunged it into the back of the robber's neck. She stood back as he collapsed, and Ridge pushed him away. Ridge looked at the man for a moment while he twitched and convulsed, and then turned an amazed face to Josephine.

She stood a few feet away, clad in a linen tunic and her heavy leather breeches. Her long hair hung wildly about her and her scratched face was like stone as she stared back at him. In her hand, he noticed the knife. Without a word, she turned and walked back to the horse.

Ridge watched her go as he rose a bit unsteadily to his feet. She could have just as easily killed him to gain her freedom, but she didn't. He hadn't seen her fight the boy, but he noted as he came upon the thief how neatly he was gutted. She had every opportunity to escape but, instead, she chose to help him. He shook his head in wonder; *why?*

Josephine stood silently by his horse, staring up the road. Ridge packed his spare sword, the one she had used, and then sheathed his primary weapon. The entire time, he stole glances at her, but she never acknowledged him.

Josephine's mind was a million miles away. She knew, in the end, there would be no escaping from the king. If she had killed Ridge, Alexander would have simply sent someone else to retrieve her, and it would only delay the inevitable. Like it or not, she was going to Edinburgh, and eventually to Haldane, and she decided that it would be better to have an ally on the inside, someone who owed her a debt. It had been a smart move on her part to kill Ridge's opponent.

Ridge would be of more use to her alive than dead.

But what of Andrew? Did he even realize she was missing? If the fighting was heavy, probably not. If he was de… nay, she couldn't even finish the thought. She could not comprehend the thought of him dying. But she knew deep down he was not dead and that he would come for her and take her away, forever.

Already, she missed him, and her arms ached to hold him. They had had so little time together. Josephine was not particularly religious, but she found herself praying honestly to the Got she'd heard stories told about. If He would only allow her to see Andrew once more, then she would become devoutly religious.

If not, then she would be dead.

Ridge paused before mounting his destrier; his eyes riveted to Josephine. She had yet to say a word.

"You disposed of that thief quite handily," he commented.

She nodded. He searched for something more to say, but could think of nothing. After a moment, he spoke.

"My thanks," he said simply.

Then she looked at him. "For what?"

Ridge wasn't used to thanking anyone. He cocked a black eyebrow at her for forcing him to say more than he wanted to.

"For killing my fat opponent," he said. "I thank you for your help. You are a brave young woman."

She clenched her teeth and squared off with him. "Allow me to make myself perfectly clear," she said bluntly. "I did not kill that man to save you. I did it because I want something from you. You are taking me to a dark realm where nothing is familiar, including the man the king would have me marry. I do not know what lies ahead for me, de Reyne, and I may have need of a strong knight to assist me. I will not ask you again to return me to Torridon, for I know you will not. But in the future, should I call upon you to return the favor that I have bestowed, then you had better come running."

He looked at her, somewhat impressed at the delicate blackmail she had woven. She had killed his opponent to extract a favor from him. Fair enough; *but what type of favor?* Despite any misgivings, he nodded chivalrously and mounted the destrier.

He settled himself and extended a hand to help her. Begrudgingly, she placed her hand in his and he pulled her up as effortlessly as one would lift a pillow. It was impossible to sit on the same saddle with him and not be intimately pressed against him. He wouldn't put her on behind him for fear she'd slide off and perhaps run again, so he put her on his lap. She stiffened indignantly as her bottom rubbed against his crotch.

But Ridge wasn't paying attention to the fact that her bottom was against his groin. He liked women, of course, but he wasn't thinking of the lady in that way. He held the reins with one hand while his other went around her waist instinctively to lend support. She hated it at first but, eventually, she became used to it as the horse pranced down the road that was quickly darkening with sunset.

With each step, Josephine moved further and further away from Torridon, and hot tears sprang to her eyes again. The motion of the horse was hypnotic, and her head soon fell gently back against his broad shoulder. She was very tired from the day's events and, soon enough, sleep claimed her.

Ridge knew she had been lulled into an exhausted sleep when she went limp in his grasp and started to snore. He pulled her closer to him so she would not topple over. He found himself feeling a good deal of pity for her situation. She was a beautiful and intelligent woman, and she did not deserve the fate that awaited her. The bodyguard for the king, a man efficient and emotionless, had a deep, softer side that no one saw. He wasn't as emotionless as he pretended to be.

His hate for his king grew in that dark night as he traveled the road to Edinburgh.

CHAPTER TWENTY-ONE

MORNING DAWNED WITH a gray chill, with a heavy fog rolling across the land. The rain had subsided during the night, leaving behind a soggy world and soggy men. But the fog hid the devastation left by the night's battle, as if the land were ashamed to reveal what its inhabitants had done.

Andrew crossed the outer bailey, heading for the castle. His left arm was heavily bandaged and blood was seeping through the wrappings. He had caught the broad edge of a Dalmellington sword that, at just the right angle, had split his upper arm wide open.

But his wound was nothing compared to the damage Torridon had suffered. The new main gate was again in splinters and when it fell, it almost took a portion of the gatehouse with it. The Dalmellington army had breached into the inner bailey and had managed to burn down the stables and a portion of the granary. The stable structure was gone, but all of the beautiful horses had been saved, now corralled in the kitchen yard. The Dalmellington men would have torched the keep itself if Andrew had not set up a frontline directly in front of the structure to keep them at bay.

He had fought harder that night than he had ever fought in his life, but it had all been for Josephine. Never once had his fee entered his mind. With every blow and with every kill, he was paying Colin Dalmellington back for all of the pain he had caused her.

Andrew stopped counting his kills after twenty and he had been very intent on finding Colin to carry out his threat, but Colin was nowhere to be found. Therefore, he continued to hack away at the enemy soldiers with the fury he felt and knew that, eventually, he would find Colin.

Strangely, he hadn't seen Josephine since before the battle started, but he assumed she had wisely retreated to the safety of the keep. Knowing she was safe allowed his mind to concentrate solely on the battle but, every so often, he would find himself dreaming of her softness and reliving the night he'd spent with her. It kept him sustained.

In his battles, occasionally, he would come across Sully. Sully moved faster than any man Andrew had ever seen, using his two hands to fight his opponent with tremendous force and then moving on to the next. He was tireless and the Torridon men followed him without question. Andrew gained new respect for his friend that night.

But when it was all said and done, the tally for the battle was grim. Four Torridon dead knights – Severn being one of them, and three lesser knights – and thirty-five men-at-arms. Andrew personally lost twenty-eight men, with scores of wounded in the great hall. But Dalmellington lost over half of his fighting force, and they retreated to the safety of the woods shortly before dawn. A weary cheer went up from the soldiers and mercenaries alike when they had retreated.

The yard was littered with bodies, like discarded dolls, as Andrew stepped around and over them. Servants and soldiers alike were hurriedly removing the dead and, soon, the smell of burning flesh would fill the air like a fog and have everyone retching. Andrew looked down at the dead, knowing they were a necessary part of battle, but disliking it all the same.

He passed into the inner bailey and it looked as bad as the rest of the grounds. He found himself eager to see Josephine, eager to hold her and to forget about the destruction of the castle. He had never felt this urge before, to touch and be touched, and it was almost uncontrollable.

As he put his foot on the first step leading to the keep, Thane came barreling out of the door and nearly crashed into him in his haste.

"God's Bones, Andrew," he caught himself. "I beg your pardon."

Andrew waved it off, looking at his friend. He looked as if he had been on the receiving end of a violent thrashing.

"Are you well?" he asked him.

Thane grinned. "Nothing a bottle of wine will not cure."

Andrew returned his smile. "Good," he said. Then he ordered, "I shall require a final count."

"Of course," Thane nodded, looking about him grimly. "This was a fierce one. I did not expect the ferocity we encountered."

Andrew followed his friend's eyes, seeing the same destruction that Thane was. "Lady Josephine is paying us good money to defend her castle," he said. "It looks like we are not worth the asking price."

"If we had not been here, there would be nothing left standing," Thane pointed out.

"True," Andrew admitted, then mounted the next two stairs. "Where is Lady Josephine?"

Thane shook his head. "You mean your future bride?" he teased. "I have not seen her."

Andrew looked slightly puzzled. "She is not in the keep?"

"Nay," Thane replied. "I did not see her inside."

Puzzlement was replaced by a seed of anxiety. Andrew looked at Thane and Thane caught on immediately.

"I will search the grounds," he said, beginning to jog away. "I will ask if anyone has seen her."

Andrew walked rapidly into the depths of the cool keep. The smell of decaying flesh and herbs filled the air as he moved into the great hall and was met with the sight of hundreds of wounded. Across the room, he spied Oletha's orange head, and not far from her was Justine. He began to pick his way towards Josephine's sister.

Justine looked up from the hand she was bandaging to be greeted by Andrew's serious face.

"Your arm is bleeding again," she said. "I must stitch it now."

He ignored her. "Where is Josephine?"

"I do not know," Justine shook her head. "I have not seen her."

"She is not outside," he said. "She must be within the keep."

Justine stood up, catching on to the anxiety in his voice. "Andrew, I have not seen her all night," she insisted. "I assumed she was with you."

Andrew stared at her, coming to realize that something was very wrong. Suddenly, he looked about the room, at the men, and at the servants.

"*Where* is the king?" he asked softly.

"He left before the battle started," Justine replied. "He and his party took what they could carry on horseback and left. They informed me that they would send for their wagons later. Did you not see them go?"

Andrew hadn't. He'd been forming lines to the rear of the fortress right before the Dalmellington forces hit. As he stood there, a thought seized him. It was a notion so terrible that he almost lost his balance.

The king had left and Josephine was missing.

Anger and horror rose in his chest like twin demons, and he spun away from Justine. His huge hands grabbed a richly carved chair against the wall and abruptly smashed it into the stone with such force that it disintegrated into splinters.

Justine yelped in surprise, with her hands flying to her mouth.

"What is it?" she cried. "Andrew, what is wrong?"

Andrew was shaking with anger, breathing like a pent-up bull. He stood over the heap of wood and silk that had once been the chair, clenching and unclenching his fists. Oletha had heard the noise and came rushing over. Now, she stood anxiously by Justine.

"The king has taken her," he growled. "By God... the bastard has taken my Joey."

Justine gasped, hands flying to her mouth again. "But she was not with him when he left," she insisted. "I saw him leave with his stewards and courtiers."

He jerked his head to her with such pain and fury that she visibly shrank. "Then where is she, Justine?" he demanded, almost begging. "She is nowhere to be found! Where is she?"

"I do not know," she whispered, her eyes filling with tears.

"*Where*, Justine?" he bellowed.

"I do not know!" she cried, bursting into tears. "Did you check her chamber?"

Andrew was gone, running to the stairs and mounting them three at a time. Justine was close behind and followed him as he barreled into Josephine's room. He tore all of the linens off of the bed as if she could possibly be hiding there, then he moved to her wardrobe and threw open the doors, too.

He was immediately hit with the smell of rose and he shut his eyes tightly; his heart aching more than his exhausted body did. He began to curse himself; he should have stayed with her, he silently scolded himself. He should have guessed that Alexander wouldn't stay and fight if there was nothing in it for him, and the king had promised to take Josephine with him when he left.

Why hadn't he had the foresight to realize what could happen?

It had been badly miscalculated on his part.

Strangely, Andrew was a bit calmer now that he knew what had become of Josephine and that she was not dead out in the moor. But his panic was replaced by such an anger that he would stop at nothing to retrieve what was his.

It was time for his life to come full circle, time to kill his brother and discover the fate of his mother. And most importantly, it was time for him to rescue Josephine. There was no more time to waste with his mercenary pursuits and with his talk of biding his time until the moment was ripe.

The moment was now.

He turned to Justine. She stood by the door watching him, with fear in his eyes. "Is she gone with the king, then?" she asked hesitantly.

Andrew nodded, raking his fingers through his hair wearily. "She is."

"And you are certain of this?"

"I am positive."

"Then what are you going to do?"

He looked at her, then, as if the mere question were foolish. "Go after her."

Justine's eyes widened and she came into the chamber. "But you cannot fight the king," she said. "It would be foolish to try."

"I do not go to fight the king," he said as he brushed past her. "I go to kill my brother and take back what is mine."

Justine watched him move, a pain in her heart like nothing she had ever experienced. Oddly enough, it took her back to the day The Red Fury arrived, the day when she had read her cards for her sister. She remembered the cards she had drawn that day, symbols that had no meaning at the time. But now, they did.

Now, she understood.

"I foresaw this," Justine said fearfully. "My cards foretold this the day you came here."

Andrew paused at the top of the stairs, looking at her irritably. "What are you babbling about?"

Justine looked at him with great depth of fear and foreboding. "The day you arrived at Torridon, I consulted my cards about Josephine's future," she said as she came towards him. "All of the cards were powerful and passionate, depicting extreme love and hate, and of a great battle. But the great battle wasn't fought last night; it is yet to come."

His jaw muscles flexed as he looked away. "I have been waiting most of my life for this confrontation, Justine," he said. "But I never in my wildest dreams imagined that the stakes would be this high. I love her, Justine. I cannot lose her. She is the world to me."

"I know," she said quietly. "I have always known."

He glanced at her, a dull twinkle in his eye. "You might have let me in on it sooner."

She shrugged. "You had to discover it for yourself," she said, then smiled. "You were in love with her the day you arrived but I doubt you would have believed me."

That was more than likely true. Andrew winked at her. "Take care of yourself and your lout-headed husband, Lady Montgomery," he said. "When I return, I shall bring your sister with me."

Justine's smile faded. The chances of him not returning at all were great. She was deeply concerned for him and for her sister, and she felt an overwhelming urge to consult her cards again.

"Andrew," she said. "Josephine is stronger than you know. She can take care of herself."

His face clouded over and she felt a chill run through her. He looked as if he were about to reply, but it faded from his lips. He took the next step.

"I know," he said softly, then descended the stairs. "But I am stronger than she is. And I will prove it."

Justine stared at the empty stairwell for a moment, wondering if she would ever see Andrew or Josephine again.

The cards beckoned her and she complied.

ANDREW MARCHED BOLDLY towards the keep entry, with his boots clacking loudly on the stone. He was exhausted, and his arm was seeping, but he had never felt so alert or fortified. Outside, it was damp and foggy, with the sun turning the fog from gray to white.

He met Thane and Etienne in the outer bailey. Etienne's left hand was heavily bandaged, Andrew noticed, but he was too preoccupied to ask about it.

"Lady Josephine is not to be found," Thane spoke before Andrew could. "The men are scouring the battlefield now in search of her... body."

"She will not be there," Andrew said, removing his gauntlets from his boot cuff and pulling them on.

Thane and Etienne looked at each other curiously, then back at Andrew. "You found her?" Thane asked. "She was in the keep?"

Andrew pushed past them. "Nay, she was not," he said. "The king took her with him when he left. I am going to retrieve her."

Thane and Etienne were rushing after him. Thane grabbed his arm, something he would never have done given a normal situation.

"Are you mad?" he hissed. "You cannot go alone!"

"He will not be alone," came a voice from behind them. Sully walked up, calmly straightening and pulling at his mail coat that had tattered during the battle. "I am going with him."

Andrew looked at Sully and knew instantly that Justine had rushed to him and spilled the entire story.

"I go alone, Sully," Andrew said. "I must."

Sully pushed between Etienne and Thane, his eyes boring into Andrew, and Andrew could see that he had a fight on his hands. He knew how close Sully and Josephine were, and he knew Sully was as loyal to her as a priest was loyal to God.

"Sully," he said slowly. "This is something that I must do alone. You know why."

Sully would not be dissuaded. "All I know is that wily bastard has taken Josephine and I shall assist you in your vengeance."

"He has taken her to my brother," Andrew countered. "And vengeance is mine. Stay here with your wife and protect your castle. I need no assistance."

Sully sighed heavily and cleared his throat. "But you may," he said. "And if you do, I shall be there. If you do not, then only time has been wasted on my part. I am going, like it or not."

"But what of Torridon?" Andrew asked. "It is in pieces. Who will supervise the rebuild?"

Sully pointed to Etienne. "I have many competent men to oversee things," he said. "Torridon will be well-tended until I return."

It seemed there wasn't anything more to say. Andrew continued to stare him down, his jaw flexing. He had no time for this and he knew no amount of arguing would change Sully's mind. He looked at Thane.

"Prepare my horse," he growled. "And prepare Sully's as well."

Sully knew that he was going to be accompanying him all along and did not react outwardly. But Andrew glared at him as Thane and Etienne headed for the burned-out stables.

"Do not get in my way, Montgomery," he growled, and walked away.

Sully knew he was hurting, but he wondered if Andrew's desire to kill his brother was greater than his love for Josephine. Sully was going along to make sure, in any case, that Josephine came back to Torridon. He feared Andrew's true motive and wondered if Josephine would suffer if *she* got in his way.

THEY WASTED NO time.

Within the hour, Andrew and Sully were both on the road heading north, with their destriers kicking up round clumps of soggy earth as they jogged down the dirt road. Both men had been silent since they left the fortress, their minds elsewhere. The tension between them was tangible, however, until Sully finally broke the silence.

"Do you think the king will keep her at Edinburgh Castle for a while before taking her to Haldane?" he asked, looking across the moor.

Andrew pretended to be interested in the countryside as well. "Mayhap," he said. "I am counting on the fact that the king's lust for Josephine will keep her at the castle for at least a day, long enough for him to try to violate her. We can find her and shadow her on her ride to Haldane."

"Why not kidnap her on the road to Haldane?" Sully asked. "That is where she will be most vulnerable."

Andrew didn't reply for a moment. "Because I have to go to Haldane if I am to kill my brother," he said finally.

"Damnation, Andrew!" Sully exploded quietly. "Your obsession with killing your brother has blinded you to what is really going on. Josephine is in peril and all you can talk of is the murder of a man you haven't seen in nineteen years. Tell me – what is most important to you? Killing your brother or getting Josephine back?"

Instead of fighting back, as Sully expected, Andrew looked at him with such pain and anguish in his eyes that Sully was instantly sorry that he had ever doubted the man's motives. Everything he needed to know was written across Andrew's face.

"You have no idea as to what my brother is like," he said quietly. "If the devil was mortal, he would be Alphonse. He was born vile; even as a child he was feared and hated. He came to the earldom only because he was the eldest. I sincerely believe that before his death, my father was plotting to kill my brother."

It was rather shocking information. Sully didn't reply as they plodded along the road, understanding now that Andrew felt he was performing a service more than fulfilling a personal obsession by ridding the world of his brother. He was coming to suspect that his reasons were not self-centered, as Sully had believed.

"And this is the man who holds your family's legacy?" he asked.

Andrew nodded, wiping exhaustedly at his eyes. "I have always believed that it was my duty to kill him," he said. "The man has caused so much pain and suffering that I would kill him as an apology to all of Scotland and England, sorry that the evil seed fell into power. My family is old, Sully. We've always been one of the most respected families in England, until Alphonse. He's all but destroyed everything every generation of d'Vants has worked hard for. I have to rid the world of him."

"But what of Josephine?" Sully asked quietly.

Andrew laughed softly, ironically, and shook his head. "All of my life, I have been an avid opponent to love and marriage. Love, as I knew it, only held pain. Thane fell in love with a woman once, and I made him choose between her and my army." His smile faded and his eyes took on a distant look. "And then I came to Torridon, looking forward to a high-paying job, and I was confronted by the most exquisite woman who has ever walked the face of the earth. I experienced feelings I have never had before, and they scared me. I thought they would somehow weaken me. But once I gave into it and allowed myself to love her, I realized that I am stronger than I have ever been. I cannot put into words my feelings for her. To think of my brother, or anyone else, touching her fills me with the rage of the devil. In answer to your question, she is my primary concern, and will always be. But I must kill my brother."

Sully understood everything now. He looked at Andrew warmly.

"As I stated earlier, I shall assist you," he said. "Until I die, I shall assist you always. Any man who can win Josephine's heart and hold it with the highest regard shall always have my respect."

Andrew smiled faintly. "And you have mine, my friend."

The storm between them had passed and now they rode together in companionable silence. The road ahead was long and uncertain, and their minds were far into the future.

They would rescue Josephine or die trying.

CHAPTER TWENTY-TWO

IT WAS MORNING on the day following Josephine's abduction from Torridon and Ridge had stopped to let Josephine stretch her legs and relieve herself, dismounting to keep an eye on her while she disappeared into the brush on the side of the road.

"I will not follow so long as I can see the top of your head!" he called to her.

She shot him a cold look but complied. The last thing she wanted was him following her into the bushes to watch her piss

The breeches she wore were leather but underneath them, she wore very thin cotton hose to protect her sensitive legs from the leather. She wished fervently that she had one of her gowns on as she fumbled with the layers of clothing. It occurred to her that she had absolutely no personal possessions with her – no comb, no soap, and no clothes. She wanted desperately to wash.

Josephine was calmer now about Torridon and its fate. She had had ample time to resign herself to the fact that what was done was done and even if she could return now, it would not change anything. But the ache of sadness was great in her heart and the fear of the unknown was greater. *Who was alive? Who was dead? Did Andrew realize what had befallen her?* She knew he would soon figure it out for himself and come for her. There wasn't much to do but wait and fight the king and the earl anyway she could.

God, she missed Andrew.

She secured her trousers and emerged from the bramble. They were nearing Edinburgh and the hills were becoming softer as the foliage decreased. She had been to Edinburgh only once as a child, and did not remember much of it. But in realizing they were coming closer to a major city, her sense of unease had dramatically increased. It was the unknown that she was most fearful of.

The unknown of a future with too many variables to count.

Ridge was adjusting the breastplate of his destrier as she walked up, brushing her hands off on her pants.

"If you were going to kidnap me, you could have at least had the foresight to raid my wardrobe first," she said. "I do not have anything decent to wear."

Ridge gave her side glance. "Forgive me, my lady," he apologized to appease her. "I shall do better the next time."

"You plan to make a habit out of abducting maidens?" she asked, as she leaned back against the massive brown animal. "It's not a very dignified line of work for the king's bodyguard. I should think you are better than that, de Reyne."

She'd struck a nerve with him. Ridge didn't like kidnapping her any better than she did. He was a man of principle, and he was serving a man who had none at all. As Ridge geared up for a reply, he wasn't aware that she had been watching his face and she saw his change in expression.

She saw the darkness sweep him.

"Then why do you serve him?" she asked quietly.

He looked at her, with his hand gripping the harness. "What do you mean?"

"Why do you serve Alexander if you hate him so?"

Ridge released the leather and pretended to busy himself with the saddle. Josephine moved out of the way and stood by the horse's head as the animal turned to sniff at her.

"I serve him because I have no choice," he said. "I was gifted to the king. It is a prestigious position."

It was only a half-truth and she knew it. He was trying to make his role sound better than it was. Ridge just didn't strike her as one of the king's spineless pigeons, but she didn't press the issue further.

The destrier's soft, whiskery lips tugged at her sleeve and she made soft clucking noises at it.

"What is your horse's name?" she asked. "He is magnificent."

"Cabal," Ridge replied.

Josephine raised her eyebrows slightly. "You know something of Arthurian lore?"

Ridge shrugged and looked at her. "I know that Cabal was his dog and Excalibur was his sword," he said. "My mother was from Devon. She raised us on stories of Arthur, Gawain, Lancelot, and Percival. Mayhap that is why I became a knight; to continue their noble deeds."

"But those knights did not steal women," Josephine said lightly, hoping he would take it in jest. She no longer wished to be cruel to him for carrying out his duty, but she was not about to let him forget the deed. "They did a host of other things that were, mayhap, not entirely noble, but stealing women wasn't one of them."

He looked thoughtful. "Lancelot stole Guinevere, in a sense," he said. "But from what my mother says, the knights of the realm were holier than God Himself. They probably did not even possess ballocks."

Josephine laughed as he realized the foul language he had used in her presence. She had learned long ago not to be upset by a soldier's crude humor. Ridge laughed a little, too, when she did, noticing her straight, white teeth and curvy smile. She was very pretty.

"I have some watered wine if you are thirsty," Ridge said as he unstrapped a leather pouch from his saddle.

Josephine accepted it and took a few sips. Ridge watched her for a moment before taking back the bladder.

"Are you hungry?" he asked. "I have some jerky if you would…"

"Nay," she shook her head. "I am not hungry."

"You have not eaten since yesterday. You probably should."

She simply shook her head and turned away, clearly moody. Ridge watched her, a tremendous sense of guilt filling him. He felt very bad for Josephine and for what awaited her. She seemed to be a decent girl and she did not deserve what fate the king had planned for her. The more he thought on it, Ridge actually found himself feeling protective towards Josephine, but he very quickly dismissed the emotion. It was not healthy or wise, and he was a man who obeyed orders above all else. Feeling sympathy for Josephine could only lead him to harm.

He sobered after a moment and stepped away from Cabal, holding out the stirrup. "Shall we go?" he said. "It is not more than another hour's ride."

Josephine didn't want to proceed, but there was no choice. Truth be told, she felt she was going to her death. Quite possibly, she was. But she proceeded to mount with a little help from him, and he pulled himself up on the horse behind her. Poking Cabal with a spurred right boot, the horse broke into a bouncy trot and they continued up the road.

Somewhere during the morning, the clouds drifted away and a warm sun appeared. In fact, it was remarkably warm, and Josephine began to sweat beneath her clothing. She pulled at her tunic and scratched, blowing her hair from her face. Ridge understood her discomfort because he was uncomfortable as well. The weather was unseasonably warm. Edinburgh was just coming into view and the castle loomed high above to the north, so there was no point in stopping. They had nearly arrived at their destination, so Ridge pushed through.

Josephine saw the castle before she even noticed the city, and her heart sank. The reality of it came crashing down on her and she felt like a trapped animal. As much as she wanted to fight Ridge again and make a run for it, she knew that she couldn't. There was nowhere for her to go that he wouldn't catch her.

It was a heartbreaking realization.

Feeling exhausted and defeated, she turned away from the sight of the castle and the city, and tried to take her mind off of what was to come.

"How old are you, de Reyne?" she asked.

"I have seen thirty-four years, my lady," he replied. "And you?"

"Nineteen years," she muttered as visions of dark castles lingered in her mind. "Are you married?"

"Nay," he replied with a chuckle. "I have no time for a wife, nor any desire."

"That is what Andrew believed once," she whispered.

He almost didn't hear her, yet caught the painful tone she used. "D'Vant?" he asked.

"Aye."

Ridge looked away, off towards the castle he knew so well. "I still find it hard to believe that The Red Fury has feelings for anyone other than himself," he said. "The man has a reputation as the perfect soldier."

She sighed. "He is much more than that," she said. Then, she paused before speaking again. "You know that he will come after me."

Ridge's jaw hardened. That idea did not appeal to him, for he knew that he himself would end up fighting The Red Fury to keep him from Josephine. And much like her, there was no doubt in his mind that d'Vant was more than likely already on his tail.

"I know," he said simply.

Josephine sensed resignation in that statement, as if there he held no enthusiasm for such a confrontation. Ridge wasn't foolish; he knew that Andrew was a spectacular fighter. But more than that, she sensed no enthusiasm from him for this entire endeavor. He'd abducted her because he'd been ordered to, but there seemed to be no glee for that task. All along, she'd sensed only duty from the man and nothing more.

His heart wasn't in it.

"Will you fight him?" she asked quietly.

"If I must."

Josephine didn't reply for a moment because an idea had come to her. She wondered if it would be something that would interest Ridge. "Will you listen to me?" she asked. "I have a proposal that could prevent all of this."

He was rather wary of any proposal. "I am listening, my lady."

Josephine shifted in the saddle to look at him. "I am very wealthy, de Reyne," she began. "Should you return me to Torridon, I would see that you are well rewarded. I promised Andrew five thousand marks to defend Torridon from Colin Dalmellington. I shall double it for you. Then, you shall be free to either remain at Torridon or leave to pursue your own dreams. Ten thousand marks will buy you anything you wish in life."

The proposal didn't surprise him. In truth, it was rather attractive. But he could not accept it and still keep his honor.

"Your offer is tempting," he finally said. "But I must decline."

Josephine wouldn't give up. "I sense that you are a good knight, de Reyne, and I do not want to see you fight Andrew over something that never should have happened. I do not want to see you killed."

He cocked his head. "I may not be killed," he said. "Did you think of that?"

Josephine refused to entertain such a thing. "You believe that you will defeat The Red Fury in combat when he is fighting for someone he loves?" she said, rather passionately. "I am sure you are an excellent swordsman, but are you *that* good? If you are worried about the king, don't be. It would not be difficult to deceive him. I can simply send word that both you and I were killed in the Dalmellington battle and he will know no differently."

Ridge didn't quite agree with her on that. "The king has many eyes, my lady," he replied as they entered the smelly, dirty outskirts of Edinburgh. "He may be an unscrupulous, indifferent leader, but he is sly and cunning. He thrives on gossip and covert information."

Josephine fell silent as Edinburgh Castle loomed closer still and they found themselves on the dirty streets of the city. In truth, she felt true defeat closing in on her. She had run out of options.

Ridge felt the heavy silence between them as it settled. The woman had tried everything to allow her to return to Torridon – fighting, running, bargaining – and Ridge had remained firm. His sense of pity for the woman was growing, but he also felt the need to reply to her offer in order to firmly establish his position. No amount of coercion was going to force him to change his mind in any of this.

His path was set, as was hers.

"My lady, your offer is most generous, and I find, much to my dismay, that I could actually consider it," he said. "But I regret that I cannot accept and I am truly sorry. I am sorry that my loyalty lies with our king."

Josephine already knew that and she didn't want to hear it from him. "As am I," she muttered.

God... as am I!

There was no more conversation after that. Edinburgh swallowed them up and Josephine found herself looking at the dark, dirty city with many levels to it. There were streets above streets, steep roads, and pale, dirty people. It felt as if they'd entered another world, one of death and darkness and strangers who seemed more like wraiths than people. Phantoms were in every corner. It seemed to her as if they moved through a maze of avenues to reach the road that led up to the massive, fortified castle at the crown of the city.

The hill that led up to the castle was rocky and steep. As the horse made his way up the grade, Josephine's gaze was on the massive building looming before them. It was made of stone, stained black from Edinburgh's damp climate, but it looked to her as if the stones were bleeding. Stained and ugly, they were, and she'd never felt more intimidated or alone in her entire life. The horse finally made it up the hill and entered into the courtyard of the hilltop fortress, where they were met by a flock of attendants and soldiers.

It seemed to Josephine as if they'd been waiting for them. Hands pulled Josephine from the stallion, but Ridge was off in a flash, grasping her protectively to prevent anyone else from getting a hand on her. She was his charge until the king said otherwise.

Two figures pushed their way through the crowd, and Josephine immediately recognized Nicholas de Londres. She hadn't even realized he'd left Torridon, but here he was, and she felt a great deal of relief at the sight of him. He looked at her with such sadness she was sure he would burst into tears at any second. The other man had black, curly hair and a thin mustache, and was of an average stature. He bowed gallantly to her.

"Lady Josephine de Carron, welcome to Edinburgh," he said, in a thin voice that wasn't quite Scottish, as if he'd been schooled somewhere other than Scotland. "I am William Ward, Chancellor to King Alexander."

Josephine simply glanced at the man. She couldn't muster anything more than that. Her attention returned to Nicholas, looking at the man as if he could help her. Nicholas' emotions were on the surface, as they always were, and he reached out and took Josephine's hand.

"Come with me," he said softly, leading her away.

Like a small child, Josephine allowed Nicholas to take her across the courtyard towards the entry. In truth, she clung to him, so very relieved to be with someone she knew, someone she knew to be kind and considerate of her situation.

William watched her go as he stood next to Ridge.

"Even dressed as a man, I can see that she is absolutely magnificent," he said appreciatively. "No wonder the king wants her."

Ridge gave William a cold glance. "He wants to wed her to the earl," he corrected.

William looked at him quickly. "Of course," he said. "That was what I meant."

Ridge wasn't so sure. He gave Ward a nasty glare before following after Nicholas and Josephine. William, seeing that perhaps the king's bodyguard wasn't too keen on the situation, wondered if the iron heart of Ridge de Reyne might have a weak spot for the lady.

It was something to ponder, in any case.

The king would want to know.

"IT IS AN absolute lie," Ridge said, struggling to contain his temper. "I do not know who told you such things, my lord, but I can assure you that I hold no feelings for Lady Josephine. If I did, she would not be here."

Standing before the king as the man sat in his private solar, a massive fire blazing in the hearth, Ridge stood tall and strong and proud before a man he was coming to hate. Now, someone had accused him of an attraction towards the very women he'd brought to Edinburgh for the king and Ridge was angrier than he'd ever been in his life.

But Alexander seemed to find some humor in it. He glanced at his numerous courtiers, who were also grinning. They all liked to taunt Ridge de Reyne because he was English, an outlander among them, but also because they knew the big man wouldn't do a thing to them, no matter how badly they tormented him.

"No one would blame you, de Reyne," Alexander said. He was exceedingly weary, still, from his harried flight from Torridon. He was still in sleeping clothes he'd put on when he'd arrived at Edinburgh. "She is a beautiful woman and you have spent two days and a night with her."

He said it rather suggestively and Ridge's jaw ticked faintly. "Because you ordered me to, my lord," he said. "I spent two days and one night with her because you ordered me to take her from Torridon, and that is exactly what I did."

Alexander was still fighting off a smile at his bodyguard's indignation as he reached for a cup of warmed wine that a servant brought him.

"What did you mean when you said that if you had feelings for Lady Josephine, she would not be here?" he asked.

Ridge wasn't sure if he should tell the king of the woman's attempt to escape and her general revulsion of the situation. It might focus the king's anger on her. But he wasn't in the habit of withholding the truth from his monarch, not even in a situation like this.

"She offered me money to let her return," he said. "If I harbored any pity for her at all, or if I was the greedy sort, I would have taken her money and returned her to Torridon. But I did not. I am loyal to my king's wishes, just as I have always been."

Alexander sipped at his wine, eyeing William Ward as he did so. It had been Ward who had told him of de Reyne's apparently sympathy towards the lady. But Ward was a gossip with the best of them and half the things he said could not be trusted.

"Of course you are, Ridge," Alexander said. "I was only jesting with you. Do not be too angry about it."

Ridge didn't reply to that. He wasn't about to forgive a man who liked to torment and shame him when the whim hit him.

"Will that be all, my lord?" he asked.

Alexander could see that Ridge was offended, still. "It will not," he said flatly. "I have more business with you before you retire. While I realize you must be weary from your journey, I wish to know when you left Torridon and what state it was in."

Ridge was essentially standing at attention in front of him, his eyes ahead. He wouldn't look at him. "I left several hours after you did, my lord," he said. "I had to wait for the right time to capture the lady, and that was difficult."

Alexander grew serious. "Did d'Vant see you?" he asked. "Were you followed?"

Ridge shook his head. "I was not seen nor was I followed, at least to my knowledge," he said. "I was able to leave by a postern gate in the kitchen yard, one that had been bolted but was not manned, at least not when I went through. Torridon sits on a rise and since I did not wish to be seen, I immediately headed to the east, through a heavy forest, and then found a smaller road that headed north."

Alexander digested that. "And Torridon? What was the state of the fortress when you departed?"

"Still intact. The siege had not started yet."

Alexander sat back in his chair, pondering the situation. "They still have several of my wagons," he muttered, glancing at his courtiers, some of whom had accompanied him there. "If they know I have taken their lady, and I am sure they will figure that out, then I wonder if I shall ever see them again."

It was a fairly flippant comment, as if he didn't take Torridon, their troubles, or what he'd done, seriously at all. As his courtiers grinned, most of them well into the wine that was being passed around, the king turned his attention to William Ward.

"Word has been sent to Alphonse, has it not?" he asked. "The man may be at his townhome in Liberton. He knew I was going to Torridon to seal the betrothal with the lady and he further knew I intended to bring her back to my castle, so he may have remained close to Edinburgh."

Ward had a ready answer. "He is, indeed, at Liberton, my lord," he said. "I have been in contact with the man and, already, he has sent gifts for his betrothed. The young woman is being tended and shall be well dressed this eve, in clothes provided by her future husband."

Alexander had a mental vision of a properly dressed Lady Josephine. "It is about time," he grunted. "The woman favors the clothes of a soldier, unfortunately. That is a habit that will have to stop. I doubt Alphonse will tolerate it."

"He wishes to meet his betrothed soon."

"He is eager, that one," Alexander said. But he didn't want the man coming too soon because Alexander wanted to spend time with the lady also. He'd hardly had time back at Torridon. "I am coming to wonder if Lady Josephine is too good for him."

"From what I saw, she is too fine, indeed, my lord."

Alexander's attention was lingering on his cousin, who was primed to make a fine royal mistress. He'd already broken one betrothal for the lady; it would be nothing to break a second. But that might provoke

Alphonse's wrath and he was unwilling to do that.

Ridge stood there and listened as the king and his chancellor continued to discuss the lady as if she were nothing more than a commodity. In truth, women were chattel and that was simply the way of the world, but Ridge couldn't help the pity he felt for the lady, increasingly sorry to have been part of the king's plan. But there was nothing he could have done – he was a pawn in this as much as Lady Josephine was. They were all following orders.

The orders of a fool.

JOSEPHINE SAT SUBMERGED up to her neck in the biggest copper tub she had ever seen. The water was strongly scented with lavender, with tiny purple petals floating in the steaming water. She had been scrubbed to within an inch of her life by several female servants and her hair had been soaped and rinsed three times, with the final rinse consisting of flat, dark beer.

Now, she lay back, allowing the warmth of the water to seep into her weary muscles and to clear her mind. God's Toes, how she needed to collect herself. So much had happened in a very short amount of time and she was still reeling from it.

Nicholas, bless him, had brought her up a back route in the castle, avoiding all of the usual king's men and the king himself. He could see she was tired and defeated, and that she needed a chance to collect herself before going head-to-head with Alexander. He had taken her to what had once been the room of a former princess, or that's what he'd told her, where a flock of maids greeted them. The apparent leader of the group, a pretty and robust young woman named Madelaine, promptly chased Nicholas away and began drilling her peers like a soldier.

In came the tub, the water, the soap, and the oils, and off went Josephine's filthy clothes. Madelaine was preparing to burn them until

Josephine stopped her, asking instead that they be washed and set aside.

All of this happened within the first hour she was there. Washing, scrubbing, and the like. The beautiful room she was in, the Princess Room, was actually part of a three-room suite. It was a massive chamber with twelve-foot ceilings and a carved marble fireplace that was taller than Josephine was. Rich rugs from mysterious places covered the floor and there was an intricately carved couch upholstered in blue silk with two matching chairs. The walls were covered with rich tapestries to create a barrier against the stone walls.

But there was more. Behind Josephine, against the wall, stood a massive mahogany wardrobe, and two carved stands flanked the bedchamber door and displayed twin alabaster vases. Surrounded by these riches, she had no doubt that she was in the castle of a king, and she found herself in awe.

After the scrubbing and washing, the servants were nowhere to be seen until she stirred in the bath and sat up. Then, they poured in from another room and rushed in with towels, brushes, and lotions. They didn't touch her until she actually stepped out from the tub, and then she was vigorously dried and oiled, and then wrapped in a magnificent purple robe. Madelaine then led her to a chair by the fire where her hair was gently combed out. A young servant girl brought her a tray of wine, bread, and fruit, and Josephine proceeded to devour the entire plate. She had not eaten since yesterday and she was famished.

As Josephine ate and the servants brushed and dried, Madelaine, the maid, stood back and watched the situation carefully. She admired the lady's luxurious hair as it dried, noticing its myriad of colors and the unearthly shine. Having been in the house of the king since she was very young, Madelaine had seen women come and go, and she wondered who this beautiful lady was and further wondered why she was here. She had heard nothing, nor had she been told anything, with the exception of Nicholas de Londres' orders to prepare these particular rooms for a guest.

But it seemed to be a very special guest. Madelaine, of course, would never dream of speaking to the solemn young woman; it simply wasn't proper. She was a maid from a long line of maids and she knew how to behave. Service was silent. But the young lady seemed very sad and Madelaine wished she could say an encouraging word to her without overstepping her bounds.

As Madelaine pondered the mysterious young woman, more activity started in the chamber. Three young maids came into the room, each bearing several richly-colored surcotes. Madelaine directed them to the giant wardrobe where they began carefully hanging the garments on the pegs, shaking them out to smooth the material.

As Madelaine supervised the garments, she happened to glance at the young woman for whom they were intended. She could see interest on the woman's face.

"Does my lady see a cote she would like to wear?" Madelaine asked respectfully.

Josephine was caught off guard by the question. No one had spoken to her since her arrival in the chamber, so she hadn't been expecting the softly-uttered question. She had no idea where the gowns came from, but she was certain the king had something to do with them. That being the case, she had half a mind to put her combat clothes back on, to display her complete dissatisfaction with the king's decision and to protest the manner in which she was being used.

But she knew that wouldn't go over well and she truly had no desire to fight tooth and nail with the king, at least at this point. She was in his house, surrounded by his men, and things could go very badly for her. She was defiant but she wasn't stupid. She would only fight a battle she could win and, right now, there was no chance of that.

But her chance would come.

"I have no preference," she said, looking away from the garments displayed. "You choose for me."

Madelaine did. She ordered the maids working over Josephine and drying her hair to work faster. The lady must be dressed, she said. As the servants began to move with a more clipped pace, Madelaine thoughtfully selected a garment she believed would suit the lady quite well.

But Josephine paid no attention; her mind was turning from the king and his complete control over her to Andrew and Torridon. In truth, her thoughts were never far from them. They'd been heavily on her mind for the past two days and continued to be. Most of all, she wondered what was happening with them at this moment. She was saddened beyond words, feeling anguish that she could do nothing about.

All she wanted to do was go home.

But that was not to be at this moment. She had to face the king and the situation at hand. Madelaine broke her from her train of thought as she came to her with a beautiful emerald-green silk with gold trim. As the woman held it up for her, Josephine realized the woman wanted to dress her in it. So Josephine stood reluctantly and allowed the woman and her little minions to dress her in fine, white shift with an embroidered bodice, another shift that was heavier and had a ruffle along the hem, before having her step into the green silk.

In truth, the surcote was as fine as any she had ever seen. With the snug V-shaped neckline accentuating her full breasts and with the long sleeves hugging her long arms, she found the gown to be most beautiful. Madelaine took a matching green ribbon and tied it about her head, pulling her hair from her face. On her feet were placed matching shoes and stockings.

It was quite a production and Josephine had never had so much help dressing. All she had to do was stand there and let the maids do all of the work. A knock at the door shattered the calm efficiency of the room and Josephine could feel her heart leap with fear. Who had come for her? Fully dressed, she moved over towards the windows, as far as she could get away from the door, while the servants scattered back into the shadows. Madelaine was left to open the door.

It was Nicholas. He entered and immediately caught sight of Josephine in the voluminous surcote. He smiled gently as he went to her, his eyes brushing over her.

"Ye look as beautiful as I have ever seen ye," he said.

Josephine smiled modestly and looked down at the gown. "Are you to thank for this?"

"Nay," Nicholas shook his head. "This is a gift from yer future husband. I understand more are on the way."

Josephine's smile vanished and she turned away. Nicholas, knowing her distress and confusion, ordered Madelaine to leave so they could have some time alone. It was only a matter of time before the king demanded audience with her and, after that, Nicholas had no way of knowing. He'd heard that Alphonse was on his way to the castle. When he came, Nicholas might not ever see her again. The mere thought made Nicholas feel ill.

When everyone was gone, he went and stood next to her, following her eyes as she looked from the window to the yard below.

"I am sorry, Josephine," he said softly. "I am sorry for the abduction, for taking ye away from Torridon so brutally. I did not even know my uncle had ordered that until we had left Torridon and de Reyne wasn't with us. I suspected something was amiss and my uncle was more than happy to admit it."

She continued to stare at the unfamiliar courtyard below. "It is not your fault," she said. "You have been a true friend, Nicholas."

Nicholas leaned against the wall, watching her. "As ye have been one to me, as well," he said. "But I should have foreseen this. I know my uncle and I know he can be unscrupulous. I should have suspected he might have done something like this."

"There would have been nothing you could do about it."

"I could have warned ye."

Josephine stepped away from the window. "Everything happened so quickly," she said. "Even if you had warned me, I am not sure anything could have been done."

Nicholas fell silent a moment, thinking of Torridon and the people there. People he'd enjoyed greatly in the short time he'd spent there.

"What of Andrew?" Nicholas asked quietly. "Does he know you were taken?"

Josephine shrugged. "If he did not at first, I am sure he has figured it out."

"He will not stand idly by while ye marry another."

Josephine looked at him. Nicholas didn't know that Andrew and the Earl of Annan and Blackbank were brothers and blood enemies. She was fairly certain no one had told him because the only person he'd really spent any time with at Torridon had been Donald, and Donald did not know the truth. But she knew she could confide in him and it would go no further.

"Nay, he will not," she said quietly. "He will come for me and he will kill the earl."

"Kill him?" Nicholas repeated. "It would do simply to take ye away from here. Killing an earl could be… complicated."

That was true, but there was a reason for Andrew's intent to kill Alphonse d'Vant. Josephine proceeded to tell him the entire story, starting from Andrew's birth and continuing until The Red Fury came to Torridon. Nicholas was truly amazed and found himself gaping at the conclusion of the tale. He knew that Josephine and Andrew were betrothed, but the entire situation was so complex that it was almost unbelievable.

Now, he understood why she was so distressed and so completely unhappy. And he doubly understood why Andrew had to come to Edinburgh to kill the man she was betrothed to.

"That is the most incredible tale I have ever heard," he said with awe. "They are brothers?"

"Indeed, they are."

"Does the king know this?"

"I doubt it. But I suspect he will soon enough, especially when Andrew arrives."

Nicholas could only shake his head, shock on his features. "Alexander's betrothal has made it possible for Andrew to have more of a reason to kill his brother than ever before."

It was the truth. "And now you understand," Josephine said. "I am afraid, Nicholas. Afraid of the earl, afraid for Andrew, and afraid of what is to come."

Nicholas didn't say anything to that because he completely understood those fears. Truth be told, he was having some fear himself. This situation was deeper and more complex than he could have ever imagined. Finally, he went over to one of the chairs near the hearth and sat down.

"The earl is on his way to the castle, Josephine," he said softly. "The chancellor sent word to him."

Josephine looked at him with stunned horror. "When?"

"Possibly tomorrow. I am not sure."

Possibly tomorrow. Josephine sank into the nearest chair, mulling that over. "Tomorrow," she repeated. "I am not expected to marry him when he comes, am I?"

Nicholas could only shrug. He had no idea. His eyes reflected pity and compassion from his deep poet's soul. He reached out and held her hand for a moment; a helpless gesture of support.

"Be brave," he told her gently. "Andrew's love for ye will make him the victor. I have no doubt he will win whatever battle ensues."

Josephine looked at him. "I pray that is true," she said. "But I have been told that the earl is a master swordsman. If Andrew wins, all well and good. But if Andrew loses, then I will kill myself. Have no doubt."

Nicholas looked at her; his eyes silently pleading with her to reconsider. "He will not lose," he said. "He is fighting for love. That is the greatest reason of all."

She thought for a moment on his words, believing them as well. She believed that with all her heart. But there would be no fight should the king see Andrew when he came for her. In fact, it was imperative that the king didn't see him at all.

"Nicholas," she said. "Will you do me a favor?"

"Anything.

Her expression was serious. "When the time comes and the duel is at hand, you must keep the king occupied," she said. "I fear that he will interfere and arrest Andrew. I could not bear it."

"I shall endeavor to do my best," he promised. "But until then, be strong. And I am at yer disposal."

She smiled gratefully at him. "I am glad I have a friend in you," she said. Then, she turned away from him dramatically. "Oh, Nicholas, why is the king surrounded by such good and noble men like you when he himself is a vain and self-centered child? Why couldn't you have been king?"

Nicholas had often wondered that himself. "God has His reasons," he said, moving for the door. "Ye must have faith, my lady. There is a reason for everything as it is."

She turned to him, a smile on her lips. "You are a philosopher as well as a poet," she said. "I think you would make a wonderful king."

He returned her smile, falling under Josephine's spell. He could see what d'Vant and the king saw in her. He paused by the door.

"Now that ye are properly dressed, would ye like to take a walk around the grounds?" he asked. "Edinburgh Castle is quite a place to see."

Josephine nodded, turning away from the window and coming towards him. "I would," she said. "It will help take my mind off what is happening around me."

"Then that is the best reason of all."

Nicholas would not soon forget the looks he received escorting the utterly lovely Josephine, for he had never felt so proud in all his life.

CHAPTER TWENTY-THREE

I T WAS LATE in the afternoon, the colors of sunset stretching across a sky that had seen more than its share of rain as of late. On the muddy road below, Andrew and Sully had made excellent time, covering a great distance quickly. Neither had eaten since the previous evening, and they'd had very little to drink, but they weren't hungry, nor did they feel thirsty.

They were focused on reaching Edinburgh Castle.

They did stop twice to allow the horses to rest and to drink. During these stops, they talked about small things; of future events, and other small talk. But during the second rest, Andrew talked of something not even Josephine knew of. It had simply never come up in conversation. It came about when the men were speaking of where Andrew and Josephine would live after they were married.

"Two years ago, I purchased a castle on St. Mary's Loch," Andrew said. "It sits on a rise overlooking the water and was built over the ruins of an abbey. It was in a deplorable shape when I purchased it from the Earl of Buccleuch, but the location is outstanding, in some of the most beautiful country I have ever seen. There is a small village near it and the villagers are a good-natured and hearty bunch. When the purchase was complete, I set the villeins and about fifty soldiers to its repair last year. It should be nearly complete by now."

Sully regarded him with some surprise. "I thought you were a vagabond," he said. "I had no idea you had actually intended to lay down roots."

Andrew grinned, lopsided. "I knew it would be wise to plan for a time when I could no longer lead my army," he said. "That time comes to us all. Josephine will love Descanso Castle. It's three times the size of Torridon and the only fortress for fifty miles in any direction."

"Sounds remote," Sully sniffed. "Did you name it Descanso?"

Andrew nodded. "It means 'rest' in Spanish. And that is what I intend to do when I live there."

Sully could well understand that. He pondered the castle in the Lowlands of Scotland, remote and rugged, and a thought occurred to him. "Andrew, if you kill your brother, you will inherit the title and the earldom," he was thinking aloud. "Will you not live at Haldane?"

Andrew didn't look too perplexed. "We can spend summers at Haldane and winters at Descanso," he said. "Haldane is the family seat, but Descanso… that is mine."

Sully was thinking other things, too, like Torridon and its future – he had always intended to return it to Josephine but if she and Andrew already had two homes, then he saw little point in returning Torridon to them. Perhaps he was destined to remain the Earl of Ayr, and he wasn't sure how he felt about that.

With a weary sigh, he stood up and went to his horse, tightening the animal's cinch. "Come along, lad," he said to Andrew. "Let us get on with retrieving your fair maiden."

Andrew watched Sully for a moment. He knew that Sully had planned to return Torridon to Josephine as soon as the circumstances permitted, and he was sure that Sully was now confused as to whether or not he should. After all, Andrew would have two fine castles. What would he do with a third, even if it was rightly his wife's? He sought to put Sully at ease.

"Sully," he said as he stood up and went to mount his horse. "Keep Torridon for yourself and for Justine. It's as much in your blood as it is in either of the ladies'. After Josephine and I are married, she will do well knowing you are taking good care of 'her' fortress."

Sully gave him a lopsided grin as he gathered up his reins. "How did you know I was thinking about that?"

"Because *I* would be thinking about it."

Sully simply shrugged as he mounted his horse. "We think alike, you and I," he said. "If you wish for me to keep Torridon, then that is what I shall do. But the title goes with it."

"I do not want that bloody title. I'll have one of my own."

Sully simply chuckled. Spurring their horses forward, they continued on their journey. They began to pass people on the road as they drew closer to Edinburgh; farmers with empty carts, merchants, and even a troop of traveling minstrels. One of the acrobats bent over backwards and walked along the road like a spider, bringing a hearty laugh from both men. Drawing closer to the city and watching the people was great entertainment, making a bright spot in a situation that lingered over them both like a storm cloud.

Darkness approached but Edinburgh was illuminated by thousands of torches and candles as the two entered into the city. Their focus was on the castle on the tall hill; they'd been able to see it for miles. It was a huge structure and was well-guarded, with only one road leading to and from it. It was a steep road, making the castle seem most inaccessible.

Now, the reality of the situation was settling as they arrived at their destination. Sully eyed the fortress, even from a distance.

"Have you any knowledge of the castle?" Andrew asked Sully.

Sully shook his head. "No, I have never been here."

"Not to worry," Andrew answered. "Let us find an inn near the fortress. It shall be ripe with information."

They wound their way down the streets of dirt, noticing how the city closed up tightly after dark. It was quiet, too; virtually no sound emitted from the rows upon rows of dingy, structures. There was an eerie feeling to the streets, as if phantoms lurked in every corner. Darkness surrounded them.

Finally, they came upon an inn very close to the road leading up to the castle called *The Falcon and The Flower* from the sign over the door. They tethered their horses at the watering trough and carefully entered the dimly-lit establishment. One always had to be on guard when entering taverns because in cities like this, they were often filled with cutthroats and rabble.

But Andrew had no intention of dealing with men at that level; he was more interested in what the inn employees or regulars knew. He spied several whores near the rear of the establishment and that was exactly what he was looking for – who knew more about their surroundings than whores? He looked at Sully, who was evidently following the same train of thought. They were both looking at the same dirty women, and they nodded imperceptibly to each other. This was where they would start.

Andrew and Sully were not hard to miss. Andrew was as tall as a tree with rich auburn hair, and Sully was fair and handsome with his pale blue eyes. The two men lumbered over to a table and sat heavily, bellowing for ale.

A barmaid and three whores came on the run. They bumped and pushed into each other as they hurried to sit next to Andrew. As the barmaid sat down two tankards and smiled a buck-toothed grin, a red-haired, skinny wench smiled lasciviously at Andrew.

"What's yer pleasure, beauty?" she asked.

Andrew gave the women his sauciest expression. "A drink and a woman," he said. "What else did you expect?"

The women at the table laughed loudly, thrilled to perhaps be part of his plans for the evening. "Then ye've come to the right place," the wench said. "We've got both!"

More laughter from the women as Andrew took a long drink of ale, smacking his lips with satisfaction. "Who do we see about renting rooms for the eve?"

"That would be Esme," said a dark-haired whore.

"Get her for me," Sully said, as he ran a finger along the woman's cheek as she fled.

They drank and made small talk until the whore came back leading a buxom blond. The woman was a very large and very shapely woman with a strong Nordic look. Her blue eyes locked in on Andrew.

"Can I be of service, m'lord?" she asked seductively.

The whores all shot her the evil eye as Andrew stood up, outwardly appreciating the female form.

"My friend and I need rooms," he said.

"I shall be pleased, m'lord, to escort ye myself," Esme replied smoothly.

Sully could see what Andrew was up to. An innkeeper would know and hear more than most. And there was one sure way to retrieve such information.

"Thank you," Andrew said, as he took a final swig and moved to follow the woman.

Sully made brief eye contact with Andrew as he left, and then turned his attention back to the three whores purring for his attention. He lit up with his handsome smile and turned on his considerable charm but, all the while, he felt he was being unfaithful to Justine. Normally, something like this wouldn't bother him in the least, but he had a wife waiting for him back at Torridon. And she was a wife he was coming very much to appreciate, so he felt guilty for what he needed to do in order to help out Andrew. But he made himself a promise – other than flirting, he would go no further.

For Justine's sake, he couldn't.

As Sully fought off the amorous whores, Esme led Andrew up narrow stairs and pushed open a warped door. As Andrew entered the room, looking about him, she closed the door softly. She waited politely while he pulled off his mail and his sword; all the while devouring his long legs and tight buttocks with her eyes.

Esme, as the owner's daughter, seldom attended the patrons herself, but she was going to make an exception in this case. This man was the most incredible male specimen she had ever seen. He moved with the muscular grace of a god. When he finally turned his gaze to her, she felt her insides turn to mush.

"Will ye be… needing anything tonight, m'lord?" The question was obvious.

Andrew took four steps and was on her, his hand entwined itself viciously in her hair and yanked her head back. His mouth clamped down so hard on hers that she uttered a small yelp of surprise. He kissed her roughly with no passion or emotion, and it was used purely for the fact that he wanted to discover everything she knew about the castle.

The woman was big, hard, and heavy as he took her to the bed. She was moaning and writhing, and was pulling at his hair as he ripped away her bodice and cruelly sucked on a nipple that was the size of a small apple. His hand went up her skirt to the most private of places, and began stroking her expertly.

"Esme," he breathed. "Do you know anything of the castle?"

She squirmed. "Like what?"

"Daily business."

She gasped as he hit a tender spot. "Mostly," she said. "The soldiers come here all of the time."

Andrew thought that might be the case. "And you see the business coming to and from the castle?"

"Always."

"Were there any special visitors today?" he asked, his lips brushing against her hard nipples. "Did you see anything? Or… hear of anything?"

The woman parted her legs, begging for his male organ, but Andrew wasn't even aroused. All he wanted was information.

"Such strange questions, m'lord," she panted. "But I did see that a woman was brought in today."

"How would you know that?"

"Because we are very close to the castle and visitors must pass by the tavern to enter the grounds," she muttered, trembling when he rubbed her in just the right spot. "She passed by with one of the king's knights. I've seen the man before; he's *Sassenach*. And a large troupe of actors and musicians also came in today. Why? Are ye an entertainer?"

He didn't answer her, but began to manipulate the sensitive nub between her legs. She bucked and cried, and Andrew felt oddly detached, watching as if he were a disinterested bystander. It was the most un-arousing thing he'd ever done.

"Where are the guests housed?" he whispered hotly in her ear. "Do you know?"

She cried out before answering. "My sister serves at the castle," she groaned. "In the past, I think she has said visitors are in the residence to the south of the gatehouse. That's where she works. But the entertainers are housed with the servants. Why do ye ask so many questions about it?"

Any more questions and she would more than likely become suspicious, but Andrew had heard most of what he needed to know. At least, he had an idea now. *In the residence to the south of the gatehouse.* He could find it once he was able to gain access to the castle. And then, hopefully, he could find Josephine from there.

His fact-finding mission was over and he needed to get away from the woman. He manipulated her quickly until she reached her climax. Then, he jumped from the bed, going over to the basin of water to wash the smell of her from him.

Esme stretched like a cat and smiled, putting herself back together as she sat up. He turned and looked at her coldly.

"Get out," he said.

Her smile faded and she looked at him questioningly, but she obeyed. He waited until she left before he pulled off his leather vest and threw it on the bed. Then, wearing only his trousers, black linen tunic, and thigh-high black war boots, he strapped on his sword and went to find Sully.

SULLY WAS HAVING a merry time where Andrew had left him. He and the three women were howling with laughter when Andrew came upon them.

"Montgomery," he said and jerked his head towards the door.

Sully nodded, patting the women as he stood up and followed. He waved and blew a kiss as if he were actually sorry to be leaving.

"God in heaven!" he exclaimed softly once they were outside. "I thought you would never come back!"

Andrew looked grim. "I had to discover what I could," he said. "Believe me when I say that I took no pleasure in it."

"What did you discover?"

"That Josephine was probably brought in today," he said. "She said a woman had been brought in by a knight. Who does that sound like to you?"

Sully's eyes narrowed as he pondered that question. "A knight brought her in?" he said. "Who could that be? The king took everyone with him when he left."

Andrew shook his head. "Clearly, not everyone," he said. "He sent a knight to retrieve Josephine and bring her to Edinburgh. Did you meet any of the knights that the king brought with him?"

Sully thought hard. "I think there were a few," he said. "But I think I saw them with the king when he left."

"All of them?"

Sully shook his head. "I'm not entirely sure," he said honestly. "But who would he have sent after Josephine?"

"His best, probably."

A light went on in Sully's mind. "What about that bodyguard who shadows him?" he said. "The big bastard. Someone told me he was an English knight, gifted to Alexander from Henry."

Andrew knew to whom he was referring and, suddenly, what Esme told him made some sense. "*Sassenach*," he hissed. "The woman told me the knight who brought the woman to the castle today was a Sassenach. It had to be the bodyguard. I met him when I went to greet the king's entourage when they first approached Torridon and he was out in front, protecting the king. De Reyne, I think his name was."

"De Reyne?" Sully repeated. "I think I ran into him once or twice, but I can't say we shared any conversation."

"Conversation or not, he is the only Sassenach I know within the king's entourage and Esme identified him," Andrew said. "He is our culprit. Esme also said that visitors are housed in a structure south of the gatehouse, so I would assume that was where he took Josephine. We have a starting point now."

"One of the vultures you left me with in there told me that her sister is a kitchen servant at the castle," Sully said with a twinkle in his eye. "She will do anything for the right price."

That was good news, exactly what they'd been hoping for. They'd reached their horses at this point and paused, determining what they were going to do next.

"Mayhap she can tell me where Josephine is," Andrew said. "How do we find this woman?"

Sully was rather smug in his reply. "Even as we speak, my new friend is sending word to her sister at the castle that there is money to be made for information," he said. "Her suggestion was that we stay until very late tonight or even tomorrow morning and wait for her sister to come to us. We will need the woman's help to enter the grounds because there is only one way in and one way out. We will need her advice."

Andrew glanced up at the massive castle behind them, perched high on a rock. The crag itself was rocky and sheer, and to try and climb into the castle would be impossible at best. He hated that he was so close and could do nothing to get any closer to Josephine; anxiety ate at him but he fought it off, knowing that there was literally nothing he could do until the morrow.

But the thought was killing him.

I am coming, Joey! Be brave!

"Very well," he said unhappily. "Then we will stay here tonight and meet with this woman when she arrives. I suppose there is nothing we can do until then, anyway."

"My thoughts exactly."

Now that their path for the night was set, they collected the horses and headed over to the livery across the road to bed them down. But after that, they would return to the inn for a good meal, a warm bed, and to fight off the women they'd so openly seduced. It could prove for a very interesting evening.

"Tell me, Sully," Andrew said as they collected their weary horses. "How did you obtain such information without resorting to physical bribery?"

Sully grinned. "Quite simple," he said. "I am persuasive as well as handsome and charming. Have you not noticed?"

He could hear Andrew laughing all the way into the livery.

CHAPTER TWENTY-FOUR

JOSEPHINE SAT AT the king's table in the great hall of the castle, but she was too distressed to eat.

God help her, this was the worst thing she'd ever faced.

When the king would turn in her direction, she would dutifully put small pieces of bread in her mouth and struggle to chew it. The king sat on her right, watching her with great interest as he sipped his wine. She was well aware that she was being watched and was vastly uncomfortable at his attention.

In fact, she was vastly uncomfortable with the entire situation.

It was horrible and disorienting. The noise in the hall was deafening because there were easily five hundred people in the hall; all eating, belching, laughing, and farting. Josephine was a little overwhelmed by all of the commotion and that contributed to her lack of appetite. But more than that, she simply didn't want to be there. She felt like a prized mare on display.

Nicholas sat on Josephine's left throughout the evening and he could see that, clearly, something was very wrong. She wasn't the same happy, sweet person he'd met at Torridon. She was sad and quiet. So, he spoke to her gently throughout the meal and tried to make her laugh with small jokes. She would smile weakly but rarely more than that as he tried very hard to cheer her. Sadly, it was a losing battle.

As Nicholas tried to entertain Josephine, there was another important player at the table who had only been introduced. Marie de Coucy, wife of Alexander, sat to the right of her husband, a darkly handsome woman with a weathered look about her. She and the king had been married for fifteen years and she had provided him with an heir. Even so, there were a half-dozen royal bastards running about, which deeply humiliated the woman of royal blood.

But Marie was a realist. She had long ago resigned herself to endure her husband's liaisons with quiet ignorance. She had too much dignity and pride to acknowledge her husband's many indiscretions, even when the results were paraded in front of her. She wasn't entirely holy, though. She was as cold as stone and possessed what some had characterized as an evil streak.

Whispers in the castle said Marie was worse than her husband ever was.

Josephine hoped she wouldn't ever have to find that out for herself. She had been introduced to her at the beginning of the meal, but the woman had barely acknowledged her. In fact, Josephine was acutely aware of the queen's cutting glances as the meal went on. Josephine was afraid of very little but, for some reason, this woman frightened her. There was something in her eyes that suggested something dark beneath.

Down on the floor below the dais, Ridge sat at the table for senior soldiers and officers, watching the dynamics happening at the king's table. He had cleaned up since his arrival to Edinburgh, clean-shaven and in fine clothing now. But he watched Josephine as she brooded over her supper and saw Nicholas' attempts to engage her. Since the moment she'd been taken away from him in the castle yard, he found himself increasingly concerned with her fate. Then at the same time, he was disturbed that he seemed to personally concern himself with it. He wasn't in love with her, even if he did find her extremely attractive, but he sensed that she was a rare woman. It was hard for him to describe, even to himself, how he felt. The closest he could come was a brotherly sense of protectiveness.

KATHRYN LE VEQUE

But sometimes, those were the most fierce.

As he sat there and mulled over Lady Josephine's situation, the music started loudly and a group of acrobats flooded forward, putting themselves on the empty floor between the dais and the rest of the diners. They flipped, juggled, and gyrated, but Ridge wasn't watching them. He was looking at Josephine as she noticed him and was now looking back at him.

He thought he could see the condemnation in her eyes.

Ridge watched as she tore her eyes away from him and glanced at the king, who was totally enthralled with some half-nude female dancers. As the man was so distracted, she turned to Nicholas and whispered something to him, and they both rose and quietly slipped from the table and discreetly left the room.

Ridge stood, took a deep gulp of wine, and followed.

Unaware that Ridge was trailing them, Nicholas and Josephine left the noise and lights of the feast and wandered out into evening. Across from the hall, tucked up against a rise in the natural rock, was a garden of sorts with a reservoir and organized plants. The night was surprisingly mild and the smell of greenery floated on the air as they strolled among the darkened area with growth and the reservoir. Nicholas glanced at Josephine, hoping her mood was lightening somewhat.

"Do ye have a garden at Torridon?" he asked.

Josephine shook her head regretfully. "Nay," she said. "Once, my mother had the beginnings of one, but it died when she did because no one took care of it. I have never had the time or the inclination to start another."

"But ye had time to paint," Nicholas said, clasping his hands behind his back. "I am still very much interested in seeing more of yer work. It is something ye should continue, Josephine, truly. Such talent his rare."

She shrugged modestly. "Mayhap, one day, I shall," she said. "Considering the state of my future, continuing a hobby seems so far away. Foolish, even."

They found a stone bench next to the reservoir, which turned out to be more of a pond with fish in it, and sat underneath the nearly full moon. Strains of music and laughter floated through the air and could be heard in the distance as they sat in silence.

Off to their left, leaves rustled and crunched. It was clear that someone was approaching. Nicholas rose in alarm, clutching at the dirk at his side, and Josephine stood, her face full of concern. As the noises came closer, Nicholas visibly tensed and Josephine looked about her to see what would make a good weapon.

But Ridge pushed through the bushes, his eyes twinkling with amusement at the look on Nicholas' face, and Nicholas exhaled sharply.

"Good Christ, Ridge," he exclaimed softly. "Ye nearly gave me fits!"

Ridge fought off a smile. "Good eve," he greeted casually, then nodded at Nicholas' waistband. "Were you planning to use that?"

Nicholas sheathed the dirk. "If I had to," he said. "What brings ye out into the gardens?"

Ridge shrugged, looking up into the diamond sky. "I longed for peace away from the screaming and twitching of the great hall," he said. "All of those people writhing about on the floor look as if they are experiencing a bad batch of ale."

Josephine laughed softly as she sat down on the bench again. Ridge watched her appreciatively.

"If I may be so bold, my lady, you look as lovely as the flowers that surround you," he said.

Nicholas rolled his eyes as Josephine nodded graciously. He knew Ridge well and had never heard him utter such ridiculous prose. In fact, he and Ridge were friends and he liked the man a great deal. But the poetry from his mouth was nonsense.

"Sweet words do not suit ye, Ridge," he said.

"Shut your lips, Nicholas," Josephine snapped good-naturedly, then looked at the soldier. "You speak them as if they were born to you. Ignore Nicholas."

"I always do," Ridge said dryly, eyeing Nicholas. "Yet in spite of my efforts, he never completely goes away. So, I am forced to associate with him and call him friend."

"The same is said for ye, de Reyne," Nicholas said, sitting back down next to Josephine. "Now, why are ye here?"

But Josephine was just coming to realize the two knew, and liked, one another. "I did not know you were friends," she said. "Nicholas, you spent all of your time with Donald whilst at Torridon. I never saw Ridge with you at all."

Nicholas lifted his shoulders. "Because he is my uncle's bodyguard," he said. "When we travel, Ridge never leaves his side, not even for a moment."

She looked at Ridge. "Yet you leave his side now?"

Ridge nodded. "There are others in the hall who protect the king," he said. "He does not need me at the moment. Besides, when I saw the two of you leave the hall, I had to come follow. You should not be left unchaperoned with Lady Josephine, Nicholas. She is spoken for."

Josephine's smile vanished and Nicholas shot Ridge a nasty look. It was a very blunt statement that had displeased them both and reminded them of why Josephine was really here. Here to face a horrific beast of a betrothed. When Ridge realized he'd been insensitive, the jesting ceased.

"Forgive me, my lady," he said quietly. "I did not mean to sound so callous."

"He cannot help himself, Josephine," Nicholas put in. "He is a cad."

Ridge nodded readily. "I am, indeed."

Josephine looked at him with sad eyes. "I would believe that," she said. "But even so, I do not sense ill from you. I never have. Somewhere beneath that knightly exterior, I would imagine you are a man of morals and character."

Nicholas nodded before Ridge could respond. "He is," he said. "And my uncle torments him for it."

Josephine looked at Ridge with concern. "Is this true?"

Ridge looked uncomfortable, asked a question he did not want to answer. But out of politeness, he was forced to come up with some

336

manner of response.

"I serve the king," he said simply. "He is not obligated to treat me any way other than how he wishes to."

Nicholas' face darkened. "Ye're a saint, Ridge," he said. Then, he looked at Josephine. "My uncle and his courtiers speak the Scottish when Ridge is around and call him *Sassenach* and English bastard, among other things. I've heard them. Ridge never acknowledges it, but sometimes I would like to punch them all for what they do. In fact, I'd be willing to wager that my uncle forced Ridge to abduct ye and bring ye to Edinburgh. Isn't that true, Ridge?"

Ridge was looking at his passionate young friend in the darkness. "I am the king's to command, Nicholas," he said quietly. "It does not matter what the order is. I must obey it."

Nicholas made a face. "I knew it," he hissed. "Rather than escort ye honorably from Torridon, my uncle took the easy way out. He had Ridge sneak ye out. That way, if Andrew caught Ridge and killed him, my uncle would be blameless. He could say that he did not tell Ridge to take ye."

Josephine was rather horrified to hear all of this. She looked at Ridge and felt very sorry for the man. "Does he truly abuse you so, Ridge?"

Ridge wouldn't acknowledge what they were driving at. He was a man of great pride, a knight of the highest order, and to seek sympathy for his treatment was beneath him. He bore it as he always did; with dignity.

"He is the king and can do as he pleases," he said simply. "And that includes directives towards you, Lady Josephine. He is the king, you are his subject, and there is nothing any of us can do about it."

That was the truth, but a most depressing truth. Josephine could see that, much like herself, Ridge was simply a pawn. Evidently an abused pawn and even if the man had abducted her from Torridon, it wasn't as if he'd taken any joy in it. He was only doing what he'd been told. As she sat there thinking about their intertwined lives, she began to feel very cold and very exhausted. It had been an extremely long day.

"As you say, Ridge," she said quietly. "As much as I would like to sit here and continue this conversation, I find that I am quite weary. I should like to retire."

Nicholas shot to his feet. "May I escort ye, my lady?"

Ridge didn't even ask; he simply reached out and took Josephine's hand, tucking it into the crook of his arm. There was a bond they shared, as strange as it was, and his brotherly instincts were taking over.

As Nicholas followed the pair, quite unhappy that he was left without the lady on his arm, Ridge escorted Josephine back to her lovely chambers where the army of servants, led by Madelaine, was waiting to put her to bed.

LATER THAT NIGHT, Sully and Andrew were ready to breach the castle.

As they waited for the whore's sister to make an appearance, Sully was forced to spend more time with the woman whose sister they were waiting for simply because he wanted to ensure the sister didn't lead them into a trap once they'd entered the castle. Vindictive women could do terrible things to a man, so Sully kept up appearances as Andrew retired to their rented room and stayed clear of Esme, who kept knocking at the door and trying to bring him food and wine.

He ignored her.

At some point before midnight, the whore's sister appeared, summoned by the message and the lure of money to be made. The whore, whose name was Ermaline, and her sister, Ermagarde, were more than happy to help Sully and Andrew find a way into the castle. Once Andrew gave a plausible story that he was looking for a sister that he believed was being held by the king, Ermagarde made the very reasonable suggestion that Andrew and Sully should pose as farmers or servants bringing their wares to the kitchens of the castle.

As Ermagarde explained it, those were the only people who were allowed free travel through the multitude of gates that led to the heart of the castle. In fact, Ermagarde worked in the kitchens and in the great hall, and she was very willing to help Andrew find his sister. Truthfully, she really didn't care why he wanted to get into the castle, especially after he paid her a gold crown. It was more money than the woman had ever seen at one time and he promised her another crown once he was safely inside.

It was an offer too good to pass up.

Therefore, Ermagarde was very serious about getting the men into the castle under the guise of bringing produce or other supplies for the kitchen. Andrew and Sully thought it rather curious that, even at night, supplies were being delivered to the castle, but Ermagarde assured them that it was not unusual. Therefore, the men stripped down to tunics and breeches, burying any weaponry underneath their clothing, but that wasn't good enough. Ermagarde and Ermaline found dirty cloaks for them to wear, taken from the slovenly grooms who manned the livery across the road, and the cloaks covered up not only their torsos, but their heads as well. Andrew rubbed dirt on his face, as did Sully, to complete their disguise.

Now, they looked like the ordinary rabble. It had not been too difficult to blend in with the villeins and other servants, but they made sure to stay clear of any soldiers who might recognize them. Even in the darkness, a suspicious soldier could blow their cover, so they kept their heads down. The road leading to the castle seemed to be crawling with soldiers, so it was imperative for them to keep a low profile.

Ermagarde was surprisingly good at helping them blend in. It was she who spied a bent-over man hauling apples up the steep road leading to the castle and the man gladly handed over his burden when Andrew paid him a few silver coins for the apples, far more than he would have been paid for them at Edinburgh's kitchens. With sacks of apples on their shoulders and Ermagarde's help, Andrew and Sully made their way through two gates of Edinburgh's main road and around the west side of the castle where they came upon the unmistakable smells of the kitchens.

There was quite a bit of commotion going on and they were scarcely noticed, much to their delight. It was obvious that there was a great feast going on as they caught the sights and smells of a massive amount of food. It seemed to both Andrew and Sully that there was something special going on, and Ermagarde was a wealth of information on that subject. When Andrew gave her another gold coin, she bubbled forth like a rain-swollen river on most of the gossip she'd heard as of late, including the rumor that the Earl of Annan and Blackbank was due on the morrow.

That was exactly what Andrew had wanted to hear.

His brother would arrive on the morrow.

Andrew had one final question of her and that was where she thought the king might house visiting female guests. Ermagarde was quick to point out the large building west of the great hall. Andrew then thanked her and the woman fled inside the kitchens, returning to her duties so that she would not be missed.

As Andrew and Sully stood in the shadows of the kitchens with their loads of apples still on their backs, Andrew appeared to settle down in what seemed to be a resigned mood.

"So… he is coming here," Andrew said quietly. "So be it. My brother shall meet his end on the morrow."

Sully raised his eyebrows with reluctant agreement. *So much hate,* he thought. It was the kind of hate that could blind one's soul.

"That is tomorrow," he said quietly. "We must find Josephine today."

With that, they headed in the direction the girl had indicated. The night was cold and the nearly full moon was bright, casting eerie phantoms over the landscape. The foot traffic lessened dramatically as they left the kitchens, making their movement somewhat easier.

They could hear the music and voices in the distant hall as they reached what seemed to be a garden of sorts. There were bushes and vines, enough to hide in, and they covertly snaked their way around the shrubs to remain out of sight. They huddled together as their eyes lifted to the massive structure in front of them, the building to the west of the hall. Ermagarde had indicated this might be the building where visiting ladies would be housed.

It was as good a starting point as any.

As they crouched in the darkness and mulled over their options, two figures approached the garden from the direction of the great hall. It was difficult to see them from where the two men were, but they could make out male and female forms. They seemed to be talking between themselves and were completely unaware of the large figure that slipped from the door behind them, heading off into the depths of the garden.

The huge, dark figure moved swiftly, but he did not appear to be making secret his appearance. Andrew and Sully worked their way around so that they could keep all three figures in view.

The male and female figures moved into the silver moonlight and Andrew's eyes widened in recognition. God's Bones, it was Josephine! He felt as if he'd had the wind knocked out of him; of all of the women in the castle, she was the one who happened to be taking a walk in the garden at this particular time. His luck was almost too good to be true, and his palms begin to sweat with excitement.

He could hardly believe it.

He glanced at Sully and saw him flash a grin; he knew they were both thinking the same thing. It would be so easy to pluck her right now from under the king's nose. The only obstacle was the man she was with – who in the hell *was* he?

Andrew moved a little so that he could see the face of the man who escorted Josephine. Peering closer, he recognized the handsome features of young Nicholas de Londres. He rolled his eyes, feeling jealousy creep into his veins. He'd told Josephine to stay away from the poetry-spouting whelp. That young man was in for a good thrashing for turning his attentions on The Red Fury's woman.

But nothing untoward happened between Josephine and Nicholas.

They were sitting a proper distance apart, talking quietly. As Andrew watched, he began to formulate a quick and decisive plan of escape. Security seemed to be heightened due to his brother's arrival on the morrow, so their actions would have to be well-planned and covert. It was too bad that he didn't ask the little kitchen servant about the soldiers' routines.

Andrew and Sully heard the leaves crunching to their left before Josephine and Nicholas did. They had completely forgotten about the third person who'd come out into the moonlight, but now they were poised and ready to strike should a hostile move be made against Josephine. Andrew could hear blood pounding in his ears and he could not remember ever feeling more alert. Sully, too, was ready to charge.

But young Nicholas had heard the noise, as well, and was immediately on his feet with a nasty-looking dirk in his hand. As Josephine rose behind him, Andrew could see how utterly lovely she looked. She was wearing a very fine gown, and the sight of her sweet face made him doubly determined to keep her from harm.

Ah, Josephine, sweet Josephine...

Ridge de Reyne pushed his big body through the bushes, grinning like a fool. Nicholas dropped his guard and spoke sharply to him, but it was clear that there was no hostility. There seemed to be some laughter going on. Andrew and Sully found themselves relaxing as well, and tried to pick up pieces of the conversation.

Even though Josephine was safe, the appearance of de Reyne was an unwelcome one – there would be no easily plucking Josephine from Edinburgh with de Reyne at her side. The man was the king's body-guard, and certainly for good reason. Although neither Sully nor Andrew had ever fought with the man, simply from the look of him, he was seasoned and surely he must have been talented to hold the post that he did. Any battle with him would be long and drawn out, and would undoubtedly draw attention.

That was exactly what they wanted to avoid.

As they sat there and assessed how to proceed, Josephine abruptly stood up and Ridge took her arm, escorting her back towards the hall and the buildings surrounding it. Andrew watched closely as the three people moved into the castle through the door with the elaborate corbel over the arch.

"Damn!" Andrew exploded when they were gone. "She was right in my hand and I let her slip through!"

"Not entirely," Sully said. "You simply showed your intelligence. It would have been foolish to attempt to rescue her with de Reyne around."

Andrew knew he was right, as much as he didn't want to hear it. "I know," he said. "But she was right here. Right here!"

Sully could hear the angst in his voice. Before he could reply, however, a light appeared in a window directly above the door that Josephine had disappeared through. Although they did not see anyone in the window, somehow, they suspected it was Josephine's room.

Now, it was time to make plans. Andrew studied the stone building from a distance. The stone was rough-hewn and it was possible there would be a way for him to actually scale the wall. But on the corner of the building was a tree, with branches overreaching the area close to the doorway. That was a possibility, too. Either way, he would get in through that window.

He would get what he'd come for or die trying.

CHAPTER TWENTY-FIVE

JOSEPHINE WAS DREAMING of Torridon and the days before her father and brother had died, when there was all the time in the world to pursue leisurely hobbies or do nothing at all. The birds sang, Torridon was in fine condition, and she could see her father's face as plainly as if he were breathing again. She was happy.

She dreamed that she was standing in the foyer with her father when the massive entry door opened of its own accord, with the wind hissing in and lightning flashing. She turned to see Andrew standing in the doorway, larger than life, as the wind blew his hair wildly, his big body clad from head-to-toe with armor and leather.

She smiled at the sight of him as her father looked on cautiously. Just like Father, Josephine thought; always wary. Andrew smiled at her and began to walk towards her, with his big boots thumping deliberately on the stone. He extended a gauntleted hand to her.

"Josephine," he said. His voice made her feel warm and tingly all over.

She placed her hand in his, her other hand going to his cheek. It was warm and scratchy with stubble.

"Josephine," he said. His voice was so… real.

"*Josephine!*"

Josephine jolted from her sleep at the sound of her name. Someone was calling to her. Before she could see who it was, however, a huge hand clamped over her mouth and she felt hot breath in her ear.

"Joey, love, it is I," Andrew whispered soothingly. "Keep quiet."

Josephine sat up in bed, throwing her arms around him faster than he could rise to the bed from his knees. In fact, she'd thrown him off balance. As Josephine clung to his neck, Andrew sat on the bed and clutched her fiercely, feeling her warmth against him. It was better than he remembered, and all the risk that he had taken to find her was well worth the price. At this moment, it didn't seem like any risk at all.

He had her.

Josephine was so happy to see Andrew that she couldn't even speak. Half-asleep, she wondered if she was still dreaming, but he felt so firm and warm under her hands. Had she gone mad, then? Tears sprang to her eyes, tears of joy and relief. Her excitement overwhelmed her as she peppered his face with eager kisses.

"Is it really you?" she gasped.

"It is really me."

Those words meant the world to her. She hadn't gone mad, after all. "But how did you find me?" she whispered urgently.

Now, his kisses were overtaking her, leaving her breathless. "Foolish Joey," he breathed. "Did I not tell you that I would always come to you? Not even death could keep me from you, sweet. And certainly not Alex the Weak. What happened? How did you get here?"

Josephine struggled to catch her breath. "Ridge de Reyne," she said. "Do you know him? He is the king's bodyguard. He abducted me at Torridon just as the battle was about to begin."

It was confirmation of what Andrew had already heard. "But how did he get you out of the castle?"

She shook her head. "I do not know," she said. "He knocked me unconscious. When I came to, we were on the road."

Andrew sighed heavily. In the long run, it didn't matter how Ridge removed her from Torridon. All that mattered now was how to get her back there. He kissed her and hugged her again, holding her tightly, feeling his mind clear now that she was in his arms. Now, he could think clearly. He had to have a plan.

"My fortress," Josephine broke into his thoughts. "What happened to my fortress?"

He released her enough so that he could look her in the eye. "Have no fear, my little solider," he assured her. "Torridon still stands."

"Is it badly damaged?" she asked. "What of Colin Dalmellington and his army?"

"They suffered heavy casualties," he said. "Now that they know The Red Fury's army is protecting Torridon, I doubt they will attack again any time soon. Their losses were severe.

Josephine was greatly relieved to hear that. "But what of my men?"

He sobered. "We lost four knights, including Severn."

Josephine's expression washed with sorrow as she thought back to her last moments at Torridon. "I hesitate to tell you that it may have been Ridge who killed Severn," she said. "Severn was with me the moment Ridge abducted me. There was a fight... at least, I think there was. I really do not know. All I know is that Severn and I were heading to the wall and, suddenly, someone hit me on the head. That is all I remember, but if Severn tried to defend me against Ridge, then it is possible that Ridge killed him."

Andrew wasn't sure how he felt about that. In a fair fight, men were often killed, and Ridge was carrying out the king's orders. Severn more than likely got in the man's way. It was brutal and it was regretful, but it explained a lot. Seeing the anxiety on Josephine's face, he hastened to reassure her.

"Anything is possible," he said. "Not to defend the man, but I hesitate to accuse him of murder without proof."

"Nor I," Josephine said. "It is sad, Andrew... Ridge seems like a decent man. He was not cruel to me in the least on our travels here. He was simply carrying out orders, orders that it was clear he did not agree with. The king ordered him to abduct me from Torridon, so he did. But I do not think he likes our king in the least. Nicholas told me that the king's courtiers taunt Ridge because he is English. They are not kind to him at all."

Andrew thought that was rather interesting. "I would not taunt Ridge de Reyne in any case," he said. "He is a very big man with a very big sword. The king's courtiers are fools."

Josephine nodded, laying her head against his chest as the excitement of their reunion died down and reality settled in. She snuggled close, feeling his arms wrapped around her. But his presence, and his closeness, reminded her of one very important factor.

"Your brother will be here tomorrow," she said.

"I know," he said softly.

She lifted her head to look at him. "You do? How do you know?"

He smiled faintly. "I have been paying a good deal of money for information around here," he said. "I was told my brother is expected shortly."

She eyed him in the darkness, her hand going up to his rough cheek. "And you will fight him when he comes."

"I will."

She knew that. She'd known it all along, but it didn't stop the tears of fright in her eyes. She'd heard terrible things about the earl and was rightfully terrified. Andrew caught the tearful glimmer.

"Do not fear," he whispered softly. "I shall not lose. I cannot. Love conquers all."

"But… everyone will be against you," she said, struggling not to weep. "It will be you and me against the entire kingdom."

"And Sully," he put in.

She looked surprised. "Sully is here?"

He nodded, amused at her expression. "He is hiding down in the garden like a good little knight," he said. "You did not think he would remain at Torridon while his mistress was in distress, did you?"

Josephine shook her head in wonder, a faint smile on her lips. "Nay," she said. "And I am more at ease with the knowledge that Sully is here. But I am still frightened for you, Andrew. I do not know what I would do if I lost you."

He kissed her gently. "Have I not told you this, Joey? Not even death can keep me from you. I will win this battle because I have the most to lose. Therefore, I cannot lose."

He sounded confident but she was still frightened. But she thought not to tell him again because he already knew her fears. She was afraid it might damage his confidence if she continued to tell him how fearful she was.

They sat in silence for several moments after that, embracing tightly and feeling each other's warmth. Josephine was completely over-whelmed by his presence, never wanting to be separated from him again. She could have remained as they were, forever.

Andrew, for his part, was deep in thought. He knew he might not get another chance to be alone with her like this, at least not for a while, and there was something he knew he must do. She was his, always and forever, and he had to taste her again. He needed to feel her warmth around him but, more than that, he had to demonstrate his love for her once more. With a battle on the horizon, he was afraid it might be for the last time.

Tipping her chin up, his lips claimed hers sweetly, tenderly. When Josephine put her arms around his neck, his kisses grew more passion-ate, more forceful, and he laid her back on the bed. Without words, Josephine seemed to know what was about to happen. Already, she was opening her legs for him, her body completely nude beneath the shift she wore.

Andrew didn't keep her waiting.

Time was passing, and the chances of Andrew being discovered greatly increased. Quickly he stripped off everything, his tunic and breeches coming off, landing in a pile next to the bed. Josephine could see his magnificent body in the weak light and she ran a finger over his chest, his belly, watching him shudder at her touch.

She was discovering the feel of a man, acquainting herself with Andrew's spectacular form, but Andrew couldn't control himself. Reaching up, he grasped the linen gown and pulled it quickly over her head, exposing her nakedness.

His hands reached out to gently fondle her breasts, unbelievably soft in his callused hands. He dipped his head forward and caught her lips in his own, and gently caressed her breasts as he suckled her lips. It was sensual, maddening, and utterly arousing, and Josephine was being driven mad, she was sure. His touch electrified her and his mouth was doing devilishly wonderful things. When he settled himself between her pretty legs, she was without fear, and when he began to thrust, she welcomed it.

Andrew could only feel extreme satisfaction and arousal as he began to move inside her, slowly at first, but then increasing in power. The strokes were measured and strong, and Josephine moved with him, mimicking his actions, thrusting her pelvis forward to meet each stroke. A delicious, tingling warmth spread from her loins and filled her veins. It was as if this action alone consumed her entire being.

The movement between them became faster and harder, and a sheen formed on their bodies as their lovemaking continued. Andrew released her hands and groped her breasts again, squeezing in rhythm with his thrusts, but then he suddenly stopped.

Before Josephine could question him, he withdrew from her body and flipped her onto her stomach. Josephine was dazed with passion as Andrew brought her up onto her hands and knees. Pulling her legs apart slightly, he drove into her from behind and immediately began firm, hard thrusts.

It was a new level of passion never before felt as Josephine experienced their lovemaking from an entirely new angle. His hands moved to her breasts, using them as anchors to keep her from moving away from him. Josephine moaned and thrashed her head about, completely oblivious to anything but his attentions. But one of his hands moved to the damp curls between her legs and began manipulating her. Then, it was all over in seconds.

Josephine's tremors consumed her, gasps of pleasure coming from her lips. Andrew followed shortly, thrusting into her one last time with a grunt of pleasure and holding Josephine to him with great ferocity as he spent himself in her sweet body. Bound to each other, they fell together on the bed.

It was a while before either one spoke. Josephine had never felt so alive, so wanted, or so loved. Her love for Andrew knew no limits as she felt the man around her, still embedded in her. It seemed that he had no intention of removing himself, which was fine by her. As she lay there and her breathing eased, Andrew kissed the back of her head.

"Are you well?" he murmured.

"Aye."

He kissed her head again. "I love you, Joey," he whispered. "For all time, I shall love you, more than my own life."

She snuggled into his embrace, her arms over his arms as they held her. "And I love you," she breathed. "If you should die tomorrow in your quest to kill your brother, wait for me at Heaven's gate. I shall not be far behind you."

Andrew's smile faded as he thought on her words. Although he was deeply touched by her devotion and declaration, the thought of Josephine dead nearly drove him out of his mind. It had never occurred to him that she would not want to live without him but, more than that, knowledge of their betrothal, when it came to Alphonse, could prove deadly for her.

"Josephine," he said after a moment. "Whatever happens, never mention to my brother that we are betrothed. I fear… I fear his hatred of me will drive him to do unspeakable things."

Josephine pulled away from him. Then she turned in his arms so that she could look at him. Her eyes filled with fear.

"He will not hear it from me," she said. "Although Ridge knows, as does Nicholas. But they will not tell him, I am sure."

Andrew wasn't pleased that two men loyal to the king knew of their betrothal, but he didn't scold her. There was no point. He simply kissed her again and wrapped his arms around her, savoring the last few moments of this precious encounter. He knew it might be a long time before he would be able to hold her again.

Each minute was stolen and precious right now and he knew he couldn't remain with her much longer. Already, he had been far longer than he'd anticipated. With one last kiss, he released her.

"I must go," he whispered as he sat up. "Every moment I spend here is another moment I may be seen. I am assuming there are servants all over the place."

Josephine nodded, sitting up in bed and watching the man as he hurriedly dressed. He was so beautiful to watch, his big muscles and sleek form. But she tore her eyes away and noticed a small, colored stain on the linens. She ran her hand across it.

"They will see this," she murmured. "They will see this and wonder."

Andrew was pulling on his leather gloves as he glanced down at the spot. It was a colored discharge from her body, which had probably not healed since the first time he'd taken her.

"Tell them your woman's cycle has begun," he said without hesitation. "That should keep the king and my brother at bay for a time."

Josephine jerked her head up to him, shocked that he should mention such unspeakable things so casually. He saw her expression and laughed.

"Do not look so horrified, Joey," he said. "It is a natural occurrence, like eating and pissing. Women are cursed with it and men are awed by it. They will stay away from you quick enough if you tell them your woman's time is upon you."

It was rather clever of him, she had to admit. But she was still slightly mortified at the suggestion. Yet, she was willing to do anything at this point to keep the king and the earl away from her.

When Andrew was finished dressing, he reached down to pull her to him, his warm mouth kissing every inch of her face. Josephine clung to him, with small whimpers escaping her lips as she realized he was saying goodbye. Perhaps even forever. Her fear claimed her and she began to cry.

"Do not leave me," she sobbed quietly. "Please do not go."

His heart was breaking as he kissed her again as he tried to pull away from her. "I shall be nearby, always," he assured her. "Nothing will happen to you, Joey. I promise."

He tried to remove her arms from him, but she was like a terrified child. "I am so afraid, Andrew," she wept. "Please take me with you."

He wasn't getting anywhere trying to pull away from her so he paused, clasping her face between his two big hands. "Joey, listen to me," he said steadily. "By tomorrow, this will all be over and you and I shall be traveling back to Torridon for our wedding. Sully and I are here; we will let nothing happen to you. Be brave, love, as I know you are. Make me proud."

Make me proud. She very much wanted to. Josephine's breathing calmed and she relaxed her death grip. She believed his words. She knew nothing would happen to her as long as he was near. Josephine was so frightened that she had to believe him. But in the back of her mind, she reminded herself that she was a de Carron, and Hugh did not raise weak children.

"Leave me your dirk," she said after a moment. "At least give me the chance to protect myself."

Andrew considered her request. He wasn't so sure it was a good idea, but he knew she would never use it foolishly. He did not want to leave her without any personal protection. Taking his dirk from the belt at his waist, he placed the hilt of it in her palm with a deliberate motion.

"Only if necessary," he whispered.

She nodded. "Only if necessary."

With a lingering stroke to her silky cheek, Andrew departed, leaving Josephine sitting on her bed with the dagger in her hand. As she watched, he went out the way he came in – through the window overlooking the entry door to the structure. Long-legged, sure-gripped, Andrew moved like a spider as he climbed out and dropped to the earth several feet below. Josephine jumped out of the bed and ran to the window, only to see him stealing off into the darkness.

Her heart was beating rapidly as she climbed back into bed, her mind whirling with the events of the evening and with what was still to come. Clutching the dirk to her breast, she fell into a fitful sleep.

CHAPTER TWENTY-SIX

JUSTINE HAD PACED the castle like a caged animal since Andrew and Sully's departure. Never had she been alone in the fortress without Josephine or Sully, and the knowledge that they were in danger, and Andrew along with them, nearly drove her mad.

Several times, she had consulted her cards and, several times, she was left confused with the results. They simply weren't making any sense. Perhaps it was because Justine was no longer a virgin and her powers had been significantly diminished. Not that she would have traded her marriage to Sully for anything but, still, she feared her powers of insight had left her.

She was no longer the witch she had once been.

Now, she was pacing the Knight's Haven, a room she seldom entered. But with everyone gone, she had called the knights of Torridon together before dawn and had given command over to Etienne and Thane. It was a wise decision on her part, for she truly had no idea how to run a fortress and was in no condition to make any kind of decision.

She had not slept for two nights. Instead, she was trying to devise a plan of action. But she was not a soldier and could not think in those terms. She was, however, a bit of an actress and a skilled deceiver, and she believed that therein lay her best offense.

Donald was still at Torridon, remaining behind when Sully and Andrew headed to Edinburgh. He thought Justine might need his help and he'd been correct; the woman had been a mess. At this early hour, he entered the Knight's Haven because he'd been summoned, with his expensive boots thudding dully against the stone as he crossed the chamber.

"Ye sent for me, Lady Montgomery?" he asked quietly.

Justine turned to look at him and he was amazed to see the change in her. She wore one of her sister's yellow silk gowns and her hair was attractively styled; not at all like the Justine of the past. Marriage had certainly done something for her.

"I have," she said. "Donald, you are not planning on leaving us yet, are you?"

Donald shook his head. The swelling in his nose had gone down quite a bit and he was feeling well enough to travel, but he couldn't bring himself to leave, not just yet.

"Nay, my lady," he said. "I had not planned on it."

"Good," she said firmly. "Donald, I have need of you. You and I are traveling to Edinburgh."

His eyes widened. There was doubt in his expression. "May I ask why?"

"Because my sister, her betrothed, and my husband are there and are in great danger," she said. "They may need our help."

Donald thought that was the case, but he wasn't sure it was a good idea. "We may get in the way of their rescue attempt."

Justine was stubborn. "I do not think that is true," she said. "It is only the three of them against all of Scotland. I cannot stand here and wait to become a widow, Donald. Please say you shall go with me. If you do not, I will simply go without you, so it would be better if you agreed."

It was a blunt way of putting it, but Donald knew she spoke the truth. He also knew it wouldn't be a good idea to argue with her about it. Justine did as Justine wanted to do, and it had always been this way.

"Have ye spoken to any of the other knights about it?" he asked. "What of Etienne or Burl?"

Justine shook her head. "They must remain here and in command," she said. "I have no duties here at Torridon, Donald. I am tired of feeling useless. I must go and help my sister."

It was a very bad idea and Donald almost said so, but he bit his tongue. Whatever he said to her would not make her change her mind. As she said, she would go without him, and that would be a terrible thing, indeed. Therefore, he sighed in resignation.

"If that is yer wish, Lady Montgomery, then we shall go," he said. "We will do what we can."

Justine nodded, triumphant. She didn't feel so helpless anymore. "Good," she said. "Let me pack my things and you will see to the horses. I shall meet you in the inner ward in an hour."

She breezed past him, heading from the Knight's Haven. Donald watched her go, shaking his head doubtfully. If truth be known, he only agreed to go with her because he had nothing better to do and he wouldn't be able to stand the thought of Justine going to Edinburgh alone. Back at his fortress awaited his overbearing father and two stupid sisters, and Donald always yearned for adventure and freedom. In helping Justine, perhaps, he was actually being presented with an opportunity to do something worthwhile.

Or extraordinarily stupid.

Donald went to the room he had been occupying since his arrival at Torridon and packed a small satchel, all the while wondering what exactly Justine had in mind. He had known the girl since she had been a small child and he never could seem to understand the workings of her mind. Hell, no one could. Justine had always been skittish and strange, and Donald was truly amazed at her metamorphosis since her wedding to Montgomery. It was as if she had finally found her place in life.

Donald, on the other hand, seemed to have yet found his particular place in this life. He knew that one day he would inherit everything from his father, but Donald wasn't content with that. He longed for the adventure of love, and although he wasn't as accomplished a swordsman as Andrew or Sully, or every other knight he had ever met, he was quick of wit and was extremely agile. Good thing, too; if he couldn't outfight his opponent, then at least he could outrun him. He was an obnoxious sort at times, he knew, and his speed had always been a bonus. So, perhaps, the venture to Edinburgh was what he'd always sought – a sense of purpose, a sense of adventure.

A chance to do something good.

With his things packed, he ordered his steed and Lady Montgomery's palfrey readied. He never had a war horse, rather opting for a white Arabian stallion whose mother had been brought back from the Crusades. The horse was quite a bit like Donald in equine form: high-strung, smart, and but needed direction. Donald loved the horse as one would love a brother.

The horses were brought forth into the inner ward and Donald waited for Justine. And waited. When she finally did emerge, she looked like the Justine of old – swathed in black, hair pulled back severely. She was trailed by servants carrying two huge satchels.

Donald cocked a wary eyebrow at her. "What is all of that?"

Justine didn't answer until she mounted the brown animal. "That, my dear Donald, is our greatest hope for bringing everyone back to Torridon alive."

He frowned. "What? Ye have armies stashed in those bags?"

She gave him an impatient look. "Think bigger, Master Muir," she said. "I am bringing all the tools of my trade. If one item does not work, then we shall try another. You'll see."

He shook his head in bewilderment. "What, exactly, are ye planning, Justine?"

She grinned knowingly. "Trust me."

Good Lord, he thought as the horses moved for the main gates. *Angels in heaven, protect us dimwits!*

CHAPTER TWENTY-SEVEN

J OSEPHINE HAD BEEN right; Madelaine did, indeed, discreetly mention the discolored stain on the linens the following morning. Doing exactly as she had been instructed, Josephine told the servant that it was her woman's time and, from the look on Madelaine's face, she had no doubt that information would wind its way back to the king.

It was just a suspicion she had.

Feeling somewhat lighter of spirit, Josephine was carefully dressed in an off-the-shoulder pale green silk that was embroidered very finely with tiny pearls. It was an exquisite dress that had Josephine turning back and forth, admiring herself in the mirror.

Her long hair had been pulled back in the front and secured on the crown of her head with a pearl clip, then the rest was braided and interwoven with strands of tiny pearls. She stood, staring at herself in the mirror, as Madelaine brought the single braid over one shoulder and secured pearl ear bobs on each ear.

In truth, Josephine was truly amazed at the riches she wore, and she felt a little guilty that she wasn't ripping the garments off in protest of her captivity. These were all gifts from the earl and she knew very well she should not be accepting them. But there was a method to her madness.

Better a complacent captive with a plan up her sleeve than a rebel who bears watching.

Madelaine approached her with a bottle of perfume and Josephine eyed it. "What fragrance is that?" she demanded.

Madelaine smiled. "Exotic oils from across the sea, my lady."

Josephine took a sniff of the very strong perfume and promptly sneezed. "That will not do," she said. "Do you have rose?"

Madelaine went back to the vanity, fumbling about the glass phials until she brought forth a small yellow bottle.

"Here!" she crowed triumphantly. "Rose, my lady!"

Josephine crooked her finger at her. "Come here, then. I want a goodly dose."

Madelaine obliged, and Josephine felt rejuvenated by the familiar scent. But it also reminded her of her home far way and, for a moment, she felt the beginnings of tears. But just as quickly, she fought them off and took another look at herself in the polished bronze mirror. It was a proud, strong woman who gazed back at her.

A worthy wife for a mercenary lord.

Squaring her shoulders and straightening, Josephine turned around to Madelaine and her busy little minions. Before she could open her mouth, Madelaine spoke.

"Sir Nicholas de Londres requests the honor of yer presence in his chamber for the morning meal, my lady," she said. "He told me to bring ye as soon as ye were ready."

Dear Nicholas, Josephine thought. *My only friend in the inner circle.* "Of course," she said.

Madelaine escorted her from her chamber and led her down a long, stone corridor, past exquisite tapestries, and up a small flight of stairs before reaching Nicholas' room. The servant knocked softly, gaining admittance for her mistress.

Nicholas was standing on the opposite end of the room, his beautiful young face smiling when Josephine entered the chamber. It looked as if he'd been waiting rather impatiently. On the table next to him were a variety of foods, and Josephine realized she was very hungry.

As she approached him, his eyes gazed at her in appreciation. "No woman in all of Scotland or England can hold a candle to yer beauty, Lady Josephine," he said sincerely. "Ye belong in a castle."

Josephine accepted the chair he held out for her. "But you left out the women in France and Spain," she teased. "Are those women so beautiful that they make the rest of us look like dogs?"

He rolled with her humor. "Those women are as hairy as bears, and just as filthy," he said. "I have been to Paris. Believe me when I tell ye that most of those women are pigs."

She looked at him in surprise. "Nicholas!" she scolded softly. "Such harsh words from the tongue of an insufferable romantic. Remember that each woman is beautiful in her own way."

He offered her a large basket filled with different types of bread. "Each man has a different concept of beauty," he shrugged. "I would believe it safe to say that ye are every man's idea of a true Scottish beauty."

Josephine broke her bread and spread a thick slathering of butter on it. "My father used to say that about my mother."

"Lady Afton?" Nicholas looked up from his plate.

She nodded and took a small bite. "He said that I resembled her greatly."

Nicholas nodded. "Ye do."

Josephine looked at him in astonishment. "How would you know this?"

He smiled as if he had a great secret. "Because her portrait hangs in the Family Hall."

Josephine was stunned. Suddenly tears sprang to her eyes and her hand flew to her mouth. "My mother?"

"Aye."

She blinked, and tears glistened on her eyelashes. "I was only two years old when she died," she said. "My memories of her are wispy and vague, as if they were only a dream. Might I see the portrait, Nicholas?"

He hadn't meant to make her weep. He was unprepared for her deeply emotional reaction, for he had only expected great excitement.

"Of course, my lady," he said eagerly. "Whenever ye wish."

She dabbed at her tears and smiled hugely. "I would like to see it now, please.

"Now?" he stammered.

"*Now*," she said, standing.

Never argue with a woman, Nicholas thought, as he stood up and led her from the chamber. He took her back down the corridor, heading in the direction of the royal apartments and the common areas. Besides, he felt so bad for upsetting her that he was eager to make amends. If seeing the portrait of her mother was her greatest desire, then he would personally fulfill it.

The Family Hall was two flights down. It was, by far, the biggest room she had ever seen, more of a corridor, really, but it was full of portraits on wood and finely woven tapestries. The longest walls, running parallel to one another, were loaded from the high ceiling to the floor with artwork. A gallery ran along both walls so the viewer could get a better view of the portraits towards the top of the chamber.

Josephine had never seen anything like it. Some paintings were quite large, while still others were much smaller, and everything in between. The hall was so large that the faint sunlight streaming in through small windows was rather insignificant in its space, and it was difficult to make out most facial features.

Nicholas led her over to one far corner. Their footfalls were sharp in the dim light. Even though Nicholas held her hand, she felt distinctively lonely and isolated as centuries of her relatives gazed down upon her. It was as if she were in a roomful of people she didn't know, with each looking at her and whispering secret observations.

Suddenly, Nicholas stopped. "Here it is," he said quietly.

Josephine's gaze fell across a face that brought hundreds of memories tumbling into her mind, from things her father had told her of her mother. The surge of emotion was strong as she stared at her mother's beautiful, familiar face.

Afton was a mirror image of her daughter with her huge green eyes and distinctive features. Her hair was darker than her daughter's, perhaps a bit browner, and it was stylishly coiffed in an elaborate veil. Her expression was serene and peaceful, radiating her kindness and gentle nature.

Josephine reached out a timid hand and drew a finger across the bottom of the painting, as if she were truly touching her mother. The more she looked, the more she realized that even more than herself, her mother resembled Justine. The two could have been twins.

A sudden peace swept over her; a peace that formed as if a missing part of her life had been found. By simply seeing her mother's face, a part of her soul had been filled. This was the woman she had never really known but loved, and greatly missed. She turned to Nicholas with a smile.

"It is like looking at my sister," she said.

Nicholas was relieved at her lightening mood. He glanced up to Lady Afton.

"It is easy to see where ye and Lady Justine inherited yer beauty," he said.

Josephine stood at the portrait a few more moments. "I must have this portrait," she said firmly. "I will ask the king. Do you think he will give it to me?"

Nicholas shrugged. "Possibly," he said. "'Twould not hurt to ask."

Josephine was smiling warmly at her mother's portrait, as if re-membering the private memories only shared between her and her father about her mother. No, it would not hurt to ask the king if she could have the portrait. All the more reason to behave herself, at least for the time being.

Josephine and Nicholas remained viewing the portrait for what seemed like ages. Josephine lost all track of time, because this was a reunion of sorts. A reunion between mother and daughter. But after several minutes had passed, Nicholas finally turned to her.

"Shall we return to my chamber and finish our meal?" he asked.

She shook her head. "I am not hungry any longer."

"Then will ye allow me to show ye the castle?"

Josephine took his offered arm. "I was hoping you would."

Josephine was soon to discover that castle life was much different from the life at Torridon. The structure itself was different from the stronghold of Torridon. The castle was tactically secure on the hill it sat upon, and what walls there were still afforded a view from every window. There were two gatehouses, the main gatehouse and then a second one behind it, and even the interior of the castle was compart-mentalized to keep different areas safe in case there was a breach. The castle also covered twice the ground Torridon did, and it possessed several levels and dozens of rooms.

It was a massive place.

There were people everywhere. Josephine had no idea why all these people were here, or what possible business they could have. Groups of luxuriously dressed women and clusters of men seemed not to notice her or Nicholas as they crossed paths, but Josephine found herself unconsciously staring at people. Living a rather isolated life as she had at Torridon, especially after her father had died, she'd had limited contact with strangers and found it fascinating that there were so many different-looking people.

Sunlight of mid-morn streamed in like golden rivers through the windows on the east and south sides of the castle as she and Nicholas toured the various staterooms. She was utterly enthralled and was proud to be a distant part of this glory. She wished Justine were here to experience a part of her lineage.

Yet, even as she was overwhelmed by the spectacle that was Edin-burgh Castle, she was wondering where Andrew was. *Was he still on the ground? Had they captured him? Or was he hiding in some house or barn, waiting until his brother arrived?* She wished vehemently that she knew because she wanted desperately to see him. In fact, she was so distracted thinking about him that Nicholas stopped the tour.

"Are ye well, Josephine?" he asked, concerned.

She paused and looked at him. *Could he be trusted?* Andrew and

Sully's lives, as well as her own, were at stake. Nicholas, for all of his friendship and gentle nature, was still the king's nephew. She liked him a great deal and knew she had his sympathy, but she wasn't yet ready to trust him with a secret like that. Not yet, anyway. After a moment, she simply nodded.

"Aye," she said. "I suppose I am simply overwhelmed."

He smiled. "I understand completely."

Josephine began to walk again, veering off the subject of her mental state. "Where do the soldiers practice, Nicholas?" she asked. "This is such a large place. Where do the soldiers drill?"

It was an odd question from a proper young lady, but not so odd coming from a young woman who had fought like a man for the past couple of years. Nicholas motioned behind him vaguely.

"Over to the north," he said, then looked deliberately at her. "I shall take ye there if ye promise not to tell my uncle."

She grinned. "I swear it."

The training arena was far larger than anything Torridon possessed. It was a big, open area by the barracks, with views from the top of the crag that went on for miles. Nicholas led her to the safety of the lists as several pairs of soldiers squared off against each other. Still others were being instructed in groups. The day was growing warm, and the dust flew as feet scuffled and blows were dealt.

Josephine was excited by the commotion, inevitably comparing the training to her own knights' training. She passed a critical eye over each man, pointing out to Nicholas what was wrong or outstanding about each. She sounded more like a general than a fine-bred young lady, but Nicholas could see she was quite thrilled with the action.

"Do you practice much, Nicholas?" she asked while her eyes were riveted to the scene before her.

"Not as much as I should," he admitted.

She nodded intently. "I should like to practice with you some time."

He was taken aback. "Me? I am not a very good swordsman."

She grinned at him. "But I am," she said. "I shall teach you a few tricks meant for those of us who are not as strong as those mountainous beasts out there."

He shrugged, knowing he should agree because she wouldn't take "no" for an answer, and turned his attention back to the fighting field. As they continued to gaze on the overall scene of men in training, they could see someone entering the area over to north.

Graceful and powerful, the massive figure strolled in, covered with armor attended by a pair of squires and several small pages. Josephine saw the figure and locked on to it, aware of who it was even from a distance.

"De Reyne," she said curiously. "So he practices with the rank and file, does he?"

He was quite some distance away, but he looked over at her the exact moment Josephine said his name. Their eyes locked and he headed over in her direction.

"If it isn't the polite maiden stealer," she said as the man came near. "Steal any other young women lately, Ridge?"

Ridge fought off a grin at her ribbing, which probably wasn't so much ribbing as it was some kind of dig at his sense of duty. "Not today, my lady," he said evenly. "But you never know what tomorrow will bring. Did you have a pleasant eve?"

It was a normal question, but her paranoia had the better of her. Josephine caught something in his tone, or at least she thought she did. Even something in his eyes that unsettled her. Did he know what had taken place in her chamber last evening? Was it possible he'd seen Andrew enter? Her expression clouded with uncertainty for a split second, but was gone.

"Very pleasant, thank you," she replied steadily. "And I have had an interesting morning; the most exciting I am sure is yet to come. Indulge my passion for swordplay and entertain me, de Reyne. I command it."

He gave her a lopsided grin. "For you, my lady, anything."

Ridge turned away from the stand and donned his helm, slapping down his visor. His pages and attendants scattered when his squire handed him his sword. From one side of the field his opponent approached, and the two men squared off.

Josephine watched, eyes glittering with excitement, as the swords came together with a mighty sound. Within the first few minutes, it was obvious that Ridge's partner was no match for the king's mighty bodyguard. Ridge moved like a lion on the prowl, and he was intelligent and quick. She had seen him fight before, of course, when the bandits attacked them on the road, but this was different. It was precisely structured and was carefully executed, like a well-choreographed dance. Ridge was the center of this exercise as he moved like he had been born with a sword in his hand.

But after several minutes, Josephine was feeling less and less satisfied with what she was seeing. Although Ridge was magnificent, it would have been more thrilling had he been fighting a tree. There was no energy to the bout, and Josephine finally jumped from the stands and onto the dirt before Nicholas could stop her.

"Cease!" she bellowed as the two men came to a grinding halt. She glared at Ridge's partner. "You, sir, are a disgrace to the order of the knight. God help you if you ever wield a sword in battle, for you shall surely perish. You may as well throw yourself on your own sword when you see the enemy approach. Now give me that sword and let me show you how it's done."

She reached out and yanked the sword from the man's hand as he stood there, dumbfounded, but Ridge suppressed a grin as she verbally battered the hapless man. Still, he did not actually believe she intended to fight him until she shoved the armored man away and turned to face him in her silk dress. She bound her skirts up, tucking it between her legs and pulling it up front to lodge in the belt around her waist so she wouldn't trip on her skirts.

Now, it wasn't so amusing. Ridge propped his helm up and looked at her with great disapproval.

"What are you doing?" he demanded.

The sword came in front of her in an offensive stance. "Shut your lips and put up your sword."

His brows came together in disbelief. "I will not fight you in that… that *dress*," he argued. "Go back to the lists where you belong."

She smiled thinly at him. "Dress or no, you shall fight me or you shall lose your manhood. Now, pick up your sword and prepare to fight."

Without warning, she lunged forward in a sharp arc, and had he been any slower she would have cut off his right arm. He parried but did not retaliate. Instead, he stood several feet back, his expression full of disbelief and disapproval.

"I told you I would not fight you," he said.

Josephine acted as if she didn't hear him. She rushed at him again, watching him put his sword up defensively. Then she spun in the opposite direction, bringing her sword to bear right at the back of his neck.

It was over in a split second. One move and Josephine could easily cut the man's neck. But Ridge didn't move a muscle; he didn't even turn his head to look at her.

"Well?" he said. "If you are going to cut my head off, then get on with it."

So he wasn't going to play with her. Josephine lowered the sword in frustration. "I am not going to cut your head off, you silly man," she said. "I promised to show Nicholas some tactics that smaller warriors like us can use against beasts like you. Won't you help me?"

Ridge looked at her, his eyes glimmering with humor. "Nay," he said flatly. "If the king saw me, I would be in for a lashing. Go back to your room, my lady. Go back there and remain there."

Josephine frowned, and she began to run circles around him, her sword defensively positioned. "I will go back if you defeat me," she said. "Lift your sword, de Reyne. I will not return to my room otherwise."

Ridge sighed heavily. He wasn't in the mood for the lady's taunts but, on the other hand, he had to admire her bravery. She was tenacious. He could see his squires looking at the lady with a good deal of shock and he thought perhaps to give the lady a taste of what it would be like to go up against a real knight, a man who had trained for years to kill men of his size.

He knew she'd been fighting at Torridon since her father died, but he suspected her knights had kept her rather insulated from the real fighting. That made her falsely confident in her abilities. That's what made her fight against him when he first took her from Torridon; she genuinely thought she could take him on.

She was about to learn otherwise.

Therefore, he stood there as Josephine walked around him, challenging him to a fight. He lowered his helm and his visor, and his sword remained lowered as well. He waited until she made two circles around him because he knew she was going to get careless and let her guard down when she saw that he wasn't going to fight her. But he was about to use the element of surprise.

Quick as a flash, he lashed out his sword, tripping her as she walked around him. As she yelped and went down on the dirt, he was suddenly standing over her, the tip of his sword to her throat. He rather hated to toss her to the earth when she was so beautifully dressed, but it couldn't be helped. Before he could demand her surrender, however, the lady brought up a foot and kicked him right in the groin. Literally, right in the balls. As Ridge grunted and stumbled back, she leapt to her feet and threw herself at him, grabbing him around the neck and using her body weight to throw him even further off balance.

Her intent was to cause him to fall to the ground, but Ridge wasn't so easily defeated. He managed to keep his balance, grab the woman who was trying so desperately to defeat him, and sling her up over his shoulder. As she fought viciously against him, he brought a trencher-sized hand down on her buttocks and spanked her soundly. Josephine howled.

"Ridge!" she screamed. "You beast! Put me down!"

Ridge spanked her again. "That is for kicking me in the ballocks," he told her. "If you ruin my chances of having a son, I will come for you, wherever you are. I will hunt you down and Andrew d'Vant will not be able to protect you."

He was carrying her back over to the lists where Nicholas was standing, open-mouthed. Ridge motioned to the young man.

"Come along," he said. "I am taking the lady back to her chambers. She is finished with the training grounds for the day. She should not have been here in the first place."

Nicholas climbed off the lists, concerned for Josephine. "Ye're ruining her dress, Ridge," he pointed out. "The king will be angry."

"Then she should not have charged me."

That was the truth and Nicholas didn't have much to say to that. What had started off as a lovely morning had turned into a bit of a fiasco. Across Ridge's broad shoulder, the more Josephine squirmed, the more Ridge spanked her. Furious, as she knew she couldn't fight the man the way he was holding her, she hung over his shoulder and reached down, pulling up the back of his mail coat.

Ridge could feel what she was doing and he spun her around a couple of times, trying to disorient her, but it didn't work – she had the mail coat hiked up and managed to get her hands on the linen breeches he wore underneath the heavier leather ones he wore as protection. Once she got a hold of the top of the linen breeches, she pulled as hard as she could and Ridge nearly dropped her.

On top of kicking him in the groin, now she was trying to cut off the blood supply to that area. She yanked hard, seriously constricting him, and he spanked her so hard that she screamed. But she didn't stop pulling. In fact, by the time they reached the entry to the wing where she was housed, she had pulled his breeches up so tightly that the man could barely walk.

"Let go," he said through clenched teeth.

Josephine refused. "Not unless you put me down!"

"I cannot put you down when you have my breeches pulled halfway up to my shoulders."

"Then we are at an impasse."

Nicholas had been watching the entire thing and he wasn't hard pressed to realize how brutally humorous it was. Josephine was stubborn, but so was Ridge. When two immovable objects met, there was often violence, so Nicholas walked around to the rear of Ridge and tried to look Josephine in the eye.

"Ye really should let him go, Joey," he said. "'Tis most undignified to see ye like this. If ye could see yerself, ye would know what I mean."

Josephine looked at him, upside-down. Her lovely hair style was all but unraveled. "He had no right to spank me."

Nicholas thought that, perhaps, the only way around her was to be firm. "And ye truly had no business trying to sword fight the man," he said. "I told ye I should not have taken ye to the training grounds and this is how ye repay me? Now, let the man go. I am hungry and want to go inside."

Josephine was reluctant to agree that Nicholas was probably right. She'd jumped into the training arena where she didn't belong, and Ridge was right to have removed her. Reluctantly, she let go of Ridge's breeches and Ridge immediately set her to her feet. They eyed each other for a moment, stubbornly, until Josephine broke down.

"I am sorry I kicked you in the groin," she said. "Are you hurt much?"

Ridge kicked out a leg, trying to pull his linen pants down from where they were bunched up in between his buttocks. "Nay," he said. "And since you are apologizing, I will say that whoever trained you to fight did a good job of it. You have excellent instincts."

Josephine fought off a smile at the compliment. Somehow, it didn't seem appropriate to smile as the man struggled to pull his breeches out of his arse crack.

"You and I have fought each other a few times since we first met," she said. "You are a worthy opponent."

Ridge couldn't help it; he grinned at the fact that she truly thought she was his equal. "I would much rather not fight you, my lady," he said. "Can we please call a truce? My groin cannot take any more violence."

Josephine's smile broke through. "Indeed," she said. "We have a truce."

"Did I spank you too hard? If I did, I apologize."

She shook her head. "With all of the skirts and shifts between your hand and my backside, I hardly felt a thing."

He laughed softly. "Then we are friends again," he said. But then, he sobered dramatically as he focused on her. "And as your friend, I would ask a favor."

She cocked her head curiously. "What is it?"

He sighed faintly, glancing around the area to see who was out and about. The king had many spies at Edinburgh, including him, and he wanted to see if he was being watched. A brief perusal of the area showed it to be relatively safe from prying eyes.

"Stay to your chambers today," he said, his voice quiet. "Do not come out again, not today and not any day from this point forward unless you are summoned. I have it on good authority from the spies on the outskirts of Edinburgh that the earl is approaching from his home at Liberton. He should be here within the next hour or two, so I would strongly recommend you return to your chamber and bolt the door. Do not give the man a chance to see you here, out in the open. Do you understand?"

Gone was the humor, the lightheartedness of the day. Gone was the just plain fun of scrapping with Ridge. Now, Josephine gazed back at him in fear.

"God's Bones," she breathed. "He has been sighted?"

Ridge nodded. "He has."

Josephine felt as if she'd been kicked in the gut. She suddenly felt sick. "I do not know why I should feel so shocked by this news," she muttered. "I knew he was coming. I have been told. Still… the reality of it is somewhat daunting."

Ridge could feel the familiar pangs of sympathy for the little soldier as well as the familiar pangs of that brotherly protectiveness. "Go back to your chambers, Josephine," he said quietly. "And if I were you, I'd keep the servants out. Madelaine is a direct line to the king. She is his mistress when the whim strikes him."

Josephine looked at him in shock. "She is?"

Ridge nodded. He didn't say another word, but turned her for the entrance with the silent suggestion she go inside. Josephine didn't hesitate; she quickly entered the building with Nicholas on her heels.

Ridge stood there a moment, thinking that even if she did lock herself in her chamber, it wouldn't do much good. All the king had to do was order her to appear before him, and before her betrothed, and she would have to appear. Ridge was supposed to practice that morning and then he had a training group he was supposed to work with in the afternoon, new Scottish recruits to the king's army. He really had no desire to work with farmers and hunters from the Highlands.

Instead, he thought he might stick close to Lady Josephine's chambers, just in case she needed him.

There wasn't much he could do if she did, but still... something told him to stick close.

HE COULD SEE the approaching army from a distance.

Using the apple man disguises, Sully and Andrew had been able to come and go freely between the castle and the inn Ermaline, Esme, and the other whores called home. It was coming to be their base of operations. Being that the inn was literally on the road leading up to the castle, it was the best place to watch the comings and goings, and that included the approach of Andrew's brother. Since they knew he was due on this day, they'd retreated to the inn and had remained vigilant, watching the road, waiting for what was to come.

And it came soon enough.

From the east, Andrew saw it first. He was preparing to ride into the city to locate a blacksmith when the approach of the army caught his eye. Troops of the highest order moving through town, heading for the castle. The banners and foot soldiers came first, trudging up the road leading to the gatehouse. The great golden bear of Blackbank was outlined on the flag coming into focus. Andrew was so engrossed with the sight before him that he didn't notice his white-knuckled fists clenching and unclenching passionately.

Men on horseback followed the foot soldiers, fierce-looking knights whose armor was familiar to him. Hell, he probably knew some of the men who wore it, for only nineteen years had passed since he'd left Haldane. He knew that all nine of the knights had been loyal to his father, and he was sure that given the choice between Alphonse and himself, they would be loyal to him.

It was a huge caravan that his brother had brought, no doubt, to show his strength. With the number of men he had brought, he could wreak considerable havoc on this city should he choose, should the situation not go well with Josephine.

And then, his brother was there, larger than life.

Alphonse d'Vant, Earl of Annan and Blackbank, sat astride a massive black animal that looked like it was borne of the demons of hell. But somehow, Alphonse didn't seem as large as Andrew had remembered, and he felt oddly relieved. Over the years, Andrew's hatred for his brother had gained him another foot in height and a hideously deformed face, but he saw that neither was certainly the case. His brother looked tamer, more vulnerable, and entirely human.

Entirely mortal.

Killing him shall be a pleasure!

But no mistaking – the man was huge. He rode on his destrier swathed in enough armor to squash a normal man, and was heading up the hill towards Edinburgh Castle. The rest of his troops followed in precise ranks, looking like a hundred trained dogs following their master obediently.

Andrew felt many different emotions as he watched his brother. It was almost as if he were dreaming because he had waited for this moment for so long. It was surreal. He felt hate and anger, but he also felt oddly relieved that the event he'd so long prepared for was finally coming to pass. Finally, his long-awaited vengeance would be realized, and he was more than ready for it.

But thoughts of vengeance turned to thoughts of Josephine, and he felt a tremendous sense of protectiveness towards her. *Damn Alphonse!* If he were standing in front of him now, he'd like nothing better than to wrap his hands around his brother's throat, not only for the pain and anguish the man had caused their mother, but now for the pain and anguish he was causing Josephine.

Of course, Alphonse had no idea that the woman he was pledged to marry was his own brother's lady but, still, Alphonse was the cause of torment for both of the women that Andrew loved.

It was time for that torment to end.

Alphonse and his entourage disappeared up the road and into the gatehouse of the castle, but Andrew continued to stare as if rooted to the spot. There was so very much going through his mind but, eventually, he came back to the world around him. Yet, his mind was still very much occupied. He thought of the coming battle, of the weapons he'd brought with him to accomplish his task.

He looked at the broadsword strapped to the saddle of his horse, a weighty thing that he'd used in battle for years. But he wanted something better. Knowing his brother had been on the approach, his intention had been to find a good blacksmith because he had some ideas about what he needed in a blade. There was something he wanted and little time to do it. For what he needed to accomplish, he needed a blade that could slice through a man's torso like a hot knife through butter.

Aye, there were many things on his mind at the moment, but something made him look up to the second story of the inn. He didn't know what or why, but he happened to glance up to the window of his room. Sully's face stared down at him, his square jaw set and his blue eyes smoldering as they locked onto Andrew's brown orbs. In that instant,

Andrew knew that Sully had seen the earl as well, and was believing every cursed thing Andrew had told him about the man.

With an ironic grimace, Andrew mounted his horse and sped off into the city.

RIDGE HAD TOLD her to stay to her chambers, but Josephine just couldn't seem to listen to the man.

She wasn't being deliberately disobedient, but it was more the fact that she hadn't seen Andrew since the previous evening. She thought for certain he would have come to her today, or at least make his presence known, but he hadn't. The longer she waited for him and the more the day progressed, the more worried she became.

Surely he couldn't have gone far from the castle. Surely he was around here, somewhere. And what of Sully? Where was he? Since Ridge had all but commanded her to return to her chambers, she'd stood at the window, watching the grounds, trying to spy Andrew somewhere amongst the many people that walked to and fro across the dirt courtyard. But he wasn't anywhere to be found and the more time passed, the more worried she became.

At her request, Nicholas had long since left her to go about his own business. In truth, Josephine simply wanted to be alone, especially if Andrew was on the grounds. She didn't want him making an appearance in front of Nicholas. But as the nooning hour came and went, it seemed certain that Andrew wasn't going to show, and Josephine was growing increasingly concerned that he might have run into trouble with the king's soldiers. Perhaps, they'd even captured him and thrown him in the dungeons. With that thought lingering, Josephine made up her mind up to look for the man.

She knew she shouldn't. In fact, even as she slipped from her chamber, she was most reluctant to go, but the idea of Andrew in danger kept her from turning back. Slipping down the corridor, down the stairs, and out into the sunshine, Josephine began to hunt in earnest for Andrew, wherever he was hiding.

Unfortunately, she didn't know the castle grounds very well and Edinburgh Castle was vast. She wandered into the garden area because she knew Andrew had seen her there the night before, but poking and peeking around the bushes didn't produce him. After the garden, she walked up towards the training grounds because there were a lot of men there, a lot of outbuildings, and many places to hide.

The training grounds proved a bit more of a challenge because men had no control when they saw a beautiful woman wandering about aimlessly. They wanted to escort her and protect her, and Josephine had to run from the training grounds because of too many do-gooders. If Andrew was there somewhere, then he was a fool, because there were far too many men around. But she didn't think he was there.

She pushed onward.

Heading away from the training ground, she came across several buildings that housed carts and carriages. There were men moving about, servants, but they didn't seem to give her any notice. As the castle was built on the top of a rocky crag, there were many instances of rocky areas, of natural holes, and there were any number of places where a man could hide.

But Josephine still didn't see Andrew as she walked past the cart buildings. The road curved around and down a great slope. She could see the gatehouse. She remembered the area from when she first arrived, so she more or less had her bearings. At the base of the road leading into the castle was the town, and there had been a dozen little inns and hostels crowded in and around the base of the road.

Perhaps that was where he'd gone.

Curiosity and concern drove her down the hill. Moving through the inner portcullis entry hadn't been difficult at all. It was guarded but there were a great many people moving in and out, so she simply walked through it with a crowd of people and continued onward. But she was nearing the main gatehouse when she caught sight of a great commotion; men were shouting at each other and the first of two big portcullises in the gatehouse, which had been half-lowered, was now being lifted.

There was so much activity going on that Josephine naturally came to a halt, curious about what was happening. There were people moving through the gatehouse, but the soldiers were hurrying them through, shouting at them to make way. Josephine tried to peer through the gatehouse to see what was on the other side, but the angle of the road made that difficult. She couldn't see much.

Then, abruptly, banners came into view.

Banners with big golden bears on them were coming up the road and the men holding them soon came into view. Heavily-armed men were at the lead and behind them came men on foot with pikes and swords. Realizing an army was about to come through, Josephine quickly looked around, attempting to locate a place she could hide. She could run back up the road to the second gatehouse, but she'd still have to hide from the incoming army, somehow, and Ridge's words came back to haunt her.

Do not let the earl catch you out.

God's Bones… *the earl!*

To her right was a wall built against the rock of the crag that the castle was built upon. There was enough of a lip at the top off the wall that Josephine knew she could hide behind it. It would be difficult, for the lip wasn't more than two or three feet high, but it could be done. Besides, she had no choice. Hoisting herself up onto the wall, she leapt over the top of it and settled down behind the lip.

She didn't dare peek out. Someone would surely see her head and her concealment would be discovered. In little time, the sounds of the army became apparent – footfalls, horses, and the creak of wagon wheels. The dust they were kicking up floated into the air and settled down around her, nearly making her sneeze. But she kept her hand over her nose, pinching it shut, praying that no one would spy her hiding behind the lip of the wall. She most certainly didn't want to meet the earl this way.

She didn't want to meet him at all.

It seemed like an eternity as the army passed by, the rumble of men in conversation, the thunder of horses. Everything was shaking, rumbling, and dusty, and Josephine remained tucked down, waiting for it to end. Eventually, the sounds began to fade, and she dared to pop her head up, seeing the tail end of the army as it passed through the second portcullis gatehouse.

The storm, for the moment, had passed.

But it wasn't over entirely. Josephine came out of her hiding place and jumped down off the wall. The main gatehouse seemed to be operating as normal, with people once again passing in and out of it, and she walked very quickly down the hill and slipped out as the guards were talking to a merchant who was trying to come in.

Josephine lost herself in the people on the road leading up to the castle, most of them simple villeins or farmers or even merchants going about their business. The castle was a very busy place, a seat of commerce as well as the seat of the king. In fact, it was rather crowded, and as she reached the base of the hill, she could hear people speaking of the great army that had just come through.

Josephine knew without a doubt who the army belonged to and she also knew that, soon enough, they would come looking for her to introduce her to her betrothed. That made finding Andrew something she needed to do sooner rather than later, and her anxiety was beginning to mount; Andrew had to know that his brother had arrived.

Looking around, it was difficult to know where to start to look for Andrew and Sully. Directly across the road were a cluster of inns, the ones she remembered from the day she and Ridge had arrived, so she supposed it would be the logical place to start. Perhaps someone would have seen Andrew and Sully; even if they didn't know them by name, she could at least describe them.

The inn directly across from the road leading to the castle was called The Falcon and The Flower, and Josephine presumed it was as good a place to start as any. Gathering her dirty skirts, she dashed across the road, avoiding horses and people, and headed straight for the entry door. She was about to open it when it suddenly flew open and a familiar face appeared.

"Sully!" Josephine gasped.

Sully could hardly believe his eyes as he reached out to steady Josephine. Having nearly run her over, she was teetering. But he grabbed hold and pulled her away from the door, all the while looking at her with a good deal of shock.

"Josephine!" he said, startled. "What are you doing here?"

Josephine was so glad to see Sully that it nearly brought her to tears. "I came to find Andrew," she said anxiously. "Have you seen him?"

Sully looked around, seeing the crowds of people in the street, and pulled Josephine with him until they were wedged into a tiny ally between the tavern and another building. It was filthy, smelling of urine and feces, but it was private.

"Aye, I've seen him," he said, looking her up and down as if to make sure she was unharmed. "And you? Are you well? Andrew said that Ridge de Reyne took you from Torridon to bring you to the king and…"

She cut him off. "It is true," she said. "I saw Andrew last night and told him this."

Sully nodded. "He told me when he returned to the tavern, very late," he said. "We saw you and Nicholas in the garden last night. We saw Ridge, too. Josephine, what is going on? Why are you here?"

Josephine clutched him. "Because I have not yet seen Andrew today," she said, quickly realizing how silly she sounded. "I did not mean it that way. I simply meant I thought I would see him today and I have not. He is not in trouble, is he? He has not been captured?"

Sully shook his head. "Nay," he said. "He is not in any trouble. In fact, he was just here a few minutes ago. Surely you saw the army pass through?"

Josephine nodded, fear in her eyes. "It was the earl," she said. "I know it was the earl."

"Who told you?"

"No one had to. We are expecting the earl today; who else could it be?"

"It was the earl."

The voice came from behind, towards the back of the ally. Josephine and Sully turned, startled, to see Ridge standing there. He did not look pleased.

"Ridge!" Josephine gasped. "What are you doing here?"

Ridge's gaze was mostly on Sully as he moved forward. Specifically, he was looking to see if the man was armed, and he was. That was enough of a sight for Ridge to bolt forward and grab Josephine, pulling her back with him so Sully couldn't get hold of her and possibly make a run for it.

But Josephine fought back, slapping at Ridge as he held on to her. "Let me go!" she demanded.

Ridge didn't let go and he didn't take his eyes off of Sully. "So d'Vant is here, too, is he?" he asked. "Where is he?"

"Gone."

"Gone *where*?"

Sully shook his head. "I do not know," he said honestly. "He rode off to the east about fifteen minutes ago."

D'Vant was off in the city somewhere. Ridge couldn't be concerned with that at the moment. He had Montgomery in his sights and needed to deal with the man.

"Truthfully, I am not surprised you are both here," he said. "I suppose I expected you to come."

Sully hadn't moved from his position by the wall, and most especially now that Ridge had Josephine. "You knew we would figure out what had happened," he said.

Ridge sighed faintly. He wasn't angry, in truth. He was rather sedate about the entire situation but for the fact he was holding on to Josephine.

"And you did," he said. "Now what? Where are you going to run to that the king cannot find you? Back to Torridon? Into England? No place you could go would be safe. And do you intend to run with d'Vant and the lady, now that you have a wife and Torridon Castle in your possession? The king would strip that from you faster than the blink of an eye. You are not thinking properly, Montgomery. You have not thought any of this through."

Sully knew that. He knew that he and Andrew had come to Edinburgh to protect a woman who, more than likely, probably could not be much protected by the two of them. But much like Andrew, he'd acted on emotion. Josephine had been taken and they had to go after her.

There was no giving her up.

But they'd made connections to get them into the castle and last night, Andrew had made contact with Josephine. Clearly, Ridge did not know that. As Sully thought on a reply that wouldn't give away the fact that they had more access to the castle than de Reyne realized, Josephine continued to beat on Ridge's hands.

"Let me go, Ridge," she demanded again. "How did you find me here?"

Ridge's gaze was still on Sully. "How do you think?" he said. "I followed you. I saw you leave your chamber after I told you to stay there, so I followed you."

She frowned and stopped trying to dislodge his grip. "That was sneaky," she said. "You have no right to follow me!"

He cocked an eyebrow at her. "Aye, I do," he said. "Evidently, you cannot be trusted to keep your word."

"That is a terrible thing to say!"

"You told me you would stay to your chamber when I told you the earl was expected. You lied."

Josephine was so angry that her face started to turn red, but the man was correct, so she couldn't very well berate him for it.

"So you have found me," she grumbled, turning away. "I suppose you are going to take me back now."

Ridge didn't reply for a moment. He turned to look at Sully, still standing against the wall. "Aye," he said. "I am going to take you back. But Montgomery is coming with us."

Josephine looked up at him, shocked. "Why?"

Ridge lifted an eyebrow. "Because he has come to abduct the betrothed of the Earl of Annan and Blackbank," he said. "Surely you know I cannot let him go free."

Josephine was horrified. "What are you going to do with him?"

"Put him in the dungeons for now."

Josephine's mouth popped open as she looked at Sully, who didn't seem all that surprised. He was looking at Ridge.

"And if I refuse to go with you?" he asked.

Ridge didn't seem too surprised by the question. "I will tell the king that you have come to take the lady back to Torridon," he said. "I will tell him that d'Vant is here, also. Given that the lady's marriage to Blackbank is an important political move, the king will more than likely send his army to Torridon and raze it. D'Vant will be an outlaw in Scotland and no Scottish laird will hire the man for fear of incurring the king's wrath. Shall I go on?"

Sully knew the threat against Torridon was very real. He didn't relish spending any time in Edinburgh's dungeons, but he suspected he had no choice at the moment. He couldn't risk Torridon, in any fashion. After a moment, he simply lowered his gaze as if resigned to the entire thing.

"Please do not do this, Ridge," Josephine begged quietly. "I am sorry I lied to you. I did not do it intentionally. I promise I shall behave myself from now on if you will only leave Sully alone."

She sounded sincere enough but Ridge was resolute. "Alas, I cannot leave him," he said. "He is a threat and threats must be dealt with."

Josephine flared. "He is *not* a threat," she said. "Please, Ridge… there is more to this that you do not know. There is a reason why Sully and Andrew are here. I did not tell you before because I did not want you to know, but now you must. I do not want you to think Andrew and Sully have come to commit foolish crimes against the king. There is a reason for everything."

Ridge cocked an eyebrow. "More lies to spare them?"

Josephine shook her head. "I swear upon my mother's grave that this is the truth," she said quietly. "You may or may not know that Andrew and the Earl of Annan and Blackbank are brothers."

Ridge didn't look so suspicious any longer. Now, he looked surprised but tried to pretend he wasn't. "Brothers?" he said thoughtfully. "I suppose it did not occur to me. The name d'Vant is not uncommon. And except for their size, they do not favor one another."

Josephine nodded. "I cannot speak to whether or not they look similar, for I have not seen the earl, but he is Andrew's older brother," she said. "When their father died, the earl imprisoned their mother and banished Andrew, so he escaped. Because of this, Andrew has sworn to kill his brother and that is why he is here. To kill the earl."

Ridge stared at her a moment in disbelief before looking to Sully. "Is this true?"

Sully nodded slowly. "It is," he said. "Andrew has sworn to avenge his mother by killing his brother. All of this – the betrothal, and of you bringing Josephine to Edinburgh, is simply an incredible coincidence. It is true that Andrew has come to protect Josephine as best he can, but his first objective is to kill his brother. He is not here to take her away, at least not yet. I swear this upon my oath as a knight."

"Does the king know that Andrew and Blackbank are brothers?"

Josephine nodded. "He knows," she said. "But he does not know that Andrew has sworn to kill the man. At least, I have not told him that. If he knows, he did not hear it from me."

Ridge sighed heavily. This was grave and serious information, something the king needed to be aware of. With The Red Fury bent on vengeance, Blackbank's life was in jeopardy. But given what Ridge thought of the man, and what he thought of this whole situation, maybe that was a good thing.

Maybe the king didn't need to know, after all.

Still, the situation was serious enough that he had to do something about Sully's presence. The fact remained that he was here to thwart the king's plans and that, on the whole, couldn't be allowed.

"You will come with me now, Montgomery," he said after a moment.

Josephine was back to struggling against Ridge. "Why? We told you the truth! Sully has not done anything wrong!"

Ridge cocked a dark eyebrow. "*Yet*," he emphasized. "I must make sure it remains that way."

Josephine geared up for a verbal battle with the man but a word from Sully stopped her. "Joey, *stop*," he said. "Fighting the man will not change his mind."

Ridge could see that Sully was surrendering. It was in the man's stance, in his manner. Frankly, he was glad he wasn't going to have a fight on his hands. Obviously, for the lady's sake, Sully would not resist. As Josephine unhappily backed down, Ridge spoke quietly.

"The sword," he said. "Drop it."

Sully looked at the broadsword strapped to his leg. "Can I at least take it inside? I do not want to leave it here in the alley."

"I said drop it."

With a heavy sigh, Sully unbuckled the sheath and the sword fell to filthy dirt of the alley.

"Now," Ridge said. "Walk to the street."

Sully turned and walked out of the alley, right into the road, and Ridge and Josephine followed, but not before Ridge stopped to pick up the sword. He wasn't going to let it remain in the alley where someone could steal it. He wasn't so cruel.

Together, the three of them made their way back up the road leading to the castle. Upon reaching the main gatehouse, Ridge turned Sully over to the soldiers at the gate with the instructions to treat him well but take him to the dungeon. The last Josephine saw of Sully was of the man being surrounded by four guards, who escorted him away from the gatehouse.

Her heart sank as Ridge took her by the arm and led her back to her chamber. He took her right up to the door, not taking any chance that she would deviate if he left her at the building entry and told her to go inside. Ridge was coming to learn that the lady had a mind of her own and even though she knew what her duty was, to obey the king, it was clear that she didn't want to do it. Nothing about her was complacent to the situation and Ridge was well aware.

The pity he felt for her, the brotherly protection, was going to get him into trouble if he wasn't careful. When Josephine entered her chamber and shut the door, Ridge could hear the sobs through the panel. As much as he thought he should comfort her and assure her that he wasn't trying to be cruel, merely following orders, he thought it best not to. She already knew his role in all of this. It wouldn't do any good to repeat it.

Trying to block out the sounds of Josephine's weeping, Ridge went about his business.

CHAPTER TWENTY-EIGHT

Later that night

JOSEPHINE SAT ON the same bench that she had been sitting on the previous night when Andrew had seen her.

It was dusk at Edinburgh and a great feast in honor of the earl was being prepared; she could smell the roasting meat and hear the sounds coming from the great hall. Servants were moving about as darkness approached and everything around her seemed very busy except for that little garden in the midst of a busy castle. It was like an oasis of dreams in the middle of a nightmare.

Josephine stared pensively into the reservoir in front of her, watching the water ripple gently. In those ripples, she saw her entire time at Edinburgh pass before her eyes – her arrival, time spent with Nicholas, with Andrew, and finally Ridge. Now, Sully was in the dungeons because of her and it was growing increasingly difficult to keep her spirits up. Where had Andrew gone today? Why hadn't he come back to her? It was all so very confusing.

And very sorrowful.

A sparrow landed within a few feet of her; its little head twitching as it looked at her with its beady black eyes. She smiled faintly as it hopped about, enjoying the little bird as a promise of life's innocence. Things weren't all that bad if birds still lived and sang, and flowers still bloomed, and rivers still flowed. If Andrew wasn't here to give her words of hope, then she could still find hope in her surroundings. At least, she could try.

She had been in the garden for nearly an hour when she heard footfalls approach. They were coming from behind her and she quickly turned to see Nicholas rounded the corner of a bush, and his blue eyes focused on her.

"I thought I might find ye here," he said. "Ye like this place."

Josephine looked about. "It is peaceful and beautiful," she said. "It is a spot of beauty in the midst of this ugly castle."

His smile suddenly took a strange twist. "I have some more beauty for ye," he said. "I think that ye should accompany me to the great hall. There is someone there who wishes to see ye."

Her face went taut. "Who?"

He took her hand and pulled her to stand. "Just… come with me."

Josephine was thoroughly perplexed, but not entirely frightened as she allowed Nicholas to lead her into the castle. He didn't seem overly concerned for her so she knew he wasn't taking her to meet the earl. But as he pulled her along, Josephine recalled the events of the day, events that had her depressed and saddened.

"Wait," she said. "I must talk to you. Have you seen Ridge?"

Nicholas shook his head. "Nay," he said. "Why?"

"Because he imprisoned Sully earlier," she said. "You must help me free him."

Nicholas looked at her, perplexed. "Sully?" he repeated. "What are ye talking about?"

Josephine didn't want to tell him that she'd been looking for Andrew but had found Sully instead. "After you and I came in from the training field, I left the castle and ran into Sully," she said. "Only Ridge was following me and he took Sully prisoner. We must devise a plan of escape."

Nicholas' eyebrows shot up. "Escape? From Edinburgh's dungeons? I think not," he said. "However, it would be no problem to slip some poor jailer a gold piece and, accidentally, he could unlock Sully's door."

He was so calm, always, when Josephine's emotions were erupting. She eyed him dubiously. "You are sure?" she asked. "He will not encounter any difficulties?"

Nicholas shrugged and resumed his walking. "Probably not," he said. "But why in the world did Ridge take him? And what is he doing here?"

Josephine paused a moment; as much as she didn't want to tell Nicholas everything, she found that she could no longer keep everything from him. He was close to her, and she knew she had his sympathy, so perhaps it was time to trust him. She decided to take that chance.

"Because Andrew is here," she said quietly. "Sully came with him."

To her surprise, Nicholas simply nodded. "I'm knew he would," he said. "I knew The Red Fury would eventually come for his lady love."

Josephine shook her head. "It is more than that," she said. "He has come to kill the earl, as he said he would."

"Good God," Nicholas swore softly. "That mountainous man? Andrew certainly has his work cut out for him."

Josephine nodded in agreement. "Have no doubt who will win, Nicholas," she said quietly. "He has much to fight for."

Nicholas smiled faintly at her. "I would like to think that, someday, I shall have a woman I would be willing to fight for," he said. "I may write poetry, Joey, but ye live it. Ye live it every day."

Josephine smiled at the sentiment. "Spoken like a man with a romantic heart."

Nicholas patted her hand as they walked in silence, making their way to the massive receiving hall. Josephine, once again, began to wonder why Nicholas had brought her here, but she did not ask again. She would know soon enough.

"He's going to do it at the wedding, isn't he?"

Nicholas had asked the softly-uttered question just as they neared the door of the hall. He sounded rather concerned about it and Josephine looked at him.

"I do not know," she said honestly. "I do not even know when or where the wedding is to be. The king has discussed nothing with me. I am living in complete ignorance of my destiny."

Nicholas felt great pity for his friend's situation. He felt her sadness and uncertainty, and tried to think of a way to lift her spirits. But, given the situation, he didn't want to sound callous about it.

"Whatever happens, my lady, and wherever it happens, ye can be assured that I and my sword will be there," he said. "I may not be very good, but I shall do my best to assist Andrew as needed."

Josephine looked at him, touched. "Thank you, Nicholas," she said. "But I hope that will not be necessary."

It was a bonding moment between them, a moment of true friendship. Josephine knew that she would call him a dear friend until the day she died.

Nicholas led her into the foyer on the way to the receiving hall. There were quite a few servants in the foyer, servants that looked strangely familiar to her. She glanced about her in puzzlement, and then the thunderbolt hit.

Justine and Donald were looking right at her.

"Torridon," she whispered in shock, then let go of Nicholas' arm and rushed into the receiving hall. "*Justine!*"

JUSTINE AND DONALD arrived at Edinburgh Castle with a caravan of wagons and servants. Justine didn't travel lightly, bringing her trunks and possessions on what was presumably a short visit. The majordomo of the castle was caught quite off guard by their arrival, but once Justine announced she was the king's cousin, she was promised suites of rooms within the hour.

The man had them wait in the great hall and they obliged, servants scurrying in from the kitchens with trays of refreshments for the king's cousin. Justine ignored the food and, instead, passed a haughty eye over the riches and wealth that decorated the room. Donald, however, was stuffing his mouth with pears in wine, all the while watching in amusement as Justine pretended the surroundings did not impress her.

The truth was that it was all a little overwhelming. They were tired from their journey and were eager to see Josephine. The emotions were mixed because of the uncertainty of the situation – what had happened since Josephine had been brought to Edinburgh? Was she well? And where were Sully and Andrew? There were a great many questions and, as of yet, no one was able to answer them.

They'd come to Edinburgh for those answers but, in a sense, were fearful to know them. But that all ended when Josephine abruptly appeared and ran at them, swallowing her sister up in her enthusiastic embrace.

It was a joyful reunion with Nicholas at Josephine's side. Nicholas and Donald reunited warmly, like the friends they were, but the focus was on the women as they hugged and gasped. It was clear there was much surprise, on both sides.

"Why are you here?" Josephine asked. "How on earth did you know to come to Edinburgh?"

Justine knew Nicholas was standing there and she didn't want to give too much away, given that Sully and Andrew were here. Knowing that Nicholas was close to the king, she didn't want to give the men away.

Justine shrugged. "Where else would you go?" she said, eyeing Nicholas with some distrusted. "How did you know I was here? We have only just arrived?"

Josephine pointed to Nicholas. "He told me you were here."

All eyes turned to Nicholas, who simply shrugged as he looked to Josephine. "I saw yer sister arrive as I was out on the grounds," he said. "There is no big mystery about it. She arrived not long after the earl did."

The mood of the reunion plunged, and both Justine and Donald looked at Josephine. "The earl?" Justine repeated. "The one you are betrothed to?"

Josephine nodded her head, trying not to show how utterly misera-ble she was about it. She didn't want to show that out in the open for all to see.

"Aye," she said, swiftly wanting off the subject. Instead, she pointed at her sister's all-black clothing. "What is this? Why are you dressed like this?"

Justine looked down at herself, clad in her usual dark attire. At least, it had been usual until she'd married Sully, but her sister didn't know what she had planned. Cards, readings, divining her sister's future... Sully and Andrew had come to Edinburgh to help Josephine one way. She'd come to help in another way entirely.

"I must dress appropriately if I am to properly entertain," she said, then put up a hand as Josephine tried to question her further. "Please do not argue, Josephine. Just... trust me."

Josephine was all set to have words with her sister, but something in Justine's tone caught her attention. The woman didn't have the usual wild-eyed look about her. In fact, there was some reason in her gaze. It occurred to her that her little sister had something up her sleeve... but what? Josephine didn't press her, however, but she most certainly would later when they were alone. There was so very much to talk about, she hardly knew where to begin.

"Very well," Josephine finally said, then looked at Donald. "Donald, I'm very glad to see you."

Donald, ever gallant, kissed her hand and openly admired her beau-ty. "Ye outshine the sun, my lady."

Josephine grinned at her flattering friend before turning turned back to her sister. "Have you been given your rooms yet?"

Justine shook her head. "Not yet," she said. "But soon, I hope. I am weary from the journey."

Josephine understood that all too well. "Then come," she said, ges-turing to a nearby table where more refreshments had been placed. "Let us sample some of this wonderful food while you are waiting.

Justine followed her, with Donald and Nicholas bringing up the rear. Justine grasped her sister by the arm and leaned in to her.

"Where is Sully?" she whispered. "Have you seen him?"

Josephine paused at the table, catching Nicholas' eye. "Aye, I have seen him," she said. Then, she lowered her voice. "He is in the dungeon."

"What?" Justine shrieked, her hands flying to her mouth. "Why is he there? What has happened?"

"Shhh!" Josephine grabbed her sister to keep her from attracting attention. "Do not worry; Nicholas will free him, I promise."

Justine looked at Nicholas in a panic, realizing he knew about Sully and Andrew's appearance. Certainly, Josephine would not speak so casually in front of the man had he not known. There was some relief to that, but there was also some fear.

"But the dungeons?" Justine gasped, tears in her eyes. "Why is he there?"

Josephine slapped a hand over her mouth because she was growing loud. "Quiet!" she hissed. "Have no fear, please. All will be well but you must trust Nicholas!"

Justine's eyes were as wide as saucers and Josephine was hit by the intensity of the woman's anguish. She was terrified for the husband she'd had for less than a week, and rightfully so. She'd never before seen such a look of intense fear on Justine's face.

But then, it dawned on her. Justine was in love with Sully. Her sister – her strange, flighty, and obstinate sister – actually loved Sully. Josephine would have let her joy show but, somehow, it didn't seem right at the moment. Sully was in a crisis and Justine was nearly hysterical. With her sister's feelings in mind, she turned to Nicholas.

"Can we do anything now?" she asked him.

Nicholas looked thoughtful. "Possibly," he said. "Does the king yet know of Sully's imprisonment?"

Josephine was at a loss. "I do not know," she said. "Why?"

"Because," Nicholas said, "I would imagine that if his two beautiful cousins pleaded with him to release Sully, he would easily give in."

"There is no need."

The statement came from the doorway near the table and everyone turned to see Ridge standing there.

Josephine's face darkened. It had been Ridge who had imprisoned Sully in the first place and she was furious with him. But it wouldn't do to harass the man, not when he possibly held Sully's life in his hands. Neither would Josephine tell Justine of Ridge's role in Sully's imprisonment. It wouldn't do for Justine to charge the man and possible be thrown into the dungeons right along with her husband.

"Why not?" Josephine asked the man. "And how long have you been standing there?"

Ridge emerged from the doorway, heading in their direction. He greeted Justine politely before returning his attention to Josephine.

"Long enough to hear you discuss Montgomery with his wife," he said. "Voices carry in this hall. I would wager to say I wasn't the only person who heard what you said."

Josephine sighed sharply, looking about the hall, not realizing voices carried in it. "So, you heard me," she said, snappish. "That still doesn't tell me why we should not make the effort to plead for Sully's release to the king."

Ridge glanced at the food and reached over to pick up a sweet oat cake. "Because I released him myself not ten minutes ago."

Josephine was shocked, looking at her sister, who reflected her own confusion. "I do not understand any of this," she said. "Why is he released? And why did you imprison him in the first place?"

Before Justine could react to the news that it had been the big, dark knight who had incarcerated her husband, Ridge focused on Josephine.

"Because," he growled. "Consider it a warning to the man. The earl must realize that here in Edinburgh, the king is absolute. There will be no half-assed rescue attempt by a mercenary and a nobleman. The king has decreed that you shall marry the Earl of Annan and Blackbank, and we must all obey the king's decree. Is that in any way unclear?"

His voice was so very hard, and Josephine's lovely face darkened with anger. Several heated retorts sprang to her lips, but she refrained. Ridge was speaking with his head, not his heart, and she knew it. She knew the man well enough to know he was saying all of that for show. *Voices carry in the hall*, he'd said. He was being smart about this, whereas she hadn't been. But looking in his eyes, she could see that he had every intention of making sure she obeyed the king and her heart sank. It was Ridge, the ever-firm upholder of the king's wishes. No matter what he felt, he wasn't going to give in to those feelings.

He would see the king's wishes carried through no matter what.

God, she hated him for it.

"Remember your debt to me, de Reyne," she countered with equal steeliness. "That is all I demand of you."

Ridge's dark eyes glittered at her but he didn't say a word. He didn't react in any way. Infuriated, upset, Josephine turned her back on him, facing the food table as she began to help herself. Justine wandered up beside her.

"What now?" Justine she asked. "And *who* is that knight?"

Josephine shoved something sweet into her mouth. "He is the king's bodyguard," she said. "He came with Alexander to Torridon. Did you not see him?"

Justine wasn't sure so she glanced at him again. "I do not know," she said. "What does he have to do with any of this?"

"He is the one who abducted me from Torridon."

Justine looked at Ridge through new eyes, perhaps newly hostile eyes. "He did?" she hissed. "And then he put Sully in the dungeons?"

"Aye."

Justine was quite certain that she didn't like Ridge de Reyne now, not in the least. "Then where *is* my husband?"

Ridge heard her. "He was released outside of the gates, Lady Montgomery," he replied, his gaze on Josephine's stiff back. "No doubt, he was unaware of your arrival. I shall attempt to locate him for you."

Josephine heard the man's offer and she almost stopped him, but decided otherwise. Ridge could find him faster than anyone else could and having Sully inside the castle would be the perfect situation – Ridge would bring Sully to Justine and everyone would assume Sully had come with his wife. No one would know he'd come days earlier with Andrew in an attempt to protect her from the earl.

Besides… Josephine felt decidedly safer with Sully close by.

"I do hope you brought your husband some clothes, Justine," she said to her sister. Her mouth was full of the same pears in wine that Donald had been scarfing down. "The last time I saw him, he was in a sorry shape, indeed."

Justine stared at her sister, still pondering her words to Ridge. As Ridge walked away, presumably going off to find Sully, Justine found that she was increasingly confused by Ridge's relationship to her sister. She didn't know the man at all but, clearly, he knew Josephine and she knew him. There was something strange going on there that Justine didn't like.

"*What* debt, Josephine?" she asked. "What did you mean by that?"

Swallowing the food in her mouth, Josephine told her. Having the king's bodyguard be indebted to her for saving his life was not a bad thing, after all.

SULLY NEARLY CAME to blows with Ridge when the knight found him on the street on his way back to the inn. Sully had thought that Ridge had changed his mind about releasing him and had come back for him. But Ridge's lips pressed into a hard line at Sully's defensive stance.

"At ease, Lord Montgomery," he said irritably. "I came to inform you that your wife has arrived at Edinburgh. If you will trust me, my lord, then I shall escort you to her."

Sully's face went from anger to genuine surprise. "Justine? *Here*?"

Ridge nodded. "And she brought Donald Muir with her."

Several things rushed through Sully's mind at that moment – to return to the inn to await Andrew, but he also felt a strange desire to see his wife.

His wife.

Sully found that he very much wanted to see her, and that was reason enough for him to return with Ridge. But another thought occurred to him. By infiltrating the castle and staying with his wife, as she was the king's cousin and therefore an honored guest, he could also stay near Josephine. He wondered why de Reyne hadn't thought of that.

Or perhaps he had.

In any case, Sully would go to Justine. Then, somehow, he would get word back to Andrew as to the current situation.

Much had happened.

Sully made the excuse of wanting to gather his possessions. He'd rushed into the inn and told Esme to tell Andrew he'd been taken to the castle. Esme agreed, and Sully followed Ridge back to the castle and all the way to the great hall. As he headed for the door of the hall, he passed by Torridon wagons and servants that were being disbanded. He recognized his people, his equipment and, once inside the hall, his reunion with Justine was rather touching. She rushed into his arms and they embraced as if they were the most passionate of lovers, as if they'd been doing it all their lives.

In truth, Sully was very happy to see her, more than he ever thought he would be. Somehow, annoying Justine had ceased to become annoying and, instead, had become someone he was genuinely eager to see. Sully wasn't sure how that had happened, only that it had, and he couldn't have been happier.

As Sully and Justine hugged with the joy of their reunion, Josephine watched from several feet away. She had been truly touched at the scene. Yet happy as she was for her sister, her heart ached with longing for Andrew. She wanted the same kind of reunion with him. The more she watched her sister, the more her heart hurt, and she finally had to turn away to compose herself.

When Justine released Sully enough to allow the man to breathe,

Josephine was calm enough to turn around and face him. Setting down the cup of wine she had in her hand, for she'd just spent the wait for Sully sampling nearly every fine food on the table, she made her way over to him.

"How were the dungeons?" she quipped. "Make any friends while you were there?"

Sully grinned, glad to see that Josephine was at least in good spirits. "No friends worth mentioning in mixed company," he said. "But to be truthful, I was in and out so quickly that I hardly had time to sit down. But I am glad to be out and glad to see my wife."

He looked at Justine and she flushed prettily. Josephine had to grin at her sister's reaction; it was truly sweet. But she interrupted the warm moment as she glanced at Ridge, several feet away as he'd come in with Sully, before speaking.

"Have you seen Andrew?" she asked quietly.

"Nay," Sully answered, glancing over his shoulder to make sure Ridge wasn't close enough to hear. "But I left a message for him at the inn where we have been staying. I told him that de Reyne was bringing me back to the castle."

Josephine wasn't pleased to hear that Andrew was still missing. In fact, she was very worried. "I see," she said, trying not to seem too unhappy about it. "I… I do hope he gets the message."

Sully could see the worry in her eyes, but he truthfully had no idea where Andrew was. He sought to ease her.

"He will," he assured her quietly. "He has not abandoned you, Joey. He would not do that. Wherever he is, he has good reason to be there."

Deep down, Josephine knew that. She forced a smile. "I am sure that is true," she said. "But it seems as if he has been absent all day and, naturally, I am concerned. I was afraid that…"

She was interrupted by an entourage of well-dressed servants appearing from the door on the south side of the hall. Their finely-shod feet made clacking noises against the stone floor of the hall, an unusual feature when floors were usually made of hard-packed earth. Josephine saw William Ward, the king's chancellor, as he entered the room with several servants, and she immediately stiffened. She didn't like the man; she hadn't the first time she'd seen him.

Unfortunately, William spied her almost immediately and headed in her direction. She kept her gaze on him as Nicholas came up behind her.

"This cannot be good," he muttered.

Somehow, Josephine knew that. "About the earl?"

"More than likely."

But she stood her ground as William came up to her, eyeing her in a way that made her skin crawl. He didn't seem to notice anyone else standing around her; not Nicholas, not Ridge, nor Sully, Donald, or even Justine. He was looking strictly at Josephine.

"My lady," he said politely. "I had gone to your chambers but was told you were not there. I was hoping you were here, with the party from Torridon."

Josephine cocked her head. "And so I am," she said. "What can I do for you, my lord?"

William seemed rather pleased to deliver his message. "The king wishes for me to inform you that your betrothed, Alphonse d'Vant, has arrived," he said. "Surely you saw the man and his army enter the grounds?"

Josephine nodded. "I did."

William was puffed up, prideful, as he delivered his message. "The king has ordered a great feast in Blackbank's honor and you are to be the guest of honor," he said. "I am to tell you to dress in the white gown Blackbank has given you and wear that to the feast this evening. The earl wishes to see his betrothed in all her glory. He wishes to inspect you and the king is proud to show you to his favored ally."

The more he spoke, the more resistant Josephine became. So she was to be inspected, was she? It was infuriating as well as degrading. Frustration filled her and it was a struggle not to react. Where was Andrew when all of this was happening? Was he truly to leave her to the wolves?

"I will be ready," she said. It was all she could manage.

William had been expecting more of a gleeful answer from a young woman about to marry a very wealthy and powerful earl, but her reaction was restrained. Unhappy, even. Puzzled, the smile faded from William's face.

"An escort will be sent at the proper time," he said, turning away in some confusion. But he caught sight of Ridge, standing over near the table that was half-filled with the remnants of food, and he paused. "The king has been asking for you, Ridge. You are expected."

Ridge immediately departed, heading across the hall and disappearing through a door. With a lingering glance at Josephine, William left the way he'd come, followed by a host of servants who seemed to orbit around him. Once he left the hall, Josephine turned back in the direction of the table, the impact of William's news taking a toll on her expression. Justine put a hand on her.

"Not to worry," she whispered. "We are here now. Nothing will happen to you."

Josephine turned to her sister, seeing such assurance in the woman's eyes. But Josephine knew it was foolish to expect that Sully, Josephine, Donald, Ridge, or even Andrew at this point could protect her from the earl. So many people had come to help her, but they were essentially helpless.

As she'd known from the outset, railing against the situation would only cause grief. The only way she would be able to create any change would be to at least show some complicity with what was happening, to lull the king and the earl into a false sense of security. She put a hand on her sister's fingers, squeezing them.

"I know," she said. "Andrew has a plan. He must have one. Until then, all I can do is pretend to go along with this. There is truly nothing else I can do."

Sully heard her. "She's right," he said, mostly to Justine. Then, he looked at Josephine. "I was truly afraid I would find you chained up because you went wild and threatened to kill everyone. You are a strong woman, Joey, but you are not stupid. I am pleased to see that you've shown some sense in all of this. Until we can figure out what to do, you're simply going to have to go along with the betrothal."

Josephine was glad that Sully was agreeing with her. "I do not want you to think I've grown spineless," she said. "But it is my hope that they believe I am in agreement with all of this. That way, mayhap they are less likely to watch me. If I do escape, they will not expect it."

Sully could see that Justine didn't quite agree. She was still thinking of resistance, of fighting, but Josephine had realized that subterfuge would be more effective. As they stood there in relative silence, the majordomo appeared to inform Justine that her rooms had been prepared.

As Donald and Nicholas escorted Josephine back to her chambers, Justine and Sully followed the majordomo to the same building where Josephine was lodged. A parade of servants followed them, carrying Justine's numerous trunks, and Sully had to wonder what she'd brought that would pack up four large trunks. He soon found out.

Once they were settled in their chambers and the servants left them alone, Justine opened up two of the trunks to pull forth all of the things that Sully had little patience with – decks of cards, a box of bones that she used like an oracle, and special tables to put them on.

Sully stood there and shook his head as Justine unpacked all of the tools he had hoped she'd given up, but he supposed it was too much to ask so soon after their marriage. Even though Justine had changed a great deal in the past few days, she was still, in fact, the Justine he'd always known. She truly believed in her cards and oracles and divining rods.

He wasn't sure he could ever break her of that.

"What are you doing?" he asked quietly.

Justine turned to look at him, seeing disapproval in his eyes. God, she did so want to please him, but she felt very strongly about what she must do. That was why she had brought all of her cards and other things with her.

"I must see what the future holds," she said. "I must see if my cards will tell me what is in store for my sister."

Sully sighed faintly. He was becoming rather fond of Justine because he could see that she was trying very hard to be a good wife. She had moved beyond that annoying woman he'd known all these years and was transforming into someone warm and wise. He appreciated watching the transformation but when he saw her cards come out, he felt as if she was taking a giant step backwards.

"Your sister's future is not in the cards," he said as he went over to her, standing over her as she held the wooden deck in her hand. "Your sister's future is divined by God and the king, and Andrew, if he can help it. You would serve her better in prayer, not witchly pursuits."

He touched her shoulder, gently, and walked away, heading to go clean himself up. Justine watched him go, her heart tugging.

"You do not approve of what I do," she said. "I… I am sorry, Sully. I know you do not like it. But I feel strongly that the cards will tell me what prayer cannot."

He paused by the door to a smaller room off the master chamber, looking at her earnest face. After a moment, he chuckled, wondering why he would want to change the woman. Her belief in the occult was part of her charm, he supposed. Like the rest of her, he'd married it and needed to accept it.

"Then play with your cards if you feel you must," he said. "As for me, I am going to take a bath. You are invited to join me if you wish."

Justine flushed a violent shade of red, grinning as she turned away from him. Sully laughed softly at her reaction.

"Or you can remain here and play with your witch's curses," he said. "It is your decision."

As Sully went to go take a bath in a smaller room attached to a large bedchamber, his last vision of his wife was as she laid out a series of cards on two separate tables, clearly intent on reading the signs. Perhaps the lure of bathing with him wasn't strong enough, and he found he was actually insulted by it. If the woman would rather play with cards than with him, then it was a fine marriage he'd agreed to. He was going to have to do something about her attitude.

Servants came and went with buckets of hot water, filling up a big, dented copper tub. When the servants vacated the chamber and Sully was about to get into the water, he looked up to see Justine standing in the doorway, wrapped from head to toe in one of those sheer dark sheets she liked to wear. He'd seen her wearing them before, with nothing underneath. But now, her appearance in such a garment was a little different for him. The body beneath now belonged to him. In fact, it was rather arousing.

He could see her small, big-nippled breasts beneath the fabric and the dark triangle of curls between her legs. Her naked body beneath the fabric drew his lusty stare.

"So you have changed your mind?" he asked, already feeling himself growing hard. "You are most welcome to join me."

With an embarrassed grin, Justine came into the chamber, her eyes never leaving his. She walked right up to him, standing still as he reached out to pull the sheer fabric off of her, revealing her naked body beneath. When Sully wrapped his arms around her and bent over, sinking his teeth into her tender shoulder, Justine forgot all about the cards.

Whatever troubles her sister had, for the moment, were going to have to wait.

CHAPTER TWENTY-NINE

EDINBURGH'S DISTRICT FOR cattle and horses was called, appropriately, the Cow Market area, and it was in this district not far from the castle where Andrew found what he was looking for.

He needed a blacksmith; but not any blacksmith. He was looking for a man who specialized in weapons because, for what he was about to enter in to, he needed something better and stronger than the weapons he already had.

He needed a giant killer.

Seeing his brother with his army from Haldane hadn't been the life-changing experience Andrew thought it would be. He thought he would feel a surge of unmitigated hate and anger, foaming at the mouth and all that. But he hadn't. The hate and anger he'd always had was there, but it didn't surge. Instead, he felt some kind of odd satisfaction at the sight of Alphonse, as if he had once again sighted the reason for the turmoil and was pleased to see no one else had killed the man yet. That privilege was reserved for the one he'd done the most damage to.

Andrew.

The Street of the Blacksmiths in the Cow Market was more like an alleyway. It was hot and full of steam and smoke, impure air, and the alley ran with dirty water and slag from the anvils. Andrew wandered down the street, looking at each man's stall, seeing what they were doing and what they specialized in.

Every smithy specialized in something. One man was making chainmail while another was working on something that looked like fire pokers. Still another was working on shields, which he had hung up along the eaves of his stall to advertise.

Andrew paused to look at the shields, as they were very well made. When the smithy came to talk to him to see if he could sell him a shield, he and Andrew began to engage in conversation about weapons as well. The smithy didn't make weapons, but he knew who did, and Andrew spent almost an hour with the shield smithy because he appreciated the man's work and inspected every one of the shields he'd already made. He found one he liked a great deal; a big tri-corner shield that was lightweight but extremely durable. When he purchased it for a good price, the shield smithy was more than happy to take him down the row of stalls to the man who produced the weapons.

And what weapons they were.

Andrew had seen many weapons in his life and he knew excellent craftsmanship when he saw it. The weapon's smithy had beautifully made daggers on display, on tables that were surrounded by heavily-armed men to protect the wares, but as much as Andrew admired the daggers, he was more interested in broadswords.

The smithy was not Scottish nor English, but from across the sea, where he had learned his trade. *Tyre*, he'd told Andrew, and when he brought forth the first of four big broadswords for Andrew to inspect, he pointed out the wavy steel patterns of Damascus steel, a secret he'd brought with him from the Holy Land.

Andrew was awed. He'd heard of Damascus steel, but he'd never seen it. And, already, he knew he was going to purchase a broadsword from this man. Damascus steel was the strongest, most durable steel in the known world and Andrew very much wanted a weapon forged of such material. Perhaps it would be that giant-killer he was looking for.

The first three broadswords were magnificent in size and craftsmanship, but they weren't exactly what Andrew was looking for. Then the man, called Abe, brought forth the last sword he had – a massive weapon with one razor-sharp straight edge and the other edge serrated, like viper's teeth. Andrew fell in love with the sword the moment he put his hands on it.

This was what he'd been looking for.

It was a spectacular piece and extremely expensive, but price was no object. In fact, Andrew paid Abe for it before he even took it into an open area next to the stall to test it out. Six gold coins ended up in Abe's palm as Andrew took the sword and began moving it around, swinging it, becoming accustomed to the weight of it. One of Abe's heavily-armed guards came out with another sword so Andrew could practice the use of the sword against the man.

There was some gentle parrying and thrusting against each other as Andrew quickly became adept with the sword, which was magnificently balanced and surprisingly lightweight for such a weapon. The swords clanged against each other but when Andrew would stop to inspect the blade to see if it was damaged, there was no such blemish on the steel. Damascus steel was nearly impervious to nicks or scratches. Andrew ran a careful finger over the blade with satisfaction.

"Abe," he said. "You are a master at your craft. I cannot believe I did not know you were here in Edinburgh. I thought I knew where all of the good weapon craftsmen were."

Abe, short and old and wrinkled, with enormous shoulders and biceps from years of hammering steel, grinned.

"I have been here for many years, young knight," he said in his heavily-accented voice. "Where have *you* been?"

Andrew chuckled. "Everywhere," he said. "My army and I are paid very well to fight other men's battles, and we go everywhere."

Abe watched him as he swung the sword around casually, adjusting to the weight. "But you have not been to Edinburgh."

Andrew's smile faded. "Nay," he said. "Not until now."

"And now you intend to fight another man's battle?"

Andrew shook his head. "I am here to fight my own battle."

Abe could see the change in his expression. "It must be a serious battle."

"It is."

Abe was an old man, wise with years and experience. He sensed this strong, young knight was not about to fight a battle for his own pleasure. There was something more behind the man's eyes, something quite serious.

Normally, Abe did business with only the elite of Scotland. He even had English lords that traveled all the way from their homes to purchase his wares. Many of these men simply put the swords on the wall and never used them, but this man was different – clearly, he knew how to use a sword, and he fully intended to do so. It wouldn't simply be a trophy piece for him. And the man had a good knowledge of metal and weaponry, as Abe had discovered during the course of their conversation. But he seemed most serious about purchasing this sword, showing there was only one purpose for it.

As if it were only meant for one thing, one event.

"Come, Andrew," Abe said, calling him by name because Andrew had introduced himself at the beginning of their business. "Come and sit with me. We must speak."

Andrew stopped swinging the sword around and came into the stall again, sitting on a stool as indicated by Abe. It was dim and hot in the stall, as two of Abe's sons operated the anvil. They were hammering away at something, working on another weapon perhaps, but Andrew had what he'd come for so he wasn't paying attention. As he placed his sword carefully on the table next to him, Abe's wife came forward with a tray of refreshments.

The woman was wrapped from head to toe in dark fabric that re-sembled something Justine might wear. It covered her head, her body, and part of her face. She set a tray down in front of her husband, a steaming metal pitcher and two metal cups, most likely pewter. Abe poured something hot from the pitcher into the cups, handing Andrew one of them.

"Drink," he said. "Tell me why you have purchased my finest weap-on. What is this battle you must fight?"

Andrew sipped at the hot drink, discovering it to be minty and sweet with apples. He rather liked the old man, who had been kind and helpful, and didn't much mind the question. But he wasn't sure he intended to answer it.

"All men have battles they must fight, Abe," he said, pronouncing the man's name as "Ah-bay", the way the old man had. "Does it truly matter?"

Abe shook his head. "It does not," he said. "But I have six sons. I have lost two to battles they were sworn to fight. I sense that there is more to your battle than simple obligation and it worries me."

Andrew smiled faintly as he sipped at the very hot brew. "Why? You create weapons, Abe. You know men purchase them because they must fight battles. Why should I worry you so?"

Abe sipped at his own brew. "Tell me of yourself, Andrew," he said. "You said you are paid a great deal of money to fight other men's battles. That makes you a mercenary."

Andrew nodded slowly. "It does, indeed," he said. "I have been a mercenary for many years."

"Are you successful at it?"

Andrew laughed. "I must be if I paid you six gold crowns for this magnificent weapon," he said. Then, he sobered. "The battle I must fight has been a very long time in coming and no one is paying me to fight it. It is one of my own choosing."

"Who must you fight?"

"I must kill my brother."

Abe blinked, perhaps hit by the impact of those words. "I see," he said, concern in his voice. "May I ask why?"

Andrew didn't see any real harm in telling the old man at this point. "Because he is a vile, wicked creature," he said. "When my father died, he inherited my father's lands and title. He imprisoned my mother and banished me, but I always remembered. My brother has enacted many evils in his life and I must stop him."

Abe looked rather sad to hear all of it. "Why did he send you away?"

Andrew shrugged. "Because I was alive," he said simply. "I was a threat, I suppose. I was very young at the time and clearly no threat, but my brother did not see it that way. I think I was lucky to escape with my life."

"And you became a mercenary."

"I did what I had to do in order to survive."

Abe nodded in understanding. "So you were chased from your home and you have spent all of these years waiting to seek revenge," he said. "But why now?"

Andrew smiled, but it was without humor. "Because I was betrothed to a woman I love," he said. "She is a cousin to the king, and the king sought to make an alliance with my brother, who is a powerful border lord. He dissolved my betrothal and pledged the woman I love to my brother. I cannot allow him to marry her. For that reason, and for the slight against me and my mother, I must kill him."

Abe's bushy eyebrows lifted as a horrible story came to light. He felt sorry for Andrew. "Then you have a terrible burden to bear, my friend."

Andrew looked at the sword lying on the table, the magnificent piece with a dreadful destiny. "I do not know how terrible it is. I only know that it is my burden. It has always been my burden. But it is something that shall soon be lifted."

Abe looked at the sword because Andrew was. Something ironic occurred to him as he gazed at the nasty blade.

"Then you have selected the right weapon for such a destiny," he said.

Andrew looked at him. "Why would you say that?"

Abe's gaze drifted away from the blade, now looking at Andrew with his black eyes. "Because I name all of my weapons," he said. "Like children, I am their father because I gave them life, so I name them all. This weapon was christened *qatal alshyatin*."

"What does that mean?"

"Demon Slayer."

Andrew was struck by the appropriateness of that name. He returned his attention to the sword, seeing it in a whole new light. *Demon*

Slayer. Reaching out, he picked it up, holding it vertically so he could once again inspect the blade.

It was the blade that would free him.

"It will, indeed, slay a demon," he muttered. "This blade will destroy the burden that has dogged me all of these years."

Abe watched Andrew's face as he studied the steel. Amidst all of the vengeance, he thought he might have seen a ray of hope flickering in the man's eyes.

"Andrew?"

"Aye, Abe?"

"When you have finished with your brother, will you send word that you have survived as well?"

Andrew looked at him, hearing concern in the old man's voice. It was strange, he thought, considering he'd just met the man, that he should be concerned for him. But it also reminded him that there were kind and genuine people in the world who did care for the fate of strangers. And with that, Abe became something of a concern to him, as well.

"I will," he said. "And from now on, I shall only do my business with you, Abe. We share a bond, you and I. With this great weapon, you have made it possible for me to achieve what I have needed to achieve all of these years."

Abe simply nodded. Leaning forward, he put a meaty, dirty hand on Andrew's arm. "I hope you find peace, Andrew," he said. "That is what I pray for you. Peace."

Truth was, Andrew prayed for peace as well. He hoped that killing Alphonse would finally give him what he sought but, as he'd seen so many times with men bent on vengeance, sometimes being successful in their revenge left them empty, as if the revenge had become such a part of them that it was difficult to find that peace once the vengeance was gone. Some men needed that hatred in them simply to survive.

Andrew didn't think he was one of those men but, soon enough, he would find out.

Soon enough, he would know.

CHAPTER THIRTY

I T WAS EARLY evening and the castle was lit spectacularly in honor of the earl's visit. The warmth of the day still lingered and every window of the castle was open, allowing the sweet fragrances of nature to waft in on the evening breeze.

A huge feast had been prepared for the hundreds of people that would be dining this evening. Servants flowed throughout the structure, assisting, dressing, serving, and bathing the revered occupants. The air about was alive with the importance of the event and the enormity of the situation.

This night had to be perfect.

Josephine was high in her rooms, waiting patiently as Madelaine finished dressing her hair. She was clad in the most exquisite silk gown, white in color, that had been part of the wedding gifts from the earl. He had sent a message along with the dress, specifically asking that she wear it to the feast tonight. The message had the tone of a direct order and she angrily obeyed, hating herself for complying.

As Josephine sat thinking about the message from the earl, the angrier she became. How dare he order her about! And how dare she cave in like a weak, spineless woman! She was Lady Josephine de Carron, cousin of the king and heiress to the Earldom of Ayr. At least, she had been. Still… she would not take orders; she would *give* them.

Abruptly, she stood up, knocking the brush from Madelaine's hand.

"I will not wear this dress tonight," she said firmly and turned to the massive wardrobe that lined one wall. "I will find something else."

Madelaine was aghast. "My lady, why not? 'Tis a lovely gown!"

Josephine swung to the maid and the woman visibly cowered. Her jaw muscles flexed and her lips pressed into a thin smile. "It *was* a lovely gown," she said as she deliberately stepped on the hem of the dress and stood up, ripping a large portion of the skirt from the bodice. "But alas, a terrible accident occurred as I was dressing and the dress was ruined. I am sure that that earl will understand."

Madelaine looked at her in shock. Then, she suppressed a grin. "My lady, yer bravery astounds me," she said softly. "His request *was* a bit demanding."

Josephine's eyebrows lifted "A bit? Make no mistake; it was a command. And I will not do it."

Madelaine's expression was one of approval. "I can see that ye relent to no man, my lady. Ye have my respect and admiration."

For the first time, Josephine felt Madelaine was on her side. Even so, she remembered what she'd been told; that the woman was a sometime mistress of the king. Still, she really didn't care if this made it back to the king.

"Then help me select a new garment," she said.

Madelaine helped her remove the dress first, handing it over to a pair of hovering servants. Josephine, in her shift, then stood alongside Madelaine as the two scrutinized the other dresses in the wardrobe.

"What of the red garment?" Josephine asked, as she pulled out a red silk surcote, studying it. "This will make me look entirely wicked."

Madelaine was looking at the collection of dresses as if hypnotized. "Or the black?" she breathed. "Black for mourning. Black for the loss of innocence."

Josephine looked at Madelaine, hearing something in her tone. There was sorrow there as she spoke, and Josephine was affected by the depth of her words. Something in her expression suggested that Madelaine knew exactly what the loss of innocence meant. If she was the mistress of the king, then it was probably something she'd experienced firsthand.

Josephine had only spent a short amount of time around the king, enough to know that he was lascivious at best. Perhaps he'd stolen poor Madelaine's innocence. She tossed the red dress aside.

"Then black it is," she said quietly.

Josephine was dressed in the exquisite black silk, a surcote with a massive skirt to it, elaborately embroidered, and Madelaine went back to dressing her hair. She pulled the front portion of Josephine's hair back and secured it at the crown of her head with a jewel-encrusted clip. Then, she gathered up the whole wonderful mane and secured it at the nape of her neck with a black silk ribbon embroidered with tiny crystal beads. The last step was the rose fragrance, daubed over her entire neck, back, and wrists.

Josephine gazed back at herself in the polished mirror, noting the long, graceful neck, the creamy shoulders, and the swell of her breasts. She had to admit that she looked rather beautiful. Madelaine finished by swabbing red-tinted salve on her lips, making them seem all the more tempting and full. The entire picture was startling.

There was a knock on the door and Madelaine rushed to open it. Josephine turned defiantly to the door, certain that it was the earl, and braced herself for a fight. Much to her surprise, it was not the earl.

It was the king.

Alexander entered the room, his eyes falling appreciatively on his young cousin. In fact, he had that lascivious look that Josephine had seen before.

"Josephine," he said, as he reached out and took her hand. His eyes raked all over her. "You are incredibly lovely. But why black? I was told that the earl requested you to wear the white dress he sent you."

Josephine curtsied formally. "My lord," she greeted. "The white dress was accidentally torn. It will not be repaired in time for the feast."

She didn't seem upset by it and that piqued Alexander's curiosity. "Then why black? There are many other colors in your wardrobe."

"Black is the color of sadness, and I am sad."

He looked at her with a pout. "My sweet little cousin," he said. "Have I made your life so miserable? You will be a very rich and very powerful woman. Certainly, that is some cause for happiness."

Josephine could tell that he truly did not understand her plight and she felt a certain amount of pity for a man who was so narrow-minded. But she also felt a great deal of resentment. He had no idea of the hell he was condemning her to and if he did, he didn't care. Either way, it was an appalling prospect.

"Nay, my lord, it is not," she said frankly. "I know you believe this to be a great honor, but it is not to me. I want to go home to Torridon and marry Andrew."

Alexander hardened at what he perceived to be an ungracious attitude. "But I am giving you the opportunity to start a new and prestigious life as a countess," he said, leaving no room for discussion. "Now, close your eyes. I have brought you a wedding gift."

Reluctantly, Josephine obeyed. She didn't like the idea of closing her eyes with this man in close proximity, and her body was taut with uncertainty. She felt something very cold go around her neck.

"Open your eyes," he commanded gaily, directing her towards the mirror.

Josephine opened her eyes and her hands flew to her neck, touching the necklace as she stared at her reflection. A bejeweled necklace clung to her skin, its incredible brilliance sparkling like a million stars. It was an expensive and outrageous gift, and she did not feel comfortable accepting it.

"My king," she breathed, her eyes glued to the bejeweled strand. "This is the most beautiful necklace I have ever seen." Suddenly, she stepped back from the mirror and faced him. "But I cannot accept it. This is far too generous."

He looked confused at her refusal. "It is a gift, Josephine. My wife selected it herself," he said. "You *will* accept it."

He was giving her an order. To defy an earl was one thing, but to defy the king was another thing. And since the queen had a hand in selecting the gift, Josephine felt as if she truly could not refuse. With a deep breath for resolve, she forced herself to curtsy again.

"I thank you, my lord."

Although she uttered words of thanks, still, she was wary. The necklace was a gift to be given from a husband to a wife, or from one lover to another. She began to suspect that the necklace came with strings attached when she noticed the lustful gleam in the king's eyes. Instinctively, she moved away and put distance between them.

Alexander noticed. One would have been blind not to see that Josephine didn't want to be near him. In fact, she'd been standoffish since they'd first met, and he suspected why. At least, he thought he did.

"You fear me, Cousin?" he asked softly. "Why? Have I frightened you somehow?"

Josephine turned to him. She felt braver with several feet between them. "I do not fear you, my lord," she said. "I respect and admire you."

If he believed her, he didn't give any indication. He simply continued to stare at Josephine until her skin literally crawled from his cloying gaze. There was something so dirty about the way he looked at her. Eventually, he closed the distance between them. He came to within inches of Josephine and she saw his hand come up to her face. It was a struggle for her not to pull away as he gently grasped her chin and looked her in the eye.

Josephine stood her ground, but she was terrified. She could not refuse him if he wanted to seduce her. And physically, she was no match to fight him. Strangely, she felt a great deal of anger at his boldness, but she also felt a great deal of disgust at herself for allowing him to have power over her.

But he was the king, and she was his subject. She prayed she wasn't going to go the way of Madelaine, claimed by a man she could not refuse. Alexander's breath was hot on her face.

"You are the most beautiful woman I have ever seen, Josephine," he whispered. "I should like to get to know you better."

She lowered her gaze, her lashes fanning against her cheek. "Ask me any question, my lord, and I should be happy to answer you," she said. "As I would like to get to know you better as well. I understand you knew my mother. Mayhap you could tell me about her, what you knew of her in your youth."

A crushing blow to the king's intentions. Josephine happened to glance at him as her words sank in, and she saw the flame of lust extinguishing. Wielding her mother's name like a weapon, the only weapon she had, it had worked the desired effect.

But Alexander wasn't pleased about it. His hand dropped like a stone from Josephine's face and he cocked an eyebrow at her. The woman was cleverer than he had given her credit for, knowing that mention of Lady Afton would remind him of the person he toyed with. Lusting after his own family, as it were.

Disillusioned, and defeated, he turned away.

"As children, your mother and I were quite close," he said. "She was a bit older than I and quite beautiful. She would be pleased to know that her daughter can thwart the plans of men with less than honorable intentions with nothing more than a few words."

Josephine looked at him incredulously, realizing he was fully admitting his lust for her. But she also caught an amused glimmer in his eye and they were soon grinning at each other knowingly. Josephine knew his mind and she had established a line he would think twice before crossing.

"Do you wish the necklace returned?" she asked.

He scratched his head with a smirk. "Nay," he insisted. "It is your wedding gift from me and Marie. That, and a manor house outside Selkirk. It comes with a village of nearly two hundred acres of land."

Josephine was genuinely touched by his generosity. Maybe he did realize the terrible pit he was casting her into and was trying to make it as attractive as possible. But she was going to press him on the issue of the manor house.

"Thank you very much, my lord," she said. "You are most gracious.

Might I make a request?"

Now he looked at her a bit warily. "What is it?"

She wasn't shy about telling him. "That the manor house, and all of its holdings, will be placed in my name only," she said. "The earl will not be able to touch it. I want it to be mine alone."

To her surprise, he smiled at her. Then, he laughed. "Josephine, you are a shrewd and wise woman," he said. "I can see that you possess more in your head than most of your countrywomen combined. Of course, the manor house will be yours entirely, as well as the title it carries. But I do not suppose you care about a title, do you?"

There was some humor in his question, surprisingly, and she shrugged. "I was once the heiress to the Ayr earldom," she said, as she cocked her head comically. "Soon, I shall be the Countess of Annan and Blackbank. What is the meaning of one more title?"

"Nothing, of course," he agreed with mock seriousness. "But the manor house comes with the title of Lady Ashkirk."

She bowed her head. "Thank you, my lord."

With all of that behind them, Alexander had a new respect for his young cousin, who was quite cunning in spite of her youth. He reminded her a good deal of her mother. A seed of respect for the woman sprouted and he held out his hand to her.

"Come, my beauty," he said. "The castle abounds with guests who, I am sure, wait at this very moment in the dining hall with strained patience."

Josephine looked at the outstretched hand, knowing he meant to take her to the earl, and all of the ease she'd felt with the conversation over the past few moments was gone. Now, she felt a good deal of apprehension. She'd already fended the king off, but she wasn't so sure her luck would hold out with her intended. The best way to fend him off would be to stay away from him, and that was exactly what she intended to do. Andrew's advice suddenly popped into her head – *tell them your woman's cycle has begun*, he'd said.

It was the best excuse she could think of.

"I am afraid I am not feeling very well this evening, my lord," she said, putting her hand to her belly. "I... I should like to meet the earl when I am feeling and looking my best. And unfortunately, that is not tonight."

Alexander peered at her. "You seem well enough to me."

She shook her head, rubbing at her belly. "I fear it has taken all of my strength to speak with you," she said. "I feel rather weak and... faint."

His eyebrows came together. "*Faint?*"

She nodded, reaching for the nearest chair and trying not to be overly dramatic about it. She didn't want it to seem as if she'd suddenly taken ill the moment the king invited her to attend him to the hall, but that's exactly what it looked like. She had to make it seem believable.

"It comes over me sometimes," she said. "*Monthly*, I mean."

Alexander was looking at her as if he had no idea what she meant until, abruptly, her meaning settled. Suddenly, he didn't seem so suspicious and, much as Andrew had predicted, he moved away from her.

"I see," he said, rather clipped. "Well... then mayhap I shall excuse you from the feast tonight. Are... are you *sure* you do not feel up to it?"

Josephine shook her head. "Alas, I would be grateful for the reprieve," she said. "My sister just arrived earlier today and I will have her brew some herbs for my affliction. I should feel better in a day or two."

Alexander eyed her somewhat dubiously, wondering why she hadn't mentioned this curse before, but he realized their conversation would have been no place to speak of such matters. He didn't even want to speak of it now. With a sigh of frustration, he moved to the door.

"The earl will be disappointed, Josephine," he said. "Mayhap, I will arrange for you two to meet on the morrow."

Josephine nodded. "If I am feeling better, I would be honored," she said. "But you understand... I do not want to greet the man and then faint because I am feeling so poorly."

"Of course not."

"Thank you for your understanding, my lord."

Alexander wasn't sure he understood, but he wasn't going to press her. He didn't want her fainting, either, because it would embarrass him. Now, he realized that this entire evening was going to be a problem because the earl had already expressed his desire to meet his betrothed when he arrived earlier in the day. Now, he would have to pacify the man somehow. Reaching the door, he paused before stepping through.

"May I inquire how you are feeling on the morrow?" he asked unhappily.

Josephine nodded. "I would be pleased, my lord."

"Shall I send my wife to you?"

"There is nothing she can do. This, too, shall pass."

Alexander left without another word, shutting the door behind him. Josephine sat there a moment, listening, wondering if he was going to enter again and demand she attend the feast. He'd appeared most displeased when he'd left. But he didn't come back and, after several long seconds, she jumped up and ran to the chamber door, bolting it and saying a silent prayer for Andrew's advice.

A smile spread across her face as she realized just how right he'd been. At least for tonight, she had a reprieve.

RETURNING TO THE rented room that he shared with Sully well after sunset, Andrew was surprised to find that Sully was nowhere to be found. He wasn't in their chamber, nor was he in the common room. He saw Esme and made haste to avoid her. But the woman called his name and rushed towards him, so he held his ground, wondering what she had to say to him. He was fully prepared to make any and all excuses as to why they could not spend time together but, much to his surprise, she had a message from Sully to deliver.

Justine has arrived at the castle and I have gone to stay with her.

Find me there.

It was a most surprising message. Now, Sully evidently had a legit-
imate reason to be in the castle being that his wife had arrived from
Torridon. He wondered why Justine had come but, in truth, it was no
great mystery – her sister was here, as was her husband, and she
probably thought she was coming to help them both.

It was not welcome news, either.

Andrew had to shake his head. His mission to help Josephine was
growing by leaps and bounds. Now it was turning into a crusade for her
sister as well as her sister's husband. He wondered who else would show
up in a valiant attempt to help Josephine. Unfortunately, the more
people who came to help her, the more difficult it would be. Soon
enough, Alexander would catch on to what was happening, and that
would be a problem. Andrew knew he had to get to Josephine to find
out what had changed since he was out purchasing the Demon Slayer.

He wished he could bring the weapon to show it to her, for he was
certain she would be impressed by it, but he had to leave it behind at
the inn. It was in a beautiful sheath, and he wrapped the blade and the
sheath up in linen from one of the two beds. Slicing a hole in one of the
mattresses, he pulled out a good deal of the stuffing and shoved the
wrapped sword up into the mattress to hide it. It was such a magnificent piece that he didn't want to take the chance that someone might
enter his room while he was gone and take it. He didn't care much
about the other possessions he'd brought with them, but the sword…
he cared about that.

It had a purpose.

Once the sword was safely hidden away, he proceeded to don his
apple man disguise that he had been using. He would then make his
way into the castle just before the sentries shut up the gates for the
night.

As Andrew slipped from the tavern, Esme was watching him. She
was so very hurt that he hadn't given her any of his time since the day
of his arrival, the day he'd given himself over to her. Esme had been

with more than her share of men, but never any like Andrew. Tall, proud, and handsome, he was too perfect for her and she knew it.

But that didn't make her want him any less.

Ever since that lovely moment they'd spent together, when he'd touched her so sweetly, she had been making plans for her and Andrew. But it had been very difficult when she couldn't even speak to him. She knew he had business at the castle, business that had him sneaking in and out of the gates. But the fact that he had no time for her hurt her deeply. If the man wasn't going to give her any time voluntarily, then she was going to have to do something about that.

She was going to have to take matters into her own hands.

Once Andrew was gone, she slipped up to his rented room and let herself in. The room was dark, having hardly been slept in since Andrew and his companion arrived. The hearth hadn't been lit in days. Over in the corner, she could see saddlebags and other possessions shoved down so they were almost hidden by one of the two beds in the chamber. The sight of the baggage gave her an idea because she knew he would have to return for them.

And when he did, she'd be waiting for him.

The man wasn't going to ignore her again.

UNAWARE THAT, BACK at the inn, Esme was making plans, Andrew was lost to plans of his own. He had done a good deal of thinking on this day. It had started last night after he'd left Josephine but, as the day dawned, his thoughts became more and more intense. He was presuming that he would win this fight against his brother, which meant he would inherit the earldom of Annan and Blackbank. It meant he would inherit a house and hold that had been ruled by a devil since his father died, and he was genuinely concerned for the state of Haldane Castle and what he would find upon his triumphant return. It would be up to him and up to Josephine to restore what had been damaged. She was such a strong woman. Already, he felt pride in her that he'd never felt in anyone, ever. With her by his side, he knew he could restore his family's good name.

He needed that chance.

But it meant giving up the life of a mercenary. As much as that line of work had sustained him, he knew he couldn't keep it up. It wouldn't be proper for an earl to continue mercenary ways and fight other people's battles. He would remain at Haldane and become the benevolent lord of the land, and raise his sons to be fine men who would honor the d'Vant name.

It was a life he found himself hoping for.

But it wouldn't be his until he could rid the world of his brother. As he entered the grounds of the castle, Andrew was becoming well acquainted with the garden that wasn't far from Josephine's chamber. As the sun set to the west, he embedded himself in the garden to watch her window and the comings and goings, making sure he wouldn't be seen as he entered her chamber. He'd managed to scale the wall quite nicely because of the uneven stones and the corbel beneath the windows. It hadn't taken him long but if anyone was around, he would be seen. Therefore, he wanted to wait until the feast in the castle commenced and people were mostly gathering in the hall. When the grounds had quieted down, he could make his move.

But it was a difficult wait. He remained crouched in the same position, behind a heavy gathering of vines that went up the side of the garden wall, for at least a couple of hours. That was hard on his joints and, more than once, he had to shift slightly to ease up the pain. But, eventually, the grounds stilled and he could hear the sounds of voices and music in the distant hall.

Knowing he had to take his chance, Andrew emerged from out of the vines and quickly made his way to the side of the building. Like a spider, he went straight up the wall, gripped the big stone corbel beneath Josephine's window, and heaved himself in.

Coming over the windowsill, he lost his balance and fell to the floor, listening to Josephine gasp. When he rolled to his knees, she was sitting in a chair with a heavy bound book in her hands. Andrew flashed her a big smile, perhaps to cover his embarrassment at literally falling into her chamber, and Josephine burst out in giggles.

The heavy book was set aside and she rushed to him just as he lurched to his feet. But she hit him so hard, her arms going around him, that he grunted by the force of her momentum and nearly fell down again.

"Where have you been?" Josephine asked. "I have been so very worried for you."

Andrew hugged her tightly, relishing the feel of her in his arms. "I am well, love," he said. "Why were you worried?"

Josephine loosened her grip enough to look him in the eye. "Because Sully did not know where you were," she said. "You did not come to me today, so I assumed the worst."

He shook his head. "I cannot come to you in the daylight," he said frankly. "Everyone would see me. Besides… after seeing my brother arrive today, I had something important I had to do. You have not yet been introduced to him, have you?"

Josephine shook her head. "Nay," she said, "although the king tried, not an hour ago. I used your excuse and it worked."

"What excuse?"

She lifted her eyebrows in a dramatic gesture. "My mysterious woman's cycle."

He grinned. "Ah," he said in understanding. "I told you it would work."

She giggled, not nearly as embarrassed as she was the first time they discussed the subject. "It did," she said, "and you were correct."

He put his arm around her shoulders and led her over to the bed. "Say it again."

"What?"

"That I was correct."

It was a show of arrogance and she turned to him, frowning. "Why should I say it again?"

He grinned, pinching her chin gently. "Because that is something I always wish to hear from your lips. I am never wrong."

Josephine shook her head reproachfully at him but didn't argue. She was too glad to see him to chide him for being so arrogant, even in jest. Sitting down on the bed, she pulled him down to sit beside her.

"So much has happened today that I do not know where to start," she said. "Where did you go today that was so important?"

He held her hands, bringing them to his lips for a gentle kiss. "To a smithy," he said. "There is a remarkable street here that I think you should like called the Street of the Blacksmiths. There are many blacksmiths making a variety of things, from mail to swords and shields. Someday I shall take you there to meet a smithy named Abe. He has made the most miraculous sword, which I purchased from him."

Josephine was hanging on his every word. "Sword?" she said, cocking her head curiously. "But you already have a sword."

He nodded. "I know, but this is a special sword," he said, sobering. Suddenly, he didn't seem so excited about his purchase. He seemed rather serious. "After seeing my brother today, I realized that an ordinary sword will not be enough. Of course, the sword I use in battle is a fearsome weapon, but I want to have something more than that. I want something forged by the gods, something that will end my brother's life without question. I am not sure how I can describe it to you, only that I had a great need for a special weapon. Something deadly and terrible. I found it at Abe's stall."

Josephine was quite interested. "Where is it?"

He squeezed her hands, fondling her fingers. "I had to leave it at the inn," he said. "I could not bring it to show you, although I wanted to. It has a name."

"It does? What is it?"

"Demon Slayer. It was named that when I purchased it, so it must be an omen. It was meant to kill my brother."

It was an ominous title for a sword. As someone who had wielded a sword for the past two years against Colin Dalmellington, Josephine appreciated a good weapon. But to hear the name of this sword… *Demon Slayer*… it sounded so terribly menacing. Somehow, the name alone instilled confidence.

"If you are happy with it, then I am happy with it," she said. "But you did not even tell Sully where you went."

He shook his head. "I did not," he said. "There was not the opportunity. But when I returned, I received a message from Sully saying that Justine had arrived and he'd come to the castle to be with his wife."

Josephine nodded. "Justine and Donald came today," she said. "But Sully… while you were buying your sword, he was in trouble."

"What do you mean?"

Now it was her turn to clutch his hands, feeling a little guilty for what she was about to tell him, as if it were all her fault. "I became worried that you had not come to me today," she said. "I did not even stop to think that it was because it was daylight and you did not want to chance being seen. I thought something had happened to you, so I went looking for you."

He eyed her, warily. "Joey, you should not have done that," he said. "You know how dangerous it can be for you."

She nodded, hanging her head. "It was not dangerous for me, but for Sully," she said. "Ridge de Reyne followed me from the castle and when he saw Sully, he arrested him and put him in the dungeon."

Andrew's expression hardened. "Damnation," he hissed. "Was there a battle?"

She could see he was worried and hastened to reassure him. "There was no battle," she said quickly. "Sully surrendered because Ridge threatened him should he not. So, de Reyne sent him to the dungeon and then released him when Justine arrived. Ridge said that he had to show Sully that the man couldn't act against the king, so putting him in the dungeon was a warning. If there is a next time, I am assuming he will put him back in the dungeons and leave him there."

Andrew pondered the situation with Ridge. "It was Ridge who

brought you to Edinburgh," he said. "And now he follows you? He could be watching the door of this chamber at this very moment."

Josephine knew that was a possibility. "He does seem to keep a close eye on me," she said. "But it is strange, Andrew… when he first took me from Torridon, I fought him, and I even tried to bribe him. I told him I would give him money if he would simply tell the king he could not find me. But he refused. He said it gave him no pleasure to abduct me, but he had to because he was simply following orders. It's as I told you before – Ridge is a decent man. I believe that he truly wants to help me but does not know how to do it and not violate his oath to the king."

He eyed her a moment. "Ridge de Reyne is a powerful knight," he said. "We know that he keeps his eye on you."

"It is his duty."

"It could be more than a duty, Joey."

It occurred to her what he meant and she was indignant. "I do not care if there is more to it," she said. "Ridge has been kind to me, at least as kind to me as he can be, but that is all there is to it. I have no interest in him. My only interest is in you."

Andrew smiled faintly, seeing that he'd offended her. "I know," he said, reaching up to touch her cheek. "But Ridge may have some manner of fixation on you. You are a beautiful woman, after all. How could he not?"

Josephine was uncomfortable thinking that Ridge might have something other than platonic feelings for her.

"I do not wish to discuss Ridge de Reyne," she said, looking away. "I only wish to discuss us and what is to come. You have purchased a terrible sword to kill your brother with. When do you intend to do it?"

Andrew kissed her hands once more before standing up and stretching his long body wearily. He noticed food and drink on the table near the hearth and he headed in that direction.

"I am not sure," he said. "Has anything been said to you about the wedding?"

She watched him pour himself a measure of wine into a fine crystal cup. "Nay," she said. "The only thing that has been discussed with me is being introduced to the earl. Beyond that, nothing more."

Andrew drank deeply before answering. "I have been thinking about this," he said. "I have thought of little else. It is my assumption that the wedding will be here, at Edinburgh, so that the king can attend. Of course, I do not know this, but that is my assumption. If I attack my brother within the confines of the castle, it is possible that I will be arrested before I can complete my task. If that happens, I will either be killed or put in the dungeons, and you will have to marry my brother. I will not be able to help you."

Josephine stood up from the bed, making her way to him. "But what of Sully?" she asked. "He can step in if you have been disabled, and…"

He cut her off, looking at her. "Do you really want Sully going up against my brother?" he asked. "Did you see the man today when he arrived?"

Josephine sighed heavily, leaning against the wall next to the table. "Aye," she said. "I saw the back of him as he passed by. And, nay, I do not want Sully fighting the man. In truth, it is not his battle."

Andrew poured himself more wine. "Exactly," he said. "It is not his battle. It is mine. Therefore, for Sully and Donald and anyone else who wishes to help you, it is not their burden to bear. It is mine. But my thoughts are this – if the wedding is here, you will have to go through with it. For the reasons I mentioned, I will not stop it. But it is my suspicion that my brother will want to return to Haldane immediately to celebrate his wedding at his own castle, meaning he will leave Edinburgh and head home immediately afterwards. I will catch him on the road as soon as he leaves the city. There will be less likelihood that I will be stopped or arrested in that case. I will find him on the road and I will kill him before he can touch you."

Josephine didn't like the idea of having to marry the man before Andrew was able to kill him, but she understood somewhat.

"Then I must go through with the wedding if it is here, at Edinburgh?"

"Aye, love."

She sighed again. "If you believe that is best."

"I am not sure where there is any other choice, as much as I hate to say it."

Josephine was feeling sad and afraid. She moved away from the wall, heading back over to the bed. "I cannot believe that I will have to marry the man, but I understand why I must," she said, throwing herself on the mattress. "So many people are at Edinburgh to help me but, in truth, no one can. The king has made this betrothal, and no one can break it. No one can stop the wedding from happening. If you try, they will arrest or even kill you. If Sully tries, he has Torridon to lose. I would not let Donald or even Nicholas help – they could not survive in a fight against your brother. Everyone is here to help me, but everyone is helpless. All they can do is watch while I am forced into a death sentence."

Andrew heard the defeat in her voice, the same defeat he heard the night before. "I know you are scared, love," he said. "I am scared, also. Mayhap, it would be better to steal you out of Edinburgh during the night and flee to France or Spain. But the truth is that my brother would still be alive, and my mother would be unavenged. I am sorry if my sense of vengeance is affecting my decisions, but I have lived with it for so long. I know that if we were to flee and never return, it would eat at me until I returned to finish what I had always intended to do. I cannot have that vengeance stand between us, Joey. I am afraid if I do not kill my brother as I have always planned, then that is exactly what would happen."

Josephine looked at him. "I know you have a strong sense of duty, of what you must do," she said. "I would never ask you not to fulfill your vow and I would never ask you to change. I trust you in that you will do what is right, for both of us."

He needed to hear of her faith in him. It was as important to him as eating and breathing. Now that they were approaching a crucial point in all of this, it was important that they had complete trust between them. Quietly, he went to sit next to her, taking her hands in his once more.

"Mayhap I cannot give up my sense of vengeance for you, but there is something I will do for you," he said quietly. "Once we are married, I intend to give up my mercenary ways. I will turn the army over to Thane, and you and I will live at Haldane and raise our children. I would rather stay with you, as your husband, than fight a thousand wars for a million marks of gold. You are what is most important to me, Josephine de Carron. I will spend the rest of my life proving it."

Josephine smiled at the sweet declaration. "As you are what is most important to me, too," she said. "I will not continue my warring ways after we are married, either. There is no need. I will leave Torridon to Sully and Justine, and find great satisfaction in simply being the wife of Andrew d'Vant."

He leaned forward, capturing her sweet lips in his. "It will be a good life, I swear it."

She wrapped her arms around his neck and his big arms went about her. "And I cannot wait to live it, with you," she murmured, her face in his neck. "You are my sun and my moon, Andrew. Never forget that."

He held her against him, thinking he'd never heard such sweet words. He was about to tell her that when her door rattled as if someone were trying the latch. The door was bolted, so they were not able to enter. As Andrew and Josephine froze, someone knocked on the door.

"My lady?" It was Madelaine. "My lady, will ye open the door?"

Josephine sighed sharply. "It is my maid," she whispered. "If I do not open the door, she will tell the king. You had better leave."

Andrew was already standing up, pulling her with him. He kissed her swiftly. "I will see you tomorrow at this time," he said, rushing towards the window. But he was also shaking his finger at her. "Do *not* come looking for me. If you need to get word to me, send Sully since he seems to be able to move about freely now."

She nodded, anxiously watching him climb onto the windowsill. "I will," she said. "Be careful!"

"I love you."

"And I love you."

He blew her a kiss and climbed from the window. As Josephine went to open the door and let Madelaine in, Andrew made his way down the wall, jumping to the ground for the last several feet. Hitting the dirt, he dashed back to the garden to hide and to make sure he wasn't followed. For a big man, he moved very swiftly, disappearing into the darkness like a wraith.

But he wasn't alone in the garden. He figured that out quickly. There was something over to his left in the garden, flush against the wall, that had his attention. It was completely in the shadows, but he could see an outline and it didn't take him long to figure out that it was a man hiding deep in the shadows.

Even if Andrew was without his sword, he wasn't without his dirk, and he unsheathed it from his cozy nook in the top of his boot. If the shadow figure moved against him, he was ready.

Still, he wasn't going to wait for Death to come to him. Staying against the wall, he moved through the darkness, heading in the figure's direction. At one point, he froze because he'd lost sight of it behind one of the many vines that cover the wall, so he simply remained where he was, waiting to see where the figure would pop up.

It didn't take long.

"Lower your weapon, d'Vant," came the quiet voice. "I mean you no harm."

Andrew didn't recognize the voice. "Show yourself."

The figure drew closer, perhaps too close for comfort, but it stopped when it was an arm's length away. Ridge de Reyne's features came into the moonlight as he stepped out from the vines.

Andrew had seen Ridge at Torridon. He'd been introduced to the man but he'd never had any dealings with him, even though he felt as if he had. This was the man who had changed the course of his life. He couldn't decide if he felt unmitigated hatred for abducting Josephine, or if he felt a kinship to him. It was an awkward standoff, indeed.

"How long have you been out here, de Reyne?" he finally asked.

Ridge scratched his head. "Long enough to know this is the second visit you have made to Lady Josephine in as many nights," he said, watching Andrew surprised expression. "Aye, I saw you go to her last night, too."

Andrew's gaze lingered on him. "She told me you had been watching her," he said. "I suppose I did not realize just how closely. Well? Are you going to arrest me now?"

Ridge didn't say anything for a moment. He simply continued to stare at Andrew in the darkness. "It is strange, really," he said, avoiding the question. "I know a good deal about a man I have never had a conversation with before, so as I stand here looking at you, I feel as if I already know you."

"Oh?" Andrew said. "What do you know?"

Ridge let out a long, deep sigh and glanced up, looking at the stars through the vines overhead. "I know that you were betrothed to Lady Josephine before the king betrothed her to your brother," he said. "I know that you clearly must love the woman, else you would not be here to try and save her. But I also know something else."

"What?"

"That you intend to kill your brother."

Andrew wasn't surprised that Ridge knew all this about him. Considering he'd spent a good deal of time with Josephine, she had evidently told the man about the situation at large. Andrew wasn't so sure that was a good idea, but it was too late to do anything about it now.

"And you intend to stop me?"

Ridge shook his head. "That is none of my affair," he said. "In fact, Blackbank is someone who needs killing from what I've heard. He is not well-liked, you know. The king is hoping that this betrothal might make the man more pliable to Scotland's wishes, but my instincts tell me that Blackbank is loyal to Blackbank. He is loyal to Alexander for what it can bring him – in this case, a rich heiress."

Andrew began to recall what Josephine had said about Ridge – that he was simply following the king's orders but that his heart, nor his loyalty, was behind his actions. Simply his duty. He could almost believe that, based on the man's manner.

"My brother is a ruthless barbarian," Andrew said. "What he cannot control, he kills, and he will not be able to control Josephine should she become his wife. The king has given her a death sentence."

"He does not see it that way."

"I know he does not," Andrew snapped quietly. "I had a conversation with the man where I clearly stated that Josephine and I were betrothed. He ignored it soundly. Instead, he chose to dissolve our betrothal and give her over to my brother. If you think I am going to stand by and watch this… this *travesty* happen, then you are sadly mistaken."

Ridge could feel the passion bleeding off of Andrew as he spoke. Had he not known anything about the man and his relationship to Josephine, that fervent outburst would have told him everything he needed to know.

"She has the same passion about you, you know," he said quietly. "Lady Josephine, I mean. She speaks of you with the same passion."

Andrew struggled to keep his composure. "That is because she loves me and I love her," he said. "And I will kill my brother before he can touch her. If you try to stop me, I will kill you, too."

Ridge believed him without question. "I already told you that it was none of my affair," he said. "Do not involve the king in anything you do, and it will continue to not be my affair. But the moment Alexander involves himself, and if weapons are drawn, I am obligated to enter the fray. Is that understood?"

"Without question."

Ridge nodded faintly. "Then we understand one another," he said. He paused before continuing. "But I will also tell you this – whilst on the road here from Torridon, Lady Josephine and I were set upon by outlaws. She saved my life. To that, I owe her a debt, which makes this a very strange situation for me. I cannot go against my king, yet I cannot let a debt go unanswered. She wanted me to let her go, but I could not. Even if I did, it would not solve the problem. The king would simply send someone else after her, someone who was, mayhap, not so sympathetic to her plight."

Andrew was listening carefully. More of what Josephine had told him was coming back to him – and Ridge just confirmed it. *Sympathetic to her plight*. Ridge had fully acknowledged that he was, indeed, sympathetic. Perhaps, it was to this man he needed to appeal to, because certainly, if he had Ridge's assistance, perhaps killing his brother would be far less difficult. But perhaps not; as Ridge said, it was none of his affair.

"That is true," he said after a moment. "But it is not my intention to take her away from Edinburgh, at least not at the moment. I have come here to confront and kill my brother."

Ridge nodded faintly. "So I have been told."

Andrew's gaze was intense, even in the darkness. "Then you know that Sully and I have only come to make sure Josephine is protected as much as we can, but my primary purpose in being here is to confront my brother," he said. "I do not know how much Josephine has told you, de Reyne, but my need for vengeance against my brother goes back many years. When my father died, he banished me and imprisoned our mother. I have sworn to avenge my mother. The fact that Josephine is betrothed to my brother is a sickening coincidence and nothing more. When he is dead, and only when he is dead, will I claim Josephine. But for now… I must be near her. I must give her strength, as she gives me strength."

Ridge heard more of that passion in his voice, of a deep love for a woman that was rare. There was such power in his words. Now, Ridge began to feel some sympathy for Andrew as well.

"I heard all of this already," he said quietly. "And I do understand the need for vengeance. But surely you must understand that Josephine will marry your brother. You cannot stop that."

"It is possible that I can kill him before he makes it to the altar."

"And if you do not?"

"Then I will kill him before he can touch her."

Ridge shook his head. "But how?" he asked. It was almost a plea. "D'Vant, there are too many variables here. If your brother marries the woman, then it is his legal right to consummate the marriage. How do you plan on preventing this once he marries her?"

"I have a plan."

"I hope to God you do because, once he marries her, no one can interfere. Not even the king." He hesitated. "But I will tell you this – I do not want to see your lady married to Blackbank any more than you do."

Those words had a massive impact on him. Andrew knew all of this would be a huge risk but, as he'd explained to Josephine, he was assuming a great deal – that his brother would want to return home after their marriage and not spend the night at Edinburgh.

But… *what if he did*?

Andrew remembered his conversation with Thane back at Torridon, telling the man to take Josephine to de Wolfe or south to Cornwall in order to remove her from his brother's reach. But that had been before de Reyne had brought Josephine to Edinburgh. But the reality was this – if he failed to kill his brother before or even after the wedding, and he himself was killed instead, then nothing was standing between Josephine and a living nightmare. While Sully was an excellent knight, he would be no match for Alphonse.

But Ridge would.

"If that is true, then help me," he said quietly. "You said that you owed Josephine a debt. If, for some reason, I am killed instead of my brother, then I ask you to honor that debt. If I die, get Josephine to Sully and see them safely out of Edinburgh. That is all I am asking, de Reyne. I am not asking you to violate your king's orders, which were wrong to begin with. I am simply asking you to honor the debt you owe her. Give her a fighting chance at life, which she will not have with my brother. Do you understand me? Get her to safety before he kills her."

Ridge's expression tightened. Andrew could see it in the darkness. The man was in a difficult position, as he'd said. He wanted to commit to Andrew's request, but his sense of duty to the king prevented it. At least, it did for now. But very quickly, he might lose that battle and side against his king in this situation. He could feel himself leaning heavily in that direction already. To save himself, and his honor, he looked away from Andrew.

"Get out of here, d'Vant," he said. "Get out and stay out of sight. I will pretend that I did not see you here tonight."

Andrew was disappointed that Ridge hadn't given him his promise but, he was certain, with time, that might change. Josephine said that Ridge was a decent man; Andrew wanted to believe that.

He was counting on it.

"I will be back tomorrow," Andrew said quietly. "If you see me tomorrow?"

"I will pretend I did not see you again."

With that, he walked away, heading out into the garden. Andrew watched him walk away, thinking that de Reyne was fairly lenient to look the other way in this matter. That gave him hope. Perhaps the man would side with them, after all.

But those thoughts of hope for the future were summarily dashed when Andrew returned to the inn that night. What he didn't know was that he was being watched, and had been since the day he'd seduced Esme.

There was an added element to his troubles that he hadn't expected. Aye, Esme was watching him and, when he entered the tavern, she knew what was in store for him. She'd been planning it for some time. For every time the man had looked the other way when she smiled him, or otherwise ignore her, she was going to make him pay.

She didn't like to be toyed with.

Aye… the man was going to pay dearly.

But Andrew was completely unaware of what awaited him. Things like Esme and vicious women were the furthest things from his mind. But it was his mistake. The moment he entered the small, rented room that he and Sully had shared, someone hit him over the head with a heavy object and the lights went out.

CHAPTER THIRTY-ONE

Two days later

JOSEPHINE COULDN'T DELAY the inevitable any longer.

It was this night she would meet her betrothed, as she could no longer put him off.

She'd managed to avoid the king, the earl, and most everyone else all day yesterday and most of the day today, her only visitors being Sully and Justine. She didn't even let Nicholas in, not even when he begged. Andrew had been missing since the night he left her, and no one could seem to locate him, not even Sully when he made a sweep of the tavern where they had been staying and most of the taverns in the immediate area. Andrew and his possessions were missing, and no one seemed to know where the man had gone.

Josephine tried not to panic over it. She knew that wherever he'd gone, he must have had a good reason for it, but Sully had no hope or advice to offer about it. Andrew was gone and, as the hours passed, Josephine struggled against despair. She needed him now, more than ever, but he evidently had something else in mind.

She would have to trust that the man would show himself at the right time.

So, she tried very hard not to think about it and soldier on. But on the second day of Andrew's absence, William Ward had made an appearance in the afternoon telling her that she was expected at the feast that evening to meet her betrothed and that the king would no longer accept any excuses. Ward seemed rather angry as he delivered the message, but Josephine didn't rise to it. She simply eyed the man until he left in a huff. When he was gone, she rolled her eyes.

So, her womanly cycle excuse would no longer be tolerated. She wondered if it was because Madelaine, or any one of the number of other servants, had noticed she was not actually on her cycle and reported back to the king. Other than the discolored stain on the bed the night Andrew had bedded her, there had been no other evidence. Therefore, she knew she couldn't put it off any longer.

She had to attend the feast.

Another note had come from the earl himself, telling her to wear the white dress, but she would not comply. Although it was mended and hanging on a peg in her wardrobe, she made sure to tear it again. She wasn't going to be forced into wearing the thing. Instead, she chose the black dress again.

As she'd told the king, black was for sadness. The message would be clear.

As dusk consumed the land and the great hall was already noisy with guests and fragrant with the smells of fine foods, William Ward came to escort her to the feast. When Madelaine opened the door, Ward was accompanied by six armed men. Josephine had to laugh at that, inwardly of course; she wondered if the men were there because the king was expecting a fight. But she gave them no fight. She willingly went with Ward down to the hall, only to be met by Alexander at the entry door.

The king greeted her politely but didn't say anything about seeing the black dress again. It seemed that he was being particularly kind, which was strange for the man. But Josephine could tell he was eyeing the black dress. Perhaps he didn't say anything for fear of upsetting her and sending her right back up to her chambers. He had her where he wanted her and he wasn't going to upset the balance. So he simply smiled, took her hand, and proceeded into the great hall.

When Josephine entered the hall on the king's arm, all noise and movement stopped. Six hundred pairs of eyes devoured and admired the strikingly pale woman in black. Josephine was somewhat self-conscious as she was led to her seat on the dais, feeling the hot stares of the room on her back.

But it was nothing compared to the fear she felt when she was finally introduced to Alphonse d'Vant. She was seated right next to him and found herself looking up at a mountain of a man; enormous, with a pockmarked face and black eyes. He looked like everything hellish she'd ever heard about him. Big hands, a big nose – everything about the man was big. His gaze was fixed on her during their introduction. His expression suggested that he wasn't disappointed in what he saw. When he spoke, however, his tone was anything but pleased.

"What happened to the white dress I sent to you?" he growled as she took her seat. "I told you to wear that."

That was his greeting to her and Josephine's palms began to sweat. God's Toes, the man scared her. But she searched her soul and found courage; courage from Andrew, and she drew on it. She had to be brave, even if she didn't feel it.

"Forgive me, my lord, but the dress was damaged," she said. "There was no time to repair it before dinner, so I chose another dress that I hoped would please you."

Alphonse studied her, his eyes glittering evilly. Josephine couldn't tell whether or not he believed her and was relieved when a pretty maid bearing honeyed fruit distracted him. In that moment, she took the time to observe her surroundings.

Men she didn't know were seated down the table from her, men who were looking at her rather interestedly. She didn't like their stares and almost turned away until she caught sight of Sully, Justine, Nicholas, and Donald, far down the table. They were all seated together. When Josephine saw them, she nearly shouted with joy. Her confidence returned with her friends and family sitting near her. Friendly faces in a sea of unfamiliar, unwelcome men.

They gave her strength.

Her gaze fell on Sully as he smiled at her, and Josephine noticed the fine clothes he wore. He was looking more and more like the Earl of Ayr. That realization brought a stab of regret to her heart, but it quickly vanished. Her father was dead, her brother was dead, and she could think of no better man to carry on the title. Except for Andrew, of course. But he had his own path to follow that didn't include Torridon, a path that she, too, would soon follow.

Now, Torridon belonged to Sully and Justine, and forever would.

But thoughts of Sully vanished when something heavy hit her trencher. Startled, Josephine turned to see that the earl had thrown a stringy piece of beef from his own trencher onto hers. Apparently, this was his idea of being chivalrous.

"Eat," he commanded.

Though she had no appetite, Josephine took a bite. She'd already disobeyed him about the dress; she didn't think he'd take kindly to her refusing to eat. As she chewed with some effort, the earl watched her intently.

Alphonse d'Vant, Earl of Annan and Blackbank, had been waiting for this moment. He'd had quite a bit to drink that evening as he waited to meet his betrothed and was feeling his liquor. With Lady Josephine in his sight, his mind wandered to the perverted and violent sexual acts he would perform with her. God, she was gorgeous. He hadn't expected such finery. He couldn't wait to watch while she masturbated with the phallic symbol he had specially made from pure gold. It was big, like he was, and he loved to watch women as they struggled to bury it deep within their soft bodies.

Already, he had plans for his new bride. As he watched her choke down a couple of bites followed by great gulps of wine, he leaned in her direction and lowered his voice.

"Lady Josephine," he growled. "Would you accompany me to my chambers this eve? We have much to... discuss."

Josephine almost choked on the food in her mouth. She hadn't expected a proposition so soon and every instinct in her body told her to run. The man's foul breath and foul ambiance was enveloping her, embracing her like the grime of an unseen plague. She could feel death about her, radiating from him. But she couldn't run; she *knew* she couldn't. With iron control, she managed to turn and look at him.

"Of course, my lord," she replied evenly. "And I believe the king also wishes to discuss our arrangement. It would be ideal for all of us to meet in the privacy of your chambers."

The earl was a bright man. He knew exactly what she was doing, calling in reinforcements so she wouldn't have to be alone with him. But he was also an insensitive brute and could not possibly feel admiration for her bravery or her cleverness. He leaned his big head close to hers.

"I have no need for the king," he whispered gruffly. "Unless the man wishes to help me inspect my latest acquisition."

Josephine couldn't help it; she visibly blanched. "I am a maiden, my lord. I shall remain so until my wedding."

He laughed loudly, and she nearly jumped from her skin. "Liar!" he said.

Josephine flared in spite of her fear. "How dare you accuse me of untruth!" she fired back, even if he had been correct.

By this time, the dining hall had quieted considerably, watching the earl glare at his newly betrothed.

"Is that so?" he boomed. "Then we shall see!"

That was the end of Josephine's bravery. King or no king, Josephine shot out of her chair in an attempt to run, but no sooner did she move than the earl was on her, grabbing handfuls of hair and nearly her entire neck in one hand. She gasped in pain, clutching at his wrist with one hand and trying to keep from stepping on her dress with the other.

Sully, witnessing the brutal move, jumped out of his chair. His face was red and his veins throbbed violently in his temples – no one was going to treat Josephine like that, and to hell with the king. He may be killed for his actions, but he wasn't going alone. That bastard earl was going to feel his sword if it was the last thing he ever did.

But his efforts were thwarted. On either side of him, Justine and Donald reacted to Sully's murderous intentions. Donald grabbed his arms while Justine tried to block him with her body, putting her hands on his chest.

"Sully, nay!" she hissed pleadingly. "Sit down! Please, I beg of you!"

Sully was struggling against Donald. Nicholas, his eyes wide with concern, tore his eyes from Josephine long enough to see that Sully was not taking the assault well. Nicholas knew that they had to help keep Sully calm, lest his blood be spilled right here in front of all of them. The king wouldn't tolerate any acts of violence against guests, and most especially against Blackbank. Quickly and silently, Nicholas slipped from his chair and caught Sully around the torso with his strong, young arms.

"Let us remove him from the hall," he whispered to Donald, who heartily agreed.

"Let me go, you little whelps," Sully demanded, fighting all three of them. "Let me go, all of you!"

"Remove him," Justine said desperately as she gave the struggling mass a hard shove towards the door. "Take him back to our chambers!"

With Donald pulling and with Nicholas pushing, they managed to get Sully several feet from the table and Justine breathed a sigh of relief as they moved away. But her hope was shattered when a booming voice rang above the commotion. The earl still had Josephine twisting in his hand and he stepped out into the room, yelling again for the exiting group to halt.

Nicholas, Donald, and Sully came to a halt, turning eyes of anxiety and hatred to the monstrous man. Sully was breathing fire.

The earl's eyes narrowed at the group. "What goes on?" he demanded. "Who *are* you?"

Nicholas knew he didn't mean him; they had met. Quickly, he straightened. He would do the talking.

"My lord, allow me to introduce Sully Montgomery, the Earl of Ayr,

and his companion, Lord Donald Muir," he said evenly. "They are...
guests."

The earl looked right at Sully, who was spitting venom from his
eyes. "What ails you, man?" he asked suspiciously.

In his grip, Josephine was nearly hysterical. The earl would kill Sully
in a heartbeat if she didn't do something. She turned her head slightly
to look at her sister, whose face was a mirror of her own – pure,
absolute terror. Before she could say anything, however, Nicholas
answered the earl's question.

"Nothing ails him, my lord," he said. "The earl has simply had too
much to drink. We were escorting him to bed."

As Alphonse eyed Sully threateningly, thinking the man looked as if
he was about to charge, the king came up behind him as he gripped
Josephine by the hair.

"Remove your hand from my cousin," he said icily.

It was a steely command, not meant to be disobeyed. Alphonse
turned to look at the king with an expression that was nothing short of
hateful. He considered bashing the king's brains out right there, but he
decided against it. He was, after all, in the king's court, and even he
couldn't fight all of the king's men. After a moment, he released
Josephine.

"Thank you," King Alexander said, but he didn't mean it. He even
looked to see if Josephine was all right as she staggered away, rubbing
her scalp. But then he pointed at Sully. "This is Lady Josephine's
brother-in-law, and that is his wife, Lady Justine. She is Lady Josephine's sister."

The earl looked at Justine. "Not a beauty like her sister, is she?" he
said cruelly. "And you, Lord Ayr, wish to challenge me for your sister-
in-law's honor? Ha!"

Sully went mad. Jerking away from Donald and Nicholas, he drew
his broadsword from its decorative sheath. "By God and King Alexander, I'll do more than challenge you!"

The earl responded by yanking his sword from its sheath. It was a huge piece of metal, as tall as Josephine. His eyes glittered coldly.

"I'll skewer you, little earl!" he declared.

The hall was alive with people dashing to leave, and with soldiers drawing their swords; shouting. Justine was chanting "no, no, no" and Josephine turned beseechingly towards the king.

"My lord!" she pleaded. "Stop this!"

Before the king could speak, Ridge de Reyne came charging into the chamber like a runaway horse, his sword drawn. He had been outside of the hall, monitoring who was coming and going, when a hysterical servant told him what was transpiring inside. Sworn on his life to protect his king, even from a giant, he charged into the great hall.

Ridge was an extremely large man. Perhaps not as tall as Andrew, but he was very wide and muscular. He had never in his life been bested in a fight, sword or fist, but he had doubts about coming to blows with the Earl of Annan and Blackbank. Prepared for the worst, he put himself in the middle of the melee.

But the king saw that, very quickly, this was going to be a bloodbath. Once Ridge entered the mix, he raised his hands in supplication.

"Cease!" he bellowed. "No blood will be spilled in this hall!"

The combatants paused, giving King Alexander a chance to continue. Somewhat relieved, he began to issue orders. He had to defuse the situation quickly.

"Lady Justine, remove your husband to your rooms and stay there. Nicholas, go with them. De Reyne, take Lady Josephine to her chamber and remain with her." Then, he fixed an intolerant eye on the earl. "You, my dear Blackbank, will accompany me."

The group broke up. Justine, Donald, and Nicholas half-carried a reluctant Sully out as Ridge moved swiftly to Lady Josephine, sweeping her into his enormous arms and whisking her from the room. In a matter of seconds, the room was nearly empty.

Alexander fixed the earl with a cold stare. He was beginning to wonder if he had made a serious mistake.

"Now, d'Vant," he said quietly. "What you do with Lady Josephine when you go back to England is your affair. But while she is under my roof and is my charge, you will kindly show her the respect she deserves. And that includes her family as well. Is that understood?"

The earl cocked an eyebrow at him.

"Clearly, my lord," he said, simply to pacify him. But he didn't mean it.

Alexander wasn't stupid. He was very astute in his dealings with men, and he could see in Alphonse's eyes that the man had absolutely no respect for the king, his position, or anything else. Alphonse was a man used to having his way, in all things, and he considered orders from the king an annoyance and nothing more.

Mostly, Alexander saw Josephine's death in the cold, black depths of Alphonse's eyes.

Now, he was starting to feel some guilt for what he'd done. He'd taken his beautiful young cousin and pledged her to a monster. Aye, he'd already known that but, somehow, now it was different. He'd come to know Josephine and knew she was an extraordinary woman, like her mother. Truth be told, perhaps that was Alexander's biggest weakness – long ago, he'd had a great love for the Lady Afton. Perhaps he still did. That being the case, he couldn't condemn the woman's daughter to such hell. As the great hall around them began to settle down, the king shook his head.

"I hope I do not regret this," he muttered, eyeing Alphonse. "Do not make me wish I had not pledged my young cousin to you. I could have very easily pledged her to another man who would be worthy of her. But because I honor our alliance, I honored you with her hand. If you make me regret such a thing, there will be consequences."

Alphonse didn't take anything Alexander said seriously. "What consequences?" he asked. "Once she is my wife, there is nothing you can do. And I will do what I wish to my wife."

Alexander's eyes narrowed. "Harm her and I will bring all of Scotland down over you," he threatened. When Alphonse merely lifted an eyebrow, as if he didn't care, Alexander's rage knew no limits. "By

God's Bloody Rood! I should have left the woman to her betrothal with your brother, but I foolishly believed I was doing what was best for her and for my throne. And you have the arrogance to refute me and tell me it is none of my affair?"

Alphonse was prepared to retort, at least as much as he dared to a king, but something the man said caught his attention. In fact, he was most puzzled by it, fixated on it.

"*My* brother?" he repeated. "What about my brother?"

Alexander could see the man had no idea what he was talking about and, in that knowledge, he felt some smugness. He was about to lay some knowledge on the man that might change the entire dynamic of the situation.

"Your brother was betrothed to Lady Josephine but I dissolved it and, instead, gave her over to you," he said, seeing a genuine reaction of shock on Alphonse's face. "Did you not know that? Your betrothed was once pledged to The Red Fury."

Alphonse's mouth popped open in shock. He wasn't any good at hiding his emotions. "The Red Fury?" he said, stunned. "My... my *brother* is The Red Fury?"

Alexander was disgusted that the man knew nothing of his kin. "Were you not even aware of that?" he said. "The greatest mercenary lord in all of England and Scotland is your brother, Andrew d'Vant. I have met the man. He is a beast of a man, although not as beastly or barbaric as you are. I took that woman away from him to give to you. So if you harm her, not only will all of Scotland come down over you, but so will The Red Fury. I doubt you will survive his wrath."

Alphonse simply stared at him, too stunned to speak. *My brother is The Red Fury?* He'd never even heard that, not in the nineteen years that his brother had been gone from Haldane. Once Andrew had run, he never heard from the man again. He hadn't kept track of him, uncaring what happened to his younger brother. All he cared about was the fact that his brother was gone for good. Since he'd not heard from his brother in so long, he had assumed the man was dead. God, how wrong he'd been.

It seemed as if the joke was on him.

Suddenly, he burst out laughing, as if he'd just heard something incredibly funny. Still laughing, he sheathed his sword.

"*My* brother is The Red Fury?" he said. "That is the most astonishing thing I have ever heard of. I do not believe it!"

Alexander wasn't sure the man's laughter was that of real humor. There was something innately disturbing about it. "It is true," he said. "You were not aware?"

"I was not. By God, I was not."

Alexander watched the man as he seemed to relax a great deal, still chuckling over the news. "Then you know what I say is truth should you harm the lady," he said. "Treat her well, Blackbank, or you shall have to answer to a great many people."

With that, the king went back to his seat and back to his meal. He was finished dealing with arrogant lords. But Alphonse didn't follow him; he'd eaten his fill, anyway, and he'd had far too much to drink. What he needed now was a woman, but it was clear he wasn't going to get anywhere with his betrothed. She had too many people concerned for her and, until he could remove her from Edinburgh, he wasn't going to make a move against her.

Not much of a move, anyway.

Still laughing about his brother, Alphonse's thoughts turned towards his bed and the women he intended to put in it this night. Too much food and wine always fed his libido, and that libido was voracious at the moment.

Leaving the great hall, the hunter went in search of prey.

THAT NIGHT AFTER the feast, Andrew had still not made an appearance, and Josephine went to bed with a heavy heart, only to be awakened by wailing in the night. Mournful, shrill wailing that sent shivers up her spine as she sat bolt upright in her bed. The silver moonlight splashed against the coverlet and the wall, and she was spooked into believing she was hearing a ghost.

The wailing sounded again and Madelaine, who was sleeping near her this night, rose from her pallet in the alcove, amazingly level-headed as she went for the door.

"Where are you going?" Josephine demanded.

"To see who is ailing so," her maid informed her. "I shall return."

Madelaine threw open the door only to find Ridge de Reyne planted firmly in the arch.

"Close it!" he boomed, and Madelaine complied fast as a wink.

By this time, Josephine was out of bed and snatched a wine-colored bed robe from the bottom of her bed. Something was going on and she was going to find out what. Jerking open the door, she jabbed a finger at Ridge before he could snap at her.

"You will not order me, de Reyne!" she told him sharply. "Find out what the matter is and ask if we can lend assistance."

"My lady…" he began firmly.

She cut him off. "Go, you big ox!" she pushed at him. "We can protect ourselves for the moment!"

He glared at her. "I am *not* leaving you."

But Josephine would not be deterred. "I told you to go," she said again, as she made a sweeping motion with her hand. "Find out what is happening!"

Clenching and unclenching his fists, Ridge marched off down the hall, muttering to himself on how very badly Lady Josephine needed a good spanking. He'd done it once; he was about to do it again if the woman didn't hold her tongue. But he dutifully went to see where the screaming was coming from, even though he had a good idea.

It wasn't something he was looking forward to discovering.

Josephine, with Madelaine behind her, stood in the doorway as he headed into the darkness, watching and listening. They could hear distant moaning and shrieking, and wondered curiously what was going on.

Several long minutes passed and the wailing subsided. The torches in the hall flickered softly, with shadows dancing on the walls and across Ridge as he returned.

"Well?" Josephine demanded.

Ridge did not look pleased. "The sound is coming from the Earl of Annan and Blackbank's rooms," he said. "But the doors have yet to open. I do not know what has happened."

Suddenly, two female servants came running down the hall as if the devil himself were chasing them. Ridge put out a large hand and caught one of them like a fish on a hook.

"Halt!" he ordered. "Where are you going? Why are you running?"

The caught woman stopped struggling long enough to recognize Ridge. "My lord!' she cried. "Oh… it is terrible! Simply terrible!"

"What?" Ridge snapped.

Both women were crying. "The English earl," the woman sobbed. "He killed a girl!"

"How do you know?" he asked, less sternly.

"A servant girl." The women were clinging to each other, talking in unison. "He took a maid to his bed. He was so… so demanding that he killed her!"

Josephine's face went white as a sheet as she looked to Ridge, who was still looking at the servants grimly. The women continued, breaking into tears. "He was too large for her and tore her asunder!" one of the women said as the other one wept. "She bled to death in front of him, while he ate mutton and watched! It was she who was wailing!"

"Oh, my God," Josephine whispered, reeling back into her rooms.

Ridge glanced at her, seeing her reaction to the news, before turning back to the hysterical women. "Go and hide yourselves," he instructed quietly. "Come out for no one. Tell them I told you to do it. Tell any other women you see to do the same. They must all hide from Blackbank."

The women nodded and fled into the night. Madelaine went with them to help them round up all of the female servants that they could. This night was not safe for any of them.

Ridge entered Josephine's room, bolting the door behind him. Josephine stood across the room with her back to him, gripping her arms tightly. He went to her quietly.

"My lady…" he began softly.

"Get me out of here," she hissed, breaking down in tears. "I do not care about the king or my standing. I do not care anymore! I will not marry that beast! Help me, de Reyne, *please!*"

He grasped her gently. God's Bones, he wanted to help her, but he was desperately torn between duty and doing what was right. "I cannot," he muttered. "You know that."

She exploded. "Damn you, De Reyne!" she yanked herself from his grasp. "You heard what happened. And by God, you have seen what the man is capable of doing to me in the presence of others. Think of what he will do to me in private!"

Ridge didn't want to think about it because the more he did, the more his resolve to his duty began to crumble. "He was drunk tonight, and angry," he said, trying to make excuses when he knew it was futile. "It is possible that…"

She cut him off, grasping at him. "Please, Ridge, help me," she gasped. "If you will not do it, then find Andrew. He will know what to do."

It was almost too much for him to bear. Truth be told, he blamed himself for bringing her here in the first place. This was all his fault, he knew; his and his weakling king. But he swore an oath to the king, an oath that bound him to the king's wishes over all.

Tears spilled onto Josephine's cheeks and Ridge swore softly. It came down to this: he was an honorable man and his king intended to do a dishonorable thing. Alexander might as well drive his sword through her right now, for he would have just as much responsibility in her eventual death by this English earl. As Andrew had said, this marriage was her death sentence.

Now, he knew for certain that it was the truth.

He could not let her go to her death. It simply wasn't right.

Ridge couldn't free her himself, but he was not going to prevent someone who wanted to. He had too much honor to knowingly let a terrible thing happen. Grasping Josephine's face in his two big hands, he forced her to look at him.

"Stay here," he instructed firmly. "I shall return."

She sniffled and looked at him. "What… what are you going to do?"

He dropped his hands and rushed to the door. "Trust me, my lady. Please. I will not fail you."

"Fail me?" she repeated, puzzled. "But…"

The door slammed in her face. She stared at it a moment before going back to her bed, but not before she clasped her bejeweled dirk to her chest. If anybody entered her room, save Ridge or Andrew himself, she would be ready.

RIDGE POUNDED HEAVILY on Sully's door. It was a matter of seconds before the door flew open and Nicholas stood firmly in the arch.

"Oh, de Reyne, 'tis only ye," he said as he turned away.

Ridge entered the room, his eyes searching out for the earl. The room was dimly lit, smelling of strange herbs. He saw Nicholas, and Donald, and finally Sully as he sat on a chair next to the bed where his wife lay. But the moment Sully saw Ridge, he jumped from the chair.

"How is Lady Josephine?" he demanded.

"Terrified, as she should be," Ridge replied. "My lord, where is Sir Andrew?"

Sully was guarded. "I do not know."

Ridge sighed. There was no time for games. "My lord, time grows short. You must tell me where d'Vant is."

Sully cocked an eyebrow. "Why? So you can bring him to the king to be executed? I think not."

Ridge was growing impatient. "If you want to save Lady Josephine's life, then you shall tell me. Only d'Vant can help her."

Sully tensed. "What in the hell is going on? Where's Josephine?"

"She is in her room, safe for the moment," Ridge said forcefully. "But if the Earl of Annan and Blackbank has his way with her, and I suspect he will attempt it before morn, then it will be most difficult to spirit her from the castle."

"You are going to help her escape?" Justine asked anxiously as she sat up on her knees.

"Nay," Ridge said flatly. "I am not. D'Vant will. But I will not be an obstacle."

"Why the change, de Reyne?" Sully asked suspiciously. "I thought you were sworn to carry out the king's wishes. You have made that very clear."

Ridge shot him a nasty look. "Ask me again and I shall turn from this room without another word. You must trust me if you value Lady Josephine's life."

Sully looked at Ridge, attempting to determine the motivation behind his apparent change of heart, while Justine and Donald and Nicholas exchanged tense glances. It all seemed very strange that Ridge should seem so determined to find Andrew but, at some point, they would either have to trust the man or throw him from the chamber, and no one seemed willing to do that. There was something in all of them that wanted to trust Ridge, to believe he was on their side. Finally, it was Justine who spoke.

"Andrew is here in town, de Reyne," she said, divulging something she didn't think Ridge knew. "He has been here nearly since Josephine was brought here, but he has been missing for the past two days. Sully has been unable to locate him. We do not know where he is."

Ridge looked at Sully. "I have not seen him for the past two days, either," he said. "I was wondering why he had not come to see Lady Josephine. You say he is missing?"

"Then you knew?" Justine said, surprised. "You knew Andrew was here, in Edinburgh?"

Ridge nodded. "I am the king's bodyguard, Lady Montgomery," he said. "There is not much that I do not know around here. I even spoke to d'Vant two nights ago when he was leaving Lady Josephine's chambers, but he said nothing about an absence or going away. In fact, he said he would return the next night, but I did not see him."

Justine looked at Sully, fear in her eyes. "You do not believe something has happened to him, do you?"

Sully wasn't entirely sure anymore. Now, he was starting to feel some apprehension. He looked at Ridge. "We must find him," he said. "I scoured the inns at the base of the castle earlier today, but I did not come up with anything. We must search again."

As Ridge nodded, Justine spoke. "Take Donald with you," she said. "The three of you can cover more ground and Donald knows Andrew on sight."

It was a logical suggestion. "Very well," Sully said. "You will stay with Nicholas, Justine. That is not a request."

Justine opened her mouth to argue but thought better of it. She wanted to go, too, but knew Sully would never let her. Besides, she was better served remaining where her sister was in case Josephine needed her.

Therefore, she stood aside as Sully strapped on his sword and pulled on his gauntlets. With Donald beside him, Sully followed Ridge to the door. At the threshold, he paused to look at Justine and, much to her pleasure, blew her a kiss.

It was sweet and touching, and Justine responded with a shy grin. But it was all for show; once they were gone, she bolted from the bed and pulled on her warm slippers.

"Where are ye going?" Nicholas demanded.

"To my sister," Justine said casually, as she was already making for the door.

Nicholas went after her. "But Sully told ye to remain!"

Justine simply shrugged her shoulders. It didn't seem to deter her in the least. With a heavy sigh, Nicholas followed. He knew it was better to go with her than to permit her to go alone. And he knew better than to argue with her. Therefore, he went, if only to keep her out of trouble. Like her sister, Justine could well protect herself.

Woe betide the man who ever truly got in her way.

JOSEPHINE'S ROOM WAS quite a distance from her own. It was located in another part of the castle, in fact. Josephine was delighted and relieved to see Justine and Nicholas at her door and did not spare the details of the English earl's latest horror. Her hands and voice trembled as she spoke, telling them just how frightened she really was even if her words would not admit it.

Justine was horrified to hear the tale, deeply terrified for her sister's well-being. As Nicholas stood by the bolted door, listening for anything in the corridor beyond, the women headed over to the bed on the opposite side of the chamber.

"*That* is why de Reyne came to our chamber," Justine gasped after hearing the terrible story. "He did not tell us the entire tale!"

Josephine was holding on to her sister's hands. "Because he more than likely did not want to frighten you," she said. "Where is Sully?"

"With de Reyne," Justine said. "They are going to find Andrew, Josephine. Wherever he is, they will find him, I swear it."

Josephine sat heavily on her bed, her expression distant as she thought of Andrew and his absence. "I am sure wherever he is, he will return soon," she said, trying to sound hopeful. "I must believe that everything is well and that he is not in any danger. I must believe that Sully and Ridge will find him and bring him back."

Justine could hear the fear and longing in her sister's voice. "I know they will," she agreed. "Until then, we will do all we can to keep you from the earl."

Josephine appreciated her valor, but she knew it was futile. No one could keep the earl from her if he truly wanted her. But more than that, she was thinking of what the immediate future held once Andrew returned.

"Then it will come," she murmured. "The battle Andrew has been preparing for nearly his whole life is coming." She suddenly closed her eyes and hung her head. "Oh, Justine, what will I do if I lose him? I cannot bear the thought!"

Justine put her arm around her sister's shoulders. "You love him," Justine stated quietly. "I have known from the very beginning."

Josephine lifted her head, smiling wryly. "And I denied it, once," she said. "Mayhap you truly are a witch if you really did know. Aye, I love him. With all that I am, I do."

Justine smiled. "I am very happy for you," she said, her smile fading. "And I have another confession. I am not… displeased to be married to Sully."

Josephine looked her in the eye. "I know," she said flatly. "I've always known. Why do you think I suggested he marry you? I could have easily married you to Donald, but I knew you would only be happy with Sully. Besides… he is the only one brave enough to handle you."

Justine laughed softly. "You are too kind," she said to the insult. "I may even give up my magic now that I am a married woman; the powers lessen once you experience pleasures of the flesh."

Josephine turned her eyes skyward, a mocking gesture. "There is a God, after all," she said reverently. "And tell me, Sister, did you enjoy your pleasures? After the first night, anyway."

Justine looked shocked, shushing her because Nicholas was in the room. But then she grinned. "What do you think?"

Josephine reached out to stroke her sister's hair. "I think that my baby sister is finally becoming a woman."

Even though Nicholas was across the chamber, he could still hear bits of the conversation as the women whispered and giggled. He was genuinely trying not to listen to the private exchange, but he was nonetheless amused and touched. He liked his cousins very much and he was glad he'd found family that accepted him as he was. His poetry didn't make them ashamed; they loved it. Nicholas had a feeling he was going to be spending much more time with Josephine in the future. At least, he hoped so. The woman deserved a happy life and Nicholas was going to do all he could to ensure she had it, however small that contribution was.

The corridor beyond the door seemed quiet enough and Nicholas moved away from the panel, heading over to another part of the room so the sisters could continue their private conversation. But just as he reached the hearth, there was a huge crashing sound against the door.

The entire room shook, and the women shrieked, which sent Nicholas into a defensive position. As he rushed to the door to ensure the bolt held, the panel splintered, sending shards of wood flying into the room.

The women shrieked as the Earl of Annan and Blackbank catapulted through the arch, broadsword in hand. Nicholas had no time to react before the earl drove his huge sword through Nicholas' gut. Nicholas hit the floor, blood pouring, as the women began to scream.

But Alphonse was oblivious to their fear, the dying man, or anything else in the chamber. He stepped over Nicholas, his gaze feasting on Lady Josephine. She was all he could see. His drunken face was gray, and his eyes were sunken black dots.

Josephine, through her hysteria, could see what was coming. Justine sat next to her, gasping in panic. Josephine, in a serious concentrated effort, gave her sister a shove.

"Get out of here," she said through clenched teeth. Her eyes never left the earl. "Get Nicholas out of here and find help for him. Then get to the king. Hurry, for pity's sake!"

The earl never even noticed Justine dashing around him. He didn't see Justine grasping Nicholas under the arms and dragging him in a trail of blood out of the room. Alphonse's eyes were only on the lovely Josephine.

But Josephine had seen everything. Her fear for Nicholas was over-whelming, but she fought it. She had to think clearly and she couldn't do that if she was worried over Nicholas' fate. As Alphonse came closer, instead of fear, she felt incredible rage. But she knew she had to control it. She had to control every emotion that was struggling to break free. Hysteria would not save her.

Only a level head would.

Josephine had never backed away from a fight in her life and she was not about to start now. She had to hold the earl off until Andrew arrived, wherever he was, and she was grimly determined to do just that, by any means necessary.

Now, the true test of her strength would begin.

"My Lord Earl," she said steadily. "If you wanted to visit me, you did not have to break my door down or gore my friend. That was truly unnecessary."

Alphonse staggered a couple of steps and let his bloodied sword clatter to the ground. His eyes blinked slowly. He appeared dazed. It occurred to Josephine that after the initial burst into her chamber, he didn't look the least bit agitated. In fact, he seemed oddly calm.

"I told you we had much to speak of at the feast," he said, slurring his words. "Now, we will speak."

"Of course. What do you wish to speak of?"

Alphonse wasn't expecting such a calm, level-headed woman. He was used to women cowering when he was around. He thought he might yell at Josephine, or even grab her, but he couldn't seem to do either. All he could do was stare at her and say the first thing that came to mind.

"Do you know that I have never in my life had anything pure and untouched?" he said. "I have decided that I will not touch you before our wedding."

Josephine was astonished to hear that. Her knees suddenly became weak and she whispered a silent, heartfelt prayer of thanks. Hopefully, he truly meant it because that declaration made all the difference in the world to her.

"I am pleased that you would respect my wishes, milord," she said, her voice trembling with relief. "Please sit, and I shall bring wine."

Alphonse looked around the room for a chair, staggering over to one near the hearth and falling into it. With a sharp crack, the chair disintegrated, depositing the earl onto the stone floor.

Josephine's eyes widened. She was positive he was going to rage. Instead, he laughed loudly.

"Can't the Scots do anything right, even fashion a decent chair?" he said, rising like a drunken sailor. He was so large that Josephine dared not help him for fear of being squashed. "I need another chair!"

Josephine pointed to a bigger, heavier chair but he ignored it. Instead, he lumbered over to the bed and sat heavily upon it, looking at the furniture before shrugging.

"Very well that this can hold me," he said, then looked to Josephine. "Now, you will tell me of my brother. I understand you were pledged to him."

Josephine tried not to show her surprise at the question and, honestly, the apprehension. She was shocked that the earl had been told of her betrothal to Andrew and she knew, instinctively, that she must be very careful what to say. Alphonse had run off Andrew many years ago and she was afraid that hatred was still there. It was a very tricky situation.

"He is a fair and honorable man," she replied steadily. "He commands an army of a thousand men."

Alphonse pondered that in his drunken mind. "I am told he is The Red Fury."

"He is."

More silence as Alphonse mulled that over. "You know that he hates me."

"I know," Josephine answered honestly.

The earl looked at her for a moment, and then laughed. "Good," he said. "I hate him, too. He was always father's favorite son."

Josephine didn't say anything. Truly, she didn't know what to say, afraid that anything she said might enrage a man who was already dangerously off-balance. But Alphonse remained calm as he continued.

"Andrew was a quiet child, and very serious. I, on the other hand, was more assertive. Father never liked that," he said. "When father died, I was going to kill Andrew. Do not look appalled; it is true. He reminded me of what a failure I was in our father's eyes, so I swore to be rid of him. But the little bastard escaped me when I banished him instead."

Josephine watched him silently. Wine certainly seemed to loosen him up, she noted. He was a pitiful creature and was absolutely terrifying at the same time, making it an odd paradox. But she had no sympathy for him. It would be misplaced as well as unhealthy.

"And what of your mother?" she asked quietly, leading him into a subject she was very curious about. "Surely she did not have favorites among her sons."

Alphonse waved a sloppy hand at her. "Of course she did," he said. "The bitch loved Andrew more than she loved me. In fact, she hated me."

It seemed to be a sore subject. Josephine knew it was probably dangerous to speak on his mother, but she couldn't help herself. For Andrew's sake, she found that she had to know.

"Does she live in your home?" she asked, pretending to be ignorant.

Alphonse shook his head, very nearly losing his balance. "She lives in my dungeons, which is where you shall end up if you do not please me."

Josephine was shocked to hear that. "She is still alive?"

"Of course." He waved another sloppy hand at her. "Her every need is tended to."

Locked up in a dungeon for years on end. *What a horrible fate,* Josephine thought. "It is cruel to keep your own mother locked away," she said boldly. "After all, the woman birthed you."

Alphonse didn't reply. He simply lay back on the bed and closed his eyes. Josephine watched him closely, wondering if he was going to fall asleep in her bed. If he did, she was going to run and run fast. She found herself praying he would fall asleep but, after a few moments, he spoke again.

"Talk to me," he mumbled. "What have you been doing since you left the feast? That big knight took you away. Who is he?"

"He is the king's bodyguard."

Alphonse's eyes opened and he turned his head to look at her. "Do you know what I have been doing since I left the feast?"

She already knew but she didn't want to tell him that. "What?"

"Fucking," he said as if he were proud of it. "Did you not hear the screaming earlier?"

Josephine felt sick to her stomach. "I did," she said reluctantly. "What happened?"

He suddenly rolled onto his side, struggling to sit up. "You see, my lady, I have a problem," he said. "My problem is that my male organ is as large as a prized bull's and women, as a rule, cannot accommodate me. So what am I to do? Give up fucking altogether? Of course not. Women are like chickens; a penny for a dozen, so I shall never go hungry. What you heard tonight was just a dying chicken."

God, was he truly so callous? Josephine had never felt such horror in all her life. "And what about me?" Josephine demanded. "Am I a chicken, too? Do you intend to use me and watch me die?"

He scratched his chin. "I have not decided yet," he said. "Mayhap not. You are to be my wife, after all, and I should like to have sons someday to inherit my title. I suppose I shall have to be careful with you."

Josephine was so appalled at the whole line of this conversation that she was beginning to tremble. "It would be kind if you were," she said. "I… I will be a worthy wife, my lord. I… I am sure I would give you fine sons."

She hated how she sounded as if she were pleading with him, trying to sell herself to him so he wouldn't think she was another "chicken" to be plucked. Anything to keep the man talking, to keep him away from her, until Andrew or the king or someone else with a big sword and the ability to overcome the earl could arrive.

But Alphonse seemed too drunk to really care. He managed to push himself off her bed, standing next to it and weaving dangerously as he looked at her.

"You had better," he said, his manner turning threatening. "If our firstborn is a daughter, I will drown both of you in the river. Remember that."

Josephine could feel the evil radiating off of him. She knew he meant every word. "I will, my lord."

He stared at her a moment longer. He could have been thinking about anything at that moment; it was difficult to tell. Josephine waited for the next vile thing to come out of his mouth but, instead, he simply turned for the door. As he walked past her, he reached out to pat her on the face. He probably really only meant a gentle pat, as one would pat a child or a pet, but with his strength and bad manners, he ended up slapping her. Josephine's head snapped sideways as he headed for the door.

"I will be taking you back to Haldane Castle on the morrow," he told her. "Be ready to travel at dawn. I will send my men to collect your baggage before sunrise, so be prepared. If you are not ready, I shall not wait. I will bundle you up in whatever state you happen to be in and toss you onto the wagon. Is that clear?"

Hand to her stinging cheek, Josephine looked at the man as he neared the door. So he was planning on taking her immediately from Edinburgh? Her thoughts rapidly turned to the plans Andrew had spoken of, how he'd assumed the wedding would be at Edinburgh. He'd been wrong, but that wasn't a bad thing – he wanted to challenge his brother on the open road. So if Alphonse was planning on leaving on the morrow, then that was perfect for Andrew's purposes.

At least, she hoped so. If they could find the man in time.

"It is, my lord," she said. "I will be ready. Good sleep to you."

Alphonse paused by the door, turning to look at her. But he was so drunk and so weary, that he simply stood there and weaved about. Unable to answer because she had given him the exact answer he had expected, and therefore had nothing more to threaten her with, he pulled back the broken panel that he'd come smashing through only to be met head-on by Alexander and several heavily-armed men out in the corridor.

The first thing the king did was push through the broken door, positive he was going to find a broken, dead woman on the floor of the chamber, but was vastly surprised to find Josephine relatively unharmed but for an angry red hand print on her left cheek. With great concern, Alexander went to her.

"Are you well?" he asked. "Did he harm you?"

Josephine was very relieved to see him. "He did not harm me, at least not intentionally," she said. "But he gored Nicholas. Is he all right? Will he live?"

Alexander sighed heavily, great distress on his face. "He is dead," he said. "There was nothing to be done for him."

Josephine's eyes filled with tears at the death of her sweet, gentle poet friend. "I am so sorry," she whispered, the tears spilling over. "He did not even have a weapon. The earl burst through my door and stabbed Nicholas when he tried to protect me."

Alexander's features tensed and he turned to Alphonse, who was still in the doorway and unable to move forward because of so many armed men. As Josephine turned away and wept over her lost friend, Alexander went into a rage.

"You killed my nephew," he cried, grabbing Alphonse by the arm and trying to force the drunken giant to face him. "I should kill you myself!"

Alphonse wasn't so drunk that he didn't rise to the threat. "What nephew?"

"The man you killed in this chamber tonight!"

Alphonse barely remembered Nicholas. "He threatened my life!" he boomed. "Am I not allowed to defend myself? He was also in my betrothed's chambers, where he should not have been. I have a right to protect what belongs to me!"

Alexander was beyond enraged. But above that rage, the sage politician was able to think clearly. He knew that imprisoning the earl would bring with it an abundance of trouble and, in truth, he didn't need or want that kind of trouble. Poor Nicholas deserved justice, but in the world of political dealings and political balance, Alexander wasn't willing to make an enemy out of Blackbank. Not even for Nicholas. But, God, this relationship was becoming more complicated, and more unsavory, by the minute.

He was starting to wonder if the alliance was worth the trouble.

"You will leave Edinburgh tonight," Alexander snarled. "I want you out of my home. Go back to Haldane and be grateful that I do not seek revenge for what you have done to my nephew. But know this, the betrothal between you and my cousin is dissolved. I will not pledge her to such a fiend."

That wasn't something that Alphonse wanted to hear. A massive hand shot out, grabbing the king by the neck as his men surged forward and tried to separate them. All the while, Alphonse was snarling in Alexander's face.

"She belongs to *me*," he said. "I will take her with me or I will destroy this castle with my army. You will have a battle on your hands if you do not give me what you promised me!"

Men were shouting and jostling around, and somewhere in the middle of it, Josephine suddenly appeared.

She had heard the king's command and it occurred to her that if she did not go with Alphonse, not only could Andrew not challenge the man once he left Edinburgh, but there may very well be a huge amount of trouble here at Edinburgh with an enraged Earl of Annan and Blackbank and the somewhat large contingent of men he'd brought with him.

Men would die if there was fighting in the castle and Josephine wasn't willing to chance that. She couldn't see Donald or Sully or even Ridge or Andrew suffer because of her. She would have to trust Andrew to catch up to them as they traveled back to Haldane.

She knew the man would save her.

It was the only choice.

"Nay, my lord," she said to Alexander as he struggled in the midst of a sea of men. "I will go with him. That was the promise and it is not worth men's lives to break that promise. Nicholas has already paid the highest price. I would not see more men dead because of me."

The jostling and shouting came to a halt as all eyes turned in her direction. Alexander, in particular, appeared stunned by her words. His face was red from where Alphonse had grabbed him around the neck and he was, in truth, still in Alphonse's grip. But he looked at Josephine as if she had lost her mind.

"Are you mad?" he asked. "You begged me not to betroth you to this man and now you wish to go with him?"

Josephine looked at Alphonse, who had the look of a killer spread over his face. "My lord," she said quietly. "Release him. I must speak to him."

Alphonse eyed her; what was the little witch up to? But he was rather softened by her pretty face and the fact that she said she would go with him. She was willing. That alone caused him to break his grip on the king and as men pulled him back, boxing him in and restraining him, Josephine took the king by the hand and led him over to the hearth, quickly, where they could speak in private.

"Why would you say such a thing?" Alexander hissed at her. "Do you truly wish to be wed to such a man?"

Josephine shook her head, still wiping at her eyes from the weeping she'd done for Nicholas. "Nay, I do not," she whispered. "But if you do not let me go with him, it will tear Edinburgh a part. He has many men with him, my lord. You know this. If he is angry enough, men will die as he fights to take me back to Haldane. Nicholas was already far too high of a price to pay for that and I do not wish for any more men to die."

Alexander could see that she was very serious. "I am sorry I broke your betrothal with The Red Fury," he said. "I see now that my choice, although something I felt strongly about at the time, was wrong. Blackbank is a beast; a beast who killed Nicholas."

It was a surprising apology about the betrothal. Josephine could see, in that moment, that he was grieving for the nephew he had been so hard on. She felt sorry for the man.

"Then let me go," she murmured. "But when I do, you must tell Andrew and Sully what has happened. They will come after me, have no fear, and Blackbank will be no more. In their actions, you shall have your justice for Nicholas. And for me."

It began to occur to Alexander what she was saying. "They will kill him?"

She nodded firmly. "It is something Andrew must do," she said, reaching out to squeeze his hand. "It is something he has sworn to do since Alphonse sent him away from Haldane when he was a youth. Andrew has carried this vengeance around with him all of these years and he cannot fail. Will you do this, then? Tell them I have gone with Alphonse. Sometimes, one man can do what an entire army cannot. Andrew will know what needs to be done. He has been waiting all of his life to do it."

Alexander could see the logic. The thought of The Red Fury punishing Blackbank for what he'd done to Nicholas was overwhelmingly satisfying.

"If The Red Fury will do this for me," Alexander said quietly, "then I can promise you that Torridon will never again have trouble with Colin Dalmellington."

Josephine could see what a beneficial deal this was for both of them. The only problem was that she was going to have to put herself in mortal danger before any of it could be accomplished. But somehow, it didn't seem like danger. She'd faced the enemy and she'd established a rapport with him. She felt confident she could hold the man off, at least until Andrew arrived. And he *would* arrive.

She was sure of it.

"For Nicholas," she said softly, feeling tears sting her eyes again.

Alexander nodded, suddenly looking very old and very sad. It was apparent that his nephew's death was more than he could bear.

"For Nicholas," he whispered.

By midnight, Josephine was moving out with the Earl of Annan and Blackbank's army, disappearing into the foggy Edinburgh night.

PART FOUR:
AND HELL FOLLOWED WITH HIM

CHAPTER THIRTY-TWO

A T SOME POINT, Andrew realized he was staring up at an old, cracked ceiling.

He didn't know how long he'd been staring at it but, at some point, it occurred to him that he was, indeed, looking at it. The ceiling was low, attached to walls that were equally crumbling and cracked, and as he turned his head, he could see the floor that was piled high with old, moldy hay.

And the smell – it smelled heavily of urine in the chamber. It made his nose twitch, but the twitching nose pulled at his mouth and made him realize that he was gagged. When he tried to move, he was also bound hand-and-foot, tied to the bed. The only thing he seemed to be able to move freely was his head, and he looked around, noticing that he was tied up on a bed frame. He had no idea how he got here.

There was some disorientation with that thought. Plus, his head was killing him. It throbbed as if he'd been on a week-long drinking binge and the stale air in the chamber wasn't helping. There was a window cut into one wall, but it was covered with a dark oiled cloth that had holes in it. He could see daylight streaming in from the holes and, beyond the window, he could hear noise that sounded like a busy city.

God Bones, he had no idea where he was, how he got here, or even what day it was. He thought back to his very last coherent memory and he could recall leaving Edinburgh after seeing Josephine. He could also recall his encounter with Ridge de Reyne. Then, he came back to the tavern, but after that… nothing.

Clearly, something terrible had happened if he was tied up in a small room with a gag in his mouth. He didn't even remember the fight that put him here. Maybe that was why his head was hurting so badly. Someone, or something, must have hit him in the head.

But that was all he knew.

So, he lay there, staring at the ceiling, realizing that he had to piss very badly. Along with the aching head, it was a most uncomfortable feeling and the minutes passed as he lay there, wondering if he should simply piss his pants and be done with it. He had no idea if he'd been left here to rot, or if someone was returning for him. Minutes turned into hours. At least, it felt like hours. As Andrew lay there and seriously considered his next move, the door to the chamber shoved open and someone entered.

Esme appeared in his line of sight and he looked at her with some shock. He knew his reaction must have appeared in his eyes because she looked at him with equal shock. Then, she smiled thinly.

"Are ye finally awake, then?" she said. "I've been wondering if ye ever would."

Andrew didn't answer; he couldn't with the gag in his mouth. Esme bent over him, her big bosom spilling out of her bodice and the rank scent of her body odor filling his nostrils.

"Can ye understand me?" she asked. "Or did the knock on yer head scatter yer brains?"

He stared at her for a moment before nodding, wondering what in the hell was going on. Nothing was making any sense and Esme wasn't someone he was particularly glad to see.

"I'm sure ye're wondering what ye're doing here," Esme said, reaching out to untie the gag. "If I remove this, ye must promise not to shout. Otherwise, I'll keep it on for good."

Andrew was quickly coming to realize that Esme had something to do with his circumstances. Until he could figure out what, exactly, was going on, he'd have to play along with her. He spit out the gag as she pulled it away.

"Now," she said. "It seems that I have ye where I want ye. 'Tis yer own fault, ye know."

Andrew licked his dry lips; his tongue, everything was dry. He struggled to speak. "What happened?" he asked hoarsely. "Where am I?"

Esme only smiled, but it wasn't a warm or humorous smile. It was something decidedly hard. "I'm going to keep ye," she said firmly. "Ye toyed with me, Andrew, and that wasn't right. Ye should never have used me as ye did. I have every right to seek vengeance for having been wronged."

So that's what this was all about? She felt used because he'd seduced her to gain information? There was no use in denying it because he had, but he didn't think she'd taken it so seriously. Evidently, he was wrong.

"What did I do that was so heinous?" he said, playing somewhat dumb. "For whatever I did, I am very sorry."

Esme cocked her head, her lustful gaze moving up and down his long body. She reached out a hand, laying it gently on his groin.

"Ye had yer way with me and then ye wouldn't speak to me," she said, beginning to rub his crotch through his leather breeches. "This is all I wanted and ye wouldn't give it to me. Now, ye're going to. And I will have it any time I want it."

Andrew's mind was working quickly. So she wanted a slave for sex, did she? Even now she was rubbing his groin and it wouldn't be long before, physiologically, he started to respond to her. He wouldn't be able to help it. Tied up as he was, she could remove his breeches and mount him, and he wouldn't be able to stop her. He'd already tugged on the ropes that bound him and they were strong. He didn't want to have intercourse with the woman, so he had to think quickly.

"Is that what you think?" he asked as if incredulous. "That I would not speak to you any longer? Why, that is not true. I have simply been very busy on business for the king. I have not had time for anyone or anything other than my duties. I was not ignoring you in the least."

Esme's expression changed somewhat, doubtful of his words. "I tried to talk to ye, but ye would run off when ye saw me!"

"Because I had no time to talk," he said, knowing that if he was going to save himself, he would have to speak sweetly to her like he did the first time he met her. She was stupid and pliable. "Esme, my love, it had nothing to do with not wanting to talk to you. I had planned to return to you when my business was done. But now you may have ruined those chances. I have business for the king that cannot wait, and I must return to him. How long have you kept me here?"

A spark of uncertainty flashed in Esme's eyes. She was becoming increasingly uncertain. "I brought ye here," she said. "When ye returned to yer room that night, two of my stable servants were waiting. They hit ye over the head and brought ye here."

"Where is *here*? Esme, you must untie me. I must return to the king."

Esme stood up from the bed, confusion clouding her face. Clearly, she was mulling over his words.

"Then why did ye ignore me so?" she demanded. "Why did ye not tell me ye intended to return to me?"

He feigned exasperation, which wasn't so much feigned as it was real. He was truly exasperated with the situation.

"Because I did not have the time," he insisted. "Had I known you felt this way, I would have made the time, but I did not know. And you... you *abducted* me because of it? Untie me this instant, Esme. If I do not return to the king, he... he will think I have abandoned him. He will send men out to execute me. Is that what you want?"

Esme was quite distressed over the situation now. Had she done wrong? She was a bold woman, but she wasn't a smart one. She had no idea that Andrew was giving her an untrue story simply to get her to untie his bindings. He seemed so very sincere and, being that she lusted after him, she was willing to believe everything he told her.

"Then... then ye will not leave me?" she asked.

He shook his aching head. "I will not," he said firmly. "I told you I will return when my business is finished, and I will. Untie me!"

Esme sighed heavily, feeling scolded and sad. After a brief hesitation, she moved timidly to the bed, pulling a small dirk from the belt at her waist to cut off the bindings. Andrew felt the first one fall away with the greatest of relief.

"All of them, love," he told her with as much gentleness as he could manage. "Now, tell me how long I have been here."

Esme cut the bindings from the left wrist and bent over to cut them from the right. "Three days."

That brought a strong reaction from Andrew. "Three *days*?"

She nodded. "My men hit ye very hard," she said. "I did not know if ye'd ever awaken."

No wonder his head was killing him and he felt groggy. He probably had a broken skull on top of everything. As the bindings fell away, he realized his arms were numb from having been tied up over his head and he struggled to bring some feeling back into them. As Esme went to cut away the bindings on his legs, he sat up, very slowly, and noticed his possessions were crammed into the corner of the chamber. He even saw his broadsword propped in the corner, but what he didn't see was Demon Slayer.

"Did you bring all of my possessions in here?" he asked as he rubbed at his wrists, trying to bring the blood back into them.

Esme nodded. "Everything that was in the chamber."

Not everything, he thought. "Is it all there? My coinage and everything?"

Guiltily, she shook her head. "I gave some of it to my stable servants for helping me," she said. "I gave them some coinage for keeping their mouths shut."

It seemed to Andrew that she intended to keep him here, as a prisoner, for a very long time. As the last binding fell away, he swung his big legs over the side of the bed and sat there, trying to orient himself.

"Three days," he muttered. God, he was in a panic to get out of there and make it to Josephine. Given how long he'd been away, she surely must have thought he'd run off and left her. "*Where* am I, Esme?"

She stood over him, looking worried. "At the inn," she said. "This is a room the servants sometimes use to sleep in. Are ye angry with me, love? I wasn't trying to be cruel, but ye wouldn't speak to me... I wanted so very much to talk to ye."

Was he angry? Of course he was. He was damn frantic and furious. But he was afraid if he demonstrated any of that, she'd call her stable servants or whoever happened to be in ear shot and he'd have a fight on his hands that he wasn't in any shape for. He wanted to get to his former room and see if Demon Slayer was still where he left it, and then he needed to get to Josephine. It made him sick to think of what could have happened to her in three days. But instead of snapping at the woman, he forced a smile.

"Nay," he said, reaching out to touch her hand. "I am not angry. But I must get to the king and try to explain why I have been missing for so long."

He stood up unsteadily with Esme beside him, wringing her hands with worry. "But ye'll return to me after?"

He nodded, almost throwing himself off-balance as he did. "I will return to you."

"Promise?"

He didn't hesitate. "I said I would. You will not doubt my word."

Esme watched him nervously as he went to the corner and picked up his belongings, both saddlebags, another satchel, and his sword. For a man she'd fought so hard to abduct, she was letting him go rather easily, mostly because he was promising to return to her. She did so very much want his favor. As she watched, he started to look around as if missing something.

"Where is my mail?" he asked. "My mail was in that chamber. *Where* is it?"

Esme sighed heavily. "The stable servants..."

"They took it?"

She nodded.

He pointed to the door. "Go," he commanded softly. "Get it back. I need it. I will meet you in front of the inn."

Esme didn't hesitate. She scooted from the chamber as Andrew lumbered out behind her, incredibly frustrated with what had happened. His head was killing him and he put a hand to it, feeling a massive lump on the right side of his head. Even after three days, it was still big and sore. No wonder he'd been unconscious for so long.

They were on the ground floor of the inn and heading straight into the kitchens from the little back chamber, where kitchen servants and wenches were looking at Andrew rather fearfully. The last time they saw the man, he was being carried between two of the big, burly stable servants.

But Andrew ignored them. He needed to make it to his former chamber. As Esme headed from the rear of the kitchens and out to the stable yard beyond, he made his way through the common room, which was half-full of patrons, and headed up the stairs to the level above.

There were three doors on this level and a sleeping loft. He and Sully had rented the room facing the street, and he went to the door and gave a shove, only to find that it was bolted from the other side. Stepping back, Andrew lashed out a big foot and kicked the door in, sending splinters of wood exploding.

Someone inside the chamber screamed, a woman's scream, and he stepped in to find a man on his back while the woman was on top of him, his body embedded in hers. It was one of the many whores who called the inn home, making her money for the day, but Andrew ignore both her and her customer as he went to the bed nearest him, shoved up against the wall, and pulled up the mattress. He could immediately feel some weight to it and he knew Demon Slayer was still where he left it. He breathed a sigh of relief.

There was the cut in the mattress he'd made, and he dug his hand into it, feeling the end of hilt of Demon Slayer. Digging deeper into the mattress, he got a grip on the sword and the sheath, and drew them out. Straw from the mattress fell all over the floor, chaff floating in the still air of the chamber. He blew bits of straw off of the sheath, brushing at it, cleaning it up as he headed to the door, which wouldn't close now that he'd kicked it in. But he didn't care; he blew from the room without saying one word to the two occupants.

Rushing down the rickety stairs and through the common room, he emerged into the street beyond, a street he had become very familiar with. His attention immediately moved to the road that headed up to the castle gates, and the road was dotted with people, which told Andrew that it was sometime in the afternoon. By the location of the sun and the dampness of the air, he guessed it that a fog was rolling in as sunset approached, and he began to look around frantically for Esme. He needed his mail, but he didn't want to wait around for it. He needed to get to the castle.

He was desperate to get to Josephine.

He waited all of two minutes before he began to walk, wondering how he was going to get through the gates without his apple man disguise, but it couldn't be helped. Sully was inside the castle, presumably, so perhaps if he said he was with the party from Torridon, they might let him in.

As he quickly headed up the incline of the road, he passed by a man who was wearing a heavy cloak, long, with a hood to it, and he yanked it off the man as he continued to walk, slinging it up over his shoulders and pulling the hood up over his head. The man yelled his protest, but Andrew ignored him. He wanted to conceal his features somewhat and remain as incognito as possible, but he truly wondered if that was going to work. He probably should have thought his approach out better, but his urgency to see Josephine was clouding his judgement.

He could only pray.

Getting through the portcullis gate wasn't difficult because all of the guards were over talking to two women, who were heavily flirting with them. Andrew was able to slip in and practically run up to the second gate, which posed more of a problem. There weren't many people at that gate, but there were many guards, and Andrew knew he was going to have to make his story good or they would not let him in. Then, he'd have to try again in the morning with the apple man disguise. As he approached the gate, two guards approached him.

"Name!" one of them boomed.

Andrew came to a halt, holding up his hands to show he wasn't holding a weapon. "I am with Lord Montgomery's party from Torridon Castle," he said. "The name is d'Vant. If you will ask Lord Montgomery, he is expecting me."

The two sentries looked at him suspiciously, but a third sentry had heard him. He was an older man and he walked up to Andrew, peering at him curiously.

"Yer name is d'Vant?" he asked.

Andrew was certain his answer was about to get him in a good deal of trouble. He didn't like the way the man was looking at him, but it was too late to lie about it now. With regret, he nodded his head.

"Aye."

The older sentry's gaze lingered on him a moment before he lifted his hand and motioned to him. "Come with me."

Andrew did, quite certain he was about to be arrested. He followed the sentry through the second gatehouse as the two of them headed up the hill and into the main part of the castle. Andrew thought it was rather odd that the man didn't arrest him immediately. Instead, he was clearly taking him somewhere, but all Andrew could think of was running off and finding Josephine.

But he didn't run, mostly because he was fairly certain he couldn't outrun or successfully hide from soldiers who knew the castle grounds. Besides... he wasn't in any shape to run. He felt horrible with his throbbing head and lurching stomach, and something made him stick to the man who was in the lead. There was something decidedly strange about the man who hadn't arrested him right away, and that had him curious.

When they reached the bailey where the ground leveled out and the garden Andrew knew so well was off to the east, tucked up against an outcropping of rocks, the older sentry turned to him.

"Ye're Andrew d'Vant?" he asked.

Andrew nodded. "I am."

"De Reyne has been looking for ye," the sentry said quietly. "He said that if ye showed yerself, I was to bring ye to him."

Well, at least he wasn't going to be taken to the dungeons, at least not yet. Andrew simply nodded, and the man continued on to a big stone building that was directly in front of them. It was two-storied, with small windows, and soldiers seemed to be coming in and out of it. As Andrew and the older sentry approached, the sentry called out to those who were milling around the building's entry.

"Do ye know where de Reyne is?" he asked.

One of the men pointed to the collection of buildings, including the great hall. "I saw him go that a-way!"

The older sentry turned in the direction of the great hall and began to run. Andrew picked up the pace and ran after him. They ran all the way to the great hall, entering the structure that was being prepared for the evening meal.

"There!" the sentry said, pointing.

Andrew caught sight of Ridge over near another door. There was no mistaking de Reyne's sheer size, so the sentry began to run with Andrew right along with him. They ran across the hall, through the door that de Reyne had disappeared into, and out into a small court-yard.

"De Reyne!" the sentry shouted.

Ridge was about to enter another building attached to the courtyard on his way to join the king before the man went to dinner. He came to a halt at the sound of his name, turning to see a sentry over near the great hall door. But that wasn't all he saw. He also saw Andrew standing there, looking haggard and pale, carrying baggage and dressed in a dirty cloak. His eyes widened as he rushed towards Andrew.

"D'Vant," he hissed. "Where in the hell have you been? We've been looking for you for three days!"

Andrew sighed heavily, raking his hand through his dirty hair. "You would not believe it," he said. "A wench at the inn where I rented a room decided I wasn't paying her enough attention and decided to abduct me. I've been unconscious for three days, tied to a bed, and only just managed to escape."

"*What?*" Ridge exclaimed softly. "Are you serious?"

"Deadly serious. Where is Josephine?"

Ridge lifted his eyebrows at the rather wild story but, given Andrew's pale appearance, he believed it. But he dismissed the older sentry before answering, sending the man for Sully and telling him to have the man come to the king's chambers. When the sentry rushed off to carry out the orders, Ridge eyed Andrew.

"Come with me," he muttered. "There is much to discuss."

Andrew didn't like the look on his face. He grabbed hold of the man's arm before he could enter the building.

"Please, de Reyne," he begged quietly. "*Where* is Josephine? Is she well?"

Ridge could see the panic in Andrew's eyes. He didn't think he would have to be the one to tell Andrew what had happened to Josephine, but there was no other choice. He had to be the one to deliver the bad news.

"Blackbank took her," he said, lowering his voice. "They left last night for Haldane Castle. You were not here, d'Vant; you do not know what a nightmare it was with Blackbank. He became ragingly drunk at the feast last night and we had to forcibly separate him from Lady Josephine. Whilst she was safe in her room, the man went on the rampage and bedded a servant girl, killing her. I was guarding Lady Josephine's door and when I left to search for you, Blackbank broke down her door and killed Nicholas de Londres, who was in the chamber with her as protection. It was a slaughter; as if a lamb went up against a lion. Nicholas never stood a chance."

Andrew almost couldn't take what he was hearing; his aching head was now spinning as he slumped back against the doorjamb, looking at Ridge with horror.

"God, no," he hissed. "Tell me he did not hurt her."

Ridge shook his head quickly. "Strangely enough, he did not," he said. "After the king discovered that Blackbank had murdered de Londres, he tried to break the betrothal but Blackbank would not hear of it. He threatened to raze the castle if we tried to break the bargain, so Lady Josephine insisted she go with him. That is why we have been looking for you; the king wishes to speak with you."

Andrew almost couldn't function. He was so shocked and horrified at what he'd been told that he could barely move, but he forced himself to, following Ridge as they went to the king's chambers. They were in the more lavish part of the castle at this point, but Andrew didn't notice. He didn't notice the polished floors, the tapestries, the arched doorways made from carved wood. When Ridge came to a halt and knocked softly on a door, it was opened from within.

Ridge and Andrew stepped into the king's chambers as the man was dressing for the feast. He was standing in front of two polished bronze mirrors, looking at himself as his chamberlain dressed him in fine silks. At first, he caught sight of Ridge but when he also caught sight of Andrew, he spun around and nearly knocked his chamberlain down. His eyes were wide with surprise.

"D'Vant!" he gasped. "You have returned!"

Andrew was feeling weak and exhausted, with his throbbing head. But he stood tall as he faced the king, the man who had altered the course of his life. It was difficult to look at the man and not hate him.

"Aye, my lord," he said. "I am here."

Alexander came towards him, seemingly greatly concerned. "What happened?" he asked. "Where did you go?"

Andrew sighed heavily, realizing that he was going to have to repeat his story, but Ridge spoke for him.

"It would seem that d'Vant was abducted by an admirer," he said.

"A woman knocked him unconscious and has held him for the past three days. He has only just managed to escape. I told him what became of Lady Josephine and I told him that you wished to speak with him, but I did not tell him why."

Alexander looked at Andrew with the same surprise Ridge had displayed when he'd been informed of the abduction by a woman. "That is astonishing," the king said. "Was she beautiful, at least?"

Andrew shook his head, slowly and painfully. "She was *not*," he said, dropping his saddlebags and satchel where he stood. He simply couldn't hold them any longer. He rubbed at the lump on the side of his head. "It is a long and ridiculous story, but I have a bump on the side of my head to prove it. And I would be eternally grateful for any wine and food you could provide me. At the moment, I am not feeling particularly well."

Ridge began barking orders to servants, who fled to carry out his bidding. Alexander grasped Andrew by the arm and pulled him over to a chair that was near the blazing hearth. Andrew sat heavily in the chair as William Ward, who had been in the chamber and had heard the entire conversation, brought forth a cup of the king's own wine for the injured man. Alexander snatched it from him and gave it over to Andrew himself.

"Drink," he said. "It is a fine Madeira, something I keep only for myself. It will fortify you."

Andrew drank the entire cup and Ward appeared with the pitcher, filling it up again. He took another long drink, smacking his lips as he looked up at Alexander, wondering why the man was being so nice to him. He was suspicious.

"So my brother took Josephine," he said to the king. "Ridge told me what happened."

Alexander nodded, taking the chair opposite Andrew. "Aye," he said, rather subdued. "He took her."

"Last night?"

"Aye," Alexander said. Then, he hesitated before continuing. "If it means anything to you, d'Vant, I am sorry for all of this. I truly believed I was making a strong alliance with a powerful border lord when I betrothed Josephine to him. I have known Alphonse for years and, although the man has always been brutal, I suppose I did not realize just how brutal he was. He killed my nephew and the man wasn't even armed."

"I know."

Alexander sat forward in the chair, watching Andrew closely as he drained his second cup of wine. He sensed the man's defensiveness, perhaps even his hostility. Not that he expected otherwise.

"You do not forgive me, and I do not blame you, but I want you to listen to me," he said, his voice earnest. "When I realized that I had made a mistake, I tried to break the betrothal, Lady Josephine would not let me. She told me to let her go because she knew you would come for her. She said she knew you would kill your brother, which would serve justice to you and to me. You would have your revenge against your brother, and Nicholas would see justice."

Ridge appeared at Andrew's side, pulling the wine cup from his hand and replacing it with a hunk of bread that had meat and cheese embedded in it. Andrew took an enormous bite, chewing slowly. It hurt his head even to chew. But he managed to swallow before answering.

"I will have my vengeance regardless," he said. "I gather from this conversation that Josephine told you I had come to Edinburgh."

"She did."

"Then mayhap she did not tell you that what I do, I do for myself. It has nothing to do with your nephew. My vengeance against my brother is my own."

The king sighed heavily, sitting back in his chair. "I want justice for my nephew," he said. "You want vengeance, as you say, for yourself. And what of Josephine? Do you not want vengeance for her as well, for the fact that your brother has taken her from you?"

Andrew's eyes narrowed. "*You* took Josephine from me," he said frankly. "You ordered de Reyne to abduct her and bring her to

Edinburgh. When I figured out what had happened, I followed. Sully and I have been skulking around Edinburgh for days, avoiding being seen, trying to avoid being arrested because I knew if you saw me, you would have me thrown in the dungeons. And now you want my help because the contract you brokered has spiraled out of control? *You* did this to her. This is all your fault."

He was rather emotional and Alexander understood why. The man had been through an ordeal, now with an added head injury, and nothing he said was untrue. Therefore, Alexander wasn't truly offended, but he was greatly remorseful.

"And so, it is my fault," he said, feeling scolded. "I said I was sorry. You do not need to accept that apology, but I said it just the same. The important thing is that you go after Josephine. She has been with Blackbank since last night. And without anyone to prevent him from having his way with her, there is no telling what has happened. When will you go after her?"

Andrew didn't like the thought of that at all. All thoughts of vengeance aside, the very real issue was that Josephine was with his brother, unprotected. He put the food aside and stood up, weaving unsteadily.

"I am going now," he said. "My horse is in the livery down by the tavern where I almost ended up a permanent resident. As soon as I collect my horse, I will be heading south to Haldane. My brother brought an entire contingent with him, which means he will be traveling at a slower pace. I cannot catch up to him before he reaches Haldane, but I will make haste to reach it as quickly as I can. If I move swiftly, I should not be too far behind them."

That was what Alexander wanted to hear. He leapt to his feet. "I will provide you anything you need," he said. "In fact, I will send Ridge with you. If you run into trouble against your brother, he can be of some assistance."

Andrew looked at Ridge, remembering what he'd said to the man the night he'd disappeared. He knew that Ridge was sympathetic to Josephine's situation. *You said that you owed Josephine a debt. If, for some reason, I am killed instead of my brother, then I ask you to honor that debt.*

Aye, Andrew remembered what he'd said, very well. In that context, he was willing to let Ridge come with him because if something happened to him, he needed someone to take Josephine and get her to safety.

Ridge was that man.

"He is welcome," he said, still looking at Ridge. "Are you ready to ride tonight?"

Ridge nodded. "I am ready when you are."

Andrew sensed a strong ally in Ridge de Reyne. Strangely enough, he also sensed one in Alexander, who'd had a shocking change of heart. He seemed genuinely concerned for Josephine. But Andrew couldn't dwell on the king's guilt. In truth, he didn't really believe it. If given the choice again, he was sure the man would do the very same thing, whatever was necessary to form an alliance for his crown.

"Then we shall depart immediately," Andrew said, moving to the spot where he'd dropped his saddlebags. "I fear we will have to stop at Torridon on our way south so that I may retrieve my heavy battle armor. I do not intend to go up against my brother without it."

Ridge and Alexander were following him to the door. "Torridon is not too far out of the way," the king said. "In fact, it is along the road you must take south."

Andrew heaved his saddlebags onto his shoulder, reaching down to pick up both of his broadswords. "It is not exactly on the road, but it is not too far from it," he said. "The delay shall be minimal."

He was just turning for the chamber door when the panel suddenly opened, spilling forth Sully and Donald. Sully's eyes widened when he saw Andrew.

"God's Bones!" he hissed. "You *are* alive! Where have you been?"

Andrew didn't want to take the time to repeat his story. He was in a great hurry. "In a siren's lair," he muttered. When Sully's features screwed up with confusion, he went to the man and put a brotherly arm on his shoulder. "I will tell you on the way. We are going to Haldane."

Things were moving swiftly but Sully was ready. He'd already had the conversation with the king about saving Josephine, so he already knew the situation, for the most part. He also knew that they had an ally in Alexander, at least for the moment, with everyone wanting the same outcome – justice for Nicholas, safety for Josephine.

But the key factor in all of it had been Andrew, who had been missing up until that very moment. Sully didn't know why Andrew had been missing, but he intended to find out as they headed off to rescue Josephine.

"I am going with you," Sully said in a tone that left no room for argument. "Let me gather my things and meet you in the gatehouse."

"I am going, too," Donald announced. He had been devastated over Nicholas' death and Josephine's situation and, perhaps, even more than Andrew, had visions of vengeance on his mind. "I will meet ye at the gatehouse!"

He raced out of the chamber, well ahead of Sully, who was close on his heels. Andrew and Ridge were nearly through the door when Alexander called out to them. They paused, but the king was looking mostly at Andrew.

"I know I should not wish you luck in killing a man, but I will do just that," he said seriously. "When you kill your brother and marry my cousin, I hope you will consider forgiving a man for making a bad decision. I could not admit that until now. And I should look forward to a strong new alliance with the new Earl of Annan and Blackbank."

Andrew could see that the man was sincere. Or, at least he thought he was sincere. But it would be good to have an alliance with the king, someone he could depend on in the greater scheme of things. A man who would be his cousin through his wife.

... *his wife.*

God, even thinking that was like music to his ears. But there would be no wife unless he got the hell out of Edinburgh, immediately.

"I believe we can have a strong alliance, my lord," he said. "And when I kill my brother, it is possible that I will mention Nicholas' name. Josephine was fond of the lad."

Alexander nodded, his mood melancholy. "As was I."

Andrew could see the emotion in the man's face, shocking for the king he thought to be foolish and weak. He didn't see that in him at the moment.

"I will not fail, I swear it."

With that, he was gone, followed by Ridge. Alexander went to stand in the doorway, watching the two enormously powerful men moving down the corridor amongst the flickering torches. It was a surreal scene, as if they were both descending into the darkness.

The darkness of vengeance.

"I hope that is not the last we will see of either of them," William Ward said over his shoulder.

Alexander turned to look at his chancellor. He came into the room, pondering that very thing.

"Somehow," he said slowly, "I do not think that will be the last time. D'Vant is led by love, I think. He speaks of vengeance, but when he speaks of Josephine, all I can see in his face is his love for her. When one is led by love, failure is not possible."

With that, he went back to his chamberlain as the man needed to finish dressing him, leaving William standing there, pondering his words.

When one is led by love, failure is not possible.

God, he hoped so.

CHAPTER THIRTY-THREE

Haldane Castle

A BEAUTIFUL DAY had dawned over a castle that looked as if it belonged on a level with Purgatory. But it was a day of diamonds in stark contrast to the terrible journey from Edinburgh.

It had taken four long days to reach Haldane Castle, and they'd arrived very late in the night because Alphonse was eager to return home. In fact, the entire journey had been hellish in the sense that Alphonse drove his men and horses very hard. He'd not stopped during the day at all and what stop they did make at night had been very brief. No one had had more than a few hours of sleep and the animals were showing serious signs of exhaustion. But on the night they arrived at Haldane, everyone breathed a sigh of relief, including Josephine.

Finally, they had reached their destination.

Josephine had never been so exhausted in her entire life. Perhaps the only positive aspect of the difficult journey from Edinburgh was the fact that Alphonse had never touched her. He'd kept her close to him, and he'd given her more than his share of lascivious glances, but he hadn't made a move against her.

Josephine was so relieved about his restraint that it brought tears to her eyes once they reached Haldane. Even then, Alphonse had only taken the time to introduce his steward to her, a man named Chauncey, before he departed to parts unknown within the enormous, dark castle.

Josephine had been happy to see Alphonse leave but, in the back of her mind, she somehow knew he would come to her at some point. Perhaps he'd made a vow not to touch her until their wedding night, but vows were sometimes broken, especially by men of lesser character.

Or men who regarded women as chickens.

Therefore, she would have to be on her guard.

Chauncey was a tall, slender man with a hawk-nose and thin gray hair. He didn't seem to have much of a personality other than to order men about to collect Josephine's possessions, what there were of them, and motion for her to follow him. She did, gazing up at the tall keep silhouetted against the night sky as they headed towards it. As the enormous entry loomed up in front of her, with servants lighting the way with torches, Josephine felt rather like she was entering the belly of the beast, from which there would be no escape.

It was a surreal and sinister experience.

Haldane Castle was a large structure, sitting near the borders of England and Scotland, and built to withstand attacks and sieges. There was an enormous outer wall with great turrets on the corners but, once inside those walls, there was a vast courtyard with a moat and a massive keep sunk right into the middle of it.

The keep itself wasn't a normal keep. It was very big, spread out over a great deal of land, with rounded towers at the entry. The entire structure was at least three stories tall and when Josephine entered the building, she was immediately in a great hall that was quite large. But it was empty at this time of night, with servants cleaning out the hearth or sweeping the room. Large iron chandeliers hung from the ceiling, with fat from their tallow tapers dripping down onto the hard-packed earth below.

Chauncey took her into an adjoining room, which was dark at this hour. Josephine hadn't seen much of the chamber other than through the light cast by the torches, and she guessed it was a solar of some kind. Chauncey then took her through the room and to a door on the opposite side, which opened up into a small corridor.

While part of the corridor led off in to the darkness, there was only one other doorway that Josephine could see, with a heavy oak and iron door guarding it. Chauncey had opened that door to take her into a chamber beyond that could only be described as cavernous.

In fact, Josephine couldn't even see the ceiling, it was so tall. The corners of the room were bathed in darkness until servants bustled in with banks of tallow tapers, setting them into the corners of the room and lighting it up with a golden glow. Only then did Josephine get a good look at the room and, although it was plainly furnished, it was absolutely huge.

Since it was on the ground floor of the keep, the windows were high up in the walls, towards the ceiling. They were small lancet windows that only let in air and a small amount of light. They weren't meant for a view or for pleasure. This was a room built to withstand a siege but, to Josephine, it looked more like a prison.

She prayed it wouldn't become her tomb.

Chauncey had mumbled something about sending her food and a companion, and Josephine really didn't care what he'd meant by the companion part. All she wanted to do was go to bed. And after peeling off the clothes she'd been traveling in for two days, she did just that. But when she awoke in the morning, there had been a heavy-set woman bustling around in the room, silently unpacking the two trunks Josephine had brought with her, putting it all into a giant wardrobe with a broken door.

Josephine had been leery of the woman at first. She didn't like strangers rifling through her things, which happened to be all of the dresses that the earl had sent her as wedding presents. Madelaine had found two serviceable trunks the night of her departure from Edinburgh and had packed everything up neatly.

As Josephine had climbed out of bed, preparing to confront the servant who was unpacking for her, a nearby table caught her eye. There was food upon it, and drink, and a big wooden bowl of what looked like steaming water. When Josephine sniffed it, she could smell the faint scent of rosemary. She could even see the little pieces of rosemary floating around in the water. Realizing this was meant for her to wash in, she quickly went about locating the oils and soaps that she knew Madelaine had packed.

When the heavy-set servant saw that the new mistress was awake, she jumped in to assist. Josephine quickly discovered that the woman was a mute, and had no way of speaking, but she communicated well enough with her hands and expressions. And she seemed very eager to help, so Josephine allowed the woman to bathe her as she literally inhaled all of the food on the table. She was absolutely starving. But the more she ate, and the better she began to feel, the more her thoughts wandered to her surroundings; specifically, to Haldane in general.

There was great curiosity because this was where Andrew had been born. It was his home. She could hardly believe so dark and terrible a place would have been his home, but she knew it hadn't always been like this. Being in the hands of Alphonse had made it a terrible place.

But it was more than simply the appearance of the place, which was dark and menacing. It was the sheer mood that settled over the grounds and structure like a cloying fog. From what servants she had seen, everyone looked like beaten dogs. Even the air was heavy and full of fear. Living with a monster would do that.

Josephine didn't want to look like they did, scared of their own shadows, and she began to seriously wonder if Andrew wasn't right behind her, having followed her from Edinburgh. God, she hoped so. She fervently prayed that he was; somehow, she *knew* that he was. She knew he wouldn't leave her here in this horrible place for his brother to feast upon.

God, please let him be close behind me!

Thoughts of Andrew were heavy on her mind as she finished her meal. The mute servant, whose name she didn't even know, helped her into a surcote that was made from the finest wool, very light, and dyed yellow from saffron. Beneath it, she wore a shift of equally fine lamb's wool, with long sleeves. The servant didn't seem to be very good with hair, so Josephine brushed her hair out with a horsehair brush, braided it at the nape of her neck, and wound the braid up into a bun and pinned it. She felt clean, and rested, and ready to see the grounds of Haldane Castle. Her curiosity about the place was growing, but she was most curious about one thing in particular.

Andrew's mother.

Thoughts of the woman had been in the back of her mind since her arrival. In fact, she thought she might have even dreamed about the woman who had been kept in the dungeons for years and years. Now, it was all she could think about. Alphonse had declared his mother to be alive, and a great part of Josephine wanted to locate the woman and see for herself. But an equally compelling part was fearful of Alphonse's reaction should he discover she'd given in to her curiosity.

Josephine was certain Alphonse wouldn't willingly let him see the woman. It was just a feeling she had. But Josephine was determined, and she wasn't sure what else she was going to do with her time here at Haldane, sitting around and waiting for Andrew to make an appearance. Why not discover for herself if Andrew's mother was still alive? Or was she simply to stay to her room, hiding away and dreading every footstep, thinking it was Alphonse finally coming for her?

But that wasn't the way she could live. Josephine refused to live in fear. She had to believe that Andrew was coming for her, and that he would very shortly be here, and that he would be deeply grateful to know that his mother was alive. He would undoubtedly be very grateful to see the woman freed from her dungeon home.

... freed?

God's Bones, Josephine knew that was a stupid idea, but she simply couldn't help herself. The poor women had been locked away for so long, caged no better than an animal. It simply wasn't right. Perhaps, she could free the woman and have her run for safety somewhere in the surrounding area to await Andrew's return. At least she'd be out of the dungeons and not a target for Alphonse's hatred.

Even as she entertained such thoughts, Josephine knew these were the ideals of a madwoman, yet she simply couldn't help it. But first, she had to find the elusive mother, and that meant discovering where she was being kept. *Dungeons*, Alphonse had once said. So that was the place she would start.

Fortunately, the mute servant didn't stop her when she left the chamber. The woman was still busy unpacking and made no move to follow her or prevent her from leaving. Josephine grabbed a nearby cloak hanging on a peg and swung it over her shoulders, and exited the chamber.

There was some apprehension as she set out alone in this foreboding place. The corridor outside her chamber was still dark, but not quite as dark as it had been. Last night, it had stretched off into darkness. But this morning, Josephine could see a heavily-fortified door at one end with sunlight streaming in through a small, barred window at the top. She went to the door, passing by a latrine alcove as she went, and threw both bolts on the door. Pulling it open, she stepped out into the sunny area beyond.

The day was bright but cool. Josephine was cautious as she walked outside, peering around the side yard that she was in and not really seeing anyone at all. There were a couple of servants over near the moat, but she couldn't tell what they were doing. They noticed her, however, and eyed her as she walked around the side of the building, heading to the front entry. They noticed her but said nothing, and Josephine moved on.

Looking up at the great structure, Josephine could see why it seemed so dark – it was made with dark stone and up towards the top, there were great streaks of white, either bird dung or some other kind of effect caused by the moisture and weather. It was as if the stones weren't wearing well. But the walls were very tall, pocked with small lancet windows here and there. Truly, the keep was a very dark place with only these tiny windows for ventilation and light but, as Josephine had observed, the building was most definitely made to withstand an attack.

And the moat… as Josephine crossed over the lowered drawbridge, with absolutely no one questioning her or speaking to her, she noticed that there were all kinds of rotting animal carcasses thrown into it, and she swore she even saw a man or two. It was appalling and the stench was overwhelming. Quickly, she crossed the moat and headed into the vast bailey beyond.

The main bailey was wide open, with stables off to the left and a gatehouse directly in front of her. The gatehouse was nearly as big as the keep, a truly gigantic structure built into equally gigantic walls, but now that it was daylight, she could see much more detail to the interior walls.

Everything was built against them, from stables to smithy shacks to barracks. The first thing that caught her eye was a large structure on the north side of the bailey, just to the north of the gatehouse. It was in the shape of a half-circle; literally, as if someone had cut a circle in half, and long lancet windows were built into the rounded edge of it. She could also see that there was precious glass in the windows, one in the shape of a cross, suggesting that it was the chapel of Haldane. Josephine thought it rather odd to find such a prominent chapel in so horrible a place.

She moved on. Opposite the chapel and on the south side of the bailey was a long, thatched-roof structure near the stables that had men coming in and out of it, and she assumed that was the barracks. There was also a second building, smaller, that had heavy smoke pumping from the chimney. Men were going into that structure, too. As she stood there and watched it all quite curiously, Chauncey suddenly appeared beside her.

"Where are you going, my lady?" he asked, mumbling like he had rocks in his mouth. "You should return to the keep."

Josephine was startled by his appearance but quickly regained her composure. "I simply wanted to look around," she said. "Do not worry; I am not attempting to escape. I am simply curious about the castle. Chauncey, what is that building over there?"

She was pointing to the long, thatched-roof structure. "Those are the barracks, my lady," Chauncey said. "My lady, we should go back."

Josephine could hear anxiety in his tone, but she ignored it. "Then what is the building next to it? The one with the smoking chimney?"

"That is where the soldiers eat, my lady. Lord Alphonse does not like the soldiers in his hall."

She turned to look at him. "He doesn't?" she said. "Why not?"

"He says they are not fit for his table and should eat with the animals," he said. "*Please*, my lady. We should return."

Josephine didn't want to. "There is no harm in getting some fresh air," she said. Then, she asked the most important question, the one she'd been lingering on since she awoke. "Where are the dungeons?"

It was a casual question, much as she'd asked about the other features of the castle, so Chauncey had no idea she was asking for a reason. "In the gatehouse," he said, pointing to the enormous building that towered over the walls. "Do you see where that soldier just emerged? That is where they are. My lady, if Lord Alphonse sees you out here, he will become angry. You must go back."

Josephine had, indeed, seen the soldier emerge from a doorway that faced the courtyard. It was built into the south side of the gatehouse and didn't look like anything special, other than a doorway, but now she knew it for what it was.

It was the gateway to locating Andrew's mother.

Insatiable curiosity had her leaning in that direction, but she didn't want to do it with Chauncey hanging by her. She turned to the man.

"I really must stretch my legs," she said evenly. "We have been riding for two days and my legs are fairly aching. I will simply walk the bailey and come back in. Tell me, Chauncey. Is the gatehouse always open like that?"

She was pointing to the gatehouse and the raised portcullis. Farmers were passing in and out, doing business with the kitchens at this time of day. Chauncey nervously looked in that direction.

"Aye, my lady," he said. "No one would dare make war against Lord

Alphonse's castle. But I do not think you should go outside of the walls."

She looked at him, seeing that the poor man was truly terrified. She forced a smile. "I do not plan on it," she said. "I was simply curious. Go back inside and I shall finish my walk and come in. Do not worry; I will not run off. I told you that."

Chauncey wasn't quite so convinced. He stood there, wringing his hands, as Josephine walked away. She didn't seem to want to listen to him but, for certain, she would listen to Lord Alphonse. The man wasn't awake yet, but Chauncey thought to check on that situation and see if his lord had risen. If he had, then perhaps he would tell Lord Alphonse about the headstrong young woman he'd brought to Haldane so the lord himself could tell her not to wander about. It simply wasn't safe. It simply wasn't done. With a lingering glance at the bold young woman, Chauncey headed back for the keep.

Oblivious to the fact that Alphonse's steward was apparently running off to tattle on her, Josephine headed for the gatehouse. She was simply going to take a look around to see if she saw anything… like a woman being held captive. She truly didn't have any plans on trying to release the woman, at least not without a plan. But as she moved to the gatehouse, she could see how very vacant it seemed to be at this hour. Smelling the smoke from the hall where the soldiers ate, she was coming to suspect why.

They were all eating their morning meal.

God's Bones! Perhaps there would never be a better time to release Andrew's mother if, in fact, she was truly in that dungeon as Alphonse had said. Would they even miss her? Was she closely watched? At the moment, it didn't seem like anyone was about, so Josephine thought that this might be the perfect time to see for herself what had really become of Andrew's mother. As she neared the door that Chauncey had indicated, she disappeared into the archway, unnoticed by anyone.

Immediately, she was overcome by the smell of mold and rot. It smelled like a thousand dead bodies were all moldering right under her nostrils. In fact, she pinched her nose shut as she began to take the stairs down into the dark, dank depths. Josephine had to watch her step and be careful that she did not slip on the algae-strewn stairs. With each step, her anxiety increased; she knew she shouldn't be here. But she couldn't help herself. She could hear nothing as she descended into the depths save the pounding in her ears.

Her sturdy boots were dull against the stone as she reached the landing below. A torch flickered down here, wedged into an iron sconce and sending black smoke against the low ceiling. As Josephine's eyes adjusted to the dim light, she could see there were two cells on this level, barred cages that were full of wet straw. There was no one in them. But immediately to her right was a door of rotting oak, held together by strips of iron, and a broken iron handle.

A door, she thought. It could open up to more stairs or it could actually be another cell. Nervously, Josephine fumbled with the bolt, and pushed as hard as she could until it finally gave and jerked from its hole. Timidly, she pushed firmly on the door until it gave way and yawned open into the dark abyss beyond.

Josephine saw nothing in the black. Hastily, she grabbed the fatted torch from its iron sconce and thrust it into the darkness. A room came into view, but not just any room; there was a neatly made cot, a table and chair, and fresh straw on the floor that led her to believe someone was inside.

"Is anyone here?" she called softly. "Can anyone hear me?"

There was no answer. Holding the torch lower, she could see a bucket in the corner for a privy, and a stool with neatly stacked blankets against the wall. Taking a hesitant step into the chamber, she was startled when, off to her right, she saw a flint spark twice before it lit a fish-oil lamp. As she looked over, a woman's face suddenly came into the light.

"Put out the torch; it hurts," the woman said feebly.

Shocked, Josephine instantly complied. Her eyes strained against the barely-visible flame from the lamp as she tried to get a better look at the woman.

"My lady?" she said in disbelief. "Are you… may I ask who you are?"

The woman tried to look more closely at her, but her eyesight was so bad in the weak light that it made it very difficult.

"Who are *you*?" she asked.

Josephine took a few steps closer and peered into the woman's eyes as her own eyes adjusted to the darkness. It took her a moment to realize that she was looking into Andrew's eyes, and the awareness made her breath catch in her throat.

My God… could it be?

"My name is Lady Josephine de Carron," she said after a moment.

The woman's eyes narrowed. "What do you want?"

What did she want? God's Bones, she wanted to help the woman! She wanted to take her out of this hellish existence and take her someplace safe until Andrew could arrive. Tears sprang to Josephine's eyes as she thought of the joy on Andrew's face when he realized his mother was alive. This was such an important moment, and one not lost on Josephine. She was so overwhelmed that she was starting to tremble.

"I came to find you," she said simply. "Alphonse said you were alive but I did not believe it until this very moment."

The woman was still suspicious. "What do you want of me?"

Josephine shook her head. "I want nothing, I swear it," she said. "May I have your name, please? I do not even know it."

The woman hesitated quite some time before speaking. "I am Elaine."

Elaine. Such a beautiful name. Josephine smiled at her, hoping to alleviate some of the woman's suspicion. "As I said, my name is Josephine de Carron. I am not sure where to start with all of this, but your son, Andrew, told me…"

That drew a strong reaction from Elaine and her voice cracked. "Andrew?" she gasped, interrupting her. "You know my Andrew?"

"I do, my lady."

"He is alive?"

"He is, indeed."

Elaine stared at her for a moment longer, utter and complete shock in her eyes, before the threat of tears became very real. As Josephine watched, tears began to trickle from the woman's old, tired eyes.

"Alive," Elaine breathed. "My prayers have been answered, then. My Andrew survived."

Josephine could see how joyful she was, but it was more than joy. It was a mother's belief in the power of prayer, the only power she had caged up in this dark and terrible prison. It was the only thing she had to cling to. When Elaine finally closed her eyes, tears streamed down her face. Josephine was elated with the woman's joy, but she also felt terrible for Elaine and the circumstances she'd had to endure. She hastened to reassure her that her beloved Andrew was, indeed, alive and well.

"He is a powerful knight," she said. "He is a mercenary, my lady, the greatest mercenary in all of Scotland. He is coming for you, I promise. He will not leave you here to die."

Elaine looked at her, confused by the suggestion. Although logically, she knew Andrew was a grown man, the last time she'd seen him, he'd been a youth. In her mind, he was still young and small and a child.

"But… he cannot, not against Alphonse," she whispered. "He *must* not. And you… why are you here?

Josephine sighed. *How do I explain this?* she thought. "I am a cousin of King Alexander," she said. "The king betrothed me to Alphonse, Earl of Annan and Blackbank. But my love, my heart, belongs to his brother, Andrew. The king dissolved my betrothal to Andrew so that I could marry Alphonse."

Lady Elaine put up a ghostly white hand. "Beg pardon, my lady," she said. "You tell me that you love my son, Andrew, yet you have married Alphonse?"

"I have yet to marry Alphonse," Josephine said firmly. As she looked at the women, she began to wonder just how long that would hold true. If Alphonse wanted to marry her on this day, she would have no choice. She started to feel rather panicky about it. "Andrew will come for us before that happens, I promise. You will not have to live down here any longer."

Lady Elaine seemed to be grasping the gist of the situation; was there actually hope on the horizon? Was it even possible? She'd spent nineteen years in this hole, although she only knew how long it had been because Alphonse gleefully told her nearly every time he visited her, which wasn't too often, thankfully.

Still, he did come. And he did gloat. But now... was it possible the end was in sight? As she stood there, her bony knees gave way and she sank forward onto the straw-covered floor. Josephine sank beside her, reaching out to grasp her ice-cold hands.

"He is coming?" Elaine breathed. "My... my Andrew is coming? He is a great man now?"

Josephine smiled at the woman, feeling flesh in her hands that was colder than anything she'd ever felt in her life. She immediately moved to untie the cloak around her neck.

"He is a great man, indeed," she said softly, swinging the cloak over the woman's tiny shoulders to try and warm her icy flesh. "He has not forgotten you, not in all of these years. But I do not believe he realizes you are alive. I believe he thinks Alphonse killed you those years ago when he imprisoned you. He has sworn vengeance because of it."

Elaine could feel the soft fur lining of the cloak against her skin, warm and comforting. As Josephine pulled it tightly around the old woman, Elaine's suspicion transformed into disbelief and, quite possibly, elation. She could hardly believe what was happening. She couldn't take her eyes from Josephine.

"But... he should not come," she said softly, her voice weak from hardly every being used. "He must stay away. Alphonse will kill him."

Josephine shook her head. "You do not seem to understand," she said, rubbing the woman's hands to try to bring some warmth into them. "Andrew is a great warrior. He will kill Alphonse and you will not have to live in this cell any longer."

Elaine could hardly dare to believe any of this. Her expression took on a fearful countenance. Finally, she asked the question she'd been thinking all along.

"Am I dreaming?"

Josephine laughed softly. "You are not dreaming. This is real."

Elaine was struggling to digest everything. Her world was one of blackness, a perpetual darkness that erased any concept of day or night. It was like a perpetual dream state, one she was now being awoken from. She tore her eyes away from Josephine, looking around the chamber that was hardly tall enough for her to stand up in. The ceiling was very low, and she'd had to walk hunched over. So, over the years she'd developed a hump in her back. She had been living in darkness for so very long, condemned to a horrific existence by a man she'd given birth to. But now, it seemed that darkness was soon to end.

Her Andrew was coming.

"Tell me, Lady Josephine," she said after a moment. "Is the sky just as blue as I remember it?"

Josephine felt a lump in her throat at the question. "Aye," she said. "It is a beautiful day today. No rain."

Elaine nodded, trying to picture a sky she hadn't seen in so many years. "I always know when it is raining," she said. "Water comes down the stairs and pools at my door. I knew it was not raining today."

Josephine continued to rub the old woman's hands, feeling some warmth coming back into them. "Nay, it was not," she said. "It is early autumn. The trees are beginning to turn colors and soon, the days of winter will come."

Elaine's thoughts turned to the trees of the land, trees that were now like wraiths to her fragile mind. Did they even really exist? She could hardly remember.

"It would be nice to see the trees again," she said. "And you, Lady

Josephine; where did you come from?"

Josephine could see the light of interest in the old woman's eyes, as if she were finally coming to understand that she was real, that all of this was real, and that there was hope for her future.

"I was born not far from here, actually," she said. "My family home is Torridon Castle. My father was the Earl of Ayr."

Elaine smiled faintly, revealing yellowed, damaged teeth. "Ayr," she murmured. "I visited Ayr once, right after I married my husband. We took our wedding trip there. It is a beautiful town."

Josephine nodded. "It is," she said. "And you shall see it someday again, very soon. Mayhap Andrew will take us to visit one day."

Elaine couldn't really grasp leaving the dungeon much less being allowed to travel freely, but the concept was exciting. Her smile broadened because Josephine was smiling so broadly at her. She rather liked the young woman who suddenly appeared in her cell, as if from a dream. She still wasn't entirely convinced that Josephine was flesh and blood. Perhaps, she was going mad and this is where it all started. But if that was the case, she could think of no sweeter madness than sitting on the floor of her cell, holding hands with a beautiful young woman. It was too good to believe. But all of that hope, that joy, came crashing down when a familiar voice spoke from the doorway.

"They had told me you'd come down here, but I did not believe it," Alphonse said, his big body filling up the tiny doorway. "Soldiers told me they saw you come down here, but I accused them of lying. She would not be so foolish, I told them. But I see that I was wrong."

Josephine had never felt so much fear in her life as she did when she heard his voice. She heard Elaine gasp as she turned to Alphonse, whom she could barely see in the darkness. All she could see was his face; his ugly, evil face.

Oh, God, she thought, feeling that, perhaps, she was about to be severely punished. In fact, she was terrified he was going to beat her to death right in front of Elaine. It was a struggle not to cower, or to plead for mercy, because she suspected either of those things might make the situation worse. Instead, she did the only thing she could. She pretended not to understand the severity of her actions.

It was her only defense.

"Did I do wrong?" she asked, sounding as innocent as she could. "I wanted to walk and stretch my legs, and I recalled that you told me of your mother. I came down here to visit her. We are to be married, after all. Should I not introduce myself?"

It was an answer Alphonse had not expected. He couldn't decide whether he was furious or whether he truly didn't care. He watched Josephine as she stood up, pulling his mother to her feet, and then helping the woman over to her bed so she could sit down.

"You should not have left your chamber," Alphonse growled. "If you wanted to walk about, you should have asked for permission. You are not free to go where you wish, Lady Josephine. It is I who gives you permission to even breathe at Haldane. Is this in any way unclear?"

Josephine thought she was quite fortunate if this was the worst he was going to do. But she felt as if she were walking on thin ice, waiting for it to shatter at any moment. Now was the time for her to ask for forgiveness.

"Then I apologize," she said sincerely. "I did not know. I am used to being able to move about freely, so please forgive me. I will ask the next time I wish to walk about and visit your mother."

Alphonse stepped into the low-ceilinged cell, bent over as his gaze moved between Josephine and his mother. The older woman was sitting on her bed, wrapped up in a lovely cloak that, upon closer inspection, Alphonse realized he'd given to Josephine as a wedding gift. With a sigh if exasperation, he moved over to his mother and snatched the cloak from her, all but throwing it at Josephine, who caught it deftly.

"That is not for my mother," he said to her. "You will not give her anything I did not tell you to give her."

Josephine felt very sorry for the frightened woman on the bed. "Aye, my lord."

She was being very obedient, not wanting to tweak Alphonse's

anger any more than she already had. She especially didn't want him to
take it out on his mother. She put the cloak on, trying to at least appear
contrite, as he glared at her. But that glare soon turned towards his
mother, sitting tiny and frail on the bed.

"Now you have met the mother of my sons," he said to her. "If she
displeases me, she will end up in this cell with you."

Elaine simply kept her head down, nodding to her son's statement
but not replying. Josephine watched the woman, thinking that she
behaved like everyone else at Haldane – head down, tail between their
legs… *like beaten dogs.* Her gaze drifted to Alphonse, who was standing
over his mother in a threatening manner.

He's enjoying this, she thought.

"I hope I will not displease you, my lord," Josephine said, trying to
draw his attention away from his frightened mother. "Now that you
have made clear the rules, may I ask you to show me your grand castle?
You have an impressive empire, my lord."

Alphonse turned to look at her and she was struck by the sheer evil
in the man's eyes. Every time he looked at her, that evil became deeper
and darker. At this moment, it seemed worse than she'd ever seen it.
There was something so terribly black and wicked inside him.

"You will see it soon enough," he said. "For now, you will return to
your chamber and you shall remain there until our wedding."

Josephine didn't like the sound of that at all. "Have you decided
when that shall be, my lord?"

He moved away from his mother, grabbing Josephine by the arm as
he went. "I believe I told you in a fit of madness that I would not touch
you until our wedding night," he said. "It was stupid of me. I was
thinking during the entire journey from Edinburgh, how very stupid it
was of me to tell you that. It must have been the drink talking. In any
case, I have decided that I will wait no longer. We shall be married
tonight."

Josephine was seized with fear; *tonight!* She had no way of knowing
where Andrew was, or how close he was, or if he would even come in
time. God, could she put this off? Could she delay? She'd already

delayed at Edinburgh with excuses of her menses. She couldn't do that again, not so soon. She couldn't run from him and she couldn't hide; there was nothing she could do to escape this.

God... help me!

"As... as you say, my lord," she said as he practically shoved her out of the cell and yanked the door shut behind him. "Will... will it be in the hall? Is there anything I can do to help with the arrangements?"

Alphonse still had a good grip on her, as if afraid she might try to escape him. They headed up the slippery stone stairs.

"You will go to your chamber and you will prepare for me," he grumbled. "Wear the white gown I gifted you with, the one you refused to wear in Edinburgh. Do not lie to me and tell me the gown was ruined, for I know it was not. You will wear it tonight. And do not wear anything underneath. I do not wish to have any encumbrances when I consummate our marriage."

They were reaching the top of the stairs and Josephine was feeling ill at the mere thought of what he was suggesting. The mental image was too horrific to entertain. All she could think to say was the obvious response, the response he would be expecting.

"Aye, my lord."

They were out in the sunshine now, beneath skies she'd once thought to be beautiful. Now, it was the ugliest day she could ever recall, a day full of fear and horror, the day she would meet her end unless Andrew arrived in time.

But he had no way of knowing the wedding would be this evening, no way of knowing she was in mortal danger. Dear God, was it really going to end this way? Would she be forced to marry this beast of a man and then spread her legs for him, only for him to tear her apart with his size and watch her bleed to death?

Women are like chickens; a penny for a dozen, so I shall never go hungry.

That was what he'd told her. They were words nightmares were made of.

Oh, God... Andrew... where are you?

CHAPTER THIRTY-FOUR

THE LAST TIME he'd been here, he'd been running for his life.

Andrew wasn't exactly sure how he felt about returning to the home of his childhood, which had been good memories until his father had died and Alphonse had gone mad with power. As he slowed his horse from the clipped pace he'd been keeping, he realized that the familiar little village on the outskirts of Haldane Castle looked dreary, starved, and worn-down. What peasants he did see didn't even seem human. They ran from him and the men riding with him, hiding back behind their worn-down hovels.

"This place looks like hell," Sully muttered beside him. "Is *this* where you were born?"

Andrew looked around, feeling greatly saddened by what he saw. "I was born at Haldane Castle," he said, his eyes flicking up to the monstrous castle in the distance. "This village used to be very prosperous, but I have not been here in nineteen years. Clearly, it has not prospered under my brother."

Sully thought that was something of an understatement. He turned to look at the men riding behind them; Donald, who was looking at the fallen village with some sadness, Ridge, who didn't show any emotion at all, and finally Thane, who had the same expression that Donald had for the most part. Thane had never been to the village of Andrew's birth, either, so this was all something of a shock to him. But it also explained a great deal.

Whatever Alphonse touched, he killed.

Thane had been at Torridon when Andrew, Sully, Donald, and Ridge had appeared in the darkness of the late evening on the day before. Andrew had only come to collect his battle armor, and their stay at Torridon had been measured in minutes and not hours. But Thane had been insistent that he come along when Sully told him what had happened. Then, nothing could keep Thane from lending a hand.

The foursome became a fivesome that night.

Since Torridon was well into the repairs since the latest Dalmellington attack, and Etienne was a capable commander, Andrew had permitted his second-in-command to come along. If anyone deserved to come, it would be Thane. He had known Andrew, and of the man's vengeance, longer than any of them, and when they departed Torridon, it was with Thane leading the charge.

They had pushed the horses harder than they should have, but knowing Alphonse had at least a day's head start on them made them push in a way they wouldn't normally push. Fortunately, the horses were hearty, with good stamina, so a trip from Edinburgh to Torridon, and then Torridon to Haldane only took around three days. Only stopping to rest and feed the horses as necessarily, they managed to make excellent time. And even as they entered the once-prosperous village on the flatlands near the sea, all Andrew could see was the dark bastion in the distance.

Like a ghost rising from the ashes of his past, the dark hulk of Haldane was his final destination.

The men slowed their pace through the village, passing through the main road that Andrew had remembered to be very busy, once. Now, it was desolate, with dog carcasses in the gutter and the occasional frightened villein running from them. He took a deep breath, trying to steady himself, trying to focus on what he needed to do and not the feelings that were being dredged up. He felt so much sorrow to see the village as it was. And he continued to feel so much hatred towards his brother. So much of it was deep-seated, something he'd never be able to shake off. All he knew was that he'd been planning for the coming confrontation since the day he'd run for his life from Haldane.

All of these years later, Alphonse was finally going to pay.

"I still do not know why you didn't let me bring the army," Thane said as he rode up beside him, breaking him from his thoughts. "Mayhap we do not have as many men as your brother has, but one of our men is worth ten of any other in a fight."

Andrew's gaze was on the castle as it loomed closer. "Because this is something that must be done with stealth," he said. "One or two of us can make it into the castle, pretending to be farmers or merchants, and I can more easily find my brother that way. Besides, if we closed in on Haldane with a thousand-man army, they would lock up the castle and we would never have a chance to get in before my brother figured out that I had come. Josephine's life would be in great danger in that case, so it is better this way. Between the five of us, some of you should be able to enter and find Josephine whilst I locate my brother."

Thane knew the logic behind it, but he still didn't like it. He thought a show of force would be better than five knights trying to sneak into a castle, but he kept his mouth shut. This was Andrew's fight, and he would let the man fight it.

He'd waited long enough to do it.

As they neared the edge of the village, the small parish church came into view. It was the church where Andrew's parents had been wed and where both he and Alphonse had been baptized. In fact, Andrew was named after the church – St. Andrew's, as it was known. He had fond memories of that church in his youth, and of a young village girl he'd been very fond of at the time. She'd been adorable, with curly red hair, but she much preferred an older boy, a farmer's son, who was young and strong and virtuous. Andrew had been short and young and rather pudgy. He grinned when he thought of his broken heart upon losing his seven-year-old love.

As he wallowed in memories of his lost romance, he noticed two priests emerging from the church yard on a small horse cart. The cart was nearly falling apart, being pulled by a little pony with a shaggy coat. By the time the priests made it onto the main road, they intersected with Andrew and the others, and Andrew pulled to a halt to allow the priests to pass. He couldn't help but notice they were heading in the direction of Haldane, so he called out to them.

"You, there," he said. "Priest! Wait a moment!"

The priests pulled their huffing and puffing pony to a halt, waiting for Andrew and the others to catch up. When the priests looked up at Andrew with a mixture of curiosity and fear, Andrew pointed to Haldane in the distance.

"Are you going to the castle?" he asked them.

The older priest, a man with rags for robes, nodded. "Aye, m'laird."

"Why? Is someone ill?"

The priest shook his head. "A wedding, m'laird."

Andrew's heart caught in his throat. "A wedding?" he said. "Today?"

"Tonight, m'laird," he said. He looked at Andrew and the others hesitantly. "Are ye friends of Laird Blackbank?"

Andrew passed a glance at Sully before answering. "Possibly," he said slowly. "Is it the laird's wedding?"

"Aye, m'laird."

By God! Andrew nearly collapsed in relief. *Just in time!* "I see," he said, struggling to contain his excitement. "And you are to perform the mass?"

The priest nodded. "Haldane has a fine chapel," he said. "'Twill be there. Are… are ye guests to the wedding, then?"

Andrew was thinking very quickly. These priests had no idea who he was, which meant he could possibly use that lack of awareness to his advantage. The fact that God had put him here, at this very moment, told Andrew that it was a sign that he should use this situation. He had to make it work for him. His mind was working rapidly as he thought of a plan, something that would bring the priests to his aid without even knowing.

God, it had to be clever.

It had to work!

He grinned. "I am a very old and dear friend of the earl," he said, trying to make the situation sound light and humorous. He gestured to the others around him. "In fact, we are all friends of the earl. We want to surprise him for his wedding, so do not tell him you have seen us. It will spoil the surprise."

With that, he dug into the coin pouch at his waist and pulled forth several coins, which he pressed into the palm of the priest. The man's eyes widened when he saw how much money he'd been given.

"Nay, m'laird, I shall not tell him!" the priest said excitedly. "If I can do more for ye, I am happy to!"

It was the offer Andrew had been hoping for. A plan suddenly occurred to him. Leaning over on his saddle, he fixed the priest in the eye.

"There is," he said. "When you enter the castle, tell the sentries at the gatehouse that you are expecting five more... priests, men to help you with the mass. Tell them to let us pass without question. Will you do this?"

The priest nodded eagerly. "I will, m'laird. It... it will be a good surprise for the earl, will it not?"

Andrew almost grinned when he thought of the truthful answer to that question. Instead, he gave a generic version of it.

"It will be a surprise, indeed," he said. "Remember – you are not to tell the earl that you have seen us. It will spoil everything and I will take back my donation if you do."

The priest's eyes widened; he didn't want to give the money back. Coinage such as this would feed them for months and to so poor a parish, money was the most important thing. Therefore, he nodded firmly.

"Not a word, m'laird," he said. "I must get along now."

Andrew stopped him before he could get away. "When is the mass?"

"Sunset, m'laird."

That was only in a few hours, and Andrew let him go after that. He waited until the men and their rickety cart were well down the road before turning to the others.

"Did you hear that?" he hissed. "I could not have planned this better. My God… what an opportunity!"

Ridge, next to him astride his big, black horse, shook his head in disbelief. "God is watching over you, d'Vant," he said. "That, my friend, was not a coincidence. God is on your side in this matter and we must make the best of it."

Andrew nodded, feeling truly blessed by the coincidence. In fact, he was in some disbelief about it. But he looked to the men around him, seeing their grimly determined faces, and it occurred to him that each and every man thought this was his fight. They all wanted to assist Andrew so badly that it was quite possible he might be pushed out of the way in their zeal. Therefore, he felt the need to make things perfectly clear with them so there would be no mistake.

"Haldane's chapel is large," he said. "There is one entrance. And when we enter, you will disperse around the church. I am the one who will confront my brother. Your jobs will be to ensure Josephine is safe. That is the only reason you are here. Do you all understand?"

Sully and Donald nodded. Thane and Ridge were slower to respond. "But what happens if you are compromised, Andrew?" Thane wanted to know. "Are we to simply stand by and watch your brother kill you?"

Andrew thought seriously on that. "If he kills me, your lives are forfeit," he said quietly. "He will not let you out of Haldane alive, not to mention what he would do to Josephine. If it seems as if I am to be defeated, then I want you all to promise me something."

"What is that?" Thane asked.

"You take Josephine and you run," Andrew said grimly. "Get her out of there. Thane, I already asked you once if you would take her to de Wolfe at Castle Questing. I will reiterate that request. Promise me…

whatever happens, that you will make sure she is safe above all else."

Thane sighed heavily; he didn't like the thought of running off when Andrew needed him, but he knew he had little choice in the matter. He had a heavy burden to bear with keeping Josephine alive should Andrew be unable to.

"Aye," he said reluctantly. "I swear she will be safe."

That was all Andrew really wanted to hear. Knowing that Josephine would be taken care of, even if he was unable to do it, was all that mattered. With the confrontation with his brother looming on the horizon, he was oddly at peace. Everything was coming together as it should, and he was content with it. This was where he was meant to be, and he accepted that. He accepted that this was his destiny.

Now, he just had to live through it.

"Thank you," he muttered to Thane. "Now, we are going into that church and find robes or cloaks that will be convincing. If we are going to pose as priests, then we should probably look like priests."

With that, he turned his horse towards the church, spurring it onward. Donald followed him, but Sully, Thane, and Ridge were slower to respond. They watched the two men ride off across the old, dusty road.

"If he gets into trouble with his brother, I cannot say that I will run away and not help him," Ridge muttered. "In fact, I know I will not. I will not watch The Red Fury cut down by a man who is wholly unworthy to do so."

Thane nodded. Although he didn't really know Ridge, he'd come to know him a little on their ride to Haldane and his impression was of a serious knight with strong loyalties. He liked him.

"Then I am comforted," Thane said. "My responsibility is Lady Josephine. To know that you will look out for Andrew gives me great comfort."

Sully was the last one to speak, his gaze lingering on the castle in the distance, wondering how on earth they ever got to this point. Not two weeks ago, he and Josephine were fighting off the Dalmellington when the king sent word of his arrival to Torridon. Now, Josephine was in grave danger from a man he didn't even know and Andrew d'Vant's life was on the line because of it. God, it all seemed so far away from those days when all he had to worry about was an attack from Colin Dalmellington.

Times had changed, indeed.

"Josephine will not be easy to remove if she believes Andrew is in danger," he finally said, turning to Thane. "I will have to help you. Trust me on this."

A twinkle came to Thane's eye. "Are you thinking she will punch me in the face much as she did the first time Andrew displeased her?"

Sully lifted his eyebrows. "You will be fortunate if that is all she does," he said. Then, he tilted his head in the direction of the church. "Come along, now. Let's get on with this."

As the three of them headed towards the little church, Sully was still lingering on the situation and what lay ahead. In truth, his concerns for Josephine weren't far off – he doubted Thane would be able to remove her if she thought Andrew was in trouble. Her instinct would be to fight for him, and that was one instinct Sully couldn't allow her to give in to this time. It would be bad enough to lose Andrew.

But to lose Josephine would be devastating.

God help us…

CHAPTER THIRTY-FIVE

T HE KNOCK ON the door came.

It was dusk when the knock came, and Josephine knew exactly what it meant.

It was time.

This had been the most miserable day of days. Her wedding day. Something that, for most women, would have been a day of joy. But to Josephine, this was the day of her doom, of her execution. She was about to be taken to her death.

And there was nothing she could do about it.

Andrew hadn't come. The moment of her wedding was upon her, and he still hadn't come. She had to believe that something awful had happened to him over the past several days and he was unable to make it to her. She could never believe that he had made the choice not to come for her; she knew in her heart that was not the case. But the only way Andrew wouldn't come for her was if he was dead.

Therefore, she had to assume he'd met his end somehow.

Grief consumed her. The entire day had been filled with sorrow and anxiety as the last threads of hope were cut. She was about to be forced to marry a monster and everyone in the world who had promised to help her wasn't there in her hour of need.

She was alone.

The knock on the door was Chauncey. The old steward was dressed in finer clothing than Josephine had ever seen him in, and he'd been admitted into her chamber by the mute servant, who seemed to be quite sympathetic to her new mistress. But sympathy wouldn't prevent any of this from happening, and Josephine rose from the bed she'd been sitting on for the past hour, wrinkling the white surcote she'd been instructed to wear, but she didn't care. She didn't care about anything any longer.

Inside, she was dead.

Chauncey took her out of her chamber and walked her across the drawbridge, the moat, and, finally, the outer bailey as he took her to the chapel where her life would come to an end. The beautiful day that had turned so ugly was now waning, and Josephine glanced up at the sky, thinking it would be the last time she ever saw it. She knew she wouldn't survive the night. Very soon, she would see her parents, and even Andrew, in the halls of heaven, and she took comfort in that.

It was the only comfort she had.

Josephine was led to the threshold of the doors leading into the chapel. The interior was surprisingly ornate, with subtle coloring gracing the walls, which depicted several scenes of Jesus' life. She suddenly found it bitterly ironic that she was to be married to such a devil in the presence of such holy images.

Chauncey held her tightly by the elbow as somewhere in the chapel strains of a flute floated through the air and could be heard by all. There were only a few people standing around, people Josephine had never seen before and didn't know. They turned to look at her as she entered in her white dress, looking beautiful but feeling sick. Sick to death with what was transpiring and having no power to stop it.

Chauncey gave her a push forward. She hadn't even realized the processional had begun. In front of her, looking especially pious, were two priests and two small, skinny acolytes carrying candles. She scoffed inwardly; some holy servants when they couldn't even see what was going on, that a woman was being led to her doom. On weak legs, she walked slowly after them.

Alphonse d'Vant, Earl of Annan and Blackbank, stood by the altar watching his bride come towards him, his dull brown eyes devouring her. She looked so pale and pure. He was grinning lewdly for all to see, thrilled at his new bride. As he'd told her, he'd never had anything pure in his life. This was to be a first. If she survived the night, then she might be able to bear him an heir. Perhaps, he would not be so hard on her as he had been with others. He hoped she would be good breeding stock.

Oblivious to Alphonse's thoughts, Josephine was halfway up the aisle, halfway to her death sentence. She couldn't even look at him. She felt such complete despair that it took all of her strength to simply keep walking. But she had no choice; there was nowhere to go and nowhere to hide, and any attempt at resistance would certainly be greeted with painful violence. Lost in thought, she was at the altar before she realized it and the light from a thousand candles bathed her in a golden glow. The earl took his position beside her and the poorly dressed priest began to immediately intone the mass in Latin.

And so, it begins...

Josephine heard the priest, but she wasn't listening. All she could think of was how she was going to handle the earl in the marriage bed. She shuddered involuntarily; her experiences with Andrew had been beautiful, loving, and exquisitely sweet. To imagine that such an act could be used as a weapon of violence and submission was nightmarish at best.

God, she prayed silently, *I have never been one to pray, but hear me now. Please help me. Please!*

The service continued, with the priest slightly off-key as he sang the mass. Josephine stared at his dirty robes, not fixing on his face or on her surroundings. Her expression was so grim that she looked hopelessly miserable. She saw nothing, heard little, and felt only pain of a life lost.

That is why she never saw Ridge slip into the church, dressed in priestly garb. He silently slipped into the shadows, his eyes on Josephine and praying his sword made no noise against his mail. Across the church from him, Sully was also wrapped in thick, brown garments. His face was hooded, and his ice-blue eyes locked on his sister-in-law. It took all of his self-control not to run to the altar, slicing through everything and everyone in his way. His protection instincts were in overdrive, but he managed to control them. He only wondered for how long.

The third priest in dirty robes, Thane, quietly enter the church, carefully taking up his position by the door. And the fourth one, Donald, enter on Thane's tail. In truth, he was here for many reasons, not the least of which was avenging the attack on his friend, Nicholas. He felt very honored to be a member of this auspicious group, and glanced about him almost too conspicuously to make sure everyone was in place. Sully saw Donald bobbing his head around like a chicken and wished he'd had a big rock; he'd have nailed him right in the head with it.

The priest, oblivious to what was about to happen, handed his Bible to a waiting acolyte and benevolently spread his arms, reciting something Josephine didn't understand. It took her a moment to realize the man had stopped altogether and, when she looked up at him, he was looking behind the bride and groom with a queer expression on his face.

The earl saw this, too. At nearly the same time, as if in slow motion, he and Josephine turned to look at whatever had the priest so muddled. With the last remnants of the late afternoon sun pouring in through the rear windows, the chapel was cast in a warm, ethereal light. For a moment, it blinded both Josephine and the earl until a bright flash of metal, like a bolt of lightning, struck out from the very back of the chapel by the entry door.

It was puzzling. Josephine moved her head a little, just enough to block the sun and, when she did so, her breath caught in her throat. A hand went to her chest as strangled gasps freed themselves from her lungs. And her head began to swim so badly that she thought she might faint.

But she fought it; dear God, she fought it, for the vision before her was something she had resigned herself to never seeing again. Before she could stop herself, she screamed one word.

"Andrew!"

Andrew stood by the massive rear doors. Like a vision from heaven, the avenging angel had arrived in a suit of armor that could only be described as god-like; silver-white rays glittered from it as it caught the light, as if it were emitting light of its very own. From the top of the silver helm to the bottom of the armor-clad feet, Andrew was an exquisite work of art. It reminded Josephine of the Arthurian legends of the knights that were nearly demi-gods because of their skill and greatness, and Demon Slayer was in Andrew's right hand, glaring in the light of a thousand candles and hungry for human flesh. Andrew looked entirely surreal and magnificent, and absolutely deadly.

Her prayers, it seemed, had been answered.

Those in the chapel, sensing something terrible was about to happen, began to scatter in terror. The huge silver knight was extremely fearsome, and it was impossible to tell where he was looking with the faceplate down. No one knew who he had come for, and it was better to run than to find out.

Josephine, however, knew exactly who he had come for. Unknowingly, she had wandered several feet towards him, with her hand clutching at her chest. Andrew was still, however, a good distance away. With great deliberation, he lifted his feet and took a few steps, pausing again to contemplate his enemy. The man was looking at him now... black, wicked eyes.

He knew those eyes.

His enemy was sizing him up as well. Alphonse could hardly believe what he was seeing but, in the same breath, there was an odd sense of pleasure to it. *Andrew.* So his brother had come for his lady, after all, and a slow grin of satisfaction creased his horrific face. He looked almost happy to see his brother.

"Andrew," he enunciated slowly. "My dearest brother. I'd hoped you would be dead by now."

Josephine heard the words. She was shaking uncontrollably as she watched Andrew intently, waiting for any word or reaction. The suspense was maddening. When a massive gauntleted hand came up to raise the faceplate, Josephine could see the hate on Andrew's features. She'd never seen anything like it before. Andrew's jaw muscles flexed as he forced a wry smile.

"Wrong, as usual, my brother," he replied steadily.

The earl's smile faded. "Not for long," he said. "You will be dead soon enough."

Josephine almost collapsed. She was fighting unconsciousness with every strangled breath. It was all too overwhelming, and her brain screamed for relief. Tears filled her eyes; tears of exhaustion, fear, and joy spilled out onto her cheeks.

Andrew dared to take his eyes off his brother, his gaze falling upon her, and an odd feeling enveloped him. With all of the black hate he was feeling, there were such feelings of love to experience when he looked at Josephine that he could scare believe it was possible to feel both simultaneously. As much as he wanted to sweep her in his arms and take her away, he knew he couldn't. He *had* to kill his brother. He fought hard to control the surging emotions.

He had to keep his focus!

"Josephine," he said in his rich voice. "Are you well?"

Josephine let out a huge sob at the sound of his voice. To hear him speak to her again was absolute music.

"I am fine," she gushed. "And you?"

"I am well now that I see you."

He couldn't help himself and smiled a smile only for her. Josephine forgot all about the earl and began to walk to her love.

"Cease, bitch!" Alphonse bellowed. "One more step and I shall disembowel you before my brother can take another step."

It was probably true; Josephine was much closer to the earl than to Andrew. She stopped immediately, uncertainty in her eyes.

But Andrew stiffened at the threat. Slowly swinging Demon Slayer from side to side, he began a slow pace down the aisle.

"My brother," he began. "I have waited nineteen long years to skin your worthless hide. My banishment alone was not reason enough to kill you, but our mother's imprisonment did, indeed, warrant satisfaction. You are an evil, vile reptile that disgraces the name of d'Vant. You are a disease that must be wiped from the face of this earth. You are from the bowels of hell, my brother, and you may consider me the wrath of God. I am going to send you back where you came from."

His last words echoed through the chapel, sending chills up Josephine's spine. She closed her eyes tightly to block out the terror his voice drove into her. Andrew was so deadly serious, so completely possessed by rage, that she almost didn't know him.

But Alphonse had a stupid grimace on his face, apparently unimpressed by the speech. He clapped his big hands together, lamely, two or three times.

"Bravo," he said drolly. "Well-rehearsed, younger brother. You say you have only come to kill me? What of your lady love, the beauteous Josephine? You did not come for her?"

Andrew nodded. "She is the reward when all of this is over," he said. "Your death is something I have waited a long time for – for our mother, for Josephine's safety, and for a young man you killed whom you were not worthy of killing. His name was Nicholas. All of these things are why I shall kill you."

The earl cocked a bushy black brow. "Oh? And what if you fail to complete your task? What of your lovely, delectable Josephine then?"

"I will not fail."

The earl grinned wickedly. "Aye, you will, and shall I tell you what I plan to do with your woman then?" he said, obtaining sick delight with his taunting. "After I kill you, I shall marry her with your disemboweled body in full view. Then, I shall strip her down, roll her in your blood, and proceed to fuck her until she faints. After I am finished, providing she lives, I shall bite her nipples off and fuck her in the arse with the hilt of your sword. Do you fully understand my intentions, Brother? Then understand that you will die easily. She will not."

Horrified, Josephine believed every word. Andrew didn't flinch outwardly, but inside he was dying. He, too, knew every word was true. Sully, Thane, Ridge, and Donald were tasked with removing Josephine, so Andrew was certain she would be spared his brother's hideous threat. But, on the other hand, he wasn't entirely sure they would leave him behind to die when they took her to safety. Therefore, it was difficult to know how many would die for him in the chaos.

He *had* to win.

"A fantasy as befitting your deranged mind," he replied coolly. "But from this moment on, you will not touch Josephine. I do not even want you to look at her." In one swift fluid motion, he waved his magnificent sword, startling Josephine and everyone else. Demon Slayer flashed in the weak light. "Prepare to burn in hell."

Alphonse, too, drew forth his massive blade with relish. The crowd in the chapel emitted a muffled groan, with people pressing far back. No one wanted to be involved, but everyone liked a good sword fight, and blood feuds were always energetic. Besides, there was not a person in the hall who didn't hate the earl passionately, and would be very happy to see him dead.

Ridge, previously pressed against the cold stone wall, pushed his way to the front of the crowd on the edge of the perimeter. He remembered his vow to Josephine, his vow to repay his debt to her, and he eagerly waited for his chance. He hoped in a small way it would make up for the wrong done to her by the king. In truth, he had also grown to like Andrew a great deal and considered him a friend.

Sully and Thane were opposite Ridge at the edge of the chapel, watching the scene unfold. Sully was nearly frantic in his desire to remove Josephine from the combat area, but she was too far away from him. Ridge was nearly directly behind her, though he was several yards back. Somehow, Sully managed to gain Ridge's attention and the understanding was that the big knight would grab Josephine at the next opportunity since he was the closest.

With nothing else to do, they waited.

"You have come back to the place of your birth to die," the earl rumbled as he leveled off into a defensive position. "How fitting."

Andrew walked towards his brother, his sword gleaming. "'Twill be your blood on the floor, not mine," he growled. "Pity, brother, that we never truly knew each other."

"I shall ponder that for the rest of my life."

Josephine was rapidly becoming hysterical. She saw the battle brewing, the war of the titans, and she could see the blood that was about to be spilled. In truth, she only wanted to take Andrew and leave this place. She wasn't interested in any battle of honor, yet her heart ached for what she knew would have to be. Therefore, she watched with sickening foreboding but she wasn't at all sure if she could watch their spectacle. In her panic, the room began to spin and as she felt her knees giving way, two massive arms went around her body and pulled her away from the combatants.

"Fear not, my lady," said Ridge. "I am here."

Josephine fell back against him. "Ridge!" she gasped. "I did not know you were here. I... I cannot watch this. We must stop it!"

"Nay, my lady," he said softly. "We must not and will not, you know that. If Andrew is to ever be free of this hatred he harbors, then he must complete this."

Josephine squeezed her eyes shut, struggling not to cry. "I know," she whispered. "But I cannot watch him die."

"I swear you will not," Ridge said. "Look across the room. See Sully and Thane? Donald is also there. Andrew is not alone."

Such joy filled her heart at the realization, but also such pain. "He would never forgive you if you interfered," she whispered. "You have all come to help, but he does not want your help."

Ridge was prevented from replying as the clash of swords filled the air, the first piercing sound of battle that was sharp as a double-edged blade. Josephine jumped at the sound, emitting a small cry, but Ridge held her firmly.

Sparks flew wildly as metal came upon metal with blinding ferocity. Again, and again, and again, the violent sound of bashing swords reverberated within the sacred walls, with each sound telling a tale of anger, hatred, and pain, and of time spent away from family, and of love as true as the halls of heaven.

Andrew was true to his nickname. His sword flew with such speed and force that his brother was having trouble keeping up with him. Over and over, Andrew pounded out years of frustration and heartache, marking each blow on Josephine's or his mother's behalf. With each strike, he remembered the humiliation, the evil intentions, and the fear cast on a fourteen-year-old boy. He remembered being made an outcast, of crying upon hearing of his mother's imprisonment, and of the vengeance he lived for every day of his life.

Now, his brother was going to pay for all of it.

And Alphonse could sense that. He was surprised by his brother's ferocity. He tried to jump over the altar to get away from Andrew, but his foot caught and he fell heavily. Andrew was nearly on top of him, but Alphonse managed to roll away from him and gain an unsteady footing. A bank of tallow candles fell over in his effort, crashing melted wax onto the floor for Andrew to slip in.

Andrew gave him no time to breathe, let alone regain his balance as he once again hammered away at his brother. This was a life or death situation, and they both understood that. In their efforts, they were both beginning to sweat profusely, yet neither one was the least bit winded. With the noise and the grunting, The Red Fury continued.

A small stone baptismal went over heavily, dashing holy water on their feet. The pretty carved banisters that separated it from the rest of the chapel were chopped to bits as Andrew's sword came down, again and again, as he swung at his brother's big body.

Alphonse would fend off a blow, dodge, and return parry with bone-shattering force. At one point he was backed against the stone wall and ducked in the nick of time as Demon Slayer came whistling overhead. He managed to roll out of the way and take Andrew's legs out from under him. A lovely tapestry on the wall had been slashed in half during this encounter.

The disadvantage of wearing armor was that it was extremely heavy and it could be cumbersome. It wasn't made for fast movement. Alphonse had the advantage of not wearing any and was on his feet a split second faster than his brother. Andrew, on his knees, threw up his sword to ward off his brother's powerful blow as Alphonse's evil laughter rang to the rafters. For the first time during the fight, the earl suddenly seemed to be gaining the upper hand.

Josephine didn't think she'd taken a breath since the clash began. Every time Andrew would strike, she would squeeze Ridge's arm tightly until her nails began to dig into his flesh. She watched as the men hacked away at each other, destroying anything and everything that had the sad misfortune to be in the way.

When Andrew slipped on some rushes, she shrieked. When the earl landed a good blow, she gasped. On and on, parry by parry, thrust by thrust it continued. The setting sun threw the chapel into a dusky light, making the fighting figures appear as phantom soldiers on the edge of the netherworld.

They were fighting behind the altar now, near a giant wooden statue of Christ. When their swords locked, Andrew shoved his brother hard and he flew back into the holy statue, sending it crashing into a small table and all three went crashing to the ground.

The earl rolled onto his feet, perhaps less energetically than he had done earlier. The tides of the battle were turning against him slightly as Andrew leapt on him, his sword flashing, and the very tip of it caught Alphonse across the chest, slicing a long, deep gash. The earl spun away, knocking over an urn that fell between them and offered the only pause in their marathon battle.

"Ah!" Alphonse breathed heavily. "You have drawn the first blood, Brother! My congratulations!"

"It will not be the last," Andrew snarled.

Flying over the urn, he charged straight into his brother. The men fell back with a crash of wood and armor, disintegrating two chairs that had once rested on that very spot. The noise they made was indicative of their hatred and the rage in their blood, and it was difficult to believe the two were blood brothers.

The battle was becoming heavy now, deep into their hatred, and the crowd was completely silent in their observance of the swordplay. Even Josephine had stopped gasping; her hands were now at her lips, folded in prayer as she begged God to spare Andrew's life. For all of the destruction they had caused the hall, they had done remarkably little damage to each other.

But, quickly, that changed. The earl, on the floor, brought his sword up as Andrew's arms were raised in vengeance. The blade found the joint between the arm protection and the breastplate, and he drove deep into the flesh near Andrew's armpit. Blood gushed immediately, coating the left side of Andrew's armor like bright red paint. The sword struck firmly in Andrew. The earl yelled triumphantly as he cruelly tore it free.

There were a few cries from witnesses in the crowd but, remarkably, not one was from Josephine. She knew this moment would come and she was somehow prepared for it. She had seen enough battle wounds to know, however, that the injury was serious. It was deep from the amount of blood that seeped from it, but no major arteries were hit. If one had been severed, he would have bled to death by now.

To Andrew, however, the wound was not only serious, it was painful as well. The gash made it difficult to lift his left arm, yet fortunately, he was right-handed. He estimated that it would be several minutes before he would begin to feel the blood loss, and he knew he needed to weaken his brother now before he grew weak himself. With a surge of adrenalin, he attacked his brother with renewed vigor.

"He is bleeding seriously," Thane growled to Sully. "He will grow weak if he keeps this pace."

Sully's piercing eyes watched Andrew's remarkable skill, even with an injury. He admired the man greatly, as much for his skill as for his character. The Red Fury more than lived up to his reputation as a fair but fearsome knight, and Sully prayed that he would triumph over his evil brother. There were too many bad knights in this world, and there were so few with Andrew's noble soul. But watching Andrew fight with an injury concerned him. The Red Fury was at a slight disadvantage from the beginning because the earl was taller than Andrew, and outweighed him by about fifty pounds. The added handicap of the wound did not help Andrew's cause.

Sully wondered what he would do if it came down to the question of saving Andrew's life or not. He swore to Andrew that he would not interfere, but he wasn't about to keep that vow, nor were the others. The question would be when to intervene, however, and Sully wondered if they weren't rapidly approaching that moment. He sensed that the situation would soon be coming to an end because the combatants were beginning to tire. They had moved out into the center of the chapel again, almost to the point where they started.

But Alphonse was coming on strong now, as if he'd gotten a second wind, smashing against Andrew and putting dents in his armor. Andrew, however, was matching his brother blow for bone-crushing blow. When the earl misjudged a particularly vicious swing, Andrew uppercut and caught him in the side, laying open several inches of flesh. Between the wound in his chest and the gash in his side, Alphonse's strength was draining.

But so was Andrew's. Two hard strikes on Andrew's sword caused him to step backwards, tripping over some debris on the floor, and he fell heavily on his side. The earl, in a fit of gleeful maliciousness, brought his blade down violently on Andrew's helm, getting in two blows before Andrew managed to bring his sword up and fend him off.

Watching this, Josephine was no longer calm. The earl's sword on Andrew's head sent her over the edge, and she struggled violently in Ridge's grasp.

"Release me!" she demanded. "I must help him! Let me go!"

She put up a good fight, but Ridge held her firm. The one thing that wasn't needed was a hysterical female running amok.

From across the room, Sully saw Josephine panic and hastened through the small crowd to reach her. He could see the fight would be ending soon and he must be with her at the conclusion.

Dazed and bleeding, Andrew managed to get to his feet and return the attack on his brother. He was not about to let himself be hacked on again, so he concentrated on discovering a weakness in his brother's strategy. He had to find one and take advantage of it, for he was feeling weaker by the second. The blows were still heavy, but slower. Sparks still sprayed as metal bit into metal, but less frequently. Both men were bleeding and tired, yet both were fighting for their lives. It was evident to everyone in the great hall that the end was near.

The church was almost completely dark now at the onset of night, with very little light coming in from the windows as the sun was nearly down. A few candle banks remained upright, flickering in ghostly silence as a prelude to the coming death. Sully finally reached Josephine, forcing her to look at him.

"Quiet, Josephine," he whispered harshly. "Calm yourself, lest you distract Andrew. He has enough to deal with without listening to you scream."

Josephine's eyes snapped to him, her oldest and dearest friend. He was the one person in the world who could make everything all right, ever since she was a girl. Sully had always been there for her, making her world safe and secure. Her eyes began to well with tears.

"Oh... Sully," she whispered. "He... he cannot..."

He brought her hands to his lips. "I know."

"Help him, Sully!" she pleaded.

"I cannot. Not right now."

She closed her eyes and the tears fell. "Oh, please," she wept. "Do not refuse me."

"I cannot," he repeated quietly. "Not... now."

It wasn't time yet for him to do anything. There was still more of the flight to be played out. The trick would be knowing when to step in. The sound of clashing metal made all of them look in the direction of the fighting men, with the swords coming together so violently that Josephine could almost feel the concussion herself. The earl was saturated in his own blood, and Andrew was covered with his own, as well.

Their blades came together and they struggled, each man grunting with supreme effort. As the straining reached its peak, Alphonse threw out his great elbow and smashed Andrew in the chest, causing his brother to grunt loudly in pain and lose some of his concentration. Then, in one swift move, the earl put his foot behind his brother's heel and sent him crashing onto his back.

Andrew was struggling to rise, but everyone in the room could see what was coming. The casual observers were disappointed to see that the gleaming challenger would soon be dead, and wondered if they would be witness to what the earl had in store for the maiden. It would seem that, this time, evil would prevail.

Josephine watched, wild-eyed, as the earl advanced on Andrew, slowly raising his sword over his head in preparation for the death blow. She began to gasp, clawing at Ridge's arm and was on the verge of complete madness. Sully's eyes widened; he was sure this was the end and he had to do something. But the first thing he had to do was get Josephine out of there.

"De Reyne," he whispered hoarsely. "Remove Lady Josephine from this hall. *Now*. Get her out."

Josephine started to scream, a bone-chilling pain-filled howl straight from her soul. Ridge was sorry he had to slap his big hand over her mouth, but he had to get her out without attracting attention. That was imperative. Meanwhile, across the room, Thane was gripping a pylon with white knuckles, not believing what he was about to see and waiting for his moment to strike. He couldn't wait much longer. Behind him, Donald was moving towards de Reyne, preparing to help him with Josephine, who was putting up a terrible fight. It was chaos all around as the worst of all conclusions to this battle was becoming evident.

As Sully and Thane positioned themselves to intervene, Andrew saw his brother coming through his haze of pain and exhaustion. He saw the sword raised high and knew he had no time to get to his feet. But he was no fool, as his reputation proved. The end was, indeed, coming, but not for him. He was going to do what he had come to do, and that was kill his brother. Hell would have one more resident come this night. He smiled behind his faceplate.

Alphonse was on him, the sword high. "Greet Father in hell for me, brother dear."

Fast as lightning, Andrew's wicked sword came up from the floor and thrust itself into Alphonse's unprotected chest. He pushed hard, grunting with incredible effort, shoving so hard that the blade pushed clean through to the other side.

For seconds, no one moved. Alphonse was frozen to the spot, his sword still held high above his head, with Demon Slayer like a macabre skewer through his torso. Andrew was still on the ground, watching his brother in anticipation of his brother's sword coming down on him, but it never moved. It simply stayed aloft.

As fast as he could, Andrew rose on weary legs and knocked his brother's frozen sword from his paralyzed hands. Looking Alphonse straight in the eye, he jammed the sword into Alphonse's dying flesh again, so deeply, that only the hilt was visible from the front. When Alphonse still didn't go down, Andrew kicked him in the stomach and sent him sprawling to the cold dirt floor.

Josephine, Ridge, Sully, Thane, and Donald were rooted to the spot, unbelieving that a situation that had looked so helpless had turned in the blink of an eye. Andrew was the only one left alive and standing, with the earl dead at his feet. It was absolutely astounding, a perfect tribute to Andrew's determination and, for several moments, time stood still. No one moved and no one dared to speak. It was almost a sacred moment, one that had been a long time in coming.

It was Andrew's moment to savor.

Clumsily, he reached up and tore off his helm, and flung it off into the darkness. His auburn hair was wet, sticking to his face, and rivulets of blood from the vicious head-beating ran down his cheeks.

Finally, it was Josephine who moved first. When she realized that Andrew was still alive, that he hadn't been finished off, she pulled gently from Ridge's grasp and took several timid steps in Andrew's direction. She wasn't sure if she should and, at some point, she came to a halt. She would go no further.

When he was ready, he could come to her.

But Andrew wasn't looking at Josephine, at least not at the moment. He was staring down at his brother, seeing for himself that the man was finally dead. Years of hatred, of angst, and of sorrow had come to an abrupt end.

Strange that he felt no great satisfaction in the end of all things, only relief. No arrogant triumph filled his veins as he had expected it would. He had spent better than half his life preparing for just this moment and he found that victory, while sweet, was also somewhat sad. He only had one brother; now he had none.

But he had Josephine. She filled his mind like an all-enveloping fragrance; sweet, overwhelming, and powerful. As his thoughts shifted to her, he turned unsteadily in her direction and his gaze devoured her to the very bone. Suddenly, he felt very weak and drained, and couldn't call to her because of the lump in his throat. She was safe, and he was free of his obsession. He had to hold her. But somehow, he couldn't seem to move.

Josephine saw his expression when he looked at her and her face crumbled, with tears flowing and great sobs releasing. Andrew tried once again to reach and comfort her, but his legs were not working properly, and he plunged to his knees after a mere few steps. But Josephine closed the gap rapidly, reaching out her arms as she ached to hold him. She wanted to take his pain away, and to tell him how much she loved him, and how they would never again be apart. But instead of words, she could only cry.

Josephine and Andrew came together in a climactic clash. She wound her arms around his head as he buried his face in her soft torso, inhaling deeply of her familiar scent. She cried into the top of his head and he held her so tightly that he thought he might crush her, but it didn't seem to matter. She was his, now and forever, and nothing in heaven and earth would ever separate them again.

His blood stained the white surcote a bright crimson, his blood all over the gown his brother had forced her to wear. It seemed like an eternity as they held each other, knowing that everything was finally right in the world again. They had come so close to losing one another that it was hard to believe they were together again, no longer in mortal danger. Andrew half-expected at any moment to awake from a dream.

The four men that had come with Andrew now stood together, watching the emotional reunion. They didn't dare look at one another for fear the others might see tears in their eyes. Donald wasn't ashamed about wiping his away as Sully put a comforting hand on the young man's head. It was a touching scene they had all hoped to witness but had doubts that they truly would. After watching the two lovers for several moments, Sully finally spoke.

"We must tend Andrew's wound before he bleeds all over the floor," he said quietly.

Ridge cocked a black eyebrow. "We may have to surgically separate them to accomplish that task."

Sully grinned. "Mayhap," he said. "I will take her; you three tend to Andrew."

"True to form, Sully," Donald quipped. "Taking the easier of the two."

Sully snorted, without humor. "Is that what you think? Then you take her and remember that remark as she's kicking your groin in. She will not be happy to be separated from him in the least."

The three men looked at him. "We'll take Andrew," they agreed wholly in unison.

Sully grinned at their reply, but he made no move to carry out his plan. He's attention turned back to the couple. It seemed like a sin to disturb such a touching scene.

"Well?" Donald finally said. "Lead on, my lord."

Sully waved his hand at him. "In time, in time," he said. "They have waited a long time for this moment. Allow them just a little longer before we go in and break it up."

A hush settled over the hall, with most people turning to leave now that the show was over. It was eerily still and completely dark, except for the soft glow from the distant banks of candles. A peace filled the room as the knight and his lady clutched each other, the spoils to the victor.

But Andrew was growing weaker and paler, and Sully decided the time had come to separate his sister-in-law from her fiancé and tend the man's considerable wounds. But as he and the others moved towards the pair, something horrific happened.

As if from a child's nightmare, a horror straight from the mouth of Lucifer, Alphonse twitched violently and rolled to his knees, bleeding entrails down his legs. His ghostly white face was twisted grotesquely and his huge, icy hands extended towards Josephine and Andrew. He moaned, and unearthly sounds that should have been coming from a hellish demon rather than a man echoed in the chapel. Those still left in the chapel froze in horror at the sight of the dead returning.

Josephine saw him first. Startled by the sight, she screamed at the top of her lungs, a cry of absolute terror. Andrew, jolted by her screaming, turned to see something he could hardly believe. His brother, in fact, was still alive. Although Andrew was pitifully weak, he drew on an inner strength, a strength he never knew he possessed, and struggled to his feet as fast as his damaged body would allow.

All the while, his mind was screaming to protect Josephine, to get her out of harm's way. Yet only when he reached his feet did he remember he had left his sword embedded in his brother's torso. And it was still there.

Alphonse was moving amazingly well for a dead man. There was only time for Andrew to push a screaming Josephine behind him before the earl was upon him, his hands clutching at him with deadly intentions.

Andrew braced himself for the fight, preparing to sacrifice his remaining energy to protect his lady. He prayed to God that he would have the strength to do battle just one more time, so he raised his good arm to ward off the initial blow, but it was a blow that never came.

There was a hollow thump and, suddenly, the hilt of a dirk was protruding from the earl's throat. Blood streamed down onto his already soaked tunic and his black eyes opened wide in surprise. For several moments, Alphonse tottered dangerously before finally toppling over onto the stone, never to rise again. The Earl of Annan and Blackbank was dead, this time, for good.

Josephine, clutching Andrew about his torso, stared down at the dead earl as her breathing came in ragged gasps. She could see the dirk protruding from the man's throat, but she had no idea who had thrown it. It was too amazing to believe that it had been anything less than divine intervention, but she and Andrew turned in the direction from whence the dirk had come.

Ridge de Reyne stood several feet away, his right hand still slightly extended from where it had been the moment he had released the dirk. When he saw that Andrew and Josephine were looking at him, shock on their faces, he gave them a victorious wink.

"I do believe I have fulfilled my vow to you, my lady," he said quietly. "But please, do not hesitate to call on me again should the need arise."

Josephine shook her head in wonder. "And I extend the same offer to you," she replied softly. "You have more than fulfilled your vow, Ridge. I feel as if, now, I owe you."

"Friends do not owe each other. There is simple joy in doing. Now, Lord Blackbank," he addressed Andrew by his new title for the first time, "the time has come that we must tend your wound."

Andrew gazed down at his left arm and shoulder; the mail was covered with red stain. He blinked, seemingly dazed, as if he was seeing the wound for the first time. Sully and Ridge moved to help him, but he put up his right hand to stop them.

"Nay," he said. "We are not leaving as of yet." He began to look around the chapel as if searching for something. "Where is the priest?"

Ridge marched a few steps into the center of the room. "Priest!" he bellowed.

Sully and Donald and Thane fleetingly wondered what in the hell Andrew wanted with the priest. *Last rights?* They thought. No one seemed to be sure but, soon enough, the fat little priest with the dirty robes emerged from a small alcove behind the altar. His eyes darted about nervously, appalled at the destruction of the chapel. When Andrew saw the man, the same one he'd given the coins to, he grabbed Josephine's hand and stumbled towards him.

"I am now the Earl of Annan and Blackbank," he said wearily. "You will marry my lady and me."

The priest looked uncertain at first, but with a whole host of heavi-ly-armed knights standing about, he nodded in agreement. The whole situation was most confusing, but he would do as he was told. As he headed for the front of the altar, Josephine suddenly turned to Sully.

"The dungeons are in the gatehouse and there is a cell at the bottom of the stairs with a woman in it," she said quickly. "Bring her here. Hurry, Sully – bring her now!"

She sounded almost panicked and Sully wasn't willing to question her, not when she had that look in her eye. He took off at a dead run as Josephine turned to Andrew, catching a look of confusion in his eyes. She smiled.

"I did not think you wished to be married without her," she mur-mured.

He had no idea what she was talking about. "Without who?"

"When you see her, you will know."

Andrew was too weak, too injured, to realize what she was meant. He should have realized it, but he simply couldn't. His mind wasn't working very well at the moment, from fatigue and loss of blood. As Josephine put her arm around his torso, holding the man tightly, Ridge, Donald, and Thane gathered around the couple. Although Josephine wanted to wait for Sully to return, Andrew was weaving dangerously and she didn't think he'd be able to wait too much longer, so she asked the priest to go ahead with the mass.

With Alphonse lying dead several feet away, the man made the sign of the cross and began the wedding mass for the second time that day.

The service was in Latin. The last time Josephine had heard Latin was the day her father was buried. Somehow, she always associated the language with death. But this was her wedding, an event she had waited a lifetime for. She listened, trying to understand what the priest was saying as she clung to Andrew's good arm.

He seemed to be growing weaker by the moment and she was desperately worried for him. She knew she should have insisted that he have his wound tended to immediately, but she couldn't seem to manage it. It was stupid and she knew it, but he seemed so urgent to marry her now, this very second, that she couldn't delay any longer. With everything they had been through, she understood urgency. She, too, felt the same urgency.

Halfway through the mass, Andrew's knees buckled, and he sank to the floor. Thane and Ridge, nearest to him, rushed to his aid but he angrily waved them off.

"Continue!" he boomed to the priest.

The priest, poor man, nervously and quickly finished the mass, ending with the benediction prayer. He was so glad to be done with this ceremony, with his frayed emotions. This entire event had been an absolute nightmare, one he was more than happy to forget, and the fact that the five knights who had told him they were friends of the earl turned out to be men with a vendetta against him, well… that was quite a tale. Not that he had any great love for Alphonse d'Vant; no one did. Now that the wicked earl was gone, perhaps the village would know joy and prosperity again in an unexpected twist of fate. One could hope, anyway.

With a sigh of relief, he smiled weakly at the newly married couple.

"Lord Blackbank, you may kiss your bride," he said.

Andrew unsteadily rose to his feet. He would not kiss his new wife on his knees but, God help him, he was so weak he could hardly stand. For the first time that day, his focus was where it should be – completely and utterly on Josephine's lovely face.

He cupped her face with his good hand, drinking in the features he loved so much and had fought so hard for. She was finally and legally his wife, and he was nearly delirious with joy and fatigue.

Josephine gazed back at him, loving him so much she was sure her heart would burst from the sheer joy of it. They were husband and wife now, and the name Lady d'Vant was music to her ears. As his head dipped low, she caught a glimpse of a sly smile on his lips before they closed over her mouth in the sweetest expression of love she had ever experienced. It was a kiss of unconditional love, of surrender, and of loyalty. They were all to each other, and would be until the end of time.

Never again would they be apart.

It was dark but for the glow of candles as the newly married couple slowly made their way from the chapel. The priests were taking charge of Alphonse's body, which was a good thing considering Andrew didn't care in the least. The man could remain there to rot for all he cared. With Thane applying pressure to his wounded shoulder to shore up what bleeding there was, Ridge and Josephine were helping the man walk as Donald brought up the rear. Just as they were emerging from the church, they could see Sully approaching from the direction of the gatehouse.

He was carrying something in his arms. Since it was growing dark, they couldn't really see what it was, but Josephine knew. She left Andrew's side to rush out to Sully, helping him with the bundle. Sully set the bundle to its feet and it was suddenly clear that it was a child or a very tiny adult. Sully had hold of one side of the person as Josephine had the other, and they slowly made their way towards Andrew.

In fact, that was when Andrew began to take notice. The more he watched, the more suspicious he became and, abruptly, he came off the steps of the church and headed for the approaching figure as if nothing was wrong with him in the least. He was moving with surprising strength.

Ridge and Thane and Donald tried to keep up with him, in case he collapsed again, but he didn't seem to need their support. But the moment Andrew gazed at the face of the tiny figure between Sully and Josephine, he began to waver. In fact, he staggered, the suspicion on his face turning into utter astonishment.

The man was in shock.

"Mother?" he whispered. "My God... *Mother?*"

Lady Elaine looked up at her tall, mighty son, her ghostly-pale face illuminated in the light torches that were in iron sconces on the steps of the chapel. For a moment, she simply stared at him. Then, a smile spread across her face, lit with the joy of a thousand happy memories.

"You have grown since I last saw you," she murmured.

Andrew could hardly believe it. He tried to move towards her, to embrace her, but his legs wouldn't work correctly. He fell to his knees again and Elaine, who had hardly been able to walk herself, rushed up to him, putting her arms around her boy. As Josephine stood back with tears in her eyes, Andrew buried his face in his mother's cold, poorly-dressed torso and wept.

It was more than he could take, more than he had ever hoped for. Everything he'd dreamed of, the longing he'd felt all of these years, vanished in those few brief seconds when his mother held him in her arms and, for just a few moments, he was a child again. A child who had terribly missed his mother.

"Mother," he whispered. "My God... my sweet mother... I did not know if you would still be alive."

Elaine held him tightly, feeling the warmth and strength of her youngest son in her arms once more. She was shockingly composed as Andrew came apart.

"I could not go without seeing you again," she said in a tone that all mothers use when comforting a child. "Somehow, I knew you would still be alive. From the moment you were born, you were a strong and beautiful baby, and I knew you were destined for great things. Your brother tried everything he could to rob you of your life, but you were too strong for him. Your light, your goodness, was too strong for his darkness. You are my angel of righteousness and justice, Andrew. I could never leave this earth without seeing you again."

Andrew pulled his face from the folds of her dirty garment, gazing at her with such love and delight that there wasn't a dry eye in anyone witnessing the reunion. It was so very sweet, and so very touching.

"I am so sorry I did not come sooner, Mamma," he said, his big hand reaching up to touch her face as if to convince himself that she was real. "I wanted to be able to defeat Alphonse, not simply damage him. I wanted to be able to punish him for what he'd done to you. Please forgive me for not coming sooner."

Elaine cupped his face with her tiny, cold hands. "You came when it was right that you should," she said, seeing his tremendous guilt. "I am still here. We are together again. There is nothing more to worry over."

To Andrew, it was as if she'd never left him. He felt like he did when he was a child, and his mother was always there to encourage and reassure him. The joy he thought he'd lost when he was separated from her returned full-force, and he stood up and embraced his mother as tightly as he dared. She was alive.

She was here.

He could hardly believe it.

But as he held his mother, he caught sight of Josephine standing a few feet away, wiping the tears from her eyes. It was such a beautiful reunion and he was so very glad she was a part of it. In fact, she had instigated it. When he reached out a hand to her, Josephine came to him and he pulled her into their embrace, holding the two women he loved best in this world.

For him, this night had brought his life full circle – married to the woman he loved, and his mother returned to him. From this point forward, his life was going to be a grand and satisfying thing, indeed. If one believed in things like karma or fate, the ballad of The Red Fury was a tale of all things great and powerful – a tale of good over evil, of wrongs that were righted, and of love everlasting.

In the years to come, as men would sing great songs of battle, of the mercenary who had killed his wicked brother in order to save the women he loved, there were those who wondered if such tales were really true, for certain, men like The Red Fury became more legend than truth over the centuries. Myth and fact often became twisted, combined to create stories of valor for men to bring them hope and courage.

Men like The Red Fury embodied hope and courage.

Passing into legend, their legacies would live on.

EPILOGUE

Summer, 1234 A.D.

IT WAS A field of yellow flowers that had her attention.

Outside of the postern gate of Haldane, negotiating with a farmer who had brought a wagon full of bushels of dried beans with him, Josephine could see the field of flowers of to the north and, like a siren's call, the lure was nearly too much for her to bear. She would have loved to have run through them. Quickly, she finished up her negotiations, paid the farmer, and had him bring the bushels in through the gate and into the kitchen yard.

But she remained outside, her gaze on the flowers.

In fact, the entire countryside seemed to be full of flowers. The sun was shining, the birds were singing, and, inside Haldane, life had changed drastically. Sometimes it was hard to believe just *how* drastically.

Josephine turned to the kitchen yard of Haldane, seeing the moated keep beyond and a good portion of the outer bailey. It didn't even look like the same place, the one she'd first come to last autumn. It had been such a dark, terrible place under the thumb of a heavy, dark man. She remembered thinking that everyone seemed to be bent over, cowering under the weight of Alphonse's oppression.

But it wasn't like that now, nor had it been since Andrew had taken the helm. In fact, the man had injected life into a dying castle, and into a dying family, like a bolt from heaven. Now, Haldane was returning to the place it was before the event of Alphonse, a name that no one mentioned these days. It was gone, erased, turned to dust and scattered upon the wind.

Haldane Castle was finally healing.

Josephine stood there a moment, reflecting on the past several months and rubbing at her gently swollen belly. Andrew's son was due in a couple of months; at least, Andrew made sure everyone knew it was *his* son, as if Josephine had nothing to do with it. It was a running gag between them these days. He would ask about his son, put his face down next to her belly to speak to the boy, and then tell Josephine how great and powerful his son would be, and how, together, they would conquer the world.

Because of this, Josephine swore she was going to run off and have the baby in secret just so she'd have a chance to bond with the child before Andrew ran off with him to raise him alone, raising him in a group of knights like a pack of wolves. Andrew thought that was quite funny. Josephine did not.

But a smile came to her lips as she thought on her husband and his great love and enthusiasm for his family. She'd never seen anyone so attentive or sweet, both to her and to his mother. It was almost as if the man was still atoning for the guilt he'd carried around all of these years. But as time passed, that guilt, too, was fading.

As Josephine headed back towards the small bridge that crossed the moat and led into a side entrance of Haldane, she saw Andrew coming towards her from the gatehouse. He waved when she looked at him and she came to a pause, shielding her eyes from the bright sun and waving back.

"How is my son?" Andrew asked.

Josephine cocked an eyebrow. "You saw me not an hour ago," she said. "He was fine then, and he is still fine, but I am growing fatigued. I believe I will go inside and lie down for a while."

Andrew was immediately at her side, putting an arm around her shoulders. "And I shall escort you," he said, worried. "We must take care of you and my son."

Josephine eyed him. "You were never this concerned for me when it was only me," she said. "I am starting to think you love this child more than you love me."

He grinned at her, that flashy grin that could always soften her. "I think I love you a little more," he said. "But only a little."

"Thank you. You are quite kind."

It was a sarcastic response and he snorted, kissing her on the side of the head as they began to head into the castle. But abruptly, he came to a halt. "I nearly forgot what I came to tell you," he said. "A messenger has arrived from Torridon, in fact. Donald is at the gatehouse as we speak."

Josephine was immediately interested in the arrival of her friend. "Bring him in!" she said. "I would see him!"

Andrew nodded. "You will," he said. "I told him to meet us in the hall. He has a great deal to tell."

"Like what?"

Andrew resumed their walk, now heading into the shadows of the keep as they moved for the side entrance. "There is a good deal that has happened these past few weeks, evidently," he said. "First and foremost, Alexander finally had a conference with Colin Dalmellington and told Colin that one more move against Torridon, however small, and the king would strip him of everything. Donald says that Sully is greatly pleased by that."

Josephine looked up at him, a smile playing on her lips. "Then he kept his promise," she murmured. "He promised he would keep Colin away from Torridon if you... if you..."

Andrew knew what she meant. She still couldn't bring herself to speak of that horrible battle in the chapel of Haldane, where Andrew avenged his mother, Nicholas, and Josephine. Alphonse's death simply wasn't something they spoke of. The man was dead, and the terror was over. That was all that mattered, and they refused to reintroduce that darkness into their lives, even in conversation. Andrew gave her a gentle squeeze.

"Aye, he kept his promise," he said quietly. "Torridon needs this peace. The last time I was there, the walls were almost completely repaired, and the structure was in good condition, so the promise of a Dalmellington peace is the best possible news. Now, Sully will have a fortress that isn't constantly under siege and your sister can deliver their child without the threat of war hanging over them."

Josephine's smile grew as her thoughts shifted from the king's fulfilled promise to her sister's impending baby. "I cannot wait to hold my nephew," she said. "Won't it be lovely that our son and Sully and Justin's son will grow up together?"

Andrew nodded, caressing her shoulder as they headed into the dark confines of the keep. "But my son will be the stronger and more intelligent of the two," he said.

Josephine laughed softly. "That is a terrible thing to say."

"It is not terrible if it is true."

She simply rolled her eyes at the man's ego. As they came in through the side entrance, it opened up into an alcove that was attached to the two-storied hall of Haldane, which now proudly flew the new d'Vant banner, something that he'd had commissioned to incorporate the de Carron crest.

Now that Josephine and Justine were the last of the de Carron line, Andrew only felt it was right to continue that line in the new d'Vant crest. Originally, the de Carron crest had been two black serpents facing each other against a field of white, but Andrew added a sword in the middle of them. *Demon Slayer*, he had told Josephine, who had wholeheartedly agreed to the addition.

In fact, Andrew stopped to admire his new crest as it hung from the beams near the hearth. Demon Slayer was also above the hearth, having been anchored there by Andrew and Sully, as a memorial to those days of vengeance that were now gone. Andrew had even sent a missive to Abe in Edinburgh to let the old man know that Demon Slayer had, indeed, lived up to its name. He knew the old man would have been pleased.

"Lady d'Vant!" Donald entered the hall, his fond attention on Josephine as she stood next to her husband. As Donald walked, he tossed off cloaks and saddlebags, leaving a trail for the servants to pick up. "Ye're looking quite well, my lady. Have ye been well?"

Josephine smiled at her dear friend. "I have," she said. Then, she held up a hand. "If you've come to tell me again that your father wants me to name my son after him, then save your breath. Andrew and Ridge have already put in their requests, so I am not in need of any more names."

Donald grinned. "My father's attention has turned to other prospects."

"What other prospects? Do not tell me he is hounding Justine to name her child after him!"

Donald laughed. "Nay," he said. Then, he puffed up a little. "It is quite possible that I have a marital prospect, ye know. My father now has hopes that I will name a future son after him."

Andrew and Josephine looked at each other, amused. "Is this so?" Andrew demanded. "Do tell, lad."

Donald looked quite proud of himself as he took a seat at the long, scrubbed feasting table in front of the hearth.

"'Tis no one ye know," he said. "There is a lass from Edinburgh that has had my attention. I met her when we went to save Josephine from her marriage to yer brother. Red-haired, delectable dimples – her father is the wealthiest merchant in town, which makes my father very happy. Paget is her name."

Josephine was genuinely thrilled. Andrew helped her to sit opposite Donald and took a seat next to her. "That is wonderful news, Donald," she said. "I am very happy for you. I should like to meet Paget someday."

Donald nodded. "Ye will," he said, "although I think de Reyne had his eye on her, too. Her father did business at the castle. That is how we both saw her."

Josephine glanced at Andrew, seeing that the man was fighting off a grin. "No offense, Muir, but Ridge de Reyne has a bit more of a pedigree than you do," he said. "Are you both competing for the same woman?"

Donald shook his head. "Ridge has gone south," he said. "That is something else I came to tell ye. Ridge has asked to be released from his oath to Alexander and, after everything that happened with Nicholas and Blackbank, Alexander released the man. Evidently, he is making his fortune now in the tournament circuit and doing very well from what I've heard. He took some of the king's inner circle with him, knights who worked closely with him. I suspect he'll be dropping by to visit ye one of these days."

It was surprising news about Ridge but, in a sense, not so surprising. Ridge de Reyne was destined for greater things than a mere king's bodyguard. Both Andrew and Josephine felt that way.

"I hope he does," Andrew said. "If he grows bored of the tournament circuit, then I know a mercenary army that could use his sword."

Donald grinned. "That has become Thane's domain," he said. "How is the man coming along, by the way?"

"He is doing very well," he said. "He maintains The Red Fury name and reputation. That has not changed, and he has more work than he can handle. But he says men find it strange that a big, blond knight bears the name of The Red Fury. They do not understand it, except for those men who worked with me in the past and knew of me. But that is a part of my life that no longer exists. The Red Fury that I was has passed into legend."

Donald watched the man's expression, seeing absolutely no remorse in that statement. The Andrew d'Vant he'd known for the past several months was a man of contentment, skill, and wisdom, as he'd proven in bringing Haldane Castle back from the brink of death. Once known as The Red Fury, that was a name that Thane now used, carrying on the fearsome mercenary tradition.

"It does not matter," Donald said quietly, his eyes glimmering warmly. "Ye'll always be The Red Fury to me, no matter who assumes the name."

Andrew gave him a lopsided grin. "Mayhap," he said. "But I am quite content being the Earl of Annan and Blackbank, as my father had wanted. I have a very big task restoring the castle and my family name. That is the greatest legacy I could want."

Donald understood somewhat. He started to reply but a small figure caught his attention, entering through the main hall entry. Lady Elaine shuffled into the room, some flowers in her arms from the newly-restored castle garden that she and Josephine had tried so hard to coax back to life.

Dressed in fine clothing, Elaine looked like a completely different person. The woman still walked hunched over as a result of all of those years in a low-ceilinged vault, but she had filled out and regained her health for the most part. She was sweet and thoughtful, and Josephine was absolutely in love with the woman. Having lost her mother so early in her life, Elaine filled a void that Josephine never really knew she had. Therefore, when the woman entered the room, Josephine stood up in spite of her husband's protests, and made her way over to Elaine and her flowers.

"Look, Josephine," Elaine said proudly. "The foxgloves have bloomed."

Josephine smiled at the woman's excitement. "There are many of them, too. This whole castle will be filled with flowers soon enough."

Elaine handed a couple of stalks to her, with very pretty deep-pink flower bells. "They are very old plants," she said. "Andrew's father's mother said they had been planted a hundred years ago. I do not know if that is true, but they certainly make beautiful blooms. It is good to see them alive again."

Living life through Elaine's eyes over the past few months had been a wondrous experience for Josephine. For a woman who hadn't seen the world in so many years, everything around her was full of excitement and joy. Josephine often thought that was how people needed to always live their lives – with joy and excitement. Since marrying Andrew, that was exactly what Josephine had tried to do. The world was wonderful again and she was happy.

She never knew such happiness existed.

It was something she has stressed to Andrew, too. Given the hell they'd both been through, it was very important to make every moment count now that they'd finally found happiness.

As Josephine accompanied Elaine and her flowers from the hall, and Andrew and Donald continued their conversation over good wine and bread, it was moments like this that meant the most to Josephine – moments of normalcy and of family and friendship. It had been far too long in coming but now that it was here, Josephine intended to relish every single second that passed.

Before she left the hall, however, Josephine passed a final glance at her husband, sitting at the feasting table and laughing at something Donald had said. It made her heart swell simply to look upon the man. She told him once that he was her sun and her moon, and that statement had only grown more true and powerful as time went on. She adored him more than words could express, this man who had reinvented himself not once, but twice – once as a powerful mercenary, and now as a benevolent lord. She knew that there wasn't anything he couldn't do if he set his mind to it.

Except one thing.

He couldn't change the sex of the baby Josephine gave birth to two months later into a boy. After a very fast and easy delivery on a rainy night in July, Josephine found herself looking at a big, healthy girl delivered by Oletha, the healer that traveled with Andrew's former mercenary army. Andrew had requested the woman be present for the birth of his son, and she was.

But no amount of checking the baby's body would indicate that the initial diagnosis that it was a girl was, in fact, a mistake, and Josephine was genuinely concerned that Andrew might be upset about it. But once the new father was brought in to see his wife and child, and handed the mewling infant, the fact that it wasn't a boy didn't seem to upset Andrew in the least. He was utterly, deeply in love with the infant as only a new father could be, but he had insisted on naming the child just the same. He'd had the same name picked out whether it had been a boy or a girl, and Josephine had tears in her eyes when he told her his choice.

Joey Elaine Nicola d'Vant.

For The Red Fury, for Josephine, and for those so deeply intertwined in their lives, it seemed that life had come full circle, indeed.

❦ THE END ❧

House of d'Vant:

Tender is the Knight (House of d'Vant)

The Red Fury (House of d'Vant)

About Kathryn Le Veque

Medieval Just Got Real.

KATHRYN LE VEQUE is a USA TODAY Bestselling author, an Amazon All-Star author, and a #1 bestselling, award-winning, multi-published author in Medieval Historical Romance and Historical Fiction. She has been featured in the NEW YORK TIMES and on USA TODAY's HEA blog. In March 2015, Kathryn was the featured cover story for the March issue of InD'Tale Magazine, the premier Indie author magazine. She was also a quadruple nominee (a record!) for the prestigious RONE awards for 2015.

Kathryn's Medieval Romance novels have been called 'detailed', 'highly romantic', and 'character-rich'. She crafts great adventures of love, battles, passion, and romance in the High Middle Ages. More than that, she writes for both women AND men – an unusual crossover for a romance author – and Kathryn has many male readers who enjoy her stories because of the male perspective, the action, and the adventure.

On October 29, 2015, Amazon launched Kathryn's Kindle Worlds Fan Fiction site WORLD OF DE WOLFE PACK. Please visit Kindle Worlds for Kathryn Le Veque's World of de Wolfe Pack and find many action-packed adventures written by some of the top authors in their genre using Kathryn's characters from the de Wolfe Pack series. As Kindle World's FIRST Historical Romance fan fiction world, Kathryn Le Veque's World of de Wolfe Pack will contain all of the great story-telling you have come to expect.

Kathryn loves to hear from her readers. Please find Kathryn on Facebook at Kathryn Le Veque, Author, or join her on Twitter @kathrynleveque, and don't forget to visit her website and sign up for her blog at www.kathrynleveque.com.

Please follow Kathryn on Bookbub for the latest releases and sales: bookbub.com/authors/kathryn-le-veque.

Made in the USA
Columbia, SC
14 January 2018